I0537327

# THE PRISONER'S CIPHER

## A NOVEL

### BY
# S.E. FRANCIS

***Schwarz Publishing House***

This book is a work of fiction. Although, some named historical figures are actual persons, incidents surrounding their names are either the product of the author's imagination or are used fictitiously. All other names, characters, places, and incidents are either the product of the author's imagination or are used fictitiously, and any resemblance to actual persons, living or dead is entirely coincidental.

Copyright © 2015 by Stephanie Sankey

All Rights Reserved. No part of this book may be reproduced, scanned, or distributed in any printed or electronic form without permission. Please do not participate in or encourage piracy of copyrighted materials in violation of the author's rights. Purchase only authorized editions.

ISBN 978-0-9961319-3-3

Printed in the United States of America.

First year of printing 2015

All maps copyright of © Google

Modified map designs by Stephanie Sankey

New York to Yonkers, page 106, Imagery ©2015 TerraMetrics, Map Data ©2015 Google –

New York to Tel Aviv, page 200, Imagery ©2015 NASA, TerraMetrics, Map Data ©2015 Google, INEGI -

Tel Aviv to Jerusalem, page 210, Imagery ©2015 TerraMetrics,  Map Data©2015 Google, Mapa GISrael, ORION-ME -

Tel Aviv to Auschwitz, page 233,  Imagery ©2015 TerraMetrics, Map Data ©2015 Basarsoft, GeoBasis-DE/BKG (© 2009), Google, Mapa GISrael, ORION-ME, basado en BCN IGN España -

Auschwitz to Treblinka, page 286, Imagery ©2015 TerraMetrics, Map Data ©2015 GeoBasis-DE/BKG (© 2009) Google -

Auschwitz Concentration Camp, page 329, Imagery ©2015 CNES / Astrium, Cnes/Spot Image, DigitalGlobe, Map Data © 2015 Google -

Kaechon Extermination Camp, Page 329, Imagery ©2015 CNES / Astrium, Cnes/Spot Image, DigitalGlobe, Map Data © 2015 Google -

Jacket Photographs by Michal Osmenda:
*The Last Road*
https://www.flickr.com/photos/michalo/396520226/in/set-72157594582519862
*The End of a Journey*
href="https://www.flickr.com/photos/michalo/505660567/">MichalOsemnda
</a>/<a href="http://foter.com/">Foter</a> / <a href="http://creativecommons.
.org/licenses/by-sa/2.0 /">CC BY-SA</a> - Michal Osmenda /Foter/CC BY - SA

Jacket Design by Stephanie Sankey

*Dedicated to Otto Francis Sankey,
from whose cloth I am cut.*


*...And to the men, women and children
who have been, and currently are, victims of
genocide and all manner of hate crimes.*

# ACKNOWLEDGEMENTS

I am tremendously thankful for and would like to acknowledge my mother, Debra, a woman whose character I can only hope to emulate. Thank you for reading my book and loving it. Thank you for being my best friend and protector, for loving me unconditionally and at all times thinking only the best of me. I love you more than infinity.

Thank you to my father, Otto, the smartest man I have known and will ever know and one of the most brilliant physicists the world has ever seen. Thank you for being a mentor and for teaching me what it means to be a good person. Thank you for reading my book in its early stages. I am so grateful for your honest critique during the writing process. Thank you for being a sounding board and brainstorming partner for the important details. I love you more than infinity.

Thank you to Robyn Sankey and Chandler Nelson; my flesh and blood. You make the world a better place. And to Holly, Nick, Tennysen, Londyn and Bragg Rodgers. You bring me joy.

I would also like to acknowledge my other pre-publication readers and critics. Thank you to Dennis Clark Hill for being my first reader. Your opinion was highly valued. Thank you for being the first fresh voice to show me the things I didn't see. Second to JoAnn Clark—Thank you for your kindness and providing me a place to write. Your graciousness will always be remembered. Thank you for being a lover of books and for offering your literarily experienced opinion. I also owe thanks to Christian Niederle, a stranger who quickly became a friend, who read my book in its early stages and who gave me his honest input. Thank you for giving me the real German perspective. Thanks are also well-deserved by my copy editor, Kathy Williamson. Thank you for your time, perspective and encouragement. And finally, to Willow Humphrey and Jade Olivia Jupp, my beta readers extraordinaire. Their perspective was invaluable to me in my efforts to best express the thoughts of my heart.

# THE PRISONER'S CIPHER

"First they came for the Socialists and I did not speak out because I was not a Socialist. Then they came for the trade unionists and I did not speak out because I was not a trade unionist. Then they came for the Jews, and I did not speak out because I was not a Jew. Then they came for me, and there was no one left to speak for me."

Martin Niemöller-Lutheran
Minister and Early Nazi Supporter
Later Imprisoned for Rebelling
Against the Nazis

# *Chapter 1*

*October 1, 1988*

Dietrich Rüpel had died once before. It was 45 years ago. His soul was slaughtered, but he hadn't felt a thing.

*October 2, 1943 – Auschwitz, Poland*

The air was cold outside as Dietrich stood rigidly silent and stared down at the long barrel of a black pistol held firmly in his hand. The only thing standing between his sharply aimed firearm and the mass grave in front of him was a young man, only two years his junior, stripped naked and weeping.

"Please. I beg of you. No!" the young man pleaded in Polish.

Dietrich didn't understand him, nor did he care to. He stood, stalwart, ignoring his victim, at the head of a solid straight line of Schutzstaffel soldiers. The soldiers answered to the SS and each one, like him, held a pistol steadily aimed at a frightened victim. A mild scattering of snowflakes fell, ushering out autumn and etching a path for the brutal winter.

Dietrich, a German Nazi, relished his well-earned top command here at Treblinka death camp. He called the shots and his subordinates followed his lead. The 76 human lives that stood in the execution line he oversaw were all naked—as vulnerable as the day they were born, yet Dietrich was unaffected by their plight. He scanned the line of frightened men and women all standing in helpless torment solely because of their religion and ethnicity. *They deserve to be here*, his mind reminded him. They're Jews;

every one of them. As they stood in torrid agony, screaming and praying, Dietrich was oblivious. Their prayers had to be silent as they faced their impending deaths, but their deafening shrieks caused them to question whether God could even hear their pleas. As he scanned the line, Dietrich wouldn't hesitate to put a bullet in their head if they tried to pray on their knees. Dietrich was pleased as he had led the march of these prisoners at gunpoint from the nearby concentration camp. The healthy Jews had been left behind. They were needed for the heavy labor at the camp as they waited in misery for their own demise. He had forced this particular group, all Ukrainian Jews, to rise to their feet and march forward with the single command, "Gehen," meaning, "Go." He had brazenly ordered each one to undress before being marched to their final resting place in the mass grave in front of them.

Dietrich took no thought in this moment, that these Jews had already endured the loss of loved ones in the days, weeks and months prior. At the inception of the Nazi cause for the mass execution of Jews, the idea of Dietrich's involvement felt surreal to him. The lives of these prisoners were in his hands. As time progressed, the screams and cries of his victims drowned the sound of his heart which hardened further as each second passed. In this moment, Dietrich gave little thought to anything that the shivering and weeping man in front of him was feeling. The Jews were responsible for Germany's loss of World War I and they deserved what was coming to them.

On that chilled morning in October of 1943, standing ready to shoot, Dietrich's actions impacted him with a mere palliative force. His soul had been stirred slightly during his early initiation into the SS, but in this moment his mind was empty and numb. He stood before the naked quivering man in front of him, concentrating only on his aim and making the perfect shot. As his victim stood on the windy platform above the grave, Dietrich thought nothing of what he was doing. He thought nothing of the life of the Jew that stood helplessly in front of him. He thought nothing. He felt nothing. His anger had turned to numbness and an utter lack of empathy.

It was in this moment that his soul died.

# Chapter 2

*September 8, 1988 – New York City*

When the telephone rang at 2:37 a.m. Charlotte Weiss thought nothing of it. With her hair awry and a dull headache throbbing in her skull, she instinctively lifted the receiver with her left arm. She was well-versed in the duties of an on-call prosecutor and hers was an automatic response when the phone rang in the middle of the night.

As one of the most senior prosecutors in the New York District Attorney's Office, homicide had become her specialty. Her nights had become sleepless, but she had few responsibilities outside of work. She lived for the job.

Above her nightstand as she sat up in bed, she caught a glimpse of a photograph of her three nieces laughing. It reminded her of her own lack of children. Now in her thirties, still childless and single, she had all but given up hope on the ideas of marriage and family. She resigned herself to the fact that her sleepless nights would solely be attributed to police calls and pleas for legal guidance, rather than the cry of a needy child. These calls filled a void in her life she didn't know how to otherwise placate.

The voice on the other end of the phone was strained, but she knew Detective Sergeant Troy Paniletti's voice well enough to immediately know something was wrong.

"Hello," she answered groggily with a light German accent.

"Charlotte," he addressed her somberly, "We need you down here tonight. 615 Black Drive."

"Excuse me?" She knew this to be Saul's address. *What could the police possibly be doing there?*

"Charlotte, he's been murdered," Paniletti repeated. "I'm so sorry."

Charlotte instantly sprung awake and as she jerked up in bed, her dull headache was turning to a pounding.

"I don't understand," she said. Although the pain in her head tipped her off to her sense of wakefulness, she probed further to ensure she wasn't dreaming.

"Saul's dead, Charlotte. I know you two were close so I know this is very hard to hear. There is a strange marking here. We need you."

To say that she and Saul were close was an understatement. He had not only been Charlotte's mentor in the District Attorney's Office, but also her dear friend. He achieved professional as well as tremendous personal success as the first black Deputy District Attorney to win the National District Attorney Association's award for Lifetime Achievement.

Saul's colleagues adored him and cops needed him. He had 17 years on Charlotte in terms of prosecutorial experience, and she made sure to capitalize on his good graces. She latched on to him the day she started the job.

Sitting, her body now frozen, her mind raced quickly back in time. She had been a citizen of the United States for only four years when she started work at the New York District Attorney's Office. Born and raised in Germany, she was living her version of the American dream as a law school graduate and now practicing attorney.

She would never forget the simple mantra of encouragement Saul routinely spoke to her. "You got this, Weiss," he would say. "You and your legal mind. You got this."

Their bond was natural and when Paniletti informed her that Saul had been murdered at home, she didn't actually need the address. She had been there many times before. Charlotte hung up and after throwing on a quick change of clothing, jumped into her car and made the drive on autopilot.

When she arrived and flashed her DA badge to penetrate the yellow crime scene tape at Saul's New York loft apartment, she was met by Paniletti as she made a beeline for Saul's body.

"There was a large part of me hoping it wasn't really him," she said to him softly as he stood beside her. They both stared at the mangled body of her deceased colleague and friend.

"This is a tremendous loss to all of law enforcement," he assured her. "He was a great prosecutor."

"One of the best," she answered with a tear in her eye.

Charlotte poured over every detail of the scene, trying to make sense of what she was seeing. It was part and parcel of her job as a prosecutor to be present at a murder scene for legal analysis. Homicide in the city was an uncomfortably common occurrence that she was called out for much more than she cared to say aloud. Sadly she had become numb to it. Numb until it was Saul.

Nearby, the wind blew the curtains of a raised window and drifted through his neat and modern living space. Saul liked to keep the window open during the summer and fall months, but it was evident the screen had not been tampered with. Such was also the case with the remaining three open windows in the top floor apartment. The fire escape was in its locked position; the rust on its hinges was untouched.

"The killer must have entered and exited through the door," Charlotte observed.

She stared as a pool of blood surrounded Saul's neck and head, with the obvious cause of death being a large, jagged cut running the length of his dark-skinned throat. The gouge revealed veins and arteries that shocked even her sensibilities and the pattern of the cut, leaving striated flesh in its wake, was unusual.

Crime scene investigators were snapping photographs from all possible angles and she hardly noticed Law enforcement personnel infiltrated every square inch of the apartment. Questioning of the few restless neighbors peeking into the doorway returned negative results. A search for foreign fingerprints was conducted, but would later produce nothing.

There was a dearth of physical evidence, but in as sadistic a manner as can be imagined, below his neckline, the killer had carved an eerie symbol into Saul's chest.

"He's been cut in the chest," Paniletti warned Charlotte as he raised Saul's bloody shirt. "It's a pretty important clue."

At her first sight of it Charlotte grabbed unconsciously onto Paniletti's arm, and then drew close to him. She buried her head in his chest, simply weeping. As she wept, she recalled her extensive research as of late. It had etched this symbol at the top of her mind and its meaning came to her immediately. She was able to readily identify it and this realization added an even larger twist of pain as the tears, now uncontrollable, flowed seemingly without end.

# Chapter 3

During the last 18 months, Charlotte and Saul had aggressively hunted members of the Aryan Brotherhood and in large part due to her fondness for her mentor, Charlotte held particular disdain towards members of this group. Rooted in the ideology of pure hate and the singular goal of white supremacy that the Brotherhood closely embraced, Saul routinely received hate mail, because of his work and his race.

Charlotte's protective instincts were ever present when it came to Saul and she despised the Aryan Brotherhood's mantra that anyone not of Caucasian descent was considered inferior—a threat to the pure Aryan bloodline. The fact that the Brotherhood was the primary source of an influx of hate crimes recently plaguing New York did nothing to lessen her feelings and Charlotte and Saul had been pounding the proverbial pavement to crack down on their criminal activity. Many of the commands to its members came primarily from within the walls of federal prisons, where its top leaders were known to take up residence.

In their pursuits, Charlotte and Saul spent a considerable amount of their waking hours tracking the movements of prisoners Sampson Barrett and Joseph Simms, two of the Brand's top ringleaders. Charlotte knew there was one powerful leader, the Grand Imperial Wizard above them, but he was without the confines of prison walls and hid himself well within the general population. His mystic identity was the intel Charlotte had been hungering for during the entirety of her career.

*If I can get him*, she thought. *I can bring down the whole institution.*

It was through diligence and patience that she and Saul worked on gathering sufficient proof to convict Barrett and Simms with the crimes of delegating the murders of five black rival gang members, but the prosecution had nothing on them yet. Barrett and Simms had been extremely careful in every action, especially those orders they directed from prison. Prison phone calls were recorded and monitored and Barrett and Simms knew it. Consequently, they spoke in nothing more than pleasantries during inconspicuous conversations on their calls. Hours spent listening to these taped phone calls bore little fruit for Charlotte until the day Barrett had finally made one false move. Luck turned in the prosecution's favor when Charlotte and Saul intercepted a letter from Barrett to another inmate, and before his death Saul had been working steadily on parceling out hidden messages buried in the text.

"It's like a puzzle we have to solve," Saul told her. "There's been a long series of murders ordered by Barrett and Simms and they belong on death row."  Charlotte had taken these words to heart and committed the symbology of the Aryan Brotherhood to memory in order to crack their code.

For Charlotte, the signifiers of the white supremacy organization consisted of more than the Doc Martens, red suspenders and shaved heads they were commonly associated with. Their tattoos and chosen markings were not just swastikas and eagles. They traced their roots far back into history and adopted an ancient symbology that went beyond what was commonly understood.

Charlotte knew the roots of these adopted symbols. Like the symbol carved into Saul's chest, the Brand often used runic symbols—symbols of Old Norse, a North Germanic language. The use of Nordic runes was propelled post World War I by Adolf Hitler. They were exemplified by the swastika which was firmly established as a symbol of German antiquity.

As she stood frozen in the now seeming chill of Saul's apartment, Charlotte's mind recalled this information in an instant. She dared to move her head from the current sanctuary of Paniletti's chest and look again at Saul's mangled body.

Paniletti's simple assertion to her, "He's been cut on his chest," did not do the brutality justice. Saul's body had been desecrated. The wounds were cut deep on his left pectoral just above his heart where a Nordic rune was very blatantly etched into his skin.

It was the Nordic symbol signifying death:

The blood was still fresh and bright red. Charlotte's mind instantly thought of its inverse, the Nordic rune symbol for life that was commonly adopted by the Aryan Brotherhood in the form of various tattoos and markings:

Through the rampant hate mail he received, it was no secret that the Aryan Brotherhood was livid at the idea of Saul, a black man, prosecuting them. Saul's work had always been salt in a wound to the Brand, and by the symbol of death carved into his chest, their motive was clear and meant to be so. The termination of his life had been drenched in hate and cruelly documented with his blood.

# *Chapter 4*

Some would say that Detective Sergeant Troy Paniletti murdered Benjamin Stansfeld; at least that's what they suspected but could never prove. Troy Paniletti was a man who had all the charm and charisma of a troupe of womanizers. His good looks and built-in swagger, coupled with the time he spent in the gym paralleling the number of hours he worked as a cop, added to his sex appeal in no uncertain terms.

Despite his handsome appearance, there remained the scattering of criminals who were sent to the hospital as a result of run-ins with him. While suspicion loomed over his conduct in these instances, Charlotte gave him the benefit of the doubt. She took a secret enjoyment from not reciprocating his clear romantic interest in her. It gave her a sense of power in her predominantly male-centered occupation. Nonetheless, her rebuffing towards him caused a twinge of guilt and she refused to consider the possibility that something was amiss about him.

During Charlotte's ten years on the job, Paniletti had been employed by the New York City Police Department and she considered his longevity as a sign of trustworthiness. For every negative comment made by one of his detractors resulting from a suspect wounded at his hands, there was always a story of justification she relied upon. *After all, law enforcement has to do whatever it takes to make it home each night and Paniletti is no exception.* Even so, given his history, he was forced to fight this position particularly hard in front of a glaring populace after the shooting of Benjamin Stansfeld. And in this case, even though Charlotte would need proof, the angry populace was right.

Paniletti fatally shot that man. Only two days after Saul was murdered, the event became widely recounted in the media. Benjamin Stansfeld, an investigative journalist, with a reputation for ruffling feathers, was known as the go-to guy when things got real in a bad way for high-ranking officials. He was always on hand to report a good scandal.

Stansfeld was not only an impressive journalist but he was a leader in the African American community and was proud to be among the leading African American journalists in the country. In his career, he saw and facilitated the fall of several corporate leaders and politicians. He made it his livelihood to ensure that those in power were held accountable and it was consequently a wonder he lasted as long as he did. While the general public was better off because of him, and he, in large part, maintained their support, for a fifty-year-old metropolitan journalist he had a lot of enemies.

It was called a tragedy when the report of his death came to light, and was labeled an unfortunate accident by each and every Police Officer who witnessed the shooting. "It began as a run-of-the mill traffic stop and became a high-speed chase when Stansfeld refused to pull over. It was a red light violation," Paniletti told his commander, "And when it turned into an all-out car chase, the threat of endangerment to the public became a very real concern."

A string of deputies had answered Paniletti's call for back up and police were led on a car chase lasting 22 minutes as Stansfeld tore through the city streets like a bat out of hell, racing towards an unknown destination. The chase traversed along the freeway and shredded through the city, causing pedestrians to dodge out of the way of the oncoming train of prey and predators.

"I can cut him off on First Street," Paniletti yelled into his microphone as the chase ensued. "I need back-up!" Through this upheaval, Paniletti rallied his fellow officers together until police were able to surround Stansfeld at a juncture where he had nowhere to turn. His car eventually collided with a berm, leaving no means of escape

Stansfeld, now defeated, was weaponless as he slowly exited the car and stood in front of the swarm of police surrounding him. Failing to drop to the ground, officers began to pelt him with beanbags shot from high-powered rifles as he stood next to his open door.

Stansfeld's shouts to police were muffled and incomprehensible as he was struck over and over in an attempt to force him into submission on the ground. The pain was too great and he had no choice in that moment but to take cover behind the open driver's side door. This move proved to be a deadly mistake. As he dove behind the metal barrier, he realized it could not provide the cover he needed and he retreated back into the open. Fully beaten, he put his hands up. He was still weaponless.

This was reckoning time—a time of full surrender; Stansfeld's back was to the officers.

The red and blue lights of no less than 20 police cars dotted the scene as Stansfeld stood still and breathless. With the exception of Paniletti, each officer had their fingers off the triggers of their deadly weapons, the immediate threat now gone with Stansfeld's position of surrender and lack of weaponry.

The accounts would later vary when the internal investigation into the shooting was done. Some said it happened instantaneously, some said time froze. It may have felt like a lifetime, but in reality it was all of 3.79 seconds between the time he emerged from the protection of his car door and his death. The time after Stansfeld fully raised his arms and turned his back to the police, submitting in full, was 1.72 seconds—And then he was shot in the back. The smoking gun was held firmly in the hands of Paniletti.

The administrative hearings for the internal investigation were conducted immediately. A doctor testified that the human brain can process what the eyes see within .025 seconds on the outside. This left a difference of 1.695 seconds which Paniletti had to remove his finger from the trigger. A full 1.695 seconds was the amount of time allotted him to make a choice. It was a full 1.695

seconds in which he could have decided to spare the life of Benjamin Stansfeld, but he chose otherwise. And now a man was dead.

Nonetheless, the DA called it a justifiable shooting and it was three days later that Paniletti returned to work. "It all happened so fast," Paniletti was quoted as saying, after which he was cleared of any wrongdoing.

Although a weapon was never found in Stansfeld's vehicle or in any surrounding area of the pursuit, "Stansfeld could have had one," Paniletti reported. "When I lost him for a few seconds going through the alley between Hazelton and Meridian I was forced to go around the block to get him. He could have gotten rid of it."

And with that, Paniletti was put back on the streets. Other than a lingering sense of solemnity for the situation and a few doubters labeled as conspiracy theorists, the DA called it, and the populace conceded, that Stansfeld was shot and killed in the name of officer safety. Even though he was unarmed, with his back turned, in the eyes of the law, order triumphed again.

# Chapter 5

*September 9, 1988 – Sing Sing Correctional Facility*

Isaac Kanzler sat calmly on an old tree stump as he watched the crowd. Donning his orange prison jumpsuit, he blended in while maintaining a distinct distance. Now in his thirties, he was stronger than both his older as well as a large percentage of his younger, fellow prison inmates. His hair was becoming peppered with gray despite his age and he was letting it grow long. It currently reached his back. He didn't care for the prison barber and forewent regular cuts, opting instead for what he believed to be a more rugged appearance. His vanity came out with the close monitoring of his strands of gray hair.

Just as he monitored his hair, he monitored his fellow inmates like a hawk. This was rec time; precious time on the yard granted by the Warden's good graces. It meant no lock downs and no mandatory inmate counts, and Isaac was there to watch it all.

He noticed the yard was busy today, yet just as he did every day during his incarceration, Isaac stayed to himself. There he sat, day in and day out, perched on the same old tree stump backed up to the cement block of the prison wall. This was his post and he was keeping watch. The spot was within arm's reach of the bordering chain link fence, which was topped with twisted barbed wire and ominously surrounded the yard. His beloved tree stump was at the top of an incline in the prison landscape and provided him an excellent view looking down on all of the prison yard's elements.

A tree had grown there once; in the place he sat. It had grown for 87 years before the prison was built. Eventually, the metal fenced and barbed wire confines of the facility closed in on the tree and it was cut down. Allowing it to thrive would have nurtured a perfect means for prisoner escapes.

Isaac took solace in the fact that where he sat stood once a living entity. The base was wide and he knew the tree had grown tall and strong. He drew strength from those remains, which now served as his resting place, and as his backside sat upon it day after day a groove developed that was all his. He and his companion became connected and he treated the stump as if it was an old friend.

Isaac had established himself in the prison yard. He was large in stature, which was magnified at least two-fold by his demeanor. His face was stone and he never cracked a smile. His lack of emotion scared the other inmates who incessantly worried about what he was capable of. That was exactly what he was going for.

He endured well the tests of prison life. From the day he had been booked in, he was judged and sized up by his peers and had plowed through hazings and trials. This was the way of things in prison. But early on when a group of three burly Hispanic men surrounded him in a combined effort to steal his cigarettes, the event later became known as nothing more than a feeble attempt on their part to overtake him. He proved himself.

It only took twelve seconds for him to knock them all to the ground. The simultaneous group effort on the part of his attackers could not overpower him and he was not shy about letting them know. One significant beating and that was all it took. From that moment on he became known for his toughness and strength; not just of physicality, but also of mental aptitude. The prison populace knew better than to mess with him.

The stump was the perfect lookout over the remainder of the yard. From where he sat, he was assured no one could get behind or to the side of him, and he had ample warning if they approached from the front. While he was always prepared, it never became necessary to defend himself.

During rec time, a barrage of criminality happened constantly and covertly, unknown to the watchful eye of the armed guards. Aside from those in the elevated watchtowers, Isaac possessed the best view. Deals involving drugs, weapons, money and contraband occurred en masse at any given moment. The prison yard was a continuous bustling center of commerce and he made sure to see it all.

Despite the dozens of business transactions happening at any given time, no one could go unnoticed by Isaac. As he too made a lot of money in that same drug industry, he knew exactly what he was looking at. He saw money changing hands on a regular basis and was well-versed in the prison yard drug trade. He knew who was in which gang and he paid particular attention to the Aryan Brotherhood. They were white men who wore their arrogance on their sleeves and dominated where they trod.

The Aryan Brotherhood was a central entity in this prison. Although they comprised in total less than one percent of the entire prison population, one in five murders were committed by the group. Just as the remaining prison population had, they too took notice of Isaac immediately when he was booked into prison. They were intrigued by his way of establishing dominance and beating those who would think anything less of his strength. He was just the type of person they were looking for to join their ranks.

On his fourth day of his first stint in prison, Barrett and Simms dared to approach him with the intention of recruiting him to their ranks. Sitting around a circular picnic bench, they invited him to a prison yard meeting wherein they detailed the organization of the Aryan Brotherhood and pitched to him the glamorous benefits of membership. This glamour came in the form of the highest level of power and opportunity you can find in prison and included protection and money. It meant a lot of money that easily came from highly priced drug sales.

Isaac made them wait a day or two, allowing ample time for them to sweat before he finally accepted. It wasn't long before he knew their secrets and he took up actively working with and for them until he ultimately established his position as their trusted watch guard.

As a current patched-in member who had earned his status of power, he knew of the various killings carried out by the Brand, often knowing about them at the inception of their planning stages and well in advance of their execution. He became acutely aware of the lengths the Brotherhood would go to in order to gain their ideal of racial purity, but unbeknownst to them, he carried a secret. He watched everything they did with abhorrence. He hid well his secret resentment towards them. He had gained their explicit trust and the Brand relied on him to provide the necessary Intel to keep their organization at the top.

Violence was the trademark of their organization, and as Isaac always proved invaluable to the group, he was quickly promoted within the organization. He wasn't at the very top but near it. And it was there where he was comfortable. He knew all the secrets of the organization but didn't bear all the responsibility. His solitary post on the tree stump also gave him the appearance of distance from his associates. It was well-established the Feds were tracking the top dogs and he was far enough removed from them that law enforcement rarely gave him the time of day.

As he sat now on his comforting stump, his first meeting with Sampson and Barrett had been eleven years in the past. There had been numerous meetings since, as he conglomerated with these heartless Nazis both within and without the prison walls. Their meetings were fairly routine for a group of cold-blooded killers, but now they had pushed the envelope too far.

It was specifically last Thursday when Barrett and Simms once again sat him down at a small circular table at the end of the prison yard and discussed the latest plan. There was trouble with someone on the outside, and not only was the Aryan Brotherhood going to extinguish the target, but an innocent family member would also pay with their life. Though not a novel concept, this was their first planned murder involving an innocent bystander as the victim to be brought into the ranks of the slaughtered.

Such an act was a line Isaac decided early on that he wouldn't cross. Propelled by a boundary of morality, he was of the very decided conviction that it was one thing to fight for the cause and to wage war to ensure racial purity, but it was quite another to degrade the organization to the point of senseless killings. That was simply going too far.

Despite his dissension, which he was not shy about vocalizing, this heartless murder plan remained in the works. The innocent target was going to be executed with or without his approval. It was two against one and he was the odd man out. There was nothing he could do to stop it. Therefore, given his opinion, Barrett and Simms not so politely suggested it would be best if he stuck to being the look-out for a while.

None of the Brand's members knew the whole story about Isaac. He kept his secrets so well, in fact, that no one in the group knew he had volunteered to work in the kitchen. When he told them the news, the Brotherhood believed this new responsibility was an assignment and was no different. They knew there would be only menial pay associated with it, which was less than insignificant next to the money they brought in from drug sales, but despite this new delegated position, they were happy to have someone on the inside.

In theory, having a man on the inside at the kitchen would mean the best of what was available at chow time and they could count on Isaac not to disappoint. As the weeks passed under his new employ, he played an integral role in preparing the prison meals and every day he gave his comrades extra rations and superior portions of the available food. Despite his recent differing opinion, he regained his status of being highly favored within the organization and this position helped him in that regard.

He reflected on that as he sat on his stump, and focused his thoughts on the present. Today was an especially good day. Veiled in the secrecy of where his heart truly lay, he looked down at a pad of paper on his lap and wrote as he sat and watched the crowd. He would write letters on occasion, keeping correspondence with the outside. He sent his mail right after rec time and brought his stamp and envelope with him so he wouldn't be required to make a stop at his cell on his way to the outgoing mail slot.

There was a routine and a rhythm to this process. He consistently brought up the back of the crowd heading back into the walls of the prison. This system was not based on chance or randomness.

On this day, the letter was signed and ready to be delivered by the time the inmates were herded back inside. Before sending the envelope, Isaac had made sure the red cross he drew on the correspondence would not go unnoticed by the recipient and as the bullhorn was heard signifying that play-time was over, no one was the wiser as to the intended recipient of his letter. The letter was boldly addressed to Charlotte Weiss, in care of the New York District Attorney's Office.

# *Chapter 6*

Charlotte reflected back on the inauguration of her boss, Brent Somers eight months prior. *The rumors surrounding the list were true.* Charlotte had been hearing them from different sources around the office for weeks but was hoping they were fiction. *No such luck.* There were ten names on the list. Ten names of ten attorneys who were to be terminated from the District Attorney's Office effective immediately. Ten livelihoods that were to be ripped away. They were all good people and all experienced lawyers, yet one by one, they were fired solely. They became victims of the "DA Massacre."

The voting public had no idea what the real Brent Somers was like as they chose their next District Attorney. The campaign signs had been up for many months prior to the election, and they were far from forthcoming about the wannabe DA. The posters displayed nothing but glowing images of him with a smiling incumbent Chief of Police standing proudly next to him. Somers was the man the popular Chief had chosen to endorse. Though the general public resoundingly liked the Chief, the glowing images of the man he was advocating for were simply an illusion. Brent Somers was anything but glowing.

The pair dubbed themselves the "Law and Order" Team. Somers spent the seven months leading up to the election shaking hands and kissing babies and his smile was as wooden as it was symmetrical. The fact that he looked like a Ken doll did nothing to harm the outside impression he portrayed of a stalwart prosecutor at the top of his game.

Aside from extensive chatter about the list, the rumor mill spun excitedly around talk of how Somers was able to fund his campaign.

"All that money had to have come from somewhere," Saul would say, "Something is fishy."

Prior to running for office, Somers was a line prosecutor in a neighboring county. He was a relative nobody with mediocre trial skills. It was an honest wonder how he garnered the monetary support to run the campaign.

Somers could not have accomplished running a political campaign alone, nor without an extravagant funding source. The donor contribution lists had been checked, and although it appeared each contribution was no greater than the maximum allowable amount, he somehow collected far more contributors than any other candidate in the history of the position. Sadly the voters were none the wiser to his shenanigans or to his plans to gut the DA's office current legal staff solely because of politics.

Despite his façade, those on the inside knew well that the premise "looks can be deceiving" applied heavily in his case. His persona to the public was a far cry from the way he operated behind closed doors. His temper was surpassed only by his ego, and his reputation among the attorneys in the office with whom he previously worked was one of a lack of knowledge. He worked hard to cloud his failings by displaying undeserved confidence.

Saul knew him from his work in a prior office. He had once hired Somers as a young lawyer and trained him. Saul was the person who warned Charlotte, "A wise man is not defined by his always being right, rather is defined by his ability to know when he is wrong. Somers is not a wise man."

Much to Charlotte's disappointment, Somers won the election and his arrogance bled into his actions even before his scheduled date to take office. Well before January 1st, Somers' plans for mass termination inside the DA's office were brewing. As arrogant as a lone rooster in an expansive hen house, he was his own biggest fan and it didn't take

Charlotte long to discover that he wrongly considered himself to be God's gift to prosecution.

He wasn't to take office until New Year's Day, but he made substantial efforts to usurp the authority of the outgoing DA. He took the liberty on New Year's Eve of firing employees before the authority to do so belonged to him. His timing was so close, however, that as the hours passed, the issue became moot and as the clock struck midnight on January 1st, ten attorneys lost their jobs, and it was a new year.

In so doing, Somers took no thought for the livelihoods of those he was terminating. He needed only 24 hours after he took office to eradicate those he didn't like and fill their positions with his buddies. Even before the ball dropped at Times Square, the office had turned into a good ol' white boys club.

What remained of the women attorneys after the fact was a grand total of two. Charlotte was one of them. She wasn't entirely sure why he had spared her. *Luck of the draw*, she thought. A former beauty queen turned prosecutor was the other. *No mystery there considering Somer's superficiality.*

Eight months after Somers took office, the totality of Charlotte's work situation couldn't have been worse. She had trouble acclimating to the new office structure and the unnerving atmosphere, and the trauma of her circumstances was only magnified by Saul's murder.

The morning after she made her reconnaissance of Saul's murder scene and arrived at work, she bowed her head in sadness and reverence at the site of his empty office. He rarely, if ever, missed a day and the sight of his office, now devoid of life, was devastating. The only pull that would bring her back to work after his murder was her need to find his killer. This desire trumped even her deep-rooted love of criminal law, which began when she was eight years old with a passion for the murder mysteries she begged her father to read to her. Being raised in Germany and taught to pursue her dreams, she was motivated in her teen years to join the ranks of the German foreign exchange students who matriculated for the period of one year at Wakefield High School in New York City.

Her stay in the United States became meaningful to her when her host father introduced her to the challenges and work of a District Attorney. Even stories he recounted about what he considered to be the minutia of his job were utterly fascinating to her. It was her dream from then on to be a prosecutor and to one day work in the New York District Attorney's Office.

Immediately after graduating secondary school in Germany, Charlotte once again said goodbye to her family and ventured into the great unknown of college in the United States and after successfully completing her undergraduate degree at NYU she went on to law school. Her passion and lingering connection with her host father got her a clerkship in the very New York District Attorney's Office where he was employed. A paid job there was a prize she kept as her focus. She gained United States citizenship, passed the New York State Bar exam, and cried tears of joy when she got her first, and up to this point, only job at the DA's office. The concept of the small government pay she would be compensated with was something that never crossed her mind. This work was what she was put on earth to do, and she would stick to it now even as it became all the more challenging.

# *Chapter 7*

*Yes, a bomb could definitely be thrown over the fence and penetrate the border of the United Nations Complex,* Peter Bremer concluded as he sat at the top of a tree. He scaled it with relative ease and was sure to position himself at the highest possible point, standing on the toughest of the high limbs. The situation was not worth breaking a leg over or otherwise falling to his death.

It was the middle of the night, 1 a.m., and the perfect time to be up in a tree scoping the UN Headquarters sight unseen by anyone else. By now his rifle was lowered and it was carefully tucked back in its holster. He had already checked it. The cross hairs at the end of the scope were still not high enough to secure any viable target from this vantage point. Other means would be needed to infiltrate the complex via gun from this location. This exercise was his sole purpose there. As the Head of Security for the UN it was his responsibility to check all possibilities of invasion. The security of the compound lay in his hands.

The dark sky covered the earth like a blanket and even from his elevated vantage point the nearby city lights blocked out the brightness of the stars in the heavens. Peter blended in with his surroundings. He was dressed in all black to avoid suspicion, but his uniform couldn't hide the twinge of nervousness he felt about his height. Though the night air was crisp, beads of sweat dotted his forehead. The bleach white of his knuckles was another tell of his anxiety.

He exhaled deeply. A large breath of air emanated from his mouth and nose into the crisp atmosphere. He stopped for a moment to regain his bearings for his impending descent. He sat relatively motionless and drew his tongue in. Previously unaware it was sticking out, he was so intently focused on both his primary objective to correctly surveil, and his secondary objective to come out of this alive and uninjured, that he hadn't noticed his nervousness revealing itself in this way.

Peter noticed that even at this height a little shy of fifty feet up, the large 39-story Secretariat Building loomed in front of him as it towered over the remainder of the UN Headquarters. It stood as a guardian over the 18-acre complex, which served as an international zone. In the relative stillness of the night, the 193 flags symbolizing the 193 Unite Nations Member States waved in the brisk air with seeming unity and peace. It was an image which could lead the otherwise ignorant to believe that same harmony existed at all times within the international community. That was just wishful thinking.

The light of the moon assisted his gaze as Peter stared, focusing on the glass windows covering the Secretariat Building's façade, the 39 stories of clear glass were striking black, reflecting the sky, and not at all like the crystal blue that was reflected in it during beautiful New York spring and summer days. As Peter made his descent, he did so with caution. He was careful to ensure he and his rifle would make it down safely.

When his boots hit the firm earth he breathed a large sigh of relief and was happy to have gathered the information he needed. Quickly he turned towards home and as he travelled on foot, his mind turned to the business that was conducted within the walls of the compound. He was fascinated by the politics of the UN, always interested to see the workings of various countries' ambassadors, particularly the US and the country of his forefathers, Germany. He kept up with the politics of the present as well as of the past, as the words of his father echoed often in his mind, "Those who don't know history are bound to repeat it."

Tonight, however he was even more so interested in the proceedings slated for the next day in the United States Senate. Tomorrow the nation's Senators would be voting on the Genocide Prevention Act of 1988, which he was closely following. As he continued to walk towards home, he couldn't help but speculate as to the day's outcome.

# Chapter 8

*November 13, 1944 – Berlin, Germany*

If it hadn't been for being ripped from their home by militant soldiers of the Sonderkommandant just after bedtime, Violet would have only remembered the way her pink, silk pajamas felt against her skin as she peacefully drifted off to sleep. She had received them that day for her 13th birthday and she felt like a princess as she lay in bed. Lying beside her was her younger brother Otto whom she was happy to share the bed with. She adored him and the feeling was mutual. He had looked up to his older sister every minute of the nine years of his life.

The two children were full of Lebküchen their mother, Katherine, had baked in celebration of her birthday. Between that and the chocolates she had lovingly made, the children were stuffed like pheasants fit for a king's feast. That day was a wonder and a rarity. Violet was old enough to recognize her mother must have saved all year to buy her gift of silk pajamas and that fact made her appreciate them infinitely more.

Sadly, and in an instant, the wonder of the day was shattered with the banging of soldiers' rifles against their small, wooden apartment door. The terror was amplified with the abhorrent screaming, "Offen die Tür! Jetzt! Offen die Tür!" Violet knew the distinct meaning of this command, "Open the door! Now! Open the door!"

Violet jolted awake and curled up next to Otto who began sobbing uncontrollably. She knew instinctively they should not obey the commands. They should not open the door. Their mother hurried into the bedroom, locked the door behind her and covered the children tightly under their thin blanket.

"Ich hab' euch Lieb," she whispered.

"I love you too, Mutti," Violet whispered in between sobs. Before Violet could process sufficient words to express her devotion to her mother, the front door swung open with a bang so loud it pained both her heart and ears as it reverberated through her body.

This was the night the sound of agony was born and Violet was there to hear it as anguished cries escaped Katherine's throat. Violet stared wide-eyed as the German soldiers penetrated the threshold of their tiny two bedroom apartment. Pounding feet shook the core of the household and smashed the serenity that had embraced the children and their mother just moments before. Violet and Otto huddled together as the soldiers pounded on the bedroom door with the butts of their rifles. It took only three strikes before the thin piece of word cracked under the pressure of the beating and flew open. The door bounced once off the wall as the lead commander struck it back again. This time the door swung back and the door handle embedded itself into the wall.

"Steh auf!" The commander shouted, ordering them in a harsh German dialect to stand up. Violet's mother lunged at the commander's ankles and grabbed them tightly. Her cries of desperation clouded the sound of the commander's orders. Begging for any small sign of mercy, she gripped him with white knuckles and pulled him with all her might away from her children.

The second soldier to enter the room took it upon himself to gain the admiration of the commander and jabbed Katherine in the ribs with his gun. She winced in pain and loosened her grip. Kicking her out of the way, the commander grabbed Otto by the arm, ripping him from the safety of the bed while his wing man was less gentle and pulled Violet by her hair, her night gown snagging on the bed post.

A third officer held a gun to Katherine's head as tears poured down her cheeks. Her sobbing was unceasing and he pulled her up off the ground as the children were torn from the bed. Once sufficiently satisfied that Katherine was smart enough to avoid further acts of disobedience in the face of a gun barrel, the commander ordered the three to gather their belongings. They were directed to bring only one suitcase.

With a gun, if not two at each of their heads, the children and their mother stuffed whatever was most convenient into one small bag each. They were given little more than two minutes. Violet's mind raced and she couldn't focus. She failed to notice as Otto packed a ratty teddy bear and wooden racecar; his two prize possessions. Nothing about these two items was essential or useful in the place they were surely being sent; a concentration camp. Violet mindlessly placed several articles of clothing in her school satchel. She was too filled with terror to assess whether she had everything she needed.

"Time's up," the commander suddenly instructed. What they had packed up to this point would need to suffice. As the soldiers with guns forced the terrified family out the doorway of the apartment building, Violet couldn't help but notice that several of the neighbors had awoken and were standing in their doorways watching. They did nothing to help. There was no movement in the family's direction or in their defense. The frozen stares with which they watched this eviction into the unknown were lifeless. There was just a touch of fear in their eyes but they didn't move an inch. They were not Jews. They had committed no offense. They didn't question at all. They just watched.

# Chapter 9

Despite Saul being gone, Charlotte was not about to give up their fight. With his death, the fire within her to fight against hate crimes burned brighter. The filth of the movement affected her in a very real way. It was now personal and she would ensure that Saul's death would not be in vain.

With the incoming District Attorney's regime, the general sentiments of pride Charlotte felt when she joined the office, were trumped by the anger she had bottled up over her dear friend's death.

As if prosecutor morale couldn't get any worse, it did so when Somers marched into her private office to talk about the latest in the news surrounding the Police Department. The killing of Benjamin Stansfeld had happened two days after the murder of Saul and consequently was the top news du jour. The fact that the rest of the world had already moved on from Saul's death bothered her, particularly when the news of Paniletti's quick comeback in law enforcement overshadowed the murder. *Saul deserves better than that.*

"I don't trust him," Charlotte had publicly vocalized about Somers and as per the usual, the rumor mill was hopping in the DA's office regarding her disapproval. Somers was aware of her disdain before the two of them were even formally introduced.

"I understand you currently sit as one of our top line prosecutors," he told her as he welcomed himself into her office. "I want you to know I value that and I value you, despite what the media has portrayed about the way I've chosen to implement change. I have solid goals for promoting justice in New York and I ran my campaign on that premise, but I need a team to make this work and I need a team attitude.

"That being said you are faced with a decision to make, Ms. Weiss," he continued. "Are you with me or are you against me? I know you are suffering like others in the office regarding the death of Saul Adler. His death is a great loss to the profession. Nonetheless, life moves on and the work of this office must continue. I'll simply leave it up to you to decide where your loyalties lie. In the mean-time, I strongly urge you to consider your desire to continue to be a part of my team."

Charlotte was taken aback at this back-handed expression of sympathy turned veiled threat. Somers spoke in no uncertain terms and the look in his eyes and tone of his voice was unmistakable. The ultimatum was clear: she would ignore any negative sentiments she had about his way of doing business and subscribe to the new way of doing things or she could find a new place to work.

As Somers walked stoically out of her office, providing no time concession for her to respond, Charlotte longed for the time when things were different. Before Somers, Charlotte was a prosecutor because she was working towards a valiant cause. It was noble to be on the right side of the law. Now, with the days of the "Law and Order" campaign gone, she felt conflicted. A crease was taking up permanent residence in her forehead, serving as a constant reflection of her inner angst. The office she once loved was led by a man she was finding difficult to work for, let alone trust.

Deep in thought about her disappointment, she was quickly pulled back into reality when she tasted blood and raised her hand to her mouth to discover she had done it again. Unconsciously, she had bitten her lip. Charlotte possessed a unique set of quirks ranging from germophobia, claustrophobia, a fear of heights and a crazy aversion to vegetables. Of them all, the lip biting, when she was nervous or anxious, was perhaps the most pronounced.

Looking out the window she could see the clouds were looming, darkening the sky and setting a mood in the world outside that paralleled the mood inside. *It's time to call it a day.* In that moment, she decided she was taking a few days off from work.

The swirl of emotions she was already experiencing combined with the ultimatum Somers served her with, were mentally exhausting. She knew herself well enough to know she wouldn't accomplish anything for the rest of the day. Prone to staying late on a regular basis, the thought of burning the midnight oil didn't appeal to her now. She gathered up her coat to fight the elements outside, even though a tornado could rage and it would have seemed like a picnic compared to her inner turmoil.

"Good night, Nicole," Charlotte said to the receptionist as she made her way out the door. "I'm calling it for the day. Don't hold your breath for tomorrow either."

"You deserve it, Char. I'd take several weeks if I were you," she countered.

"Maybe I will." Charlotte really liked the sound of that idea.

Charlotte then walked behind Nicole and reached into her designated mail slot. She pulled out a single envelope with the intention of addressing her mail when she got home, and with that, mustered up the energy to give Nicole a quick smile before proceeding out the door.

After walking on autopilot, she made it into her car and locked herself inside. Reaching into the glove compartment, she pulled out four capsules from her trusty bottle of sedative-laced pain reliever with an added sedative. Although she felt the onset of a headache on top of the sick feeling brought on by anxiety that had formed in her gut, it was the diphenhydramine in the pills she was really going for. Diphenhydramine would dull her anxiety and put her to sleep. Soon she would be completely unconscious and oblivious to her current reality, thus achieving the desired effect. She felt almost like a drug addict with the way she used the pills and in a sense she was. This time she swallowed two more than usual; she would be home just in time to pass out in bed. Swallowing the pills quickly and inhaling a deep breath, she stopped to take a moment and look at her mail.

It was only a single letter addressed to her from the Sing Sing Correctional Facility, 30 miles north. It was always intriguing when prison inmates drafted their own correspondence to her, and unlike when it was addressed to Saul, it never bothered her if it came in the form of hate mail.

Looking down at the envelope, she read the front. The sender was *Isaac Kanzler, Inmate #P027626*. His name was neatly printed in the top left corner of the envelope. Below it was his current residential address: Sing Sing Correctional Facility. His pod, cellblock and bed numbers were also inscribed for ease of return mail. Isaac Kanzler was a name she was vaguely familiar with. Though she couldn't place his face immediately, she knew she had prosecuted him in the past and his name was on her master list of white supremacy gang members.

Now even more intrigued, she carefully opened the letter and found a simple handwritten note inside.

> I have information about the man you're looking for.
>
> Please come see me.
>
> Sincerely,
>
> Isaac Kanzler, #P027626

"*I have information about the man you're looking for. Please come see me.*" It was signed, "*Isaac Kanzler, #P027626.*"

Under his name, in red ink, was a simple cross. The lines were thick and it was meticulously drawn.

Alarm bells immediately went off in Charlotte's head as she processed the simply written words. The message perplexed and intrigued her and she glanced up at the clock on her dashboard as she debated whether or not she would go see him then. She knew that by the time she got to the prison visiting hours would be over. For tonight, she decided she would sleep on it. She would go in the morning after the splitting of her headache subsided and her heart received a little more time to acclimate itself to the unsettling events of the day.

# Chapter 10

Alexander Card liked to go by "Alex," always considering "Alexander" a little too uptight to be relatable. Despite his preference, he went by his formal name for professional purposes, which was appropriate given his position as the United States Senator for the State of New York. His typical easy-going nature wasn't readily evident as of late. His expression was often stoic and it was virtually impossible to tell whether he was angry or overjoyed. For that reason, he was quite often perceived to be moody. The safe default was to presume that he was annoyed whenever there was a question about his constitution. It was best to tread lightly.

Things hadn't always been this way when it came to his personal interactions. It was mainly during the last year in which a drastic change occurred. Alex possessed a wicked sense of humor that was dry as a bone, but those moments of hilarity were seemingly now few and far between. The old Alex was much more preferable to the discontented part of his personality that exhibited itself at present.

As of late, it was a banging on his office wall which was the tip-off that a new senator was in town. At first it came as a shock to his colleagues, especially those with offices on either side, then quickly became a routine as it occurred on most occasions when his wife, Eliza, called him at work.

Alex strived to be a good husband, but despite his love for her it became increasingly difficult to keep up with her demands and the lifestyle to which she had grown accustomed in her formative years. Eliza came from money and throughout her life her parents did nothing to hide that fact. She had a nanny from birth until the day she left home for boarding school and her every need and whim was taken care of.

The consequence of this life of luxury inevitably caused her to lack all skills pertaining to cooking, laundry and domestic chores in general. He would often look the other way when she showed her severe sense of entitlement and despite her becoming spoiled early in life, she was beautiful and sophisticated and he loved her. She had a charisma that was irresistible and was a draw for him that even time could not diminish.

As his mood darkened during the past year there was rampant speculation in the political realm that they would be divorcing soon. He confirmed to a very few close friends that the stress in his marriage had escalated over the years and was magnified by the reality that the couple was unable to conceive. At every stage of their marriage, Eliza, for all intents and purposes, had wanted to have children yesterday, and Alex was not opposed to this plan. He wanted to please her and a large part of him wanted to be a father. With the success he had attained in his life, it was the perfect time.

Sadly, after four miscarriages in as many years, their marriage became strained beyond either of their abilities. Eliza was sick both physically and emotionally due to the losses of the babies.

"It's your body that's causing the rejections," the doctor said, and the toll it took on her was insurmountable.

Alex tried to remind her of his love daily, despite their arguments, but this assuaged her sadness only superficially.

Six months after the fourth fetus passed lifeless through Eliza's body, they all but gave up hope until a miracle occurred in the form of adopting a curly-haired, brown-eyed daughter from Sudan. They named her Brielle. Alex could see in Eliza's eyes when she looked at Brielle that she had never loved anyone to the same degree. The wall pounding stopped and Alex appeared markedly less disturbed with the new addition to his family.

It was now the 10th of September and he was back at home in the Hamptons after a stint in Washington D.C. It was the day after the final day of the legislative session and there had been much agitation the day prior. It was more than the usual politics. The hot item had been the *Genocide Prevention Act* and its purpose was to render sanctions to Iran for their acts of genocide. Alex held a staunch position and he stuck to it as unpopular as it was. He was of the strong opinion that the Act would do little to rid the world of genocide and the economic burden it would place on the United States far outweighed any potential benefit. Through his advocacy, he led the path towards defeat of the bill.

He had arrived home late that night after being in meetings all day. His wife and new child slept soundly and there was a remarkable feeling of contentment in his home, which continued when he went to bed.

The next morning, he awoke later than usual. Glancing at his alarm clock, he saw nothing but red lights blinking "**12:00**." *The power must have gone out in the night.* Blurry eyed, he stumbled out of bed, his mind foggy. It took him just a moment, but then cognition kicked in and he realized that Brielle was eerily quiet. She was seven-months-old now and he had grown so well accustomed to her cries that he hardly noticed anymore when he heard them. The lack thereof was more startling to him than their presence ever was.

Checking his own bed, Eliza was laying sound asleep, sucking up every possible ounce of rest she could while she had the chance, but when he went to Brielle's room to check on her, nothing but an empty crib loomed in front of him. His jaw dropped and he immediately started a desperate search for his daughter. *There's no way she could have gotten out alone, but I need to be sure.* His running around didn't awaken Eliza, but he startled her with a yell.

"Brielle's gone!" he screamed.

He literally bumped into Eliza as he ran back into Brielle's room hoping fervently he had missed something. He prayed his eyes were just playing tricks. The tears were plummeting down Eliza's face as she proceeded out of the small child's pink colored bedroom with a note in her hand.

"This was in the crib," she cried, handing it over to him. "My baby's been kidnapped!"

# Chapter 11

Alex couldn't keep himself from dwelling on his awful situation. News of the kidnapping had been explosive in the days that followed Brielle's abduction. As much as Alex desired that it not be the case, the event was the straw that broke the camel's back of his eight year marriage. His relationship with his wife would be unable to withstand this blow and shortly after the abduction, Eliza was gone.

Alex was now left alone, and found even in his hours of solitude that he was unable to pull himself away from the trauma. At this time, the police were still in his home investigating. He felt powerless and was unable to do anything more than mope and fret. In essence, he had lost everything he held dear and had nothing more to lose.

Two treacherous days after Brielle's abduction, Alex walked somberly into her bedroom. She was still young enough that she needed a crib, but he knew no sooner would he be able to blink than she would be ready for a big girl bed. Or so he hoped. He hoped he would get her back. The empty space where she slept now felt large and daunting. This room, which was supposed to be a haven for her, had been violated and it tipped Alex's world upside down.

As he entered, the room was perfectly quiet. He could hear the sound of his feet hitting the padded carpet beneath him, but was otherwise silently alone in his thoughts. Her bedroom, which felt cold and lifeless, offered him no solace at this time of tragedy.

*Maybe I should fly back to D.C.*, he thought as he rubbed his head in grief. He had spent the last 52 hours awake and in shock and he wondered if it wouldn't just be better if he left town. He couldn't bear to be at home. Despite police working fervently to do everything they could to track down his daughter, just as they had been doing for the last 48 hours, this did little to quiet Alex's soul.

Alex was present during a thorough search of the home. The police focused on Brielle's bedroom window, which was now identified as the clear point of the kidnapper's entrance and exit due to it having been found open when Eliza was sure she closed and locked it the night before.

"The intruder must have gotten around the alarm system when the power was out," Alex surmised to police.

Alex was present for the dusting of fingerprints and for the introduction of the bloodhounds to his daughter's scent. It was supposed to put his mind at ease when the police detective explained to him the latest and greatest news in canine detection.

"Dogs have up to 300 million olfactory receptors in their noses. Humans have a mere 6 million in comparison and the portion of a dog's brain that is dedicated to analyzing smells is 40 times greater than ours. They are our best bet in tracking your daughter's scent," the K9 detective explained to him.

The bloodhounds brought to Alex's house were heavily subjected to odors from Brielle's bedding and her previously worn unlaundered clothing. To serve as a reminder for the dogs, these items were then wrapped in plastic and accompanied the trackers as they pursued her abductor and sniffed out the trail she was last taken down.

Alex did take some degree of solace in the sleuthing canines. They were garbed in police vestiture in the form of a collar and neckerchief with "Police" embroidered in gold. His hope sustained, however, only until day three rolled around and they came up with no long-term leads.

Despite their prowess, the dogs and their handlers worked all day and all night, but inevitably came up short-handed. Alex would routinely sit in a padded rocking chair in the pale pink-themed, teddy bear-themed bedroom where his baby daughter was last seen. Despite the dogs' lack of success, he returned often hoping that being near her padded crib would ease his mind. So far it didn't.

Alex couldn't keep his mind from replaying the events of that fateful morning over and over. He reported it to the authorities as soon as Brielle's abduction was discovered.

He had struggled to communicate with police dispatch, hardly finding the words as Eliza stood crouched in the background crying and shrieking.

When Eliza uttered those shocking words, *"My baby's been kidnapped!"* Alex's mind raced and spun. The words were strange and shocking to hear. The pain of the situation was further deepened in finding that the kidnapper left no evidence of their identity.

Even more enigmatic, was the mysterious pairing of words written just as if they were answers to a crossword puzzle. Neither Alex, his wife, nor the police knew what to make of it. The words were written in scarlet red ink, with the letters connecting to make the shape of another cross:

```
        C
    SHOES
        A
        M
        B
        E
        R
```

# Chapter 12

Katherine and her two children were stuffed in the back of a wagon being pulled by an SS police cruiser. The night air was cold and Katherine wrapped Violet and Otto lovingly with their coats she managed to bring. These items took up most of the space in her one bag but it would keep them warm.

The ride was bumpy and uncomfortable and they were alone. *There are no other Jews on our street*, Violet thought. That was the reason why they received a private trip to the destination they ultimately discovered to be a train yard. Otto cried as Katherine held her children close to her and whispered words of comfort. Unfortunately, Violet was in too much shock to register what she was saying.

Their privacy was not long lasting. After this dark period of the unknown, they arrived at a train yard filled with swarms of other Jews. The entirety of the surrounding mass included people who were ripped from their homes just as Violet's family had been. The fear in the air was palpable and the sadness was tangible.

Violet would remember vividly the train ride which followed next. The train car was packed with people—it was standing room only. To make matters worse, the body heat and close quarters of the confined space was the perfect recipe for the foulest of stenches. The air surrounding them was thick and the Jews crammed in the train car choked on the odor of their neighbors.

Violet studied her surroundings, clinging tightly to Otto who was clinging tightly to his mother, his knuckles turning white. Her eyes struggled to acclimate to the darkness of the enclosure and she was able to see very little. Notwithstanding, fear clearly glared through the darkness.

The train's passengers exchanged stories of their capture and consoled each other with the tales of their own misery, hoping to soften the harsh blow the others had been dealt. No one was there alone.

Violet fought sleep, struggling to try and make sense of it all. The shock of her trauma kept her awake for a time, but was soon overshadowed by her need for rest. She managed to fall into a deep sleep as she and Otto slipped down to the ground. They were small enough to huddle under Katherine and settled between her feet and those of a ragged old man pushed up beside her.

Twenty nine hours later the jolt of the train's abrupt stop shook Violet awake, and she quickly learned the awkward position her body had collapsed into had caused a painful kink in her neck. Her eyes were sore as she strained to see the early morning sun. It was pushing its way through the train car's crevices which served as the passengers' only source of air and light. Violet was still huddled next to Otto who remained in his refuge beside her, and Katherine was still standing with nowhere to lie, leaning against the wall, her eyes closed.

Violet quickly noticed that an additional wool coat was wrapped around the shoulders of she and her brother. It had kept them warm in the night. She felt comforted as its satin lining draped over her pajamas and skin and she recognized it as the coat belonging to the frail elderly man beside her. He was now scrunched in a ball in the corner with his eyes firmly shut. The fragility of his frame gave the appearance that he would break any minute and his paper-thin skin was almost translucent. It appeared it would tear easier than her delicate nightgown. She saw that his name, Erich, was embroidered into the lining of his black, wool coat. As she gently pulled the coat off and placed it gently over the old man, she didn't know it, but this coat was his second most prized possession. He would need it more than they did.

No sooner had the train stopped at its destination than the locked door to the train car slid open. Par for the course on this journey, the occupants were given no opportunity to adjust their eyes to the incoming flood of light before they were herded like cattle out of their cage. There were two sets of reactions to this façade of freedom that was the open train door. First were those who clamored out, anxious to be rid of their boxed prison. Violet was separated from her mother for a moment with their mass exit. Her small frame was bullied from either side as those eager to escape pushed their way out.

She, her mother and her brother were among the others in the second group who reacted quite differently. They were those who were not so trusting; those who hung back. Part of her thirteen-year-old brain shared the view of the bolder crowd. *Anything is better than where we are. Our circumstances couldn't possibly get any worse.*

When the barrel of ten guns showed themselves in their threshold to freedom however, Violet knew she was terribly wrong. Things could and were about to get much worse. Her life again depended on her following the soldiers' orders, and she reluctantly exited her train car prison. It somehow now felt, in comparison to the unknown lurking outside, more like a sanctuary. Outside the train car, they were faced with even greater unknown. She looked upon it from the back of the line of those deboarding the train. Along with her family, she was second to last to exit. The last was Erich, the frail old man. He slowly struggled to make his way out, his shoulders hunched from the weight of a lifetime.

Upon his weak embarkment into the light of day, the entire group was gathered. It was at this time they were met by the others. There were 11 cars full of people who were just like Violet in one respect: they were Jewish. The large group of people was surrounded entirely by bars and fences and then of course, the guns, which forced the crowd into a large open field. This was the Auschwitz Concentration Camp.

Violet immediately saw there was no way out and there was no escape. She tried to ease her mind with the thought of the wildflowers scattered among the grass. They were the one joy, which had not been mowed out of the prison, and they were calling her name. She took particular interest in the wild daisies as the thought of strings of daisy chains stood in front of her as possibilities. She would make a necklace for her mother and a necktie for Otto, she decided. That would be sure to calm her brother's fears.

Violet moved closer to Otto, took his hand and brought his attention to the new find. For the first time since they had been ripped from their beds did a small smile creep across his face. As would be telling of the next few months in their new home, Violet and Otto's shred of happiness brought on by the flowers was short-lived. The soldiers began separating families. Fathers were forced into one group with the men. Mothers were forced into another group with the women. As Violet's mother was pulled into line with the other women, she stood directly across from her children. Again, the soldiers' rifles served as a divide.

Violet clutched Otto's hand tighter as she looked into her mother's eyes. She knew those eyes, and although the look her mother gave was one of feigned soothing, Violet knew another message lay behind them. It was a look of knowing. This was good-bye and it was final. As the tears streamed down Katherine's face, she knew they would never see each other again in this life on Earth. Her mother was sent off for a shower with the line of other women. After that shower, they would never return.

# Chapter 13

*November 28, 1944 – Auschwitz, Poland*

After the horrific witness of Katherine being led away with the other mothers, Violet and Otto were separated from the rest of the remaining crowd. The elderly and the children had been separated and led to a different encampment in their new prison home and each child was surrounded by a mass of their peers in the same situation. They had only each other now, each suffering from the loss of their family members. The commonality of their environmentally induced stress drew them together and they huddled into a mass of small bodies. Each one shook in their boots under the pressure of the soldiers surrounding them with guns.

A brash Nazi soldier made a beeline through the frightened group, once again ripping many apart from the grips of the only loved ones they had left.

Otto cried out to his older sister as she was shoved to the side and their clenched hands were ripped apart. Violet ran to him in answer to the call but was pulled away by her collar. She looked up in shock and found herself staring directly into the face of the tallest man she had ever seen. His bright blue eyes stood in stark contrast to his starched Nazi uniform.

The remaining shreds of Violet's strength were sucked away when he put his hands on her and she couldn't prevent her eyes from welling with tears. In that moment, something else happened, which she would never forget. Staring through the sting of the saline irrigating her eyes she saw a miraculous change in his face. As he looked at her he momentarily softened. A glimmer of light shone in his eyes for a brief second and he let her go. The officer watched her as she paused briefly, unsure of this blessed release, and then ran to her brother's side, enveloping him in her arms. She wondered in fear what might come next as he continued to stare back at her, but she breathed the slightest of sighs of relief when he stoically walked away.

The children were led by force to a dirty warehouse where they were issued miniature prison striped clothing to fit their tiny bodies. Their scant material possessions were stripped from them and collected in a large trailer, which was then hauled away. They were left in a warehouse for the night. Each in the mass of children was hungry and they were all locked in together, neither bed nor bunk available to them.

When dawn broke the next morning, Violet's hunger pangs were severe until three rough soldiers made their way in and threw a small piece of stale bread to each child. The blue-eyed soldier was among them and he targeted Violet again, grabbing her by the hand and leading her to another large stone building.

The shock of the entire experience was beginning to dull her senses. She didn't feel much when this happened. The trauma of the life she now knew was definitely taking its toll and when he led her into the building she saw it was filled with mountains of clothing, shoes, suitcases and other personal items. It was a strange sight and Violet couldn't immediately comprehend where she was.

"Arbeit!" he said. "You will work here." He explained to her harshly that she was to spend her days sorting these mountains of personal possessions.

A handful of adult women were already busy at work. They were strangers to her but she took a small amount of comfort in the fact that they were females. *Maybe this is where all the mothers are.* She was hopeful. As soon as the soldier turned his back to her she scoured the aisles and stacks for her own mother, but Katherine was nowhere to be found. Soon realizing that if her mother was still alive, she was not there, Violet gazed around and took inventory of what was happening around her. This was partially for curiosity's sake but mainly for self-preservation purposes. The women were busily sifting through the large piles and meticulously inspecting each item. They checked the pockets and felt the lining of every garment, searching for something. Anything really; anything of value.

Despite the utter monotony of this position, Violet learned in the days that followed that this job was a privilege. It served as a welcome break from the sheer horror of the camp where she and her fellow prisoners were confined outside the walls of this warehouse. Although she worried about Otto each day until she returned in the evenings to the barracks they were later placed in, she was grateful she had a task. When the tall, blue-eyed soldier would slip her an extra piece of bread each night, she would give it to Otto, grateful she could provide something for him.

Down the middle of the spacious building, Violet saw several well-placed wooden trunks with large slits in them. The women selected to work in the warehouse were to place anything of value that they found into these boxes. The openings were large enough to slip money and other small valuables in, but not large enough to put a hand in to retrieve items.

The women found all manner of items hidden in the clothing. Each one was a treasure that the imprisoned Jews had brought with them, but were stolen away from them. The women were watched like hawks as they worked. The Nazi guards paced continuously backwards and forward keeping a watchful eye. It was their job to make sure the prisoners were doing their jobs and not embezzling any of the loot.

Despite this, Violet knew the wooden trunks lining the aisles of the warehouse were not completely theft proof. She routinely observed one particular guard taking items from the bounty and filling his uniform pockets. The other soldiers turned a blind eye because they were doing it too, and the women never said a word. For the prisoners' part, they were searched each day before returning to their squalid bunks to ensure no contraband was smuggled out.

The daily search was humiliating as they were patted down in the most inappropriate of ways. Violet closed her mind when she saw the women being led away with the soldiers after hours. She would realize later that what went on was just as unspeakable as the terror happening in the rest of the camp.

A physical bolt of pain shot through her heart on one especially difficult day when she came upon a familiar coat in one of the piles of ransacked clothing. It was black wool and she easily recognized the name "Erich" stitched into the lining. It was this coat that had kept her warm many nights ago. It belonged to her old Jewish friend.

Violet had seen Erich a few times in the camp since their train ride together and she witnessed his already fragile body wither even further. Their harsh surroundings and lack of nourishment were taking a toll on him in a major way. Watching as he progressively deteriorated was a very close second when compared with the horror she felt as she watched her mother walk away. Violet ran her hands along the smooth lining of his coat and grasped the wool. She rubbed it along her face and took momentary comfort in the feel of a familiar garment. As her fingers made a final descent down the length of the coat, she faintly felt something small which had made its way to the bottom.

Looking more intently, she observed the item appeared to be sewn into the lining. Not wanting to destroy the coat, but epically curious as to what Erich would have hidden, she looked around to make sure there were no eyes on her and she carefully began to break the stitching at the bottom seam with just her hands.

One by one, she broke the stitches until she created a hole just large enough to access the item, which she could now see was metallic gold. She delicately pulled the item from its casing and was surprised to see that it was a small golden cross on a chain. This confused her given her young age. *A Jew with a treasured cross?* She wasn't familiar with this, but she wanted him to have it back.

Just as she resolved to return it to him, she heard loud footsteps approaching behind her. She recognized it could only be the sound of Nazi boots and she quickly hid what she was doing by throwing the coat in a pile of already checked clothing.

"What are you doing?" an angry guard asked her as he sidled up behind her.

"Nothing," she replied sheepishly. "I'm just checking the garments."

"Keep working," he barked back and then moved on with a grimace.

Violet clung to the golden cross for the remainder of the day, hiding it cleverly in her underwear. At day's end, she placed the small pendant and its chain cleverly under her tongue. She knew this was one place the guards wouldn't check when she left. Despite her ingenuity she was nervous to make her exit, but when the time came she handled herself with poise and swelled with joy when she was able to return to the barracks undiscovered.

Her good deed was not to go unappreciated. Violet was able to find Erich and he wept with joy at his most prized possession's return. He placed it around his neck even knowing it would mean his doom. He slept soundly that night and moments before he was awoken in the morning by, Karl Unreich, one of the Nazi guards a look of peace rested on his face.

Erich's calm quickly turned to one of anguish. The prisoners knew Karl had a reputation throughout the camp as being among the cruelest of the cruel. He ripped Erich from his bed and confronted him about the cross.

"How dare you wear this emblem!" he yelled. "You are a Jew and not worthy of the cross!"

In a calm voice, the old man responded matter of factly, "The Jews share a culture with Christians. We all have prophets. And, yes, I am a Jew but we are the same. Your God is my God and my God is your God."

By now, the entire camp was awake and the prisoners in the barracks turned their complete attention to the scene. They looked on with expressions of shock and amazement. Violet was astounded as Erich professed his conviction with quiet strength to his persecutor. It was then, that Violet saw with her young eyes, Erich transform into a strong giant of a man. An indescribable feeling of power filled the barrack and he seemed for just a moment to be a being that was not quite of this world. There was a heavenly light surrounding him, which was only visible to Violet because of her own purity. His spirit and inner goodness radiated before her.

"We are not the same, you dog! You are nothing!" Karl snapped, stabbing him with his gun and ripping the cross from his neck. Karl continued to beat him until he felt it no longer pleasurable, and in the days that followed, Erich died of resulting internal injury and malnourishment. His physical body finally succumbed to his harsh and cruel environment. Violet was quick to observe the renewed look of peace on his face even in death, and it made her heart smile a little even as it broke more at his passing.

# Chapter 14

*September 11, 1988*

Charlotte thought twice about her decision to go immediately to the prison to see Isaac Kanzler. Her headache hadn't yet subsided the morning after she received his letter and the pain lingered. On her second day off, however, news of the kidnapping reached her and she was taken aback at the symbol of the red cross in connection with the abduction that was reported.

This intrigued Charlotte enough that on the second day she decided to make the trip. She wondered about the simplicity of the message, *"Please come see me,"* and why it was paired with such an enigmatic symbol, a red cross. Her curiosity was sparked in large part because of knowing Isaac Kanzler to be deeply entrenched in the Aryan Brotherhood—*the same organization responsible for Saul's murder!*

She awoke on this morning with anticipation and it was with nervous excitement that she entered the main gates to Sing Sing. As she did so she was engulfed in a sea of concrete, steel and barbed wire. This was a maximum security prison. One had to enter cautiously and no handbags, extra clothing or unnecessary items were allowed past the main doors. One needs a form of identification and lawyers needed a State Bar Card to gain entry. It was of the utmost importance that everyone and everything be accounted for with precision within the prison walls.

Charlotte grasped her wallet with the necessary documents and made her way up the narrow ramp to prison administration. She also brought a legal pad, which she knew would be allowed. Her mind raced with each step towards the entrance. *What does Isaac Kanzler want? What information does he have for me? And what does the red cross mean?*

Upon approaching the entrance, she identified herself and without a moment's delay she was buzzed in through the main steel doors. Because she was responsible for putting some of the facility's most dangerous offenders behind bars, she was recognizable to the prison staff and well known to the guards all the way up the chain of command to the Warden.

Jeff Barker, head officer of the prison lobby, welcomed her immediately with a friendly smile and way too much enthusiasm.

"Hey, Miss Europe," he greeted her. "Are you here to accept my offer of a date?"

Jeff was not the first member of law enforcement to hit on her. Charlotte had always been impressive to men who, with few exceptions, considered her beautiful. The trace of a German accent was attractive to many and she was often paid superficial compliments. Though she hated hearing them, she put up with it with extra stalwartness on occasions like these when she needed something and she knew her appearance would get her things.

"I'm here to see an inmate, Isaac Kanzler," Charlotte responded, hiding all traces of annoyance.

"How are things at the office? I've heard the new boss is about as good at managing attorneys as fish are at climbing trees," he said as he typed into his computer.

"It's always interesting adjusting to change," she replied dismissively.

"I'm sure. The stories are going around. You know how the rumor mill runs in this place. Nothing is sacred, especially when we're down ten experienced DA's."

Charlotte cleared her throat, taken aback at his blatancy. "Is Isaac Kanzler available? Inmate number P027626."

"Oh, right. He's in Pod D. I'll radio the guards to bring him out. And you know the drill."

"Yes, I know the drill, Jeff," she responded, grateful that their awkward exchange was over.

Charlotte dutifully locked her wallet in a locker, cleared the metal detector and walked down the initial hallway to the visitation rooms. The hallway was dotted with windows, and she soaked in the last light she would see before making her way through the dim, empty corridors leading to the rooms specifically designated for attorney visits.

The invisible guards controlling the prison's video surveillance hub watched her on cameras as she passed through an elaborate series of intermittent steel doors. Using their mighty powers harnessed through the innovation of electronic video, the guards sat behind the scenes in their security room and let her pass through each bolted door as she approached. Charlotte was then led by yet another guard, Todd Collins. He was mealy looking and took no effort in hiding the fact that he was counting down the minutes until his shift was over. He escorted her into a small visitation room at the end of the final hall and brashly prompted her to take a seat on a sturdy, metal chair bolted to the floor in front of an equally securely fastened table.

Charlotte sat down and waited for Isaac expectantly in the sterile prison visitation room, all the while tapping her fingers on the metal table hiding her crossed legs. Several minutes in, Charlotte heard the clanking of metal and saw a face she recognized as that of Isaac Kanzler. She could see the passage of time in prison was taking its toll on his outward appearance. He seemed a disproportionately older version of the criminal she prosecuted years prior compared to the actual amount of time that had passed. It didn't feel as though sufficient time had passed for the creases in his face to have taken as deep a root into his skin as they had.

Shuffling into the room, his wrists and ankles shackled, Isaac was escorted in by Collins and seated on the metal chair opposite Charlotte. Collins handcuffed Isaac's wrists to the table and quickly exited.

"Buzz me when you're done," he rehearsed, pointing to a button on the wall next to the table before he exited the room.

The time was 10:30 a.m., and as was customary for an inmate meeting with the District Attorney, it had been announced that Isaac Kanzler was going to medical. Charlotte notified the prison in advance and the Warden was aware there may be a possible defector who could aid the prosecution. *The nurse will be administering my insulin,* is the story Isaac told the other inmates. He led them to believe his health required it.

As Isaac entered, Charlotte's mind raced. *He probably has the Nordic rune for "Life" as his signature tattoo. That or an iron cross—another trademark symbol of the Aryan Brotherhood. Maybe he's going to confess some role in Saul's murder. After all, Saul and I were the last prosecutors to put him in prison.*

# Chapter 15

Collins' departure left a momentarily tense silence in the tiny space of the visitation room. Charlotte and Isaac stared at each other for what was just a few seconds, but felt like hours.

Charlotte broke the silence as she cleared her throat, "I told the warden you wanted to see me and I set you up to break away from the general population. Did it work?"

"Sure did. I told the others the nurse needed to give me my insulin shots." Then changing the subject he said, "I see you got my letter."

"I did."

"And you're intrigued?" he questioned almost cajoling her.

"Slow down. Don't flatter yourself. I want to know why you used the symbol of a red cross and I want to know about Saul Adler," she demanded.

"Ms. Weiss," he addressed her seriously, "I am prepared to defect and give you valuable information. I know about your friend's death as well as the red cross symbol involved in the abduction of Senator Card's baby, but I want to be listed as an Informant. There has to be something in it for me."

"First, tell me why you're doing this," she ordered. "You've been a patched-in member of the Aryan Brotherhood for over a decade. You expect me to believe you want to flip after all that time?"

"It's because of Barrett and Simms. They're going too far," Isaac told her. "The Brotherhood is making moves that even I can't get behind. I'm 36-years-old and given my criminal history I'm looking at 15 to 20 years on the new charges I'm in on. I don't want to die here."

"I took the liberty of bringing your RAP sheet with me," Charlotte told him as she began to flip through it and rattle off his prior crimes. "Possession of Narcotic Drugs, Sale of Narcotic Drugs, Auto Theft, Aggravated Assault, Disorderly Conduct, Attempted Homicide. The list goes on and on. Would you like me to continue?"

"I get it. I have a history but I also have connections. I can get you felony arrests."

"You do realize you've been through the criminal justice system far too long for the prosecution to take it easy on you. You're going to have to be able to produce results of epic proportion about white hate crimes."

"And I can do that. The Aryan Brotherhood is much further reaching than you think," he told her. "They're not just local and their roots run deep. They've woven themselves into the tapestry of society like an infectious disease. They're everywhere and they don't always wear the uniform."

"Sounds like a tough time to try and get out now."

"And it will only get harder. Let me be very clear about something," he continued. "The Aryan Brotherhood is not satisfied to remain a stagnant organization. They will bleed into every component of society if they can. Their ideal is not just racial purity, but extinction of all others. Like an ever-growing organism, they are not content to be small. They will expand in any way possible and seep into every pore of the earth."

"And what does that have to do with the red cross symbol left with Senator Card? I want information about that and Saul Adler's killer," Charlotte reminded him.

"It's quite simple when you consider the fact the Senator has adopted a black baby while he himself stands as a symbol of the country. The Brotherhood will not stand by and watch the mixing of races whenever they see an opportunity to intercede, and I came to you for that reason. You have the knowledge required to make a difference. You have experience with the Aryan Brotherhood which can be instrumental in stopping them. You must help the Senator."

"Are you saying that the abduction of the Senator's baby is related to Saul's killer? That the Aryan Brotherhood is behind both of these crimes?"

"I'm saying I'll give you as much information as I can. Believe me when I say you want to know what I can tell you. I can get you the information you need and you can help me in return."

"I'm listening," Charlotte responded unequivocally.

"I understand you've been trying to pin down Barrett and Simms and you've been intercepting their mail."

"How do you know that?"

"The entire Aryan Nation knows. It's why they've been so hard to catch. They know you're reading their mail so they use a code that is seemingly so difficult, you'd need a team of NSA code breakers to decipher it."

"That would explain why I've had no luck so far."

"What would you say about making me an Informant if I told you I can help you with that?"

"I would say, 'Let me draw up the contract.'"

"I trust then you'll do that right after you leave here because you're about to get a big break in your case. Do you remember what Joseph Simms wrote in his last letter?"

"Yes. I have it with me," Charlotte said, pulling a piece of paper out from her legal pad. "He wrote this last one to Rocky Dobson who's in Alhambra State Prison in California. They're both AB."

"I know," Isaac cut her off. "Rocky was transferred to a prison on the West Coast last winter. He and Barrett are extremely close."

Charlotte placed the letter gingerly in front of him.

"I hope you can make sense of this because I've been staring at it for weeks and have still gotten nowhere."

Isaac took a brief glance at the letter she had been pouring over and then much to her surprise quickly responded, "It's right in front of your eyes because the answer is in the letters. The coded letters are in the letters."

"The coded letters are in the letters?" Charlotte asked quizzically. "That doesn't make any sense."

"May I?" he requested, motioning to the correspondence.

Charlotte slid it closer to him.

"There's no change in the font, the spacing or the thickness of the lettering. It remains consistent throughout," he remarked. He then read the letter aloud:

> Hi Rocky!
>
> How's everything there? Are the conditions in Alhambra better? Like always your charm and wit are needed greatly around here. I am not alone when I say, "Come back, friend." I desperately desire close friends around me.
>
> A grandson was born into my family last November. Wow! I'm thrilled about being his grandfather. He's strong and healthy just as I am.
>
> Miss you buddy.
>
> Best wishes,
>
> Joey Barrett

"It seems fairly blasé to me," Charlotte admitted. "I've been struggling to find any type of deeper meaning."

"It's called the Baconian Cipher," Isaac responded as if it was nothing. He took one look at the letter and immediately knew how to find the hidden message. "The Brotherhood has been using this method of encryption for a while because they've had so much success in keeping it covert."

"The Baconian Cipher? What is it?"

"It was invented by Sir Francis Bacon, a Renaissance man by definition who was in the prime of his life in London at the turn of the 17th century. His life was peppered with various accomplishments in politics, law and science, but to the Brand he's most beloved for the Baconian Cipher he developed in 1605.

"It's a substitution cipher which substitutes each letter of the message for an algorithm of five binary letters specifically using 'A's' and 'B's.' Words beginning with letters of the alphabet A-K are assigned an 'A' while words beginning with the letters 'L-Z' are assigned a 'B'. Once the decipherer has figured out those sets of letters, they are grouped into sets of five. In other words, the first five words would produce a series of five letters in some combination of 'A's' and/or 'B's.' There's a specific alphabet employed wherein each letter of the English alphabet is assigned a string of five letters...I'll need another sheet of paper."

Charlotte ripped a sheet of yellow paper from her legal pad and passed it to him. Then looking around to make sure she wouldn't be reprimanded for giving a sharp object to an inmate, she handed him a pen. Quickly he got to work writing down each of the 26 letters of the alphabet and its accompanying string from memory. In less than two minutes he proudly pushed the page back to Charlotte to show her his work. At first blush, what he had recorded was even more puzzling.

| | | |
|---|---|---|
| A=aaaaa | I/J=abaaa | R=baaaa |
| B=aaaab | K=abaab | S=baaab |
| C=aaaba | L=ababa | T=baaba |
| D=aaabb | M=ababb | U/V=baabb |
| E=aabaa | N=abbaa | W=babaa |
| F=aabab | O=abbab | X=babab |
| G=aabba | P=abbba | Y=babba |
| H=aabbb | Q=abbbb | Z=babbb |

He continued to explain further, "In Barrett's letter, for example, the first five words written to the sect in LA were: 'Hi Rocky! How're things in...' First, we have to establish the first five letters in those first five words. 'H' is between 'a' and 'k,' giving us an 'a'. 'r' is between 'l' and 'z' giving us a 'b,' another 'h' gives us another 'a,' and so on. That gives us the string 'abaab.' Using that string and applying it to the key we get a 'K,' and there we have our first letter in the message. Once you have a basic understanding of the cipher it just takes time and patience. Soon you'll be able to decode much lengthier messages quickly and easily."

Though he had taught her the method, Isaac patiently walked her through the entire letter using the code to decipher the hidden message. With each set of five words he obtained a string of "a's" and "b's" and matched them to their corresponding letters. When he finished Charlotte was horrified at the message and instantly angry at herself because she hadn't seen it before. Isaac had very predominantly written the letters which comprised the fatal order:

## Kill Black Pride

The message was clearly referring to the four members of the Black Pride group who had recently been stabbed to death in Sing Sing. While their backs were turned to their white enemies as they socialized in a cell, each one of them had been fatally stabbed with homemade shanks, by four members of the Aryan Brotherhood. But for their skin color, it was an otherwise senseless set of murders ordered by Barrett. With this information Charlotte had the evidence to prove the crime was racially motivated.

"This was an order for the killing of the Black Pride members in Alhambra State Prison last week. We're too late—," she remarked despondently.

Isaac tried to restore her hope. "While you may be too late for that hit, you've got them now. You can save lives with this. You can convict Barrett and Simms for conspiracy to commit murder as a hate crime."

"Unbelievable," Charlotte said to herself. She was taken aback at what had been staring her in the face for weeks, but what she failed to see.

"Now you know and this information will serve you well," he told her.

"Thank you," she said.

Charlotte paused for a moment of contemplation. "Please," she implored of him, shifting topics. "Tell me what you know about Saul. You have to know something. The Aryan rune for death was carved into his skin. It was clearly the work of the Brotherhood."

"You're right, they are behind his death and it would be foolish to overlook the relationship between a murdered black prosecutor and the abduction of the black baby of a Senator."

"Are you saying the two are connected?" Charlotte asked astounded.

"I'm saying you and Senator Card can help each other. When you help him you will find your answers."

Isaac's eyes softening, he responded, "I'm sorry, I can't tell you who killed your friend without putting your life in jeopardy. You have to find out for yourself and save your own life. I feel it imperative to warn you of one important thing, however. There was a green light on your former partner and now a green light on you. The Brotherhood is and will continue trying to kill you."

Charlotte winced at this harsh reality.

"Oh, and one other thing you might find interesting," Isaac piped up. I can get you the information you need to stamp out the key leadership of the Aryan Brotherhood completely. I can get you to the ultimate leader in the Brand—The Grand Imperial Wizard."

"Who is it?" Charlotte asked failing in an attempt to hide her excitement at the question she had been desperate to have answered for the last 10 years.

"I've given you a lot, Ms. Weiss, but it won't be that easy. I can't let you take away my leverage without an informant deal. I'll give up the name when I have it in writing that I'll be out of prison sooner than later. For now, let me tell you that you're on the right track. You recognized the meaning of the carving in Saul Adler's chest as the Aryan rune for death, the inverse of the Aryan rune for life. Take notice, that red cross I sent is the great divide. If you combine the two Aryan runes, the shape of a cross marks the exact middle. The middle is where the answers are found. Look for the symbol of the red cross wherever you go."

The next thing Charlotte knew, Collins was entering the room and began to retrieve the prisoner.

"Time's up, Kanzler," he said. His timing could not have been more inopportune.

"Now, wait just a second," Charlotte demanded. "That's it? The middle is where the answers are found?"

"That's all I can give you," Isaac responded, making a quick glance at the guard. "Just remember the red cross. Look for that symbol wherever you go and you'll find your way. Let me know if we can help each other further. You know what I mean by that."

Forcing the conversation to end, Collins questioned Charlotte, "You know your way out of here?"

Charlotte, though thoroughly annoyed with him, said everything she needed to simply with the look she gave him as he ushered the prisoner out. She then quickly stood up to leave as Isaac was led down the hallway leading back to his cell. She was determined, as she watched him walk away, that she would be back with the paperwork first thing tomorrow. She would need to work fast before word got out she had learned the code.

Charlotte retraced her steps back through the prison now deep in thought. *The middle is where the answers are found. Look for the symbol of the red cross wherever you go.* She repeated those words to herself and her thoughts swirled as she tried to decipher the cryptic message.

# *Chapter 16*

Despite her focus on the tragedy of Saul's murder, the news surrounding the abduction of Senator Card's baby had reached Charlotte almost immediately after it happened. It had been virtually impossible to avoid. The media coverage had been the reason she was able to speculate as to its connection with Saul's death when she met with Isaac.

During their visit, Isaac instructed her that she was necessary in helping the Senator find his baby and in solving the mystery of Saul's death. Even as she lay in bed the night after her trip to the prison, she was restless, drifting in and out of sleep as she tried to make sense of everything. *The middle is where the answers are found. Look for the symbol of the red cross wherever you go.*

Her mind was groggy the next morning, but she bounced awake when she picked up the newspaper and saw the bold letters draped across its front page:

---

**STRANGE CLUES SURROUND THE KIDNAPPING
OF U.S. SENATOR ALEXANDER CARD'S BABY**

---

Scanning the front page of the newspaper, she quickly read the main story regarding the seven month old robbed from her cradle at home. The details of the story made it clear that police had eliminated the possibility of the situation being any type of custody dispute or familial quarrel. This crime was clearly the work of an outsider. As the media made sure to mention, not only was this a worrisome situation for the Senator's family, but it could be one of potentially international gravity were this determined to be the doing of a rogue foreigner. Charlotte's heart went out to the Senator and she remembered what

Isaac had said about her helping him and the fact that they had both received letters with the strange marking of a red cross.

The previous article had described: "With no fingerprints, hair or any other physical evidence identifying the abductor, something of a good-bye letter was left in the child's crib. It's a cryptic message that breathes a greater sense of gravity into the situation confronting Senator Card. Even more mysterious and disturbing is the mark of the words 'shoes' and 'chamber' in the shape of a cross. A pair of the child's shoes was left in her crib with the note. The Senator has reported no knowledge of its meaning and investigators are stumped."

All things considered after her prison visit as she read the article it was clearer to Charlotte than ever that there was a lot of work to be done. *I have to get to the bottom of this.*

# Chapter 17

Alex lived in the Hamptons where beautiful homes dotted the lush, tree-lined streets. Due to the extent of the news media's coverage, video footage of Senator Card's home was widely publicized and the viewing public was shown the abduction scene from a variety of angles. Because of the publicity, Charlotte found the location of his home was unnervingly easy to find.

Charlotte approached the Card residence and made it to the front gate on the outskirts of the property. The home's palatial theme was immediately obvious from the exterior and it appeared to be seemingly ripped right out of the pages of a luxury home magazine. This particular home sat in a wrought iron fence enclosure and was surrounded by tall deciduous trees. A private electronic gate protected the structure from any n'er-do-wells and riff raff.

It was late afternoon when Charlotte decided to pay a visit to the Senator. She needed to attend to this before she went back to see Isaac. When she arrived, she noticed the police presence had called it a day at the Card Estate and a newly appointed armored guard stood at the entrance. *Rightly so.*

Charlotte drove confidently up to the gate, firm in her resolve to speak to Alexander Card. She rolled down her window and stoically addressed the on-duty police officer guarding the premises. Flashing the gold D.A. badge emblazoned with her name, she identified herself and was waved in. *That was easy.* Not wanting to question the guard, she drove up the stone driveway slowly as if speed would cause her vehicle to careen out of control and disturb the crime scene. Yellow police caution tape was strung entirely around the area and she was careful not to touch it as she parked and walked to the front door.

Charlotte rang the doorbell and knocked loudly, breaking the eerily quiet stillness. She knocked five times as it took an inordinate amount of time for Alex to come to the door. As she waited, the feeling in the air was cold and shot through her body like a dagger. It came in stark contrast to the beauty of the home and the exterior flowers meticulously lining the home. Subconsciously, she felt the presence of something drastically amiss as she waited, then heard heavy footsteps on the other side of the wooden door. It slowly cracked open.

It was then that Charlotte saw the poster child of degradation. Alex appeared visibly ragged with stress and worry. The bags under his eyes were puffy and dark and there was a slack to his face revealing he felt as hopeless as he looked. The stress of losing his child was a burden that was visibly a hair's length away from swallowing him whole.

"Can I help you?" he demanded in a tone signaling he was not to be trifled with.

All too familiar with this similar air of chauvinism and condescension she recently experienced in the workplace, she stood her ground and gave him the benefit of the doubt. *Under normal circumstances, he surely wasn't so mean spirited,* she reassured herself. *Enduring the heartache of a kidnapped child has likely caused this reaction. This is an anomaly.*

Charlotte introduced herself by name, but Alex didn't give her the opportunity to identify her profession before he blurted out, "You're trespassing on my property. How did you get past the gates?"

Charlotte was taken aback by his prompt dismissiveness. "As I was going to tell you," she went on. "I'm with the District Attorney's Office. I'd like to talk to you about the letter you received from your daughter's abductors. I was recently mailed a letter with a red cross on it and I think there may be a connection to the red cross encryption you received."

Charlotte pulled Isaac's letter out of her purse and showed it to him, pointing specifically to the red cross.

"Where did you get this?"

"An inmate in Sing Sing sent it to me."

"I'm sorry. What did you say your name was?" he asked her condescendingly.

"Charlotte Weiss, New York District Attorney's Office."

"Well Ms. Weiss, at last count the police have received 136 calls from people claiming to have information about my daughter's whereabouts. I even had one old woman in Pittsburgh call and make a report about her neighbor, who she could hear talking to himself through the walls, showing up this morning with a black baby. Turns out she's a paranoid schizophrenic and the child was his granddaughter he was seeing for the first time.

"With all due respect to your position, Ms. Weiss, because I know I'm going to be relying on your office when we find the heathens who took my daughter, I don't think it would be wise for me to consider your letter when not even the police have any credible leads. I'm certainly not going to trust some lunatic prison inmate trying to send me on a wild goose chase. I understand they've got nothing but time on their hands there in Sing Sing."

Despite Charlotte's desire to scream at him about the urgency of the situation, she paused to be cautious in her words and made sure to exercise extreme sensitivity.

"If that's your decision I will respect it," she said after carefully selecting her words. Handing him a business card, she added, "This is my card. I will be available to you if you need anything or change your mind."

And with that, she walked away with poise and grace as her mind flooded with questions. *How am I going to convince him to help me and more importantly how am I supposed to help him?*

He wouldn't listen to her tell him she had no doubt as to Isaac's veracity and that she knew not just the answers to the mystery behind Saul's death, but also the life of the

Senator's child, were on the line. Unfortunately, though, making him more upset would only worsen the situation.

As she made her way home, she decided she was not giving up on this. She would go it alone if she had to.

# Chapter 18

As the days and weeks rolled by, Violet continued to grieve the loss of her mother and now that of Erich whom she liked to have said was her friend. Nonetheless, she found strength in being an emotional rock for Otto. She consoled him through the trial of what they were forced to endure and encouraged him to use his child-like imagination to entertain himself. It also lifted Otto's spirits when soon enough both children found a new friend in the form of a 12-year-old boy named Mathias. They loved his antics as he entertained them and the other children in the camp with magic tricks. Violet and Otto were mesmerized by him.

Mathias routinely pulled flowers from a basket he had woven from sticks and made innumerable rocks disappear and reappear from his new friends' ears. He formed a special bond with a rat there in the prison and his audience loved his sidekick, especially when he made his little buddy disappear. Even though Violet knew Mathias simply pushed the rat into his sleeve for the great disappearing act, the trick was a favorite of she and Otto. Violet would watch him with joy, but her joy was always undercut by sadness. She wished nothing more than for Mathias to use his magic to make her disappear from this place.

Violet found further distraction in the crowded barracks with the Jewish prisoners' frequent talk of escape. After the death of Erich, Violet wholeheartedly resolved to be saved from this hell on Earth. She watched sadly as the general health and welfare of the prisoners at the camp shrunk into almost nothing. As that occurred, she recognized the likelihood of escape was also shrinking. Even as the prisoners' ambitions grew, their strength declined. Few made the attempt to escape, and none were successful.

Matthias had told her of his plan to dig out from under the fence one night, but even as he told her about it she had a strong feeling she would never see Mathias again. She was right. She closed her eyes that night in anguish as the silent tears leaked out of her eyelids at his capture and murder. She allowed herself to grieve only until morning at which time she would turn her attention back to survival.

After Mathias' failed attempt at escape, an internal fire was lit within Violet. Her numerous and tragic losses were making it almost unbearable, but for Otto's sake she knew she had to overcome the odds.

Day in and day out she would dream about escaping. Shell shocked by Mathias' failed attempt, her innocence had all but been ripped from her as she processed thoughts with a clarity that was beyond her years. By now she counted herself fortunate to be in the organizing warehouse. It was her luck of being in that situation which eventually gave her the idea of the delivery trucks.

Other than the 1939 convertibles which were the favored method of transportation for high ranking Nazi Officers of the SS, the delivery trucks were among the few motor vehicles entering and exiting the camp. Violet was careful to note a schedule when it came to picking up loads of items from the warehouse.

*How can Otto and I escape undetected in one of those trucks?* She wondered. She needed the perfect plan to stow away.

It came to her one sullen afternoon. By carefully paying attention to their schedules, she learned that every two weeks three dump trucks with uncovered beds arrived to be stacked with piles of clothing that were previously ransacked and searched for valuables. The trucks would stay in the warehouse overnight and when the morning came, they were driven out of the camp. Violet didn't know their destination, but that was of no consequence. The one thing she was sure of was that the trucks left the camp.

By this time, winter was in full swing and the snow was thickly blanketing the ground. This was the perfect time to make a go at freedom. Violet stayed on alert for the next shipment to go out. When the time came, the trucks were packed and loaded as usual. Nothing, not even the weather, would deter her. She awoke in the middle of the night and snuck out of the barracks, taking Otto with her. Other than a last ditch will to live, Otto was the only viable thing she had left in this world.

For the escape, Violet made sure they wore their one pair of worn down Nazi issued shoes out into the cold and they quietly made their way to the warehouse. She was careful to cover their shoeprints in the snow using a stick. She knew the truck was packed and ready to leave first thing in the morning. They would wait until then. Of course, the waiting would be easier said than done. When they arrived at the warehouse door, to her horror, the door was latched closed with a padlock. The large cargo door on the opposite end of the building would be too heavy to open even if it wasn't locked.

Because of her meticulous planning, however, all hope was not lost. She had thought this situation through and had an alternate plan. Earlier in the day, when the watch guards were busying themselves with grubbing money and valuables from the day's collection, she risked wedging open a small lower window. She did this meticulously in terms of timing and was careful to do it minutes before the end of the day so as not to alert anyone should they feel the outside air infiltrating the building more than usual.

Now that the depths of night had fallen and the chill in the air grew, Violet rushed to the window from the outside to ensure it was still cracked open. She found it was, but as she attempted to raise it further she quickly discovered it was stuck. The freezing cold had caused ice to form in the crevices and the frozen window would simply not budge. She furiously tried to push it open further, even just minimally. Her fingers shot in pain from the cold as she continued pushing and prodding the window. Finally, there was success. She broke the icy barriers and got the window to budge just enough to open it.

Quickly, Violet turned around in excitement to retrieve her brother and hoist him up, but her face drained of all blood, becoming as white as the snow which lay before her when she saw there was no Otto! Her eyes captured a line of small footprints in the snowy carpet. The imprints were quickly filling in with consistently falling snowflakes and she hastily followed the path around the warehouse. She ran until she neared the border of the camp where she could make out the silhouette of her younger brother standing in the darkness at the chain link enclosure at the northeast corner of the camp.

Horror stricken, her mind reverted to the fate of Mathias in that same location. Impulse and adrenaline continued to flow as she sprinted to Otto's side and grabbed him by the shoulder. He stood rigid as she tried to pull him away but he remained staring forward and pointing ahead.

"There's a man," he said, "A man on the lake."

"Komm schon! Let's go!" was Violet's immediate response. "We'll get caught." Seemingly dragging him back to the window, time forced her to rely on the snow to cover their tracks. She dodged behind the warehouse, trying desperately to personify an unseen ninja, which was proving difficult with her small companion in tow.

"You could have gotten us killed," she chastised him as she hoisted him up and through the open window. "Squeeze through," she directed until he emerged on the other side.

When her younger brother was soundly in, Violet hoisted herself up and then carefully locked the window behind them. She took no time in hurrying Otto to the loaded truck. She knew that once they were safely in the truck, they could get warm and hide under the stacks of clothing. As they situated themselves inside the truck's bed toward the bottom, she was careful to make sure neither of them suffocated under the weight of the load.

As she lay cuddled next to her brother in the softest, most comfortable bedding they had enjoyed since their abduction earlier in the year, Violet fought sleep. She lay awake enjoying the soft material against her skin but anxious about what was to come.

Eventually, despite her boldest of efforts, sleep did overcome her, which she learned several hours later when her eyes sprung open at the sound of the truck's engine starting. Her joy was great when she realized the soldiers had not spotted them and she looked carefully through the stacked clothing and metal bars of the truck, ready to see the world outside...

# Chapter 19

*It looks good*, Peter thought to himself as he prepared the final report on his exterior United Nations security check. He sat in the UN security room surrounded by walls of television screens, computer equipment and audio and video recording devices. As the head of Security, he lobbied for the latest surveillance equipment and he took great pride in his work. He managed a crew of 100 employees and was wildly intent on having the job done right. Even when it placed him in precarious situations, including extreme heights, he was willing to take on any required task to ensure the safety and security of the UN.

The effort he expended surveilling up in the tree recently served him well. It was his final analysis that the tall tree posed no immediate threat or opportunity for a sniper, but it was nonetheless his suggestion that the upper branches be trimmed. His report was written up and would be filtered to the UN director and handled accordingly. Based on his report, the UN facilities department would be tasked with trimming the tree to ensure it posed no threat.

With the printer printing out his final report, Peter moved on to the higher priority issue at hand. Sliding a videocassette into the surveillance machine's recording compartment, he memorialized the relevant footage taken at 1:52 p.m., the day of Benjamin Stansfeld's death, by making a copy.

He paused for a moment to reflect on Benjamin who had been his closest friend. Peter first became acquainted with him when he was stationed in the military on the Northern Border of South Korea. Benjamin was there on the front lines of the Korean conflict doing what he did best, investigative journalism. He was perfect in the role, investigating the guts out of any topic he was researching, and then putting on paper the oftentimes harsh realities of war and a world no one wanted to think about.

Benjamin was a Jew but the topic of religion never came up between the two friends and Peter admired him almost to his detriment. There were few people in the world Peter would have laid down his life for willingly, and Benjamin was one of them.

The other was his wife, Myung-Hee, and as Peter left work that day, he would return home, sit on a chair at the foot of the bed where she, the love of his life, lay.

The television screen now in front of him was paused with an image on the screen as if frozen in time. He brought a copy of the UN surveillance footage home for safekeeping of the video evidence documenting his friend's murder. The screen blasted the image of Benjamin Stansfeld with his arms up in the air, hands empty and facing away from the police officers who were aiming at him. It was an image of the moment right before Stansfeld was killed by the bullet that would be called justified.

This footage was taken from a camera on the west wall of the UN compound that faced First Avenue in New York City. Peter made a backup copy for extra security and packaged the only other remaining videocassette copy in a manila envelope and sealed it closed. He then hid the backup tape in a false panel in a leather case, and knowing he was the only person to have a key to it, he locked it up. He had erased the segment of the surveillance footage of interest and deleted it from the computer hard drive at work. It was imperative the information not be inadvertently leaked, yet at the same time needed to be preserved to ensure it was siphoned to the proper party; the District Attorney.

# *Chapter 20*

Feeling like she had hit a dead end, Charlotte was back at work after only a few days of leave. She felt she might be able to clear her mind better if she focused her mind on something else for a while. The toxicity of her office environment hung over her like a looming cloud that would not dissipate, however. The threat to her job that Somers made still echoed in her mind. Nothing about their most recent conversation sat well with her and she continued, just as she had since it happened, to wonder: *Does the satisfaction I receive from my job outweigh the fact I'm working for such an arrogant man whose sense of ethics are increasingly becoming more suspect?*

As she sat at her faux wood desk with mahogany veneer, momentarily lost in contemplation over these questions, her office phone rang.

"Charlotte, you have a delivery up front," the office receptionist informed her. "The man says he's from the UN and wants to give it to you personally."

"Thank you Nicole. I'll be right up."

Mail and other deliveries were typically received or signed for by the front desk receptionist. It was rare that an outsider would approach her with a personal delivery but Peter Bremer had called her earlier and she was expecting his arrival. He informed her that a video camera at the UN Complex had caught the face-off between Benjamin Stansfeld and police. There was a video recording of the final moments before his death.

"You must be Mr. Bremer," she greeted him cordially as she stepped out into the office lobby. His face looked familiar to her, although she couldn't place it.

"Yes, as I said on the phone, I have something I believe will be of extreme interest to you."

"I will review it thoroughly. Thank you," she replied.

"My pleasure. I understand you have a reputation as a strong advocate for justice and I'm confident in your abilities," Peter said to her. Then nodding his head he gave her a friendly, "Good day, Ms. Weiss."

Having accomplished the delivery of the package, he ended the conversation abruptly and turned on his heels and walked out.

Charlotte hurried back to her office and placed the tape into a VCR. She watched with anticipation as the video unfolded and was amazed to see that it was indeed a recording of the shooting of Stansfeld, and though she was expecting it, she sat in complete shock as she saw right before her eyes that the shooting of Benjamin Stansfeld was anything but justified.

Charlotte watched in horror as the video streamed. She watched it over and over in real time and slow motion. It was clear to see that this shooting was in no way done in self-defense or defense of others. *This was murder.*

Charlotte blinked in disbelief. She had run the idea of an Informant Contract for Isaac past Somers and he had instantly put a stop to the idea, citing it would be giving up too much to such a heinous criminal. She paused momentarily, now gathering her thoughts, and then made a choice. *It's go time now. All bets are off.* She was recruiting Isaac as a Confidential Informant and that would be the end of that. *Somers made an unrighteous call about Stansfeld's death and the video proved that. He is not to be trusted.*

She quickly drafted the Informant Contract. Though it was office policy to have Brent Somers' approval first, it would be executed without his blessing. She was about to tow a line of insubordination and was happy to do it. It was time to take a few more personal days.

# Chapter 21

The truck moved slowly at first as it made its way out of the concentration camp. The driver stopped at the main gate to greet the guard at the entrance and Violet could do nothing but lay in horror as she recognized the voice of the man behind the wheel. It was unmistakable and was none other than the leader of the camp, Dietrich Rüpel, who was lending a hand with that day's clothing delivery. He was the tall man who had given her the warehouse duty. She hadn't known his name at first but she later came to know it all too well.

The situation she and Otto had found themselves in seemed now exponentially more terrifying. Upon hearing his unmistakable voice she found herself clenching her teeth in anticipation of the worst. It felt like an eternity before the wheels of the truck again slowly turned, propelling the truck forward and out of the borders of the camp. Violet lay underneath the piles of clothing near the edge of the truck. The truck bed was made of metal slats that she could see through and she dared herself to look out at the outside world. She tried to focus on the view of the open space and land surrounding them. She maintained a fervent grasp of Otto's hand, stroking it lovingly and silently soothing him.

Once outside the camp, the truck moved quickly, but not fast enough for her liking, away from the hell they were leaving. Eventually, it made its way to a yard, and while the ride was a mere 20 minutes, it felt like an eternity. She passed the time by focusing on the next stage of the plan, but despite her best efforts she still didn't know what to expect when the truck stopped. They would be acting on a whim and a prayer, taking the events as they came and adapting to the circumstances to make it out of this situation free and unharmed.

As the delivery truck came to a halt, the vehicle rotors moved and creaked as the truck bed turned over on its side. She quickly pulled Otto closer and the two burrowed themselves further into the clothing pile.

"Hang on to me," she whispered to him as they were plunged from the height of the towering truck bed and catapulted to the ground. The clothing acted as a cushion to their fall and they were also covered with clothing as the truck continued to dump its load.

When the delivery was complete Violet laid tensely, her breath heavy. She confirmed her hand was still gripping Otto's by squeezing it, being careful not to rustle the mountain in which they lay or otherwise alert anyone to their presence. Violet slowly turned her head toward him. Unable to see him, she desperately wanted a confirmation that he was okay. Weakly he returned the squeeze of her hand and a sudden sense of comfort filled her heart.

She felt instantly calm as the words came to her mind, *Whatever happens, stay still. Keep your eyes closed and count to 100 in your head. When you open them, there will be magic.* She heard the voice of her mother speaking the words to her mind and she quietly whispered them to Otto.

Violet knew he couldn't count to a hundred, but that he enjoyed the attempt and that the task would preoccupy his mind for a lengthy period of time and would keep him still. Otto whispered to her that he understood her directions and immediately closed his eyes and began silently counting to himself.

No sooner had Otto started the task than Violet felt a gut wrenching cold breeze drift over her calf. A brisk wind uncovered a portion of her leg and her heart beat out of her chest as she felt the firm grip of a large hand grab tightly around her ankle. She was slowly being pulled out of the pile. Hesitatingly she released her hold of Otto, being very careful not to take him with her. Tears welled in her eyes and her body became increasingly cold as she was dragged further out into full exposure. When she felt the light of the sun hit her clenched eyelids she knew it was time to face the inevitable.

Her now water logged eyes opened into the cold brightness and as sure as she lived it was, in fact, him. It was Kommandant Dietrich Rüpel. Without a word he yanked her up and pulled her into the truck cab. She was going with him whether she liked it or not. Though dying on the inside, she made sure not to cause a fuss.

Dietrich belted her in and she cautiously looked in the rear view mirror as he visually searched the stack again. It was nothing short of miraculous that he didn't notice the still hidden Otto laying amidst the clothing pile counting to himself. He was doing just as Violet instructed him. Violet's heart lifted and as Dietrich drove her away in silence she knew her brother would be saved. Her cross to bear, whatever it was that was coming, would be lessened knowing he was safe.

# Chapter 22

Charlotte took the video from Peter Bremer home to view it again and collect herself before returning to the prison to see Isaac. The video recording was paused at a pivotal point on the screen in front of her when her phone rang. Wondering who would be calling she answered the phone. Still pondering the circumstances surrounding Stansfeld's death, her "hello" was quiet and her attempt at a greeting was feeble. On the other end of the line she was stunned to hear the voice of Alex. After his icy reception and complete disinterest in what she had had to say she was sure he would not be contacting her further.

"Ms. Weiss," he addressed her matter of factly. "I've changed my mind. I'd like to work with you."

Though this sudden turn of events was strange to say the least, she wasn't about to ask any questions. *Two minds are better than one.* She would be much more successful with him along.

"That sounds fine," she responded casually.

"Good. Then I need you to come now."

Alex waited at home patiently for Charlotte to arrive. He wouldn't tell her just yet why he changed his mind, but he was glad she agreed to come. He sat anxiously on the rocking chair in Brielle's bedroom. It, along with the entire house, was still cold and empty, filled only with his feelings of guilt.

*I was in Washington for too long. I should have come back more on weeknights instead of just the weekends.*

In the back of his mind, he knew that idea was unreasonable, but in hindsight he couldn't help but feel ultimately responsible.

Eliza had told him on several occasions she was exhausted and even before Alex arrived home the night of Brielle's abduction, Eliza knew of his homecoming and took the liberty of placing some of the worry on him at his return. She was out like a light before he even got home. Alex kicked himself for not being trustworthy. Neither of them heard the intruder enter their home or leave with their precious child. His wife had been relying on him to help her and he had failed. He began to understand now why she left him.

# *Chapter 23*

Charlotte arrived at Alex's home a quick 20 minutes after his phone call. Though his demeanor was still softened when she arrived, she knew she needed to continue to tread lightly. Charlotte stepped into the marbled entrance of the home and took a seat in a front room where high arched ceilings and a crystal chandelier reflected the sunlight flowing in through a wall of windows. The light shone in stark contrast to the mood permeating the mansion. Charlotte took a seat delicately on a plush loveseat and inhaled deeply in anticipation of the account she was about to make of her visit with the prisoner.

"I'll get right to the point," she told him. "I received a letter from an inmate in Sing Sing requesting I contact him and out of curiosity I paid him a visit. The red cross drawn on his letter pulled me in because it was so mysterious."

Charlotte then went on to explain her conversation with Isaac Kanzler in its entirety. She was careful not to omit any of the details, knowing that Alex could possibly shed light on some of it.

Through the entire discourse, Alex sat across from her motionless. He was taking it all in as worry embedded itself even deeper into the creases on his face. Alex appeared to be aging right in front of her as she talked, but when he began to speak, the things he shared with her were crucial. He explained to her what she had seen on the news—he had received a letter and a pair of his daughter's shoes was left with the letter in her crib.

"May I take a look at the letter?" Charlotte asked.

"Sure," he said, handing her a sheet of worn paper. "The police didn't find any fingerprints on it, but they took the original anyway and left me with a copy. You can take a look at the copy."

The words were handwritten in heavy black ink and though he had read it an innumerable number of times he knew she needed to see it.

> *Alexander Card:*
>
> *You must respond. A horrific atrocity exists for a people who are in grave need of assistance and aid. Through a figure in authority is how help will be brought. Achieving benefit for humanity must be urgent for those in a capacity to bring about drastic change.*
>
> *Senator, as a chieftain, a great obligation is currently given for which action must transpire. Be admonished. Your life and safety for your precious Brielle is contingent upon a change regarding an ideology you continually embrace. Your daughter's fate is in your control. Be ever warned.*

"I have no idea what to make of it," he began, but was immediately distracted by Charlotte's furious note taking on a separate piece of paper laid on the table in front of her.

"What are you doing?" he asked, puzzled.

"I just need a minute. I want to check something."

As she worked, Charlotte recounted to Alex the roots of the Baconian Cipher she had researched after her meeting with Isaac. Alex waited patiently as she worked and simultaneously explained to him what she had learned.

"As a method of steganography, Sir Francis Bacon's method of hiding secret messages lies in the presentation of text rather than its content. That makes it much more difficult to decipher," she told him. "A standard code may substitute letters, numbers or symbols for directly correlate letters in order to form a message, but Bacon's cipher requires revealing a message using a series of the letters 'a' and 'b' in various permutations. Because of its simplistic complexity, the Aryan Brotherhood was quick to latch on to this method of encryption when it was discovered by an early founding member. Modern day Nazis have, up until now, kept the secrets of the cipher known only to those in their ranks. They use it as a sufficiently obscure method for hiding messages in correspondence that law enforcement has been unable to crack."

Still decoding, Charlotte surveyed her notes on the Baconian Code she had taken during her meeting with Isaac. With those on hand, it took her only a few minutes to finishing up with what would hopefully be a proper translation, she finally took a moment to exhale as they both stared at the letters she had written on the page:

## HANNIBALSBARYONKERS

"Hannibalsbaryonkers? What in the world does that mean?"

"It's likely not one word, but a series of words." No sooner had she explained this to him than it came to her as she stared at the string of letters

"Hannibal's Bar Yonkers!" she blurted. "That's our clue. That's where we have to go."

"What are you talking about?"

"I used the Baconian Cipher to decode your letter."

"Whoa. Wait a minute!" He stopped her abruptly. "You mean to tell me the Aryan Brotherhood is responsible for my daughter's abduction?"

"I can't say that with certainty, but it's worth a try to follow this lead. So far it's the best we've got."

Alex was frustrated, but didn't argue with her. *She's here to help.* He felt extraordinarily helpless on his own just waiting for the police to come up with some semblance of a credible lead. Eliza had checked herself into a psych ward, he had learned. When she discovered their baby missing, the shock literally pushed her to the ground. Finally, after 18 hours of fervent weeping, she had to leave. Her sense of pride was quashed by the trauma she was experiencing and she didn't care in the slightest if the press found out about her becoming the local psych ward's newest patient. Their baby had been kidnapped and she blamed Alex. The words resonated loudly with him when she accused his politics of putting them in this situation and the trauma of the situation was now simply unbearable. This clue from the letter was something of a lead and it was definitely better than sitting around the house moping.

"I guess we're going to Yonkers," he conceded.

# *Chapter 24*

*September 13, 1988 – Sing Sing Correctional Facility*

It had taken him many months to collect enough of what he needed. Isaac had received a string of mail and he clung to the envelopes like they were gold.

"They're letters from my girl on the outside," he told people. "She's white and faithful and after all we've been through together she won't abandon me now. She writes to me every day."

In reality, this adoring woman on the outside was fictitious. The truth was that each precious envelope that arrived for him was laced with Cylcon-B cyanide. It was sent in such a way that even the prison mail guards couldn't detect it and no member of the Brotherhood was the wiser. Isaac collected the poison-containing-envelopes under his thin prison mattress. When the guards came in for searches of the cells they routinely put their hands into everything and overturned the mattresses, but they did nothing to bother these envelopes. *They're simply remnants of harmless correspondence.*

Not having to worry about prison guards, Isaac also demanded the respect of his top-bunk cellmate, Justin Vincent, when it came to his personal mail. Just as it was intimidating to other prisoners in the facility, Isaac's large stature was intimidating to Justin. Justin was an aspiring patched-in member of the Aryan Brotherhood, but quickly learned that staying to himself was the best way to avoid the air of tension created by Isaac. He didn't dare cross Isaac. Isaac would know if he so much as touched his letters and there would be severe consequences.

Isaac needed exactly eleven grams of the Cyclon-B. Eleven grams would take care of the Brotherhood including his cellmate, Justin, whose eagerness to impress the

Brotherhood's leadership was aggravating and uncomfortable. He had over a decade of life on the kid who was barely 22, and had little patience for this lack of knowledge in the ways of the world.

Tonight was the night Isaac would be executing his plan. Last night, he had obtained a small piece of plastic wrap from the prison kitchen. Pressed up against his skin, he was confident it would go undetected. He was prepared for tonight's chore.

Tonight, as Justin lay quietly listening to his cellmate, the shouts of other inmates echoed through the cement walls just as they did every night before, and it wasn't until 3 a.m. on this night that the rallying died down completely. Now you could hear a pin drop. That is, except for his bunkmate below.

Justin lay still on his shoddy mattress he had earlier shifted around to obtain maximum possible comfort. He had been in the prison system his entire adult life, which up to the present time ran a course of four years. He was used to less than ideal sleeping conditions. His past also included a long list of sundry juvenile offenses including truancy and underage alcohol consumption. These smaller offenses led him to commit the worst of his offense to date on his 18th birthday—Aggravated Assault. *Don't bludgeon a Mexican.* That was the lesson he was to learn with his current time in prison. Sadly, the lesson was lost on him as a staunch follower of the white supremacy movement. This time in prison was empowering him if nothing else.

Justin's father, who died when he was 17, would have been proud of his son who was booked into prison immediately after the beating. A witness called police and he was arrested still with his victim's blood on his hands. Justin did his best to fit in with prison life. He inked his body in obvious places with gang markings starting with a rebel tattoo on his left bicep. Now after four years in prison he had upgraded to a swastika. The red of the ink was well pronounced against his blond hair, pale skin and striking blue eyes. He wore it proudly on his neck and with it there was no mistaking what he stood for.

The memory of his father was the driving force behind his decision to get his body tattooed. Although he was a mean drunk and often absent, leaving Justin and his mother alone, Justin adored him. It was no secret within the community that Justin's father was a man who pulled tremendous weight within the Aryan Brotherhood. He had earned every bit of the respect he was given by the Nazis.

Justin's father instilled in him a sense of white supremacist beliefs. He gained strength from the organization and passed its ideals on to his son.

"Its leaders are to be revered," he told him. "They are the surest way to accomplish the goals of racial purity. The non-whites must be eliminated. They are marrying and breeding with each other and propelling the world into a society that can do nothing but crumble under the pressure of its own weakness."

His father indoctrinated him with racial hatred of the most severe form and made it the source of his identity. Racism was his heritage.

With the words of his father reverberating in his head, Justin liked to think he was carrying on his legacy and took pride in the fact he had gotten there in defense of a pure society. Justin watched the leaders closely and emulated their movements, yet he was not given the regard he felt he was entitled to. He tried a little too hard and dropped his father's name a little too often for their liking. They refused to allow him to ride on the coat tails of his father.

As Justin lay in his bunk that night, he was determined to glean whatever information he could from the actions of his bunkmate below. Justin was well aware of Isaac's position within the hierarchy of the white supremacists, but he noticed him watching others and was wary of his intentions.

Gossip was rampant within the prison culture much like a cruel high school environment, and Isaac was not immune to it. The rumor concerning the DA paying a visit to the jailhouse had spread.

"The woman DA showed up today," was the report of an unsavory prisoner who liked to talk. Yes, there were others who had visitors that day, but they for the most part were quick to divulge the identity of their visitors. Many of them received visits from their baby mamas or significant others and some had family come. All were happy to let others know they had people who cared. Justin found it unlikely timing that Isaac would begin an insulin regimen on the day the DA was present.

During the three months and two days they were locked in the same 84 square foot cell, Justin's suspicion about Isaac had turned into an itch he couldn't scratch and the development of the old man's fascination with the letters tonight fueled the fire to an intensity which was difficult for him to tolerate. *What was Isaac doing? Why examine the letters in depth now when he had seen them all many times before?*

It was in this moment that Isaac gently collected the trace powder from the envelopes' linings by scraping it with the thin edge of his pen cap. Slowly but surely he scraped the white crystal powder into the stolen plastic and sealed it off with a torn string from his bed sheet. Justin sought sleep and in order to hear what was going on he remained perfectly still. It wasn't until he heard Isaac replace the letters under his mattress and heard his gentle snore that he determined it safe to actually fall asleep. He would wait until the morning and would watch him closely. Perhaps he would gather information to provide Barrett and Simms about the Brotherhood's own intel officer. *What a way to climb the power ladder of the Brotherhood.*

# *Chapter 25*

When morning broke the next day, Justin was quick to awaken despite his norm. Sleeping in was a simple pleasure of prison life. He had grown accustomed to his uncomfortable mattress and took full advantage of the groove in the middle he had carved for himself.

His muscles were sore this morning from yesterday's workout. He spent an inordinate amount of time in the prison gym and touching essentially any part of his body one would feel it was hard as a rock. He took pride in this as he had little else to be proud of—a rock was an unfortunate comparison to his level of intellect.

Soon after his eyes sprung open he heard Isaac rustle beneath him and waited until he arose from the bed.

"Good morning," he greeted him.

He was treading on thin ice with this unusual greeting which was met by a glare and the simple response from Isaac, "Morning."

"I'm not feeling too well today," Justin went on. "I think I'll stick around here for a while."

Isaac shot back at him a look of suspicion and then paused before continuing with his normal activity. Isaac then left as he did every day to spend time outdoors in the rec yard.

Justin was trying to get in his good graces, hoping Isaac would mention something about the night before. What Justin didn't know was that Isaac was carrying his plastic bag, holding it securely under his arm when it wasn't in his pants pocket. At the hour appointed to prepare for dinner, Isaac headed to the kitchen with a determination he never previously demonstrated. Today was an important day.

As evening approached, Justin hadn't seen his cellmate at all, which he felt was playing in his favor. It was just as the dinner line was starting that the prison guards conducted cell searches.

The cells, the showers, the inmates and all their bodily crevices were subject to search at any time. With Isaac away in the kitchen, Justin stood by with an armed guard as the entire bunk bed and the items within their shared cell were tossed around and checked. The toilet snake was even pulled out. After a thorough search, there were no items in violation of prison code found and the guards left without cleaning up after themselves. Justin was quick to notice this also worked to his advantage. Isaac's letters had been thrown on top of his mattress.

This was a golden opportunity Justin was not about to miss. As the prison guards moved on to the next cell, he verified he wasn't being watched. This was his one chance to do some snooping through the letters. He was faced, however, with the ultimate disappointment when he furiously checked each envelope and each came up empty. *Isaac must have destroyed the contents.*

Justin did take note that although the senders failed to identify themselves, the envelopes were all postmarked from Germany and with the exception of one they were predominantly sent from Berlin. The last one received was sent from a striking place that left Justin speechless: the Polish city of Auschwitz in the infamous location of the Auschwitz-Birkenau concentration camp.

Justin's mind raced as he attempted to make sense of this shocking information. *Isaac is receiving mail from the site of the world's most infamous Nazi death camp.* His eye caught Isaac's bed post and the message Isaac had scratched into the metal. "AB—Always Remember," it said and instantly Justin knew he had made a major discovery. Always believing the "AB" inscription was a representation of Isaac's loyalty and commitment to the Aryan Brotherhood, now he knew it was just the opposite. "AB" was not an acronym for the Aryan Brotherhood, rather was for Auschwitz-Birkenau. This coupled with Isaac's visit with the DA made everything clear.

Isaac was playing for the other team and was definitively not a servant of the white pride movement as he claimed. This was the nail in the coffin for Isaac and Justin was going to tell the bosses. He would alert them immediately.

*When Barrett and Simms find out about Isaac's traitor status they'll notify the Grand Imperial Wizard, Isaac will be killed and I will be promoted. I have to act fast.* Justin's release date was the next day and he needed to establish credibility while on the inside before he lost touch with the Brotherhood's leaders. This vital piece of information would secure him a place in the higher ranks for the rest of his life.

As Justin was relishing the idea, a large grin spread across his face and he made the decision to act immediately. He resolved to track them down in the chow hall. Walking with intensity, he was startled by the loud blare of the warning alarm. The prison was being placed on lockdown. Quickly Justin rushed back to his cell to avoid incrimination in any ill-doings that could possibly extend his release date. His moment in the sun with the Brotherhood would have to be delayed for a few hours. He would tell the Brotherhood the first opportunity he got; as soon as the lockdown was over.

# *Chapter 26*

As usual, the Brotherhood made their way to the front of the chow line expectantly to meet Isaac, their man on the inside. Sausage tortellini, a rare treat on the prison menu, was being served this evening. The Brotherhood wasn't taking any chances today of not getting the best, and they were duly rewarded with more than their fair share. They enjoyed the meal all sitting together at the head of the dining hall, as usual marking their territory as the dominant group in the room.

Justin, known to them as the man-child, was markedly absent in the line. Isaac hadn't bought his flimsy story about being sick but there was nothing he could do about that now. He had counted on Justin to make his usual attempts to weasel his way into the front of the chow line with the rest of the white supremacists, but he couldn't delay his plan just because of one missing target. Justin's life would be spared for now, but he wouldn't get very far. *He's foolish and feeble minded and the Brotherhood on the outside will kill him before they ever let him get close to the top*, Isaac thought.

As each modern-day Nazi dipped into their heaping piles of pasta and relished the taste of it sliding down their throats, they were ill prepared for the physiological damage they were within moments of experiencing. The first eleven trays of inmate food were poisoned. The cyanide mixed into their meals by Isaac would quickly enter their blood stream and the damage would begin.

One by one, just as expected, each of the 11 members of the Brotherhood started to feel the effects of the drug. For many it started with a headache and dizziness and then quickly turned to vomiting. Some skipped directly to rapid breathing and a racing heartbeat, but all of them began to seizure moments before their deaths. They had each received lethal doses of poison.

When the news of the killings spread to him, Justin suffered a legitimate shock. The entire population of the Aryan Brotherhood in Sing Sing was executed, all with the exception of Isaac Kanzler. All 11, including Barrett and Simms, were gone and there was no one left to lead from the inside. There were no more white supremacists left to roam the prison yard or take up bed space in the cellblocks.

The prison personnel did a quick investigation into their suspicion that Isaac was the correct murder suspect. The evidence convinced them to put Isaac in solitary confinement, not only for punishment, but for his own protection.

Justin began packing his meager belongings. The consequences of Isaac's murdering and betrayal against the Brotherhood would be serious and Justin determined it was his job to move forward the administration of those consequences through the Brotherhood. Although, he would have to wait until his release to reveal what he knew, Justin was sure of what he had to do.

# *Chapter 27*

It was Charlotte and Alex's joint decision to reconvene later in the day to head to Yonkers. It would be better to hit up Hannibal's Bar in the evening and Charlotte still had a Confidential Informant Agreement with Isaac to execute, and planned to discuss the trip to Yonkers with him. Once the agreement was locked in she was sure he would be giving her much needed inside information about the Aryan Brotherhood and Saul's killer. In exchange she was more than happy to cut him a deal for possible early parole. The terms were all set and clearly spelled out in black and white. Charlotte just needed his signature on the document.

Among the several legal provisions in the contract was the most important:

> "Any and all current and historical information and knowledge ISAAC KANZLER has about gang related activities including but not limited to: Formation of the Aryan Brotherhood, Recruitment Process of the Aryan Brotherhood, Illicit activities conducted by the Aryan Brotherhood, Past members of the Aryan Brotherhood, Current members of the Aryan Brotherhood, Rival gangs to the Aryan Brotherhood and Connections to other gangs."

With paperwork in hand, Charlotte arrived at the prison. Although it was early evening she had to see Isaac now. As she made her way through the prison doors, she wasted not even a second on Jeff's unrequited flirtations and immediately informed him, "I'm here to see Isaac Kanzler."

"A woman on a mission. I like that," he said to preface the news. "Unfortunately he's been taken into solitary and can't have visitors."

"What?" she questioned. "What are you talking about?"

"I'm talking about Kanzler," he replied. "He's been sent to solitary confinement. He killed all 11 of the other Aryan Brotherhood inmates we have here. There was only one affiliated survivor who skipped dinner."

"What difference does it make that he skipped dinner?"

"All the difference in the world. It was a decision that saved his life."

"How? In what world does a single man murder 11 of some of the most powerful gang members in the prison system?"

"It's easy with poison. Isaac Kanzler worked in the kitchen and served them up a deadly combination of tortellini sauce and cyanide. The Medical Examiner confirmed all 11 were poisoned to death. Afterwards, a cell search of his personal belongings revealed that he'd been receiving mail laced with cyanide. Now he's in solitary. He's made an enemy of Justin Vincent and the entire Aryan Brotherhood."

"Who's Justin Vincent?"

"The lone survivor I mentioned. He follows the AB around like a lovesick puppy. It's pretty sad...What a day it's been. I better get back to work."

With that, Jeff left her alone. Charlotte had a million more questions but it was clear she wasn't getting anything else out of him. *I'll need to start at the beginning*, she thought to herself.

Feeling downtrodden at losing her strongest lead, she walked back to her car to leave. On her way, she glanced back more than once at the prison walls, knowing Isaac was physically so close and possessed information she desperately needed, but wouldn't be able to get.

It suddenly struck her like a lightning bolt. *The killings were a premeditated act on Isaac's part. He knew this was coming and he knew he would be stuck in solitary for it. He flipped on the Aryan Brotherhood and gave me information, but he didn't really want out. He wanted to accomplish his own agenda. The information he's given me so far will have to do.*

Charlotte slid into the front seat of her car and turned on the ignition. Looking in her rearview mirror she was surprised to catch a glimpse of Paniletti driving up the narrow road leading to the prison entrance. *What is he doing here?* He didn't have a convict in the back of his car to book in; in fact he wasn't transporting anyone at all. Charlotte watched him enter the prison through the back. Her expression turned to a scowl, however, because it was too soon to make an approach without first finding Alex's baby and figuring out the motivation behind Saul Adler's death, she drove away perplexed and distraught. She needed to think.

# Chapter 28

Charlotte had little time to dwell on her Paniletti sighting. She found herself worrying more about her life later during the drive to Hannibal's Bar in Yonkers. Alex was behind the wheel and because they strategically waited until late evening he was anxious beyond belief to get there.

"It might be nice to get there in one piece," Charlotte commented as they raced down the freeway. Even though it was well after rush hour, insanity would be the appropriate word to describe the traffic. Alex was doing nothing to navigate it wisely.

"I told you. I'm not taking any risks. We can't lose time," he responded, clearly failing to see the irony in those statements. Charlotte wondered if she would survive the car ride and when they hit even heavier traffic she was grateful.

The roadway turned to bumper-to-bumper traffic, and the terror of impending death didn't feel so closely upon her as they drew near to their destination. Additionally, the slow-down gave her time to review her surroundings. Ghetto was the theme of this neighborhood. The buildings looked as dilapidated as city code would allow without being condemned. Trash littered the sidewalks. It was dismal and hope was blatantly void in this part of town. Its dearth of light or thriving life was tangible.

Charlotte's eyes rested upon a shallow-faced man sitting against a brick stone building. He was begging for change. The hollowness in his eyes and the involuntary fidgeting of his brittle hands were a dead giveaway that he had victimized himself with drugs. Her heart went out to him even though she had seen the sadness of illegal drug use far too many times in the people she prosecuted.

"I think this might be it," Alex's voice boomed, snapping her out of her thoughts. The brightly lit sign of Hannibal's Bar was directly in front of them. "Yes, this is definitely it," he confirmed.

"Where will we park?" Charlotte inquired, seeing no empty spaces anywhere close.

"We're going to have to go around the block."

As Alex slowly drove past, Charlotte noticed there were several people trickling into the bar. Although appearing innocuous enough on its face without regard to its name, the combination of the drug-addicted homeless man on the corner and the quality of the people walking into Hannibal's Bar exuded the essence of sketchiness.

Alex passed the sordid entrance and continued to drive the dirty streets navigating his way through this unfamiliar territory until he found a place to park. It was a tight spot, but lacking in any other option for leaving a Mercedes he took it. The two exited and made their way on foot to the entrance of the bar. The entire way, Charlotte peered at her surroundings with a fearful intensity.

Trepidatiously, they opened the door to the establishment. The strong smell of alcohol and hookah wafted out of the building as the rants of a heavy metal group blared on stage at the end of a spacious hall. The bar was now packed.

The interior of the establishment was larger than it appeared on the outside. It was a place devoid of propriety and angst permeated the air. The crowd was comprised of predominantly scruffy men, who seemed in large measure to have misunderstood that the hair on their head was supposed to be on top rather than on their chins. The bar patrons socialized with the obvious odor of liquor on their breaths.

With few exceptions, their heads were all shaven bald, yet this wasn't the most obvious of the signs signifying they were members of the Aryan Brotherhood. The vast majority were clad with tattoos, many of which were swastikas worn pervasively on their bodies. Some bore the words "White Power" on various visible parts of their bodies. *This is just the tip of the iceberg.* What was visible to the observer was just a fraction of what could be seen emblazoned across their bare chests or backs.

These were all marks of the Aryan Brotherhood that served as symbols of allegiance to the white power movement. Charlotte watched the crowd lingering in the establishment, imbibing ever increasing quantities of alcohol, and staring at the disproportionately fewer women in the club. For the men's pleasure, the bartenders and servers were all female and scantily clad. Their tattoos, if they had them, were much less obvious butterflies or Asian symbols of peace. The women had little or no allegiance to the Brotherhood. They were there for the money and were being paid for how attractive they made their appearance while serving the white supremacists their alcohol.

Although sticking out like sore thumbs, Charlotte and Alex made every attempt to blend in. They were fortunate the number of doubters was few and the majority of the crowd was too wrapped up in themselves and the women behind the bar to notice them. A waitress approached them seconds after they found an ideal seat in a small booth in a dark corner. Her hair was dark, almost black, with dirty blonde roots creeping out near her scalp. Her scarlet red lipstick and eye make-up were heavy, although it was hard to tell whether this was an expression of her identity or a job requirement.

"I haven't seen you here before," she noted. "You new to the area?"

"Somewhat," Alex responded as he flashed a flirtatious smile. "I think we're ready to order."

"I'll be right back with those," she responded, equally charmingly after she took their drink orders.

While waiting for their drinks they continued to scan the club and look for clues, but nothing was readily apparent. Aside from the clientele who all clearly shared the same bigoted values, nothing was out of the ordinary.

"There's got to be something here that stands out," Charlotte said after the waitress brought their drinks. "We're just not seeing it."

Alex flagged down the waitress for one final question. "Who's the Hannibal behind the name of this place?"

"That's Johnny," she answered. She pointed in the direction of the bar and motioned at a gruff, muscular man behind it. He was busy glad-handing patrons, encouraging them to tip the buxom bartenders and overseeing the operations of the business.

"He owns the place," the waitress continued.

"It's a good scene," Alex commented to dissuade any notion he may be meddling.

"I'm going to look for the restrooms and check out what's in the back. You stay here and see if you can get any more information from Little Miss What's Her Name."

Charlotte rose from her chair and wandered her way through the smoke and bodies. She feverishly searched for their next clue only slightly expecting Alex's baby to be stashed somewhere in the building. Brielle was ultimately what they were looking for, but in reality Charlotte didn't know what she was supposed to find in the bar.

As she moved, she felt an unsettling air about the place that bred discomfort. She felt strange in her own skin and her heart was beating rapidly.

Shortly after beginning her exploration, she found a darkened hallway and walked towards it. As she made her way down the hall, the area grew less congested and the music grew increasingly softer. She passed a set of smoke filled lavatories and pressed forward until she reached a red velvet divider. The sign hanging from the divider stated, "Employees Only." Looking behind her to make sure she wasn't being watched, Charlotte ignored the sign and turned a corner to find yet another hall hidden in even greater darkness.

At the end of it was a door again marked "Employees Only." Hearing no voices behind it, she slowly began to twist the knob open. Just her luck, it was locked. Deciding that such a shady establishment wouldn't likely have the latest in security, she pulled a credit card from her bra, and slid it in the doorjamb.

It worked and she found herself peering into the darkness of another room. Immediately she heard the sound of footsteps approaching in the adjacent hallway. Somebody was coming.

Quickly she jumped in, careful to close the door behind her. She heard it latch shut as she stumbled her way behind an armchair sitting in the corner of what she could slowly begin to discern was an office. Her eyes began to acclimate to the darkness giving her just enough time to situate herself in her hiding spot before the door was unlocked and opened and the light turned on. She crouched down even further, hidden behind the chair. The ominous person entered and though she couldn't see him, he identified himself as a man by the masculine sound of a large throat clearing.

The growing smell of smoke filled her nostrils as the foreboding presence sat at a nearby desk she was huddled within feet of. A stack of papers was shuffled around to clear a space on the table and she heard the clank of a piece of glass laid down followed by the sound of a small razor cutting on the glass.

The drug ingestion process took all of two minutes as she listened intently to the extended sniffs and exhales.

The desk chair squeaked as the man reclined back. Charlotte was breathing without making a sound, which was difficult considering how hard and fast her heart was beating. Through the dulled rock music playing from the bar, she could almost hear as his nose began to drip from the aftermath of his nasal drug ingestion. It was cut off by the loud ring of his desk phone.

"Yeah, man," a male answered. "I'll be right out."

Then, just as quickly as he came, he was gone and turned out the light again. Charlotte breathed a sigh of relief. From her hiding spot she had been able to distinguish the bald head as it exited and immediately recognized the man to be Johnny, the owner of the bar.

Despite the risk of being caught, the hiding spot beyond the chair did her an enormous amount of good. As she looked up towards the ceiling a few minutes earlier with the light on, she noticed a mirror hanging on the opposite wall. In the reflection, which she could see without being spotted was a picture of Isaac with his arm around Johnny. They were posed for the camera with smiles on their faces and the distinct image of brotherly love. The photograph was neatly displayed in a picture frame and it showed the two men leaning over an antique Enigma machine.

This was quite the revelation in more ways than one. Charlotte had researched Enigma machines in her work on the Barrett and Simms cases. This had been in an effort to understand Nazi cryptology in order to help her crack the codes of the Aryan Brotherhood. At this point she was more well-versed in Nazi code machines than anyone should probably ever be.

When it came to the Enigma machine, she knew all it required was an enciphered message and a key for the setting of the machine. With that, an enigma enciphered message was yours for the taking. She had learned the Enigma machines were used by the Nazis at the inception of and during World War II to circumvent any enemies of war who may have otherwise intercepted the plain text of their radio messages. Coded messages were enciphered through its use and then sent in radio frequency to their intended destination via Morse code. The beauty of the Enigma was that it scrambled the letters of a message in a series of letters that only the intended recipient, with another Enigma machine set with a correlating key, could decipher. All that a would-be enemy interceptor would find would be a string of letters that were about as useful as toilet paper with no means of deciphering them. It's the sheer complexity of the machine that assured privacy and thus gave the Germans an unnerving feeling of power during World War II.

The Enigma machine acts as an automatic letter scrambler, she knew, making for a perfect supposedly uncrackable code with its almost infinite permutations and possibilities for the key. The machine can be set up in approximately 159 million million million ways, through the use of rotor positions, a plugboard and a random key.

Historically, through complex methods designed to exceed the complexity of the Enigma, the British had been able to eventually crack the code which lead to the demise of Germany in battles such as that fought on D-Day. These discoveries hastened the end of World War II.

Excited at seeing the photograph containing an Enigma machine, Charlotte came out of her hiding spot and turned on a small lamp next to it. She was right. It was Isaac and Johnny. Up close Charlotte could tell they both had tattoos draped across their chests. Johnny proudly wore a swastika and a shamrock with the words "White Power" perfectly centered above his navel, but Isaac's ink was less conspicuous.

The location where the photograph was taken was curious to Charlotte at first. In it the Enigma machine appeared to be sitting out of its wooden box on a table, which she surmised was a chest of drawers. Next to the machine was a small lamp, reading glasses and aftershave. A pair of Doc Martens lay loosely on the floor nearby next to the corner of a bed which could only be the bedroom. Above the chest, hanging on the wall, was a sign reading: "Hannibal's." It was another rendition of Johnny's logo. *That has to be Johnny's bedroom.* Although the Enigma machine was striking to her in and of itself, she was taken aback at the sight of a small first aid kit sitting on the right side of the chest displayed in not so prominent view. Though fairly innocuous to an impartial observer, Charlotte picked up on it right away. The first aid kit was enclosed in a white box with a red cross printed on it, and Isaac's words again flooded to her mind, "Look for the symbol of the red cross wherever you go and you'll find your way." She knew now the Enigma machine was what they were looking for. *We have to get into Johnny's house.*

No sooner had excitement overtaken her thoughts than she heard a creaking sound outside the office. Charlotte held her breath, horrified someone would enter the room. She paused for a minute but soon realized it was a false alarm. *That was close.*

Eradicating all possible signs of her presence, she made sure the scene looked exactly as it did before she arrived. She made sure the light was off and the door locked as she exited and she wasted no time in returning to their table where the waitress was leaning over the table seductively and feeding into Alex's charm.

"Come on," Charlotte ordered him abruptly. "It's time to go."

Alex, knowing she meant business, handed a wad of cash to the waitress and gave her a look of eagerness. "I'll call you, Chrystal," he said.

"I can't wait, Trevor," she responded.

"Trevor?" Charlotte remarked with a smile. "You went all out for this role."

"Not too shabby if I do say so myself," he told her as they hauled out of the bar.

Their satisfaction at his performance was short-lived, however. As they made their way to the hard fought parking spot she had the impending fear they were being followed. Even when Alex turned the car's heater on full power she felt unshakeable chills. She turned to look out the rear window but saw no one.

Getting back to business, she addressed the news of the topic at hand as they left the area.

"Good news. I found the 'who' that we were looking for, but we're going to have to do more leg work to find the 'what.'"

She proceeded to explain to Alex what she saw in the photograph of Isaac and Johnny and informed him that with Isaac in solitary confinement, Johnny was their strongest lead.

"We're going to need to get to him from the inside," she went on. "We'll need to get close enough to him to track down the Enigma machine, which I'm convinced he stores in his bedroom. He must have it there for safekeeping. It's a valuable commodity for the Aryan Brotherhood as there are few machines that have been preserved since World War II. Many of them are in museums but a few are with private owners."

Charlotte explained to him further that she was positive the Enigma machine wasn't in the club. She had been in Johnny's locked office and other than the photograph, it was nowhere to be seen. With the way Johnny and Isaac beamed with joy posing with the antique machine, Charlotte knew it would be stored in a safe place and the bar was far too risky.

"And how do you suggest we get close enough to Johnny to track it down?  He's a white supremacist. He's not exactly going to divulge his secrets to total strangers," Alex queried.

"We're going to have to go undercover," was Charlotte's matter of fact response.

Going undercover was not a concept Alex was immediately keen to. They did fine playing the role of the unsuspecting couple trying out a new bar, but what she was proposing included taking on roles much more specific and character driven.

"Undercover?  What? Do you live in some sort of covert spy operation fantasy world?"

Alex was clearly going to be a tough sell when it came to this plan.

# Chapter 29

For Charlotte the idea of going undercover was gold. She relished the idea of working as an undercover spy. She loved the fact that undercover police officers appeared as anything but police in that line of work. They were often unshaven with long scruffy beards and multiple tattoos to give them credibility when trying to infiltrate a gang or take down a drug dealer.

Charlotte had similar visions of grandeur when it came to their current situation.

"We saw in the club the exact style of people we need to model in terms of our appearance," she explained to him. "We have to look like one of them if we want to find the Enigma machine."

"And how do you suggest we do that?" he asked her.

"I just hope you're not afraid to lose your hair," she answered decisively. "Our main problem isn't so much getting to the Enigma machine, but rather figuring out the message and the key we need to input into it to provide us with our next clue. I'm going to have to go over your letter again to find the key."

"What do you mean key?" Alex asked.

"The key is the setting for the machine that provides for the proper decryption of the message," Charlotte responded. "Without the proper key all efforts are futile. It is impossible to be assured you are deciphering the proper message without it."

"It's all falling into place," Alex responded.

"What is? What do you mean?" Charlotte inquired.

"The message. The key. I have it."

"What do you mean you have it?"

"I have it right here around my neck," he informed her, pulling a string hidden underneath his shirt. "I wasn't sure how much I could trust you in the beginning so I didn't mention it to you before."

Alex recalled to himself how he came into possession of the item. During the two day period in which police infiltrated his home and set up command for "Operation Find the Senator's Daughter," Alex had failed to shower or bathe, but his lack of personal hygiene wasn't a conscious neglect. To call it such would be disingenuous. It was a symptom of depression. His mind was so wrapped up in the dire situation at hand that to consider adding another task to the mix of already mind-draining concerns was simply too difficult.

He was spared from his own stench in the first 60 hours after the discovery of his missing daughter, but eventually caught the near fatal whiff of himself. *It's time to bite the bullet and take a shower.*

Though the shower had been seemingly calling his name, he heard even more loudly another voice pulling him towards the attic. He really needed a drag. The police canvassed the entire house but he was hardly nervous they would find his stash of weed he desperately needed. It was carefully hidden in a locked box under the attic insulation in a remote corner of the attic that not even the canines, which were trained in human rather than drug detection, had caught the scent.

He made the journey up into the spacious attic and found his treasure. Just one joint. It would be all he needed for now. It had been a long time since he pulled out his stash of marijuana, but desperate times called for desperate measures and he was in crisis mode.

By the time he finally stepped into the shower he was officially high, but not enough that he wasn't coherent. He went to the shower closest to Brielle's room. It made sense to do that now. If the sensation of cool water running down his body granted him nothing more, he hoped minimally for a further sense of relief.

That, however, was not to be. The events of the day had provided him with nothing but disappointment and the shower proved to be no different. He turned the faucet handle up to full capacity, but the showerhead offered nothing but a small trickle of water running only weakly. Alex was getting colder by the second.

Not wanting a piece of plumbing to get the better of him and determined to fix the problem, he unscrewed the showerhead and was shocked to find a small key buried within it. It was silver in color with an octagon-shaped head. Rubbing his thumb across the top of it to get a clear view of its detail, Alex observed engraved in tiny print across the top were the letters *"oświęcim,"* and below them were the letter groupings *"stacja"* and *"kolejowa."*

Engraven atop this strange set of words were three symbols, which just like the letters meant nothing to him:

Although the symbols' meanings were a mystery, the key held the possibility that it opened a lock somewhere in the world which could lead him to his daughter, and it would now become a part of him. He carried it with him always from then on, as it was attached to a chain hung securely around his neck. The mystery enshrouding Brielle's kidnapping was becoming ever more elusive, but he found hope in clinging to this new and odd piece of evidence. The concept of a simplified kidnapping of his daughter for ransom was long since gone, and after he finished his shower and toweled himself dry he picked up the phone to join forces with Charlotte.

Now, as they continued to drive away from Hannibal's Bar he decided it was important to reveal the key to Charlotte.

"This is our key AND another hidden message," he continued to tell her as they drove away from the bar.

"This key with the help of the Enigma machine will guide us where we need to go next. Why on earth wouldn't you tell me this before?" Charlotte questioned, punching him solidly in the bicep as she stared at the key.

"Hey, my daughter's life is on the line here. I couldn't take any unnecessary chances with some strange woman I just met. I'm telling you now. I have complete trust in you now."

"Thanks a lot," Charlotte responded sarcastically. "That makes me feel so much better."

Despite Alex's being unaware, Charlotte vaguely recognized the symbols on top of the key when he showed it to her. Just as she was familiar with the Nordic rune chiseled into Saul's chest, she was familiar with the runic alpha and numeric symbol systems.

Charlotte quickly determined she would need to check her book of runic symbols. It was a book Saul had gifted to her. "You need to know their culture if you want to understand and beat them," he told her.

When Alex dropped her off late that night after their trip to Yonkers, she headed straight for the book. It was easy to find being lined up perfectly on her alphabetized bookshelf in its assigned place. Pulling it from the shelf she flipped to the numeric portion.

She meticulously recorded the symbols on the key at the top of a blank sheet of paper and as she checked her reference she noted the symbols for the following numbers:

## 12, 22, 23

Much to her dismay, these results meant nothing in and of themselves. She stared at them for quite some time trying to figure out what they represented, but only came up short. She took hope in the fact that they might be the key to the Enigma machine. After a while, her head began to nod and her brain literally began to hurt. She was not solving this now. Sleep took over.

# Chapter 30

It was true what they say in the case of Justin Vincent. Never trust a man with two first names. He was nothing but bad news and there was no one who would speak up in disagreement of that fact. His release from prison, just the day after his cellmate was exiled to solitary confinement, was a joyous occasion for him but he had no one to share it with. He no longer had friends on the outside and with both his parents gone and the recent passing of his grandmother, there was no one to welcome him home; wherever home was.

His friends from his pre-prison days had either moved on or were in prison themselves. For many, their days of donning shaved heads and wearing Doc Martens with red shoelaces were over. They had wised up and suppressed their ideas of the master race in favor of fitting into society.

To Justin, those former so-called friends weren't true soldiers. Because of their disloyalty he reasoned it was for the best he no longer maintained contact with them, and he sufficiently convinced himself he didn't want them anyway. This was his method of self-preservation and as he exited the gates at Sing Sing he was determined not to think about them.

When he was initially booked into prison four years prior, Justin had little more than the shirt on his back, but it was all returned to him upon his release. As he ventured out into the world, these possessions consisted of his few articles of clothing, a pack of four-year-old cigarettes, what appeared to be a *Bible* and a ten-dollar bill. With the exception of the *Bible*, these items were confiscated at his booking and stored with his clothing while he served his incarceration period. The ten dollars was the only money he had to his name. He would need more money to accomplish his present goal and there wasn't much time to acquire it. Remembering from years past the areas he knew he could go to get cash, he immediately headed away from the prison and walked determinedly in that direction. *I wonder if the old stomping grounds have changed in the last four years.*

He walked for an hour before he arrived at his destination and was wholly pleased to find nothing had changed. His familiar destination was still encapsulated within a main drug corridor of the city and he knew the area like the back of his hand. While this familiarity would prove to be helpful he also needed to be careful.

Justin had gotten sober in prison and didn't want to tempt himself. Heroin was the cause of his father's death and he owed it to himself to follow the traditions of his family in strengthening white power, but refrain from those things his father had done to cut his life short. His parole officer too wouldn't be easy on him if he had any missteps involving drugs.

Despite the lingering negative influences of his old stomping grounds, Justin was silently happy to see that some things never change. Reaching the end of the main roadway, he arrived two hours after his prison release at his final destination. And there it stood; Mega Mart. He knew the products sold there were all encompassing and that for a would-be thief it was like a golden metropolis of possibility.

His plan was simple, find a discarded receipt for a preferably high dollar item, enter the store, find the identical item on the receipt and go to customer service to return it for cash. Although it was less than ideal to risk getting arrested right after leaving prison, this was an emergency. He needed money badly. Just like old times, Justin marched through the store's large parking lot and started rummaging through the garbage bins. Discarded receipts could always be counted on to be strewn throughout the parking lot, but were more likely found in garbage cans near the store's exits. *The key to rummaging for receipts is covertness. It's important to act completely naturally.* Justin learned it was best to do advance surveillance and when the coast was clear give the impression you had garbage of your own to discard. Justin did this many times in his youth and of those countless occasions he was proud to claim that only one such act of theft caused his incarceration in juvenile detention. He was reckless that time in thinking he was invincible, but he was older and wiser now.

On this particular Wednesday afternoon as he went about the task, there was initially very little to show in terms of the fruits of his labors. The receptacles were fairly devoid of receipts. His luck quickly changed, however, when he saw an overburdened mother with three children in tow, having just purchased two car seats. She was hardly able to cling to her sanity let alone the receipt she had been handed moments earlier.

Sure enough, right outside the store's exit, she tossed the ancillary piece of paper in the closest trash can. And like a vulture to a piece of fresh road kill, Justin nabbed it. He would now wait until tomorrow and return in the morning. It was much more likely that a person would return a pair of car seats after having tried them out overnight. The total purchase price was $320.98 including tax. $320.98 including tax was an amount worth holding out for so he resigned himself to sleeping under a nearby bridge that night, smiling to himself over his own cleverness.

# Chapter 31

Dietrich watched in awe as the crowd responded to Adolf Hitler. When it came to Hitler's infamous rallying, the people revered him and took from his voracious speeches feelings of passion and empowerment. Although it came as no surprise to Dietrich, or anyone for that matter, Hitler rose to power seemingly overnight. Using an inordinate amount of cunning and stealth he lulled the people of Germany into a false sense of security, turning the country from a democratic republic to a dictatorship in an instant with a platform of the Nazi party.

For Dietrich, these notions of Aryan supremacy were planted in his youth. His early years were rooted in a palpable hatred towards the Jews, which was nurtured by growing up in 1930s Berlin. Times were tough then, and this hatred was ingrained in him like a bunker, seemingly impenetrable and deep. Feelings of abhorrent Anti-Semitism ruled his family's views. Local Jewish traders and bankers were consistently cheating them, they believed, and Dietrich had to set things right. In later years, his initiation as a soldier in the SS was the natural thing to do as WWII began.

All members of the SS were instructed that orders of mass extermination were justifiable and lawful. The orders came directly from Adolph Hitler and bled down the chain. The Jews were to be looked upon only as enemies and the reasons behind the extermination program were rationalized as truth. Through this system, no soldier-turned-executioner questioned under what authority and to which end they were serving.

At the time, unemployment was near the 20% mark, leaving one out of every five Germans without a job. Nazi propaganda fueled the fire that Hitler started with a fanatical enthusiasm, which successfully brought Germans together, for the first time since WWI, in a sense of determination and hope for a brighter economic future.

Already a member of the Nazi party before Hitler joined, Dietrich observed the leader as he climbed the ranks. He made sure to associate with Hitler whenever possible. Due to their acquaintance turned friendship prior to Hitler's incarceration, there was a bond present between the two that allowed Dietrich to latch onto him after his release. The fact that he sent letters to Hitler periodically in prison, while making specific reference to his adoration for him, certainly didn't hurt him in furthering his position in the party.

Dietrich was more than happy to do whatever it took to further the movement and push the party line. He made sure to be on hand for the Reichstag Fire. The burning of this German Parliament building to the ground was the work of Dietrich and his comrades and had all been in the name of the Nazi cause. Incidentally, the Nazis blamed the Communists for this atrocity in order to further play on the fears of the Germans.

The burning of the Reichstag did well in elevating Hitler to a higher level of power. It was as a direct result of the fire that German President Paul Von Hindenburg enacted the Reichstag Decree. With one single, new law, President Hindenburg eradicated civil rights, liberties and freedoms afforded to people under the German Constitution. Cloaked under the false auspices of being for the protection of the people and the country, the Reichstag Decree was enacted and promulgated on February 28, 1933. Even in its first two Articles, it single-handedly tore down the personal rights of the people:

"On the basis of Article 48, Section 2, of the German Constitution, the following is decreed as a defensive measure against Communist acts of violence that endanger the state:

§1 Articles 114, 115, 117, 118, 123, 124, and 153 of the Constitution of the German Reich are suspended until further notice. Thus, restrictions on personal liberty, on the right of free expression of opinion, including freedom of the press, on the right of assembly and the right of association, and violations of the privacy of postal, telegraphic, and telephonic communications, and warrants for house searches, orders for confiscations as well as restrictions on property are permissible beyond the legal limits otherwise prescribed.

§2 If any state fails to take the necessary measures to restore public safety and order, the Reich government may temporarily take over the powers of the highest state authority."

And with this new law, Germany was hoodwinked and would never be the same.

Although, he also felt distrust for Hitler, President Hindenburg drew him closer, naming him Chancellor, the head of the German government, in an effort to keep him at bay. Never to be outdone, Hitler stabbed Hindenburg in the proverbial back and as Chancellor abolished the office of President immediately upon taking office. Hindenburg was consequently ousted and Hitler became the sole leader of Germany. He became its dictator. He became *Der Führer*.

Although there were those in the general populous who opposed the Nazi movement, they disliked democracy more. The democracy of the Weimar Republic was the force that had plummeted them into a recession so deep that a savior was needed emergently.

Veteran police officers were compelled to form battalions of Nazi officers and the chain of command now went directly to and from Hitler in executing this new form of government. In furtherance of the Nazi agenda, the police unwittingly and egregiously violated civil rights, initiated the criminalization of groups deemed to be inferior, and facilitated and excelled the process of deportations to concentration camps.

In the beginning, prior to being slowly desensitized to the terror, there were some in positions of authority who questioned things. All officers in the Nazi regime, when called to take an oath of service, came to understand that it was an "Oath of Allegiance" to Hitler. There was no allegiance to God, no allegiance to country, it was simply and solely allegiance to Hitler.

Many took the oath solely because the consequences of failure to do so would lead to termination. They would lose their jobs and in the current economic conditions couldn't afford that. Most were left in the dark about the grave consequences of their work.

Overall, these law enforcement officers were not crazy, sadistic or evil men. They weren't even generally unkind men. They were ordinary men who followed the orders of their commanding officer and who felt helpless to take a stand against the beginnings of a massacre. When they took the "Oath of Hitler" they let the directives of the dictatorship speak for them. Pledging their allegiance and power to Hitler, each one was forced to state:

> **"I swear by God this sacred oath that to the Leader of the German empire and people, Adolf Hitler, supreme commander of the armed forces, I shall render unconditional obedience and that as a brave soldier I shall at all times be prepared to give my life for this oath."**

Dietrich was among those who took the pledge boldly and proudly, but the Nazi agenda was successful not entirely because of those, like Dietrich, who were avid supporters, but rather because of the failure of those who knew they should, to speak up and stand against the dictatorship. Their failure to act became a slippery slope downhill to the depths of hell. This slow process of desensitization resulted in an end that rightly appeared abhorrent at its introduction, but ultimately became accepted and ignored. This end resulted in millions of Jews and minorities being imprisoned in camps and led swiftly to their deaths. Most non-Jewish Germans failed to see what was right in their backyard—the Holocaust—true genocide.

As for Dietrich, one of the furiously valiant ones, he acquired for himself the role of a heavily trusted ally and friend in the eyes of Der Führer. Dietrich was initially named the Commander of Auschwitz-Birkenau. Much to his displeasure, however, Rudolf Höss, a fellow Nazi or "the heathen," which Dietrich referred to him as, later surpassed him in popularity with Hitler and the control of Auschwitz was eventually given to him. Hitler put Dietrich in command of the smaller, nearby camp, Treblinka. Although, angered by this, Dietrich vowed he would work himself to the bone in his new position and would become even more revered than Höss.

In the beginning, it was likely his intellect which attracted Hitler to Dietrich. Dietrich was endowed with an inherent gift for chemistry and some who knew him wondered if this talent was given to him to offset the abrasive and harsh disposition he was also born with that caused him to be not well liked by many. That was of no consequence in his mind as his knack for chemistry, on the other hand, would translate into a very useful asset to the Nazi's utilization of the gas chambers in their numerous concentration camps.

Hitler encouraged him in using his expertise in chemistry to accomplish the eradication of Jews and non-Aryans in what they called the "Final Solution."

With Hitler's blessing, Dietrich went about testing chemical compounds best suited for human fatality. He eventually found the most success in a form of cyanide called Zyklon-B, otherwise known as Cyclon-B, which caused a chemical reaction fatal to the human system, and the formula eventually became beloved by Hitler as a pivotal chemical reaction that would provide the Nazis with great success in their demented ambitions for mass murder.

# Chapter 32

Perhaps it was Dietrich's lust for power, or the evil in the core of his heart, that led him to believe his actions were right. These traits led him to improve his scientific discovery for the sheer purpose of maximizing the murders that were taking place. In the alternative, perhaps it was the shriveling of his heart that followed the death of his oldest daughter, Eva.

Prior to her death, he and his wife Ingrid had two children. Both were girls and both were beautiful, but Dietrich regarded his daughter Eva as more beautiful than her younger sister, Brigitte. Eva's tendrils of curly blond hair were offset by the piercing blue of her eyes and the radiance of her smile which dimmed at her death at the age of 11 from typhoid fever. The loss of that light tipped Dietrich over an unfathomable edge and was a primary source of his mania.

His obsession led him to disobey Hitler's command when at the conclusion of WWII and the brink of liberation for the Nazi-imprisoned Jews, it was decided that a quick absolution to the end of the war would be necessary. Hitler mandated all evidence of the Nazis was to be destroyed. Nothing could remain. No trace could be recovered of their records. They would deny everything.

And so it was for the most part; Dietrich did as he always did. He went along with Hitler's commands, but with one exception. Before starting his reassignment from Auschwitz to Treblinka, he decided there was one item he would not and could not decimate and he had already taken a drastic measure to make sure it was never destroyed. It was his leather bound journal in which he lovingly kept photos of his family, including Brigitte and Eva, and a lock of Eva's hair.

In this chronicle he documented his innermost fears as well as successes and accomplishments during his time as commander of Auschwitz. Within the record was also evidence of his crimes. It was of utmost importance to him that his record be hidden in a safe place. He would come back for it.

Dietrich had carefully placed the journal in a sealed bag within a sealed box, and his designated hiding spot, the Sola River, ran the length of the eastern side of Auschwitz and provided the perfect hiding spot. In the name of preserving his recorded legacy, he boarded a small wooden boat and rowed his way out to the middle of the river to a location close to the border of Auschwitz. It was there he submerged the sealed book within the box. He would now trust it to the water's depths, rather than trusting in Hitler's command.

As he went on to establish continuously new versions of toxic gas, and manage the labor and killings of his tasked camp, he never forgot Eva. He clung to each aspect of her memory with almost perfect clarity and it was that memory which led him to believe he saw her again after her death.

One cold winter day in November of 1943, Dietrich was confronted with a miracle when a new batch of Jewish prisoners entered the Treblinka death camp. On that day, it was almost as if he was willing Eva back to life when he set eyes upon Violet. Violet was gorgeous and looked exactly like his daughter would have looked had she lived to the age of 13. The striking resemblance left him breathless and in awe. Dietrich saw her first in the middle of the labor camp huddled with a young boy.

It was as if he was dreaming when he laid eyes upon her, yet he knew he was not. This was a girl of living flesh and bones who in every manner of appearance was his little Eva. The thought of this angelic being in this camp was almost unbearable. *If this is not Eva, it is her perfect likeness. I must get her out of here!*

Freeing Violet from the camp would take some planning on his part and in the mean-time; he would keep a close watch on her. A glimmer of mercy revealed itself when he placed her in the warehouse where he could keep a careful watch on her as he pondered his course of action in bringing her into his family. It was after a time of careful contemplation on this that he believed the heavens to be smiling upon him. He found the heavenly presence outside the camp. She had stashed herself in a pile of filthy Jewish clothing to be discarded.

Immediately dismissing the grave infraction of her escape attempt, it was on that day he took her into his home and finally introduced her into his family as their long lost child.

"You're crazy," his wife told him in response, and Brigitte concurred. "You have literally lost your mind."

In the years that followed, Brigitte developed bitterness in her heart towards this stranger, "the new Eva," and there appeared to be no salvation for Ingrid and Brigitte, who were forced to live with the lunacy of their patriarch. It was Dietrich's sincere belief that Violet was, in fact, his daughter Eva. This psychosis lingered with him through the entire duration of his life.

# Chapter 33

*September 16, 1988 – Millwood, New York*

The day after his release, it was mid-morning when Justin noticed a throng of shoppers develop at that the Millwood Mega Mart. He had been keeping watch since dawn. There was little respite from the sunlight, now shining intensely, under the bridge he had called home for the night, and he awoke with the sun.

He made his approach now that it was less likely he would be observed by security making a fraudulent return and upon entering the store, headed straight back to the baby care section and sought out the car seats. His excitement turned to disappointment, however, when he realized only one was left. Without a complete set he couldn't approach the clerks and return two items that he didn't have. He would have to go with the one, which would mean a return of only half of what the true purchaser paid—$160.48.

*Not a bad haul for one receipt*, he thought to console himself as he approached the customer service counter.

When it was his turn for service he was greeted warmly by a store clerk. It was a welcome thing to be exposed to pleasantries which simply didn't exist within the concrete walls of Sing Sing.

The clerk was young and sweet. Her blond ponytail swung as she talked as if it were moving with the rhythm of her words. Justin wasted no time and immediately recounted to her the lie he concocted about his oldest child being too big for the car seat.

"They grow like weeds," he joked to her.

"I know what you mean," an old woman behind the counter responded from the next register over. "And before you know it, your babies will be having babies. Enjoy them while you can."

He had passed the legitimacy test when the clerk handed him the refund for the stolen car seat.

"Thank you," he said sweetly. "You ladies have a pleasant day now."

No one was the wiser to his scam and he was $160.48 richer. This would be enough to get him where he needed to go.

After buying his one-way Greyhound ticket to the small town of Hannah, North Dakota, he still had $27 and change left. *Perfect. I'm starving.* He spent this remaining money on provisions for the bus ride which would take him across a large part of the country and all the way north very near to the border of Canada.

Hannah, North Dakota, was the small town where he knew he would find the man known as August Bäcker, the Grand Imperial Wizard of the Aryan Brotherhood and a legend in the white supremacist movement. His old age precluded him from being actively involved, but his blood ran thick with long held racial hatred. Justin revered this person he was about to meet.

Justin knew that these days, instead of using the sweat from his brow or any amount of physical strength, August Bäcker was the primary source of financial support for the Aryan Brotherhood. Although the Brotherhood sustained itself well on proceeds from drug sales, August was often footing the bill for various enterprises in furtherance of the cause. This role was what he now lived for and was where he found his worth. The entirety of the white power organization was indebted to him for it.

Justin knew he could go to August for support in this time of need. He desired now more than ever to make a name for himself, and with a large number of the central figures in the regime wiped out, he needed to make his move quickly. He had the inside information on what went down in Sing Sing and possessed vital information about its greatest defector. He was sure to gain favor in the leader's eyes and thereby make a name for himself. He had all 52 hours of the bus ride to ponder this when he deboarded in the sleepy town of Hannah. His stomach was tied in knots from the nerves and excitement; he was going to see the Grand Imperial Wizard. His father would be proud.

# Chapter 34

It was the Vatican that made Dietrich and his family's voyage to America possible. It was called "Operation Paperclip" and it was aptly named. It was with a paperclip that the false identity paperwork was bound to the photograph of each prospective Nazi who was secretly recruited by the United States. Conducted by the U.S. government's "Joint Intelligence Objectives Agency," The intellectually best and brightest were brought into the country to lead the post war scientific revolution with the rationale being that the Communists posed a genuine threat to the survival of the Catholic Church.

As for the United States government, their first post World War II priority was to offset budding signs of the impending Cold War. The Vatican was happy to assist in this effort as it meant the stifling of Communism. By recruiting German scientists to advance their own ends, the United States, with the Vatican's help, derailed any plans these imported intellectuals may have otherwise made to relocate to England or the Soviet Union, or worse yet, rebuild Germany. At the end of the war Hitler was dead, but the U.S. knew there would be others waiting in the wings. Operation Paperclip was formed to extinguish any possibility of a Nazi comeback.

President Harry S. Truman issued a directive excluding all Nazis from consideration in the program. In an effort to circumvent this, it became necessary for the Joint Intelligence Objectives Agency to strip the Nazi scientist candidates of all proof of their former selves and any outward affiliation with the Nazi agenda. Enter the false identity paperwork and the paperclips that bound it together. The Nazis were provided with security clearances for work in the United States and were recruited in various areas such as electronics, physics, rocketry, intelligence and medicine.

Dietrich was one such recruit based on his expertise in chemistry. His new identification paperwork was shining and pristine. It could withstand any act of scrutiny that might call into question its authenticity.

New identity in tow, Dietrich was a coveted new addition to the chemical industry in the United States. He thrived professionally while the truth behind his identity remained shrouded in secrecy. After World War II, he was no longer Dietrich Rüpel, but was rather August Bäcker. He shed the stain of his history with his new persona. He hid it well, along with the secret surrounding Violet, as his family started their new life in the United States. Just because his start was fresh didn't mean it was easy. Always looking over his shoulder August lived in fear of discovery and was forced into perpetual cautiousness.

Nonetheless, he was unable to leave behind the inner substance of his being. Only six years into his new life he plunged head first into the dark underworld of the Aryan Brotherhood. Here he found a piece of home in this foreign land.

The ideology of the Nazis was highlighted in the beliefs and by-laws of the Aryan Brotherhood. August took on major roles within the organization including, as time moved forward, the discriminations that spurred the Civil Rights Movement of the 1960s. He was also an avid member of the Ku Klux Klan, a group that imbued him with power and status he was missing from his days during the execution of the Holocaust. Shrouded in secrecy with the Klan's capes and hoods, he felt a sense of security in knowing he could remain invisible in his beliefs even as he built a life in the United States.

# Chapter 35

Isaac's solitary confinement left Justin without a cellmate, which was an opportunity that was not wasted. Just as soon as he heard the news, he seized the opportunity to do a thorough search of his former cellmate's possessions.

The search bore no fruit at its inception. Justin found only a few blunt pencils, miscellaneous junk food items from the cantina, and a *Bible*, but each of these was a usual possession of prisoners in Sing Sing. Nothing appeared out of the ordinary. Thoroughly unimpressed, he took the liberty of eating one of Isaac's Twinkies. As he snacked, he picked up the *Bible. Might as well read it while I have the chance.* Justin knew that the very thought of him looking through his *Bible* would infuriate Isaac and that put a smile on his face.

As he opened the leather bound book with worn pages, he noticed it was different than what he had seen in the past. Not particularly religious, he was unfamiliar with the format but knew enough about the books within the *Bible* to recognize this was not it.

The cover was legitimate, with "*Holy Bible*" embossed in gold type across the front, and the spine also reflecting the title and specifying it was the King James version. Justin recognized those indicia, but noticed the blatant absence of any reference to Matthew, Mark, Luke or John, and if there was one thing Justin was sure should be in there, it was *Genesis.*

If nothing else, he had read the first chapters of *Genesis* multiple times over the course of his life. He had the first few verses memorized and definitely knew that "In the beginning Cod created the heaven and the earth." He knew with absolute certainty there was no *Book of Bereishit* in the *Bible* as the book he held in front of him contained in the place where the *Book of Genesis* should have been.

Upon reading, he was greeted with the first words that, although similar to *Genesis*, were clearly not the same:

> "1  IN THE beginning God created the heaven
> and the earth.
> 2  Now the earth was unformed and void, and
> darkness was upon the face of the deep;
> and the spirit of God hovered over the face
> of the waters.
> 3  And God said: 'Let there be light.'
> 4  And God saw the light, that it was good;
> and God divided the light from the darkness."

Within the text, Justin was drawn to the peculiar circling of many of the letters in red. He vowed these markings in this non-Christian text would be the proverbial nail in his coffin with the Aryan Brotherhood. Armed with this information, he knew that if Isaac didn't die by state execution, the Brotherhood would be sure to finish his life. He would make certain of it. Justin took the book as his own and slid it under his mattress in the top bunk for safekeeping until his release.

With no further competition from the Brotherhood on the inside due to their deaths, he would take the book with him to approach the Grand Imperial Wizard. Isaac's secret would no longer be hidden.

Upon his arrival in Hannah, Justin kept in mind the well-known fact that the house belonging to August Bäcker was in the most remote area of this remote town of Hannah, North Dakota. The lack of activity he saw was indicative of the extremely sparse population. There were a mere seven people living in Hannah when August, already under cover, first arrived in the area in 1945. *Yes, Hannah is a city*. There were no towns, villages or hamlets in North Dakota. There were only cities, even if the city, like Hannah, was only .19 square miles.

Now, almost 50 years later, Hannah had blossomed to a population of 18, but the other 17 never bothered August even now that he lived alone after the death of his wife and both Brigitte and Violet leaving as soon as they could. He was a recluse among recluses and his home was blocked off with trees like a fortress. No one was observed ever going in or out and this was especially true now. The overgrowth on the property had developed into a jungle.

The compound August built for his home was little known to anyone outside of the Aryan Brotherhood. Those in the know were best advised to head on foot straight east through the thick forest lying on the outskirts of the city to get to it. The driveway August maintained was carefully hidden. The house was 12 miles as the crow flies from the closest bus stop but anyone would be hard pressed to find it without explicit instructions or at a minimum knowing the lore about its location. Justin had heard all about it in prison and he had no qualms about making the long trek there.

After deboarding the bus, it took Justin a little under four hours to traverse the thick brush intertwined amidst the full pine trees en route to August's property. As he finally approached the house he had heard about only in rumors, he was greeted by the wild overgrowth of the property. *August must be too weak to keep up with it.*

As he made his final approach, August sat quietly on his front porch and rocked back and forth on a rocking chair. August gripped a large AR-15 firearm with his bony hand. As Justin approached the fence line of the property, August raised his weapon to him, aiming at his chest.

"Sieg Heil," Justin said, as he raised his right arm in front of his body in true Nazi fashion. The threat was now neutralized. August returned the gesture and walked slowly to the entrance gate to remove the fortress-like series of locks. Justin was quickly invited to sit on a second wicker chair on the porch as August returned to his station and they were soon in deep conversation. Justin quickly filled him in on the purpose of his mission.

"They're all dead?" August confirmed after hearing the news. "All 11?"

"Sadly, yes, and Isaac Kanzler is a defector," Justin told him. "His loyalty lies with the Jews. He has masqueraded himself for years as a true supporter of the Brotherhood, but all along he has been playing us for fools."

August listened with silent attention.

"It will be hard to recover from the blow of our lost brothers," Justin continued, "I will do anything within my power to cut this enemy down."

"How do you know this?" August asked him.

"I lived with the guy in prison for four months. I always knew something was off."

Justin went on to detail the contents of Isaac's *"Bible"* and went on to explain his experience with the envelopes and the "AB" inscription the night of the murders of the 11.

"Isaac Kanzler orchestrated and carried out the killings," Justin emphasized, "I'm convinced that he's not going to stop there."

Justin made no hesitation in presenting the *Bible* to August whose eyes opened wide when Justin showed him the red circled and underlined letters hidden in the text. Justin began to read from the beginning of the book at which time August quickly responded, "I hate that book. Do you have any idea what it is you're reading?"

"No," Justin responded, feeling embarrassed.

"It's the *Torah*; the vile Jews' sacred writing. It's a mockery to mankind."

Now Justin was reeling at not having known that. He certainly wanted the Grand Imperial Wizard to know he was knowledgeable about all aspects of their cause.

"It's disgusting," Justin responded, faking familiarity now that August identified the text.

Staring at the circled red letters in the text of Isaac's *Torah*, August asked him, "Are you fluent in the Code of the Brotherhood?'

"No, not fluent," Justin responded. He heard on occasion rumors about the Code, but was never enough a part of the group to be in the know.

August looked at him with the distinct expression of annoyance dominating his face.

"This is definitely Baconian Code," he confirmed to Justin. "Isaac must have been trying to send a message to someone. Now all we have to do is decipher it and figure out who he was trying to communicate with."

"Rumor was he was talking to the DA."

"Which one?" August asked him quickly and excitedly.

"I'm not sure. I just heard it was a woman."

"That has to be Charlotte Weiss," August said then got lost in thought. *There's a hit out on her but she's a damn workaholic. We haven't been able to get her yet.*

Focusing back on Justin and the message, he addressed him with renewed fervor.

"Isaac leaked information to the DA and unless Charlotte Weiss is stopped, it will be leaked everywhere. You really should know the code," August continued, pointing to the first letter circled in red. It's the AB Code. In this instance, the 'a' or alpha letters are circled and the 'b' or beta letters are underlined in red. My eyesight isn't what it used to be. You'll need to identify each of the letters and write them out in sequence. Write big."

August slid a pad of paper over to Justin, who quickly picked it up and began documenting the highlighted letters. Barely literate, he pulled this off by simply copying what he saw. It felt like an eternity to August as he waited the 15 minutes for Justin to complete his task. When he finished August took the listed letters and set about deciphering them. Given his age, this process was slow and now it was Justin's turn to wait impatiently.

As he was deciphering the code, August learned there was a key Charlotte would have in her possession. The key would be crucial. He also learned that along the way Charlotte would be sent on a path taking her to Yonkers, New York and then on to a destination in the Middle East.

"You must get on a plane immediately!" August cried upon deciphering the code. "If you leave now you will certainly beat her there. You must meet her there. You must catch her off guard in a city we have a chance she is unfamiliar with. That is where you will make your attack. This woman is a disturbing threat to the Brotherhood."

Justin listened intently, his ears perking up when August told him he wanted him to go to the Middle East and track down Charlotte. *This mission is getting exotic!*

As he continued to translate, August eventually finished deciphering the entirety of the plan as encrypted in Isaac's *Torah*. He spoke quickly but at the end the blood drained completely from his face, leaving his complexion white as the driven snow when he realized the ultimate intended destination for the DA.

Now armed with that information, it was a simple matter of Justin saying the word regarding how much money he would need to finance his trip and accomplish the intended goal of stopping the enemy in her tracks. August had connections for a fake passport and it was made within the hour once a photo of Justin was taken.

August provided him with plenty of money for the flight and extra for new weapons and ammunition for his arrival. In terms of remuneration, August promised him another $100,000 once the job was complete and Justin immediately began dreaming of what he would buy with the proceeds. *Life in the Aryan Brotherhood is shaping up to be better than I ever dreamed.*

After a lengthy conversation, the details were set and Justin had cash in hand. August was clear to advise him he had a much more specific plan in mind for Justin than just killing Charlotte.

"You must come back with what I asked you for," August warned him. "Now knowing the entirety of Isaac's notes, it's no longer enough to just kill the girl. You must return to me what I've asked. Our cause will be destroyed if you are unsuccessful."

"I will stop at nothing," he assured August.

At the conclusion of their meeting and as he made his departure down the long, dirt driveway of August's secluded home, Justin held his head high. He exited the property through the same metal gate he had arrived through and turned around one last time to see August still waving him good-bye. A smile plastered his face all the way back to the bus stop.

# Chapter 36

*September 15, 1988*

Alex awoke the next day with a bald head. It was the morning after their infiltration of Hannibal's Bar and Charlotte's brave escape from Johnny's office. His memory of becoming bald the night before was largely faded and a reminder came only when he groggily stepped into the shower. He was blessed with a full head of naturally colored chestnut brown hair, and although still in his thirties, he wanted to ensure a lifetime of luscious hair and therefore used designer shampoo. He had a habit of reaching for his large bottle of the product first when he stepped into the shower, and on this particular occasion as well he forgot he didn't need it.

Never at any time before had he entertained the idea of shaving his head to the point of baldness, and was dismayed about the complete smoothness of his scalp where a coif of hair normally rested.

"You have to do this," Charlotte reminded him as she put a razor to his head after they returned from Yonkers. "It will help you blend in."

"I'm still not loving this whole undercover idea," he told her as he ran his hand over his hairless scalp and grimaced.

There was no time to worry about it this morning, however. He and Charlotte planned to meet within an hour of the time he awoke and he needed to be in proper costume.

"Yes the plan is risky, but it's our only option," Charlotte had told him.

"I know. I have to do this to find Brielle."

Charlotte planned it down to the very last detail. The agenda dictated that Alex pick her up at precisely 11 a.m. They would arrive at Hannibal's Bar early in the day, minutes after it opened, with the singular goal being to establish a rapport with Johnny and secure more information about the Enigma machine's whereabouts. Alex would be wearing a discreet wire and Charlotte would be feeding him information from the car to establish his authenticity. She prepped him at length the night before.

Charlotte had deduced from the photograph as a focal point in Johnny's office that he and Isaac were good friends, despite Isaac's incarceration.

"Your story is that you grew close with Isaac Kanzler in prison. You will use that to bond with him," Charlotte directed.

*It's all or nothing now*, Alex thought to himself as he removed the long past five o'clock shadow from his cheeks. He made a point not to shave his uncharacteristic goatee and let the scruff that developed over the last 24 hours give him just enough facial hair to look as if he didn't make a habit of keeping up with it. To this skin-headed, scruffy chinned appearance he combined a pair of dirty jeans and a t-shirt. These ragged items were tucked away as grungies for his occasional gardening hobby.

The final details of his costume included a pair of classic black military boots, which were the remains of his early military days. He roughed them up and with that, his get-up was complete.

"Wow, I hardly recognize you. You definitely look the part," Charlotte assured him as he met her at her home at exactly 11 o'clock. "You remembered the key, right?"

"Of course I did. It's been hanging around my neck since day one," he said as they got in his car to make their way back to the bar.

"Good, because I'm sure it's our key for the Enigma machine. Immediately when we find the Enigma, we're using it to decipher the message inscribed on it. Once we decode it, I'm sure we'll know where to go from there."

"Where I'd like to go from here is the place they're keeping my daughter," Alex responded.

"Just remember, the fact that we've gotten all these clues has to mean she's still alive. Whoever is behind the abduction wants us to follow their leads and it wouldn't make sense to keep us going if she was dead. They want something and we have to follow their clues to give it to them."

After this sobering conversation, the remainder of their drive back to Hannibal's Bar was largely in silence. There was a smattering of small talk, but they were both too nervous to discuss anything substantive. Upon arrival, seeing Hannibal's Bar in the light of day, it was easy to discern the marked trashiness of the neighborhood. They could clearly see the bar had just opened for the day and it appeared quiet and uninhabited. Charlotte and Alex watched as Johnny placed a sandwich board outside the front door signifying he was open for business. It contained scant items on the lunch menu to attract a crowd who may not be drinking at this hour.

Alex parked his luxury vehicle in a discreet location on the opposite side of the street. According to the plan, Charlotte would remain there regardless of how long it took. Her role in this undercover operation was to serve as a look-out and a get-away car if needed. Looking at it as being closely akin to a stake-out she was more than happy to do so. She would be sitting in the car with a pair of binoculars and listening to the audio transmitted through the microphone taped to Alex's chest. Her hidden desire to take down bad guys made her not the least bit bothered that her responsibilities in the current situation were rather menial

Charlotte watched as Alex crossed the street to his destination and she took comfort in the fact that even if the car was noticed an onlooker would not be able to look inside. *I need to thank the inventors of tinted windows.*

As Alex entered the bar, he noticed that Chrystal, their waitress from the night before, was working this shift. Anxious to test the legitimacy of his disguise, he made a beeline for the bar, intent on his purpose and without a trace of not belonging. He ordered his drink straight up despite the hour.

"Give me the hard stuff," he requested and Chrystal served him without even the smallest hint of recognition. *Success.*

Casually he looked around and noticed in the light of day, just minutes after his arrival, a mood much mellower than was present the night before. Luck struck early and his target Johnny emerged from the back of the establishment. Alex jumped on the chance to engage him in conversation.

Alex was as confident as he was going to get having rehearsed his new persona, "Danny," since the night before. *Danny was a new in town member of the white supremacy movement. He dropped into the establishment by way of his release from prison because he had heard about the place and needed a drink. They don't serve alcohol in the penitentiary so this was to be a nice treat.*

Alex's game plan was to be as covert as possible, and in an effort to avoid being too obvious, he forewent outright mentioning that he had just gotten out of prison. *A true ex-con wouldn't flaunt that fact.*

"You Johnny?" Alex led with.

"Yeah. Who wants to know?"

"The name's Danny." There was an awkward pause here as Alex tried to regroup. *Come on, don't screw this up.*

"Nice place you got here," he said to Johnny, redeeming himself as he sipped his drink.

"Thanks," Johnny responded, wiping down the counter. "It draws a good crowd."

"I knew I could trust my buddy Isaac when he told me about this place."

Johnny's lack of response told him he had been too vague. He would have to up his game. "Yeah, he gave me a lot of good advice out in Sing Sing. Prison, that is," he continued.

"Isaac? What's his last name?" Johnny asked, his interest peaked.

"It's my boy Isaac Kanzler. He and I have gotten tight over the last several years."

"Isaac Kanzler? Shamrock?" Johnny questioned him, using Isaac's gang moniker.

"Yeah, man. That's him."

"Shamrock's been in prison five years this last time around," Johnny told him. "What were you in for?"

"'parently cops don't like you beating up niggers and they sure don't like nigger beaters with weapons," Alex blurted.

The racial slurs burned his mouth as he said them.

"I can't believe you're tight with my buddy, Shamrock. He's like the big brother I never had."

"Yeah? He had plenty of good things to say about you and this place. I woulda thought you were some kind of demi-god by the way he talks."

"I'd say we have a mutual respect for each other," Johnny said with a smile on his face. "I'm sure he told you we've been friends since grade school. We were inseparable and he proved himself to be a solid soldier for the causes he believes in. I respect the hell outta that guy, you know what I'm sayin'? He's kept up with the Brotherhood on the inside."

"I got you," Alex said.

"Yeah, he's tough; in the Brand through and through. Spent his life workin' his way up the ranks. Patched in now and fully ranked. He told me he got "AB" tatted across his chest after going into prison this last time. He's fully ranked. That dude deserves all our respect."

"He said the same thing about you," Alex said. "About deserving respect, I mean. Said you don't get as much as you deserve."

"I envy you for the time you got to spend with him. You're probably a stronger patriot for it."

By the way Johnny was talking, Alex knew he had gained credibility as Danny and this was confirmed when Johnny extended an invitation.

"So Danny, man, a bunch of us boys are gettin' together tonight after quittin' time for an after party at my house. I'd love for you to come. I'll introduce you around. You in?"

"Hell, yeah. Any friends of Shamrock are friends of mine. You cool if I bring my sister?" He smiled inside for thinking on the fly to get Charlotte involved like that.

"She cool with us?" Johnny asked.

"Oh, yeah. It's a family thing," Alex assured him, referring to racial.

"She cute?"

"Ah, man, I don't want to talk about my sister like that. You can see for yourself."

"Nice," he said with a smile. "I'll see you both around three a.m. then," he confirmed, writing down his address and handing it to Alex on a scrap of paper.

"We'll be there," he confirmed, handing Johnny a ten-dollar bill as he downed the last drop of his drink.

"Nah, man. This one's on me."

"Thanks, brother. I have a good feeling about you." Because of the tone of his good-bye, Alex cringed with worry that he had slipped up. It was hard for him to hide his excitement about the proposition of being invited to Johnny's house.

*The Enigma machine has to be there.*

Alex looked warily back at Johnny to confirm his excitement hadn't made him. Thankfully Johnny didn't seem to notice.

*That was close.*

Alex walked down the street, passing Charlotte to ensure he wasn't followed as he left. Charlotte caught up with him several blocks away and as she met him he entered the car.

"We did it! We've got a ticket to Johnny's house. We're headed right into the lion's den."

"Nice work I heard the whole thing," she congratulated him.

"Yeah? You heard about your new role as the sexy, available sister?" It's your turn to shine, honey," he gloated.

# Chapter 37

Not even remotely as concerned about dying her hair jet black as Alex was about shaving his head, Charlotte donned her new hair color with pride and plastered on the red lipstick. Her look closely competed with Alex's in terms of authenticity.

Her choice of attire was also dark. Having taken fashion cues from the waitresses at the bar the night before, she embraced a Gothic style. She donned a black tank top, jeans and high boots and she well looked the part she was going for. It was very Aryan Nation.

Charlotte and Alex were careful to do a drive by Johnny's house and scope out the surroundings after leaving the club earlier in the day. They knew they could check it out unseen. When they got there they noticed it was in a surprisingly inconspicuous middle class neighborhood, although Johnny's house was slightly nicer than the other homes in the area. Johnny's status as a relatively successful business owner seemed to be paying off and was visible by the size of his home. A shiny Harley Davidson was parked in the side yard behind a fence and two large pit bulls stood nearby as lookouts. Other than those two warnings to intruders, the house and property looked relatively unassuming in the sleepy neighborhood. Alex and Charlotte continued driving by. They would return later.

***

The scene was modestly different when they returned at precisely 3:15 a.m. By this time, there were already a number of vehicles parked in front of the house and the party seemed to have fully pilled over from the bar after closing.

Charlotte and the Alex walked trepidatiously to the front door. A twinge of intimidation came out of reserve at the prospect of the two of them surrounded by a house full of Aryan Brotherhood and the damage that would be caused should their ruse be discovered. Upon entering the house, they were welcomed in by Johnny who was quickly introduced to Charlotte by Alex.

Johnny made his feelings known when he boisterously exclaimed, "No reason for you to be shy about it, Danny. She is a cutie." Winking at Alex, he escorted them around the house, careful to stay close to Charlotte.

For the remaining early hours of the morning, the two spies pretended to enjoy the company of the party. Drinking almost nothing, they carried glasses of wine and beer around with them throughout the duration of the gathering in a successful effort to look like they were getting progressively drunker. Their actual soberness gave them the upper hand against their host and the remaining party guests.

Getting much more information than they had hoped for or actually needed, they sat in on a discussion of the more bold members of the organization who were present at the party. With their loose alcohol-coated lips the others unknowingly let them in on some of the inside workings of their press for white power. Discussing many topics ranging from a national Neo Nazi rally in Montana the next month to who's done the worst thing to a minority, the conversation was putrid. The truest of their colors shone through when a drunken game of "Would You Rather..." began.

"Would you rather be born with black skin or give up alcohol for the rest of your life?" was asked of Johnny when it was his turn to choose the hypothetical lesser of two evils. Charlotte listened intently, craning her neck in the direction of Johnny. *Which will he choose?* As she had mentally documented in the last 24 hours, Johnny's world revolved around alcohol.

"I'd rather be relegated to drinking urine the rest of my life than be a nigger," he answered.

Charlotte closed her eyes, forcing herself to concentrate on not cringing, showing her disgust or making an outburst. There was too much at stake to stand now in defense of all the black people who were actually human and were not the bigoted scum she was currently surrounded by.

The majority of Johnny's guests stayed until dawn, during which time, Charlotte made every attempt to slyly break away to look for the Enigma machine. Unfortunately, and much to her annoyance, Johnny was stuck to her like glue and she never got the chance.

*I better just play along,* she conceded to herself.

"Danny tells me you know his last cellmate," Charlotte said to him with interest. "He says you both were pretty tight."

"He's like a brother to me," Johnny said, taking yet another sip of Bourbon. "We take care of each other," he went on. His words were grossly slurred.

"You taking care of him while he's locked up?" Charlotte asked in response, attempting to capitalize on his uninhibited state,

To her surprise, he took the bait. "I'm not going to leave my brother stranded. He's been giving me information from the inside and I've been taking care of some of his assets, if you know what I mean. I've got his Harley here and no one's getting near it. I've got some sentimental items too. Just little things he doesn't want to lose track of and most importantly something he would never trust with anyone else.

"What is it?" Charlotte asked.

"Shhh!" he whispered drunkenly, oblivious to the fact that no one was listening. "You've probably never heard of it," he warned her. "It's a decoder from World War II. Nazi stuff. Big reason they had success wiping out the inferiors and strengthening the Aryan race."

"What kind of decoder?" Charlotte pried further, covering her true intentions.

"The Enigma machine kind. It decodes messages. Shamrock bought it from a private dealer and it's like his prize possession. I keep it upstairs in the bedroom, but it's in a secret hiding place. I don't want anyone wandering up there to see it."

"Can I see it?" she asked him flirtatiously, "I love secrets."

"Ah ha, I see I've got you hooked. What kind of a man would I be if I took you up there when we weren't alone? I would miss out on a golden opportunity to get you in my bedroom and out of those clothes."

"What do you say I come back a little later, maybe in something a little more comfortable?" she said to him seductively. "I'd love to see what you have to show me."

"I can show you plenty of things," he creepily whispered into her ear.

Despite the fact that she wanted to throw up in her mouth at the prospect of being intimate with this man, Charlotte smiled slyly, covering her pride in this accomplishment of making him believe she was interested in the idea.

Having sealed the deal on a hot date with Johnny several hours down the road, Charlotte signaled to Alex it was time to go and he was eager to oblige. As they walked out the door, Johnny kissed her on the cheek and hugged her a little too tight. She reminded herself how much was at stake and feigned a smile he took to be genuine.

"You owe me," she said to Alex as they drove away. He simply laughed at her demand, which she didn't mind at all. It was good to see him smile. Charlotte filled him in on the final effort to decode the latest message and her upcoming meeting with Johnny. Sighing, she conceded to him it was their only option.

"I need to get to a smoke shop. I know exactly what we need," she directed him. The plan was simple: Seduce Johnny, drug him and then find the Enigma machine.

# Chapter 38

Other than the location of the Enigma machine, perhaps the most helpful thing Charlotte learned at Johnny's house was that he was a fan of bourbon. He mentioned it several times during the course of the night; almost as many times as he sucked down a glass.

Charlotte and Alex had managed to catch a few hours of sleep before the party but they were both still tired. They would again be relying on the adrenaline pumping through their veins to keep them awake as they purchased a bottle of bourbon at a 24 hour liquor shop and covertly obtained a vial of GHB at the smoke shop.

GHB is Gamma-Hydroxybutyric acid to the chemistry world, and it was through Charlotte's working drug and sexual assault cases that she knew where to easily obtain GHB, also known as the date rape drug.

With alcohol and drug in hand, Charlotte made sure to dress contrary to what she was comfortable in, but what was very appropriate for her private visit to Johnny's house in a few hours. Normally dressing in a conservative, professional manner, the blatant presentation of her cleavage into the public was a cameo she would not be quick to replicate.

"That skirt is a little too short," Alex admonished her in a protective tone.

"We have to go all out on this," Charlotte reminded him. "One slip up and we have to come up with a new plan. Remember listening to them talk last night? These people are for real. They are in the business of hate and they are not backing down."

"You know how much of that stuff to use?" he questioned her. This was his attempt to change the subject and confirm she was still as well versed about GHB as she was five minutes ago when they discussed it last. Alex was hesitant about the use of a drug in their plan.

"I know what I'm doing," she assured him again. "In order to make sure he's out, but not necessarily permanently, I'm going to give him half of what I have. If I need more, I'll use more. This guy is vile, but the law doesn't look too favorably on homicide."

"You've got to be careful."

"Alex, I can handle this. I'm a big girl," she told him. "I can take care of myself."

At this point Alex had no alternative but to trust her as she asserted herself with the drugs, the bourbon and his key with the mysterious symbols on hand.

# Chapter 39

It was decided that Charlotte would drive herself to Johnny's house. There was a grave emergency at Alex's downtown New York City office, but he told her he would be just a phone call away. It was when Charlotte found out that he would not be with her that she realized how much she was beginning to rely on him.

Despite her desperate desire to maintain her tough girl attitude, she wished he was going with her. She was on her way to meet one on one again with a pretty heavy hitter in the underworld of the white supremacists; only this one wasn't bound by shackles and chains.

"I feel fine about going alone," she lied. Although Charlotte had never been a bigot, she could fervently claim she held an intense and abiding hatred for the Aryan Brotherhood. Everything they stood for was ugly and weak and that was the reason she was doing what she was doing.

She took a moment to re-check her make-up when she pulled up to Johnny's house shortly after parting ways with Alex. *This is the moment of truth.* Puffing a cigarette for authenticity, she wasn't a smoker but was no stranger to the idea as she had experimented with it in her younger days. She hated it then and she hated it now but decided it was best to tolerate it for show as she made her way to the entrance of the lion's den.

Taking one final deep breath, she rang the doorbell and it took only a matter of seconds before Johnny opened it to her widely. He was dressed in a bathrobe and clearly happy to see her. Immediately taking control, Charlotte quickly introduced the bourbon she brought for the occasion, sat him down and poured them both a glass.

"I like a woman who knows what she wants," he said with a grin. "And this'll hit the spot, baby. I'm a little hung over."

With Johnny none the wiser to her tactics, Charlotte stealthily waited until he turned his back and poured half of the GHB into his drink. She made her next move by suggesting he throw some pillows on the couch for some foreplay before heading up to the bedroom.

Although she wasn't willing to go anywhere near the level of intimacy he was seeking, Charlotte was not subtle in letting him think the opposite, just to get to the Enigma machine. In her sober state, she was calling the shots while the drug was soothing him to sleep, all the while playing a serious game of hard to get and ramping him up with eager anticipation.

By her count, as he continued to down the aged bourbon, it was only 13 minutes from his first glass when he began to exhibit signs of passing out.

She watched him closely as his head dipped down and his body became limp. She removed the glass from his hand as he looked at her in a disoriented fashion. "Wow, I feel odd," he said before closing his eyes.

"Maybe I can make you feel better," she responded still going along with the ruse. Moments later, his breath deepened and he was asleep. She kissed him once on the mouth to ensure unconsciousness then laid him fully extended on the couch. She was careful to position him on his side to ensure he didn't swallow his tongue or vomit and choke.

With her roadblock now out of the way, Charlotte wasted no more time and made her way upstairs. She had had plenty of time to surveil the home while she was there earlier that morning and had noticed the bedrooms were located upstairs. She hurried up the steps and checked each door, until she found Johnny's bedroom. She honed in on the dresser in the photograph only to be struck with horror that the Enigma machine wasn't on top of it. She saw the first aid kit that had brought her there to begin with, but there was no Enigma machine.

Quickly, she entered the room and furiously searched. "A secret hiding place," she remembered him saying. *What could that mean?* The room was surprisingly sparsely furnished, which Charlotte chalked up to Johnny's bachelor status. The closet and under the bed yielded no Enigma machine and she was out of hiding spots and running out of time. *What if the drug wears off? What if Johnny finds me up here?*

Just as these thoughts crossed her mind, she heard Johnny stir downstairs. Bounding out of the bedroom, she went to check on him. In the event Johnny had awoken, her mind quickly contrived an excuse. *I'll tell him I couldn't find the bathroom.*

Charlotte was pleased to find that Johnny had simply rolled over to his other side. *I have more time,* she thought, and wasting none of it, ran back to his bedroom. Standing at the doorway, she was reassessing the scene when her eye was struck by the unlighted "Hannibal's Bar" sign hanging above the dresser. It was crooked. *This is my last option here,* she continued to think as she walked towards the wall to examine it. Carefully she lifted it slightly away from the wall and found that behind it, in fact, was a secret hiding spot. It was a safe. And it was a safe big enough to hold an Enigma machine, but she only had one option for the code— the seemingly impossible three digit combination from the mysterious symbols she was planning to use to set the Enigma's rotors, "12, 22, 23."

"This has to work," she quietly said to herself as she removed the sign from the wall and slowly turned the safe's lock.

She inhaled a large breath as she turned the handle, hoping for a miracle. She held her breath as it moved and only exhaled when she heard the click. *It opened!*

The Enigma machine inside was a beautiful sight as she moved towards it slowly and with wide eyes. After removing it from the safe and placing it on the dresser, she took just a moment to marvel at its age and imagine the places it had been, before she excitedly pulled Alex's key from the token hiding spot in her bra. Given that her chosen clothing for the morning was selected with an eye towards seduction, it was skin-tight and kept the key close to her body. *She glanced again at the door. It's still closed. I'm safe from discovery at the moment.*

Placing her hand on it, she marveled at the infamous Enigma machine. It was a cryptography apparatus whose methods were as abstruse as its name implied. At first blush it appeared to be little more than a glorified version of an archaic typewriter, but it stood before her much more complex and elaborate than met the eye.

Just as time had been of the essence for the allies in cracking through the complexities of the Enigma machine, Charlotte now stood in her own race against time. Though her task was simple, her palms were sweaty. *Focus Charlotte. All I have to do is use the key and the encrypted message, "oświęcim stacja kolejowa," to decipher the code and get the next clue.*

Her heart raced and the adrenaline pumped as she set the rotors according to the numbers "12," "22" and "23," represented by the Nordic runes engraven into the key. She prayed it would work. Then, cautiously she pushed the first button on the keyboard. "O" from *"Oświęcim."* She awaited the response with a shaking finger. Though she knew it was coming, she was almost taken aback when instantaneously the letter "P" lit up before her eyes. It was now only a matter of time before she would see the fruits of her labors in message form.

Her fingers continued to shake, yet she steadfastly worked as she typed in the letter groupings, contained on the key, *"oświęcim,"* without the accent marks, *"stacja"* and *"kolejowa."*

Rhythmically, she began plugging in each letter in succession as they were engraven on the key. Charlotte watched as each typed letter reverberated from her fingertips to the decoding mechanisms and then back to her where a new letter appeared illuminated. She was careful to notate each new letter that appeared even as her heart beat out of her chest at the thought of Johnny walking though the door.

Charlotte was moving quickly considering her constant fear of being discovered. She only had three more letters to go when she heard a fateful knock on the front door. *Who could that possibly be?*

Johnny's house party was long since over and she was counting on no new arrivals. If she was caught she would be trapped with no legitimate excuse readily coming to mind.

Charlotte raced to the bedroom window, which incidentally looked out over the front entrance, and gasped in horror at the sight she saw. It was Paniletti! Not only was it Paniletti, but it was plain-clothed, no-uniform wearing Paniletti.

*He's not here on police business. This is personal, but he sure didn't forget to leave his gun at home.*

Any benefit of the doubt she ever gave him evaporated then into thin air. A personal visit with a white supremacy leader such as Johnny sealed the deal in terms of his absolute malfeasance.

The face of Brent Somers flashed in her mind and upset her even more. Standing at the doorway, Paniletti demonstrated the same conceit and arrogance she routinely saw in Brent Somers, and was reminded of that arrogance rearing its ugly head at his meeting with her before she took this brief sabbatical from the New York District Attorney's Office.

Focusing again on Paniletti, she cringed as she saw him look over at her car. As modest and non-descript as it was, given she lived on a government salary, she knew he had seen her driving it before. She prayed he wouldn't put two and two together and more importantly that he would just go away.

Unfortunately, that was not to be her luck. Charlotte retreated from the window and looked down from the hallway onto the living room couch to confirm that Johnny was still out despite the ruckus at the door. Paniletti resorted to pounding on the door.

"Johnny!" he shouted repeatedly.

He rang the doorbell, which then set off the barking of the dogs in the backyard.

Charlotte refocused her efforts on finishing deciphering before hatching an escape plan and made the quick decision to close the bedroom door.

"That will buy me a whole two seconds," she said to herself dishearteningly.

As her fingers punched in the last symbol she watched with bated breath as the machine produced her result, which was immediately followed by a gunshot. It was a gunshot that busted the front door lock and was followed by a loud kicking in of the door. Charlotte didn't need to see him to know Paniletti had gained entry and was rushing in.

# Chapter 40

It didn't take much for Paniletti to decide something was amiss when he barged in and saw the scene in front of him. There on the leather couch laid his friend, passed out drunk, and surrounded by the lingering smell of woman's perfume. That combined with the sight of a small, woman's handbag, aroused his suspicions entirely. He followed the scent trail to the stairwell and headed up the stairs to the bedrooms. With his hand on his gun attached to his hip, he inched up and scoured his surroundings.

Charlotte was in a scrambled to find an escape. For a brief moment she considered hiding. Under the bed sounded good at this point but given the gravity of the situation she knew she would be easily found. Much too soon for her liking the handle to the door moved and she knew she had only seconds. Paniletti was behind the door and he would not be happy to see her. The flimsy lock would be no match for him.

Although the door was locked he would undoubtedly get in. *It's now or never.* Charlotte looked toward the window. *Looks like that's my only option.* There was no level of certainty that she wouldn't break her leg or neck for that matter, but she had no other choice. Outside, she noticed a well-placed tree, which appeared to have a strong potential to serve as her salvation. Having no time to think it through, she decided on her escape route and climbed out the window onto a semi unstable tree branch that hung close to the windowsill. Struggling to keep her balance, her jet-black hair became wrapped in the leaves and the branches scraped up her arms as she awkwardly descended.

The deciphered code was tucked into her bra, written on the slip of paper she brought in with her. She was left with this as the only place she could store it as she realized she left her handbag containing her driver's license downstairs.

*Not that it matters if Troy finds my ID,* she thought as she reached the bottom of the tree. Paniletti had penetrated the bedroom door and was looking down at her with his gun aimed precisely in her direction. She saw the spark of recognition on his face through the dense foliage. It was clear he knew who he was dealing with, but that recognition didn't stall him.

Two shots rang out in that instant. *He is really after me! Thank heaven the tree blocked his view.* Given the vegetation Paniletti wasn't going to have any success without firing a slew of bullets and getting lucky. Consequently, he ran back downstairs and through the front door of the house to confront Charlotte on the ground.

Charlotte rushed to her car and swung the door open, propelling herself inside and onto the driver's seat. Without hesitation she reached for the door locking mechanism and secured it in its locked position. Breathing heavily, she turned on the engine and double-checked to confirm she hadn't lost the ever important handwritten decryption in her mad dash back to the car.

About to shift into gear and propel the vehicle forward, she noticed an obstruction on her rear view mirror. *Wait a minute. I definitely locked my car doors before going into Johnny's.*

A chill ran down her spine as she realized someone had entered the locked car and intruded on her personal space. Affixed to her rearview mirror was a lock of curly black hair affixed to a piece of paper containing the following pairing of words in bright scarlet lettering:

Charlotte paused to think for just a second about its meaning, but as she had yet to decipher the first message of a similar nature that was left in Brielle Card's crib, she simply stopped and removed it. It came down easily and she could see once again behind her in the mirror. And not a moment too soon. As she looked up, she saw Paniletti running rapidly towards her, gun in hand. She had an initial uncomfortably short lead after a very untimely stalling of her car, but quickly shifted into drive and slammed her foot on the gas. She raised a ruckus as her tires screeched forward and gained momentum by spinning in place for the space of three rotations before shooting forward.

She saw Paniletti stop and take aim and heard her rear window crash as a bullet penetrated and lodged itself into the back seat. It stopped short of her body and her heart began to beat faster with the knowledge that he was literally trying to kill her.

Soon the distance between them was too great for him to have any likelihood of getting off an accurate shot, but he continued trying nonetheless. As Paniletti continued to shoot, Charlotte steadfastly sped forward until she found an intersection. She swerved to the right, scarcely pausing to step on the brakes. With her focus being purely on survival, she drove with her knuckles gripping the steering wheel, white from clenching. The screeching of the tires continued until she was safely down the street and sufficiently satisfied she could suspend the process of driving like a maniac. Only then did she return to a semblance of safe but fast driving back to Alex's house.

With her life spared, as she drove her thoughts returned to the mysterious message on the mirror. *Who could have possibly gotten into my car while it was locked? And why? It definitely wasn't Paniletti. He was too surprised by my presence when he barged into Johnny's house.*

*This made her shudder. Whoever did leave the message was clearly the same person who left the message for Alex, which meant it was the same person who abducted his baby. The abductor is remarkably close.*

"I hope there are no fingerprints on this because I don't have time for testing," she said aloud.

As for Paniletti, after he was left in her dust, he cursed her name as she drove away. Johnny was passed out and he gathered Charlotte had been using the Enigma machine. *What the hell business does she have with it?* He was going to get to the bottom of this.

Not before having the opportunity to process what she transcribed, Charlotte pulled over as soon as she found a safe place and looked at the crumpled piece of paper stashed in her bra. In her scribbled handwriting, she read:

---

**PIEREIGHTYEIGHTSUNDAY**

---

This was their next clue. Pier Eighty Eight on Sunday. Her mind couldn't help but reflect on "88" as a symbol of the Aryan Brotherhood. She was aware that "H" was the eighth letter of the alphabet and they had adopted the number "88" to represent "Heil Hitler." It served as a symbol of their Nazi beliefs. For her purposes, Charlotte knew exactly where Pier Eighty Eight was along the Hudson River and there was not a moment to waste. Tomorrow was Sunday.

# Chapter 41

Paniletti dusted of his muscles and ego after his prey evaded capture and made his way to the prison. He walked in like he owned the place and immediately began barking orders to Jeff, who was ever on duty.

"I'm here to search Isaac Kanzler's cell," he demanded. "Quickly, before his possessions are moved. I'm investigating the Aryan Brotherhood murders."

Jeff didn't so much as blink before leading him to the desired cell.

"You know, your stupidity has just about cost you your life on this one, Barker. Once the Brotherhood gets word of this I can't help you. Watch your back," Paniletti warned him as they made their way through the secure hallways to Isaac's cell.

"I didn't know about Isaac Kanzler. He was good at keeping his secret. Acted real legit white supremacist all the time," Jeff responded submissively.

"I paid you to know, bonehead. That was your job."

"I did my job, boss. I promise. I kept a really good watch on him. Even when Charlotte Weiss came to talk to him, I had a bug in their visitation room, but slacker Collins stepped on it when he brought Kanzler in. That was the end of that."

"Excuse me, what did you say?" Paniletti piped up, forcing him to repeat himself.

"I said, 'Slacker Collins stepped on it when he brought Kanzler in.'"

"No, I mean what did you say about Charlotte Weiss? She was here?"

"Yes, and I tried to record the visit but like I said slacker Collins stepped on the bug."

"Enough about Collins. Why didn't you tell me she was here?

"Here it is," Jeff announced when they arrived. He swallowed hard and pointed Paniletti to Isaac's cell, trying desperately to change the subject.

Paniletti's glare almost penetrated his skin. Jeff began to break into a sweat and meekly whispered, "Please, I beg you."

"Thank you. I'll take it from here," Paniletti announced, utterly disregarding Jeff's plea for mercy.

Jeff hunched his shoulders, picking up on this not so subtle hint and turned to leave. *He's definitely going to report me to his bosses. I may need to skip town.*

There was no reasoning with Paniletti who would spend the next several hours in the cell looking through the remainder of Isaac's belongings only to wind up empty-handed. He was there to find traces of motivation behind the murders of the 11 or at a minimum something that could lead him to additional defectors. The *Torah*, covered with the binding of a King James' version of the *Bible*, was ostensibly a marker of Isaac's loyalties and he swore under his breath again at the incompetence of Jeff for not noticing this and advising him accordingly.

Paniletti had been in contact with August Bäcker. He knew the entirety of Isaac's plan encoded in the *Torah*, but he was at the prison to collect more dirt on him. Paniletti knew that Isaac was aware of his own affiliation with the Brotherhood and the plan to murder Benjamin Stansfeld.

*That fool better not have mentioned anything about me to Charlotte.*

As Paniletti finished up canvassing the cell, the reality of the situation stared him in the face like a blinding light. Isaac was a defector and he was divulging secrets of the Brotherhood to Charlotte. Paniletti knew it and he was going to have to act fast. There was too much at stake for him. Charlotte escaped him once, but he was going to find her and kill her. This was his focus now.

# *Chapter 42*

Having previously been out late several nights prior doing reconnaissance up a tree outside the UN compound, Peter sat and enjoyed his day off. It was past dusk now, and he was reading his favorite newspaper, the *Deutsche Allgemeine Zeitung*. The soft whir of a circular fan soothed him and for the first time in a long time he was in complete peace. He sat on a reclining chair with his legs up on an ottoman as his eyes grew tired from the combination of small newsprint and the soft glow of a lamp overhead. He set the paper on his lap and looked over at his prized possession, his wife, Myung-Hee. She was in the kitchen cooking Korean food they would soon sit down and eat together. His heart filled with tender feelings for her as he watched.

Myung-Hee was a stranger to this part of the world and a stranger to any quality of life that included things like the comfortable beds, hot showers and moderate temperatures she currently had access to in the cozy apartment she shared with Peter. She was North Korean and she was a living witness to the atrocities happening in her native country.

Peter recalled three years prior. It was by pure chance he first had the privilege to lay eyes on her. On one particular evening around dusk, he had crossed into the demilitarized zone that served as a buffer between North and South Korea. There he entered by flashing his military ID. It was actually by mistake he was able to make it as far as the zone overlapping the borders.

*God must have put me here for a reason*, he thought when he realized the mistake.

It was on that night he discovered the beauty that was Myung-Hee. Seeing her for the first time put him in literal shock. *She's the most beautiful woman I've ever seen.* Myung-Hee was on the other side of the DMZ, often seen standing in the area of, and subservient to, an abrasive looking North Korean guard. She was there for his pleasure and nothing else.

Peter was not the only one who was struck. She saw him too and their eyes locked through lines of chain link and barbed wire. This moment was fleeting as the guard pushed her to the side with his body, but it was in the simplest of terms, magic. He smiled in her direction even as the moment had passed. He would be back.

The next evening at exactly the same time, he stood as close to the border as he could get, nearest to where he was standing when he first saw Myung-Hee. Ever cognizant of Deity, he believed he would see a miracle eventually. When he saw her again the next day, his heart literally leapt for joy. This time he was able to offer up to her the smile she missed the day before and she returned the favor.

And so it went, day after day. Their eyes locked at the same time, the same place, even if only for a brief second. He had the advantage of the military uniform to give him this opportunity and his world began to revolve around it so much so that terror struck him on the 47th day when she was not there. The guard she was there to service was present but there was no sign of her.

He waited for a time that night with no sighting and then dejectedly began the journey back to the barracks at the Army base. Along the way, he did a surprising double take when he saw a flash of long black hair about a quarter mile up the length of the fence. This was unusual to say the least, as the border between North and South was guarded heavily by stoic looking men on the North.

Cautiously but excitedly, he made his way to the area where he had seen the flash of female hair. Arriving at his destination, he looked intently through the wire fence to examine whether he could confirm what appeared to him to be a mirage. The area was covered with trees and shrubbery on the North side but his eyes were able to discern a folded piece of paper stuck in the ground. There was just enough open space between the chain links at that location to reach down and grab the paper with his fingers. He opened the note and read the simple message.

"Help me," it said in Korean, a language which he had learned enough now to understand. "In three days I will be at the water's edge in Songang-ni. I must escape."

He could hardly believe what he was seeing, but processed it quickly enough to formulate a plan. *This is from her. She risked her life to deliver this message. I must help her.* It was a current trend that some brave attempts were being made to escape from North Korea by way of the Yellow Sea. In order to get to Songang-ni, which lay on the eastern edge of North Korea on the shores of the Yellow Sea, Peter knew Myung-Hee would have to cross the Ryesŏng River. This journey, although very risky, would be a proverbial walk in the park compared to the journey she would have to make across the Yellow Sea into China. This worried him to say the least. Many attempted this method of escape, but few succeeded. If they didn't die in the process, they were apprehended by the North Korean government and sent to a prison camp.

At the appointed time, three days later, and having the benefit of military gear, Peter took off shift early and journeyed again off base to pursue this inexplicable connection with the beautiful North Korean woman who was depending on him.

There were almost unbeatable odds that needed to be overcome, but he had faith in the idea. It was imperceptible initially, as he took a small steel boat he acquired out into the depths of the Yellow Sea, but he felt a force beyond his control steering him in a direction that defied his instinct. The raft began to take a clearly desired route and he had no option but to go with it.

Three hours passed after he finally stopped and tread water at the beach of Songang-ni. There was no sign of life out in the water's depths. Peter began to lose the confidence he started with. His faith was shaking from the experience just like his body was from the cold.

It was in a moment of sheer hopelessness to match the now darkness of the night sky when he saw a light and heard the nearby splashing of water. Quickly and with a burst of excitement, he rowed toward it and saw, like an angel fallen from heaven, Myung-Hee, clinging to an inflatable raft. Floating in the great depths of the dark sea, she was clinging tightly to a burlap sack. It was the only thing she brought with her aside from the clothes on her back.

Feverishly Peter rowed up to her side and hoisted her up into his small vessel. He quickly wrapped her in his coat to abate her shivering from the cold. He embraced her tightly then turned the boat around to begin the tiring journey en route to the porous area of China. *There will be refuge for her there. I will make sure of it.*

***

Though their journey was riddled with a fear of being caught, they succeeded. Peter delivered Myung-Hee safely to a house of refuge in China and later brought her safely through Berlin and then on to New York City. It meant walking out on his duty to the military to accomplish this, but that was of little consequence to him. Their success renewed his trust in the power that bound him to Myung-Hee and he felt content about his choice to forfeit the military career that had defined his life. She would be his life now. Everything was as it should be.

On this night three years later, he was happy. For now she was cooking Korean food in the warmth and safety of their home and it did his heart good.

# Chapter 43

Time was on their side for Alex and Charlotte. Granted, it was by the skin of their teeth, but they pulled off the feat of decrypting the Enigma machine code in sufficient time to make the Sunday appearance at Pier 88. Charlotte's near death experience when crawling out the window of Johnny's house had happened the day prior, requiring immediate action the next morning to travel to Pier 88.

Alex was both mortified and relieved to see the mysterious lock of hair found in her car when Charlotte showed it to him.

"That has to be Brielle's," he asserted. "She must still be alive." His relief in making this statement was evident, but was trumped by his frustration as to how Pier 88 could fit into the equation of the journey they were embarking on.

"What's that supposed to mean?" Alex blurted when Charlotte had revealed her translation from the Enigma machine.

"It seems pretty self-explanatory to me," Charlotte replied.

"Self-explanatory? How is it self-explanatory? It tells us nothing. It just gives us another location and leads us on more of a wild goose chase."

"Look Alex, I get it. I'm sure this is excruciating," Charlotte responded kindly. "The only thing I can tell you is that there has to be a reason for this process. Without a living, breathing daughter of a Senator, this goose chase would be absolutely unnecessary. I firmly believe that Brielle is alive. We just need to get through this. We need to get to the end, wherever that may be, and find her."

Charlotte's response calmed Alex slightly but he still remained worked up. Unbeknownst to Charlotte, after they finished planning and retired to their separate residences for the evening the night before, Alex drove by the Pier. He noticed they opened their gates at 5 a.m., and it was clear when he arrived at her home exactly at 4:30 a.m. to pick her up that he was going to make sure they were there at the crack of dawn.

Alex was much earlier than Charlotte anticipated, but she didn't complain and quickly showered and prepared herself for the day. The earliness of the hour allowed them to make record time to the harbor.

"I didn't sleep last night," he told her. "I can't possibly sleep knowing Brielle is out there." There was a specific solidarity in this statement and Charlotte remained quiet while silently respecting it.

Despite the dreariness of their situation, the sun was beautiful as it rose. *I wish we were headed to the pier for a cruise,* Charlotte thought to herself. *A 24 hour ice cream bar sounds pretty great right now.*

Upon arriving, they parked the car and Alex was careful to lock it not knowing how long they would be gone. They walked to the gate leading to their destination. When they arrived at the harbor, Alex's Senate identification badge got them through the gates much more smoothly than anticipated.

"Impressive," Charlotte responded.

They walked through the gate and traversed the harbor's path. Paying close attention to their surroundings, they saw several massive boats, ferries and cargo ships lined up at the docks waiting to be let loose. Again, Charlotte couldn't put her finger precisely on what they were doing there or what they might find. She certainly didn't like the idea of water combined with a small child.

"There's Pier 88," Alex blurted, snapping her out of her worry.

Charlotte looked in the direction he was pointing and saw an oversized cargo ship being loaded with large cargo boxes, which were in turn being lifted by cranes. The ship appeared to be nearly fully loaded, with just a few more cargo containers remaining to be airlifted on board.

The ship was well marked as a Scandinavian vessel with an Icelandic flag, which with its blue background and the predominant red cross, waved proudly in the wind.

"Look at the flag, Alex," Charlotte exclaimed excitedly. "It's a red cross."

I guess we're in the right place then," he said, sharing in her excitement. "The problem is how are we going to get on board?"

"Great question."

"You stay right here and I'll go find out," he instructed her as he rushed his way over to an early twenties shipping yard attendant, Mikey Harris.

Mikey was directing one of the cranes, ensuring that the last of the items were properly placed on board the ship.

"Excuse me," Alex said when he approached him.

"Yes, sir."

Alex identified himself, again flashing his U.S. government badge then asked, "Where's this ship headed?"

"Ah, Senator Card. I've been expecting you," he responded.

"You've been expecting me? What do you mean? How can that be possible?" Alex asked.

"I can't give you any details but I've been well paid to make sure you get on this ship and hide there until it docks."

"Paid by whom?"

"I can't tell you that either, but I can tell you I don't get my $20,000 until you get on this ship and stay there until it docks."

"Are there any other passengers riding?"

"No sir, this is a cargo ship. Ship crew only. No passengers."

"What time is it leaving today?"

"9:05, sir. We still got ourselves a coupla hours to get her loaded and get on out of here. I'm glad you made it in time."

"Are you riding it as well?" Alex pried further trying to squeeze out as many details as he could.

"No, I'm not crew on this trip. I've been on that thing for the last three months and I'm anxious to get home and have my leave. I hate being out on the water for months at a time, you know what I mean?"

Based on his choice of words it was obvious Mikey had forgotten he was addressing a United States Senator.

"Can I at least get you to tell me where it's going?"

"I'm sorry," Mikey responded. "I forgot and—"

"Let me guess, you can't tell me?" Alex cut him off.

"Like I said, I'm being paid to just get you on the ship and tell you where to stow so you stay hidden and get off when the boat docks. Those are my only responsibilities."

"I can pay too," Alex answered back. "How about $1,000? Will that refresh your memory?"

The young man considered this for a moment. "Fine," he conceded. "If you've got a grand in cash, I'll tell you where it's going, but you can never let anyone find out that I told you."

Mikey counted the money Alex readily handed him then revealed, "It's going to Israel; the beaches near Tel Aviv." Then, with a twinkle in his eye, he said, "I'm sure you'll love it, Senator. You'll definitely love it more than your ship accommodations for the next eight days."

"What accommodations?" he asked suspiciously.

"The only place you'll be safe and remain undetected is in the cofferdam. You'll need to stay there the whole trip."

"For eight full days we're going to be staying in a tiny cofferdam?"

"That's right," he confirmed. "Don't shoot the messenger."

"Got it," Alex responded, wishing desperately that what little news he received could have been better news.

Charlotte stood back watching this exchange between the two. *Alex has some great social skills,* she thought.

"What are you up to?" she asked him coyly when they were out of Mikey's earshot.

"Well, turns out it's a cargo ship there and we've got to get on it."

"How exactly are we supposed to do that? Your status doesn't quite pull rank when it comes to boarding cargo vessels, I don't believe."

"Yes, but that kid there probably has a girl anxiously waiting for him to come off leave. I'm thinking he'll want to surprise her with something nice. Status and money talks. Apparently he's being paid to smuggle us on board and told me where we're hiding out on the ship."

And he was right. The next thing Charlotte knew, Mikey was ushering she and Alex as they climbed into a cargo container. As Mikey closed the lid he reminded them a final time, "Remember. The latch on the inside will get you out. When the coast is clear you'll need to make your way to the electrical hole. Follow the directions I gave you and remember YOU DO NOT KNOW ME! You gave me your word."

"And $1,000," Alex reminded him.

Their presence on the ship was a security breach, which was an obvious point of concern for Charlotte. Alex warned her to be silent and do everything he instructed her, but as Mikey slammed the lid shut on the cargo container, he seemingly hammered the nail in her coffin both literally and figuratively.

Despite this seemingly fatal end, the second Charlotte found the opportunity she asked, "Why do you have $1,000 cash on you?"

"I have some extra cash just in case," he responded as they were patiently waiting for the ship to depart. He didn't want to disclose yet where they were headed for fear she would try to get off the ship.

"What are you, some kind of Mafioso?" she asked him. "I thought we were supposed to be trusting our government officials."

"Have you ever been forced to prepare for something like this? Following a series of random clues to find your only child?"

"No."

"Exactly. And neither have I. I have no idea what we're in for at any given moment in this thing. I figured several stashed bills may come in handy. That and a credit card and passport. Since we can't involve the authorities and I'm fresh out of patience, I have no other resources."

"You're quite the boy scout. I always have my passport on me for a spur of the moment trip into Canada, but I'm unfortunately not prepared like you on the money," Charlotte responded.

The airlift into the cargo ship was substantially unnerving as the crane held the container by a hook on the lid. Charlotte was biting her lip. *How are we not going to die right now?* Either the lid will pop off, forcing us to plummet to our deaths, or the lid is on so tightly we won't be able to escape and will suffer a slow death by suffocation.

"The kid gave me explicit instructions about how to open this thing from the inside," he tried to reassure her as if reading her mind. "We won't be trapped."

Charlotte made a fervent attempt to take some solace in that statement. *I better trust him*, she figured. *After all, he trusted me to guide him on this quest to save his daughter. If we don't rely on each other neither of us has anything else to rely on.*

"Why can't we just take a flight to wherever it is we're going? That would seem like the rational thing to do."

"Has any part of this been rational?" he quipped back. "We've been sent on a hunt with only small, vague clues to lead us to Brielle. There must be a reason for all of it that we just have to figure out. I don't expect this to be in any way easy given what we've already been through."

*Excellent point*, Charlotte thought as their bodies shook and the cargo box landed on the ship with a thud. Two and a half tense hours later, the ship set sail. Charlotte could hear the laps of water hitting its sides as they glided through the water. Under any other circumstances it would have been a peaceful sound, but as it were, it wasn't. She didn't have much time to wallow in her misery, however. As soon as the ship departed, Alex took the necessary steps to quietly open the cargo box. Mikey had warned them the sailors on board would be conducting checks of the cargo containers—they needed to move out fast.

# Chapter 44

Peter's seat was definitely not bad for a last minute purchase. The flight was packed to the gills and since they had no remaining space for him in coach he was upgraded to first class at no extra charge. This meant, of course, at no extra charge above and beyond the sky high price he paid for a last minute ticket overseas. Peter was following Charlotte with an unsettling amount of dedication, essentially stalking her since he dropped off the UN surveillance video. He was on the next plane to Israel as soon as the naval ship left the dock.

Boarding with him was an elderly woman who was relegated to the back row. Her gray hair framed her tired face, wrinkled from the hardships she had experienced in life. It was a natural thing for him to exchange his first class ticket to take her seat.

"Thank you. That's one of the sweetest things anyone's done for me in a long time," she said, kissing him on the cheek. A tear developed in her eye.

Peter was happy to help the woman, not bothered by the fact he was giving up an opportunity to sit comfortably and stretch his legs in front of him as far as they could go. In fact, he preferred the back row. It meant no passengers behind him and he could keep a lookout on all passengers in front of him. After leaving Korea, he had pulled the plug on 15 years serving for the United States Army, yet his military training and need to surveil lingered with him in his current status as a veteran.

For a moment, he glanced out the window and reflected on his life and the reason for his need of level red awareness at all times of the day and subconsciously at night. If there was one life lesson that had been codified for him in the military it was that you never turn your back. *Never turn your back on your enemies; it could cost you your life. Never turn your back on your fellow service members; it could cost them their lives. Never turn your back on those you love, the bonds of love get weak with abandonment. Never turn your back on what you believe; the human soul gets weak with no purpose.*

He had learned these lessons the hard way. Time and life tested him and had shown him bitter truths. He could never claim, however, a regret of the lessons he learned through his struggles.

Peter had enlisted in the military when he was 16. He successfully convinced the recruiters he was old enough to join based on his appearance and a forged birth certificate. This was the surest way he knew to find purpose in his life. The military gave him much needed structure and the constant drills and instruction of his training offered him a security he never before knew. His military career had been lengthy and the moment he walked away from it to rescue Myung-Hee marked the end of his long-term commitment. To him the military was life and became his home. He knew others viewed him as making sacrifices for his country but he never perceived that to be the case. Starting from nothing, his service actually gave back to him more than he felt he was giving.

He was separated from his family at a young age. His mother died when he was young and his father committed suicide. It wasn't his father's fault, he knew. He couldn't be blamed for his actions. It was the fault of the outside influences of the world he was eventually unable to withstand. Nevertheless, the absence of a proper childhood often gave Peter pause about whether the world was a place he himself wanted to remain in, but such dreary thoughts were all before he met Myung-Hee.

Now, even after having handed in his resignation to the Army, he continued to wear his military fatigues. They were a warm blanket, offering safety and security and an anchor in the storm of life that even through this moment, kept him afloat.

As he sat now on the plane, he recalled his last post of duty in South Korea was less than 20 kilometers from the North Korean border. Having been stationed in a military camp with the nearest city being Dongducheon, and conditioned due to a lifetime of being constantly on alert, there were few things that struck or surprised him much. Shock and awe was not a concept which often passed through his consciousness. Nevertheless, as he took his first subway ride through Dongducheon, he was struck with the imagery of biomedical gas masks being stationed at each train stop. The threat of war breaking out at any time was ever present and there was no one in the country which that fear didn't touch.

Having lived all over the world at various stations, Peter's military duty took him to many parts of the world. As he made mental note of the subtle and extreme differences in the different areas of the world he lived in, he would watch the comings and goings of the people and remarked that one thing above all others was true. *The desires of human beings are universal. It wasn't just similarities that unite the people of the world,* Peter learned, *but their differences that bring unity and beauty to the world.* This was a truth he firmly believed in, and was the reason he was on the plane.

# *Chapter 45*

*September 17, 1988*

Being airlifted onto a barge in a cargo ship was decidedly something Charlotte would never be recommending to her friends. As if she was not already well aware, it was extremely unsettling to be confined in a box suspended a hundred feet above the air. Heights and small spaces; those were Charlotte's biggest fears.

"You come by it honestly. These conditions have been passed down through the generations," was what her mother told her.

Considering the source, that was either the truth or her mother lovingly said it just to ease her insecurity about it. Charlotte suspected the latter.

Immediately after they set sail and per the instructions of Mikey at the dock, Alex and Charlotte bravely sought to venture out into the unknown geography of the ship.

"No one will find you in the electronics void," Mikey informed Alex. "The electronics void is the open space between the ship's lowest deck and the hull," he explained. "You're lucky this is an Icelandic style ship. American style ships run their electrical cables along the topside of the floor's surface. Quarters are tight all around on those ships and there is very little space under the subfloor of the deck. They don't have electronics voids and there would be no place for you to hide. It will be a tight fit," he informed Alex, "but aside from that crevice, there won't be one square inch of real estate on the ship that isn't filled with cargo containers or used in some capacity."

The slightness of the space was a detail Alex had spared Charlotte of until the last minute. She was more than vocal about her fear of heights and small spaces during their flight in the cargo container and he didn't feel it appropriate to cause her more anxiety than necessary until he absolutely had to; that and he didn't want her to change her mind and possibly blow their cover.

"You'll be able to feel it when the ship sets sail," Mikey told them.

And for obvious reasons, they needed to be as silent as possible. Mikey gave Alex specific instructions for finding their way to the metal panel in the floor that constituted the doorway to the electronics void. He had Alex sync his watch and move only at a precisely given time when the crew was focusing on their work on the opposite end of the ship.

The opening to the electronics void, also known as the cofferdam, would be at the end of the ship closest to the stern. This ship depended on these cofferdams. They were insulating spaces between two watertight decks. As per usual, the cofferdam on this ship was a void; a small empty space whose purpose was to ensure that any toxic chemical cargo which may be on the ship didn't leak into the machinery spaces. On this boat it was a mere nine feet long, five feet wide and four feet tall. It didn't provide much by way of headspace but it wasn't meant to. Another of its primary functions was to store the ship's electrical wiring.

Alex was happy to be in control of the situation. He had information that Charlotte didn't about the ship and that gave him a feeling of power regardless of how slight. Professionally, he possessed a measure of power which many did not; however, when it came to his personal life at the present time he had never before felt so powerless. *My wife is gone, likely forever, and my only child has been abducted.*

At the appointed time he opened the cargo container slightly and peered outside. All was quiet on this side of the deck. Motioning to Charlotte, he boosted her up so she could climb out. He then followed behind her as Mikey instructed them to do.

"Keep to the sides of the ship," Alex told her. "We don't want to be out in the open."

Charlotte followed, fearfully obedient.

When they reached their destination at the opening of the electronics void, Alex silently pointed her in the direction of the floor panel and raised it open. Her eyes grew wide with angst at what she saw underneath. It was not at all what she was hoping for. The space was narrow and dark. They would be crawling from here on out.

She shuddered as she looked down the hole in the floor that was her only salvation. She begrudgingly followed Alex into the crawl space and winced when he pulled the panel shut on top of them. Charlotte let out a deep breath and sat steadfastly with a look of trauma plastered across her face. For the most part they both sat in silence during this, their initial hazing in the cofferdam.

"We're going to have to get used to this," he told her.

When she outright ignored him, he knew he better let her dictate the conversation. Consequently, it was no less than a full hour of awkward silence before Charlotte finally murmured, "This is not what I signed up for."

"Hey don't look at me," Alex replied in the dim light, responding defensively. "I'm not the one who jimmy rigged this ordeal. I would much rather be sitting at home in front of a fire drinking a beer and watching my little girl grow up."

"Touché," she responded.

He called her out just like she had called him out and she knew she deserved it. Her wallowing in misery was not making this easy on either of them.

"But Isaac was so persuasive," she attempted to rationalize. "He told me if I followed the clues I would discover who killed Saul Adler, be led to the topmost leader of the Aryan Brotherhood and find your daughter. Unless this ship doubles as a covert Neo-Nazi base, there has to be a better way than this to find the killer, the financial source of the world's most prevalent white supremacist criminal syndicate and your daughter."

"You have no idea how much I wish there was a better way," he responded.

"You're right. I'm sorry," she apologized sincerely. "I can't imagine how difficult this must be for you. Despite my ranting, I firmly believe we'll see the fruits of our labors here. As odd as it sounds, there was something inherently good about the prisoner when I saw him. It's almost as if his sense of justice when it comes to the cause he believes in is so strong it casts a shadow over the terrible crimes he committed."

"I have a hard time sharing your sentiment. I can't for the life of me figure out what would motivate a man, who has information about the whereabouts of a kidnapped child, to be so evil as to torment a parent for such a seemingly intangible cause."

"Chalk it up to working in a job where you're surrounded by criminals on a daily basis. You learn to distinguish between the scum."

Moving on to a new topic of conversation and trying to deflect some of the blame for the situation off of herself, Charlotte asked, "How long is this ship supposed to be on the water for anyway? I'm assuming it'll be stopping at the next harbor by morning before it moves on. We'll need to deboard at the first stop."

"The ship is only making one stop before it unloads," Alex informed her.

"Fine with me."

"Not especially. He said we'd be on the water for eight days. We're headed to Israel." He cringed at the thought of what her dramatic response might be.

"What? Eight days?" she gasped. "And Israel? We'll starve to death! Why didn't you tell me?"

Her crankiness was already rearing its ugly head due to a lack of food. They hadn't known prior where their trip to Pier 88 would lead them and consequently weren't aware that carrying food or water would have been an extremely good idea. The very large, well-stocked ship should have been a tip off when they saw it but she had managed to miss that detail. They were running on pure adrenaline and they were exhausted. Their deductive planning skills were clearly not operating on all cylinders at present.

"We won't starve before we die of dehydration," was Alex's stoic response. "Besides, why didn't you tell me it was going to be a wild goose chase to find my daughter?"

"I didn't know we'd get in this far," she said angrily. "I'm just following the code. We don't exactly have many other options at this point."

"And we may very well starve in the process."

"Did I mention I'm claustrophobic?"

"Yep. Right after the lengthy explanation about your fear of heights. The cargo container, remember?    It happened about an hour ago."

"Well, it's true," Charlotte retorted not the slightest bit apologetic that she was repeating her complaint. "But it's not my fault. It was passed down to me from my father and to him from his father. I come from a long paternal line of severe claustrophobics."

"At least you have a general idea of where you came from. You get to blame your grandfather for your phobias. I was never afforded that luxury. My parents mentioned a total of ten words about my dad's side of the family and the only thing I know about my dad's dad is that he was the epitome of health throughout his life. He had seemingly no health problems and I was bred from healthy genetic stock. My father's mother died of heart disease in her forties but my dad has yet to have any medical problems. My parents were anal about making sure we stayed healthy. I wouldn't have minded so much if they wouldn't have forced me to eat an ungodly large quantity of vegetables and flax as a child."

"Flax?" Charlotte asked. Due to her utter disregard for health foods, she was unfamiliar with wheat germ packaged for the extremely health conscious.

"Yes, don't ask."

"Hey, you don't want to get into the dark secrets of your past, I certainly won't press you," Charlotte responded sarcastically.

Suddenly, Alex piped up, "I've really got to go."

"Neither one of us is going anywhere. You'll have to wait eight days, remember?"

"No I mean I have to go to the bathroom."

Charlotte scoffed. "It doesn't look like our 50 square feet has any type of fancy accommodations, like, oh, say, a toilet. Again, you'll have to wait eight days."

"I say we designate the end of the corridor as the pee corner. I can give up a lot of things for eight days but there's no way my bladder can make the same sacrifice."

Alex's statement was more of a declaration than a request for her opinion. Deeply disturbed by the prospect as Alex went about his business, Charlotte closed her eyes and visualized herself anywhere else. Her mind wasn't clear enough to visualize any particular location; rather she imagined a sandy beach feeding into a crystal blue ocean that morphed into a wooded forest with beautiful green pine trees. After a while of this, she succumbed to exhaustion and drifted off to sleep. Although she wasn't in the most comfortable of positions, sitting with her knees tucked in and her arms crossed over them as her head fell, her body eventually overcame her mind and forced her into a temporary shutdown.

This period of rest was short lived, however. She awoke 10 minutes later. *Oh, no. Now I have to go.*

She had no choice as she retreated via a crawl to the previously designated corner of the cofferdam. By now Alex was asleep or at least pretended to be to give her some privacy.

Relieving herself in a dark corner was a new low for Charlotte. She was feeling hungry, not to mention thirsty and she wondered if she would make it eight days.

*At least the cofferdam is climate controlled.* She tried weakly to cheer herself up. *I suppose this experience could be worse although I can't imagine how.*

# Chapter 46

The dimness still encapsulated Charlotte when she awoke several hours later, but the dull pounding in her head that had developed was muted. There was a coat that had been placed, compliments of Alex, under her head while she slept. Charlotte recognized the tremendous beauty in this small act of kindness and this simple thing was the ultimate icebreaker. Charlotte realized that hiding her vulnerability was going to be more trouble than it was worth and as much as her thirst for justice was at stake, the life of Alex's daughter was more importantly also at stake. She thought as she looked at him lying uncomfortably on the cement floor in his own attempt to sleep and restore some energy, *I need to be kinder. Things are already bad enough.*

It was now 3 a.m., but they had no way of knowing that. Charlotte's internal clock suggested to her it was sometime in the middle of the night but the walls of the cofferdam were so closed off she couldn't be at all sure.

After successfully falling back to sleep, she awoke again several hours later. This time Alex was awake and desperately wanting to get some things off his mind. He went right into it.

"I always swore things would be different for me," he said. "That the experiences I grew up with wouldn't be repeated when I was a parent. My children would be raised with a white picket fence wrapped around the most beautiful house in the neighborhood. They would not grow up like I did, poor with my father working to the bone at a low paying job just to make ends meet.

"It's been a rude awakening to see that my ideal life has not panned out the way I'd anticipated. I've achieved the American dream in the very literal sense and I've provided the beautiful home and the beautiful fence exactly like I dreamed, but I never realized it would come at such a cost. It has cost me my time and my mental energy and I screwed up my marriage and my family because of it. Looking back, I would do things very differently. With Brielle's abduction, it has become crystal clear to me what is most important. Life is about time. It's about relationships. A house doesn't always make a home. It requires work." He paused before continuing, "My wife blames me, you know? That's why she left."

"I'm so sorry," Charlotte responded, turning to face him more squarely. "I don't know what to say."

"Now I've got you speechless," Alex said, cracking a weak smile.

By now Charlotte's head was pounding hard from a lack of food and water and her mouth was feeling more and more like a mixture of cotton and straw as the seconds rolled by. It was hard to think.

The oral draught had taken up residence in her mouth overnight and had sucked her completely dry of all internal moisture. She knew the rule: *Three minutes, three days and three weeks. A human can't live without air after three minutes, without water after three days and without food after three weeks.* She was most concerned about the water.

"I saw a mouse crawl through here last night after you fell asleep," Alex reported, interrupting her feelings of self-pity. "I considered killing it and eating it. I went so far as to reach out my hand to grab it, but the mouse was having none of it. He took off before I could get a swipe in. That's how hungry I am."

"It's probably for the best that particular culinary delight didn't come to fruition," Charlotte responded. "The last thing you need right now is rabies."

"I have a surprise for you," he responded. "My Eagle Scout badge hasn't been completely for naught. I have managed one small triumph."

Alex extended his arm toward a top corner of the cofferdam and directed her attention to a metal plumbing pipe adjoined to a second perpendicular pipe with a metal elbow. Charlotte noticed the pipe had a slow leak. It produced a drop of water every 20 seconds, but even so, Charlotte wasn't willing to resort to standing underneath it with her tongue out for hours at this point.

Charlotte observed Alex had tied a thick piece of string to the elbow joint, where it was hanging. He obviously ripped it from his coat before he surrendered it for her to cushion her head with. Sure enough the slow drip from the pipe ran down the length of the string, and drop by drop, they were able to slowly quench their thirst with the water run-off that Alex was collecting in a cup crafted from a small piece of cardboard he found in his pocket. Charlotte marveled at his resourcefulness and didn't think twice about the patience required to wait for each precious drop to fall. They would collect it until they had a drinkable quantity. *We've got nothing but time.* The tiny drops were as precious as cocaine to an addict.

With a renewed sense of hope in their dreary environment they began to talk of more meaningful things. "I never told you why I'm here," Alex interjected.

"You're here because you want to find your daughter," she replied.

"No, I mean I never told you why I suddenly changed my mind and decided to come with you."

"I know. I wasn't going to ask questions. With your help I'd be able to track down Saul's killer and I didn't want to say anything that would make you change your mind again."

"For one thing I found the key in the shower head like I already told you and I knew I needed to take serious action. Secondly though, and perhaps more importantly, I had a dream after you left. I only got about two hours of sleep that night, but I had a dream. It was as clear as day and unbelievably real. I've never dreamt anything like it before."

"What was it about?"

"It gave me peace. I had been feeling nothing but hate, vengeance and bitterness towards God for letting this happen to my family. I fell asleep with a grimace and my teeth clenched, but that all changed when I had a visitor in the night. It was a young girl with long, curly hair almost like spun gold. She looked like an angel but approached me in the dream in a very human form." He paused for a moment before continuing. "And then she came to me, grabbed my hand and told me everything would be alright. For some reason I believed her and I knew everything would be alright. She told me to follow the red cross and I had absolutely no reason to doubt her. I trusted her implicitly."

Charlotte was caught speechless. She had never had any such experience, but knew she couldn't argue with it. Even though they were currently confined in a space no larger than the size of a large sedan, she gained confidence from his dream that they were on the right track.

"It must have been an angel. The way you described her. If there was ever a time to believe in God, now would be it," she reassured him.

Her response put them in a lighter spirit.

"Where are you from originally?" Alex ventured to ask her.

At this point Charlotte didn't skip a beat in answering his questions. They were going to be confined for a very long eight days and if either one of them had any hesitation about getting to know the other on a very personal level such notion was not to last long. Alex found it fitting to get the basics out of the way and had been wondering about her light accent since day one. He felt it safe to assume it was either German or Austrian but was more interested in the precise location.

"Freiburg im Breisgau," she responded.

"Where's that? I've never heard of it."

"Sure you have," she reassured him. "The Black Forest in Germany, cuckoo clocks, thick clumps of pine trees."

"The black forest? I guess I need to brush up on my world geography."

"Especially being a member of the United States Senate. Aren't you guys supposed to know about other parts of the world?"

Charlotte paused. *Ease up,* she thought to herself. *You've given him enough of a hard time as it is.*

"Don't beat yourself up," she continued. "Most Germans only think of the US in terms of three main sections: New York, Los Angeles and then everything in the middle. The Grand Canyon is thrown in their somewhere. I grew up around a lot of people who were fascinated by cowboys and the West and stereotyped everyone in the West as working on a ranch and living the cowboy lifestyle."

"That's a bit of a stretch."

"And so is the American idea that all Germans wear Lederhosen and chug beer."

"I can see you're very particular about heritage," he commented.

"You never forget where you came from."

"Do you go back often to visit?"

"Not as much as I'd like too. It's hard sometimes to go back. It was my home what feels like a lifetime ago, but I do miss my parents."

"They both still live there?"

"Of course. My dad thinks I'm crazy for leaving the motherland to come to the U.S. He always reminds me he never saw the point. His soul is planted there and my parents have very strong European sensibilities. My mother was born in France just near the border of Southern Germany in a town called Strasbourg. Strasbourg is where she was also raised but she met and fell in love with my dad when she was 16. He was 20 and born and raised in Freiburg. They married when she was 17 and he brought her over the border to live with him. They joke that their love transcended European borders when in reality they grew up 20 minutes apart. My parents have been fortunate in that regard, having found each other at a very young age and continuing to keep each other happy throughout their lives. You really don't see that much anymore."

"And what about you?" he probed deeper. "I've told you about my wife. Is there any romance in your life?"

"Now that is extremely personal."

"Hey, this cement box we're trapped in is quite personal and I dished on the sordid details of my personal business, so I really see no other option for you...Oh, and I won't stop bothering you about it until you tell me. That could make for an extremely long trip across the water."

Charlotte sat quietly for a minute as she considered her options. She had been in love once but quite literally never spoke of it. That man betrayed her trust resulting in the end of the relationship and the person she once thought was the love of her life was gone in an instant. She rarely thought of it anymore and never spoke of it. It was a memory she fought hard to forget.

Since then Charlotte lived a lonely life, filling the voids with her work or dulling her pain with meaningless relationships. She found occasional moments to spend time with a would-be suitor but she was a tough sell when it came to dating. She was very hard to impress and somehow no one could ever measure up to her former love. It made her sad to think she was vastly unimpressed with the spectrum of men who attempted to court her. She wished that she felt a connection, but she would never admit the life of a doting housewife was her deepest desire. Sadly domestic bliss didn't appear to be anywhere on the horizon and she lived a life unsettled in that regard. She bounded from one man to the next with superficial encounters, hoping to fill a void, and wanting to get the most out of life even though there was no one to share it with.

Charlotte glanced up at Alex as all of these thoughts raced through her mind. He was married but his marriage was in shambles and his wife had left him. He was heartbroken but acted like he wasn't. His wife said cruel things to him and he was trying to move on. She looked at him with an understated longing, secretly enjoying the time she was able to spend with him.

Alex interrupted her thoughts. "We could talk about your job instead," he said. "I read in the paper a while ago about the "DA Massacre," sounds like things aren't going so great under the current administration."

"Absolutely not. Work is the last thing I want to talk," Charlotte responded, still feeling anxious and upset about the current culture of the office.

"Alright, then tell me about your love life," Alex encouraged her. "You've got to give me something here."

"Fine," she conceded, scooting just an inch closer to him. "I'll tell you. Yes, I was in love once and I followed him to America, which is how I wound up at NYU for law school. We were both 18 and he wanted to come to the United States. He was so passionate about it and I loved him and wanted to support him. I would have followed him anywhere."

"Then what happened?"

"America is what happened. His passion turned to an obsession and he devoured everything about it—American food, American media and American women. And that's when I became not good enough. By that time I was already working on my law degree and none of it would transfer to Germany. I would essentially have to start all over again if I wanted to be a lawyer so I stayed and I've worked in New York City ever since. That's been it really. I try not to think about it."

"Wow, I'm sorry," he said.

"Well," she said, shrugging it off, "We can't all be lucky in love. What my parents have is priceless and something so rare that I've given up on finding it for myself."

"I'm convinced that good things come to good people," Alex said trying to lift her spirits.

"That's just a platitude people use to make themselves feel better."

And with that their conversation stopped. There, in the soiled and dark depths of the ship, Alex knew she was right and somehow neither one of them felt like talking anymore. They sat in silence in the cramped space, confined as they floated through the middle of the Atlantic Ocean. Alex's wife had left and it was just Charlotte there with him.

He scooted closer to her in the cramped space and she inched her way next to him. He hugged her in an act of comfort. Their skin was now touching and Charlotte felt a warmth run through her body. He leaned in to kiss her and she reciprocated. Hard. Just for the night this kiss made the dreariness of their circumstances melt away as they focused on each other, both wanting to forget the sadness they were feeling. Charlotte knew she was currently the other woman, but found as he kissed her she almost preferred that status. It meant she couldn't get hurt.

# Chapter 47

Paniletti made it a point to visit August Bäcker on a regular basis; if not monthly then at least several times per year. He was well on his way to high rank in the Brotherhood, having been groomed by August at a young age. August adored Paniletti's grandfather who had befriended him in Montana shortly after his arrival. He was often August's partner in crime through the years when the blows of the white power movement and the Ku Klux Klan hit the streets.

Paniletti's grandfather died in prison after spending 46 years there for the murder of a black family, leaving August heartbroken. Consequently, he adored Paniletti, who by the mere association with his grandfather gained the attention of the Grand Imperial Wizard and destined to one day take his spot.

To that end, August often welcomed him into his home and Paniletti was well familiar with it. Today, as he walked up the dirt path to the front entrance after traversing the seldom travelled road to his house in Hannah, Paniletti's mind filled with memories of his childhood and he reminisced about the time when his passion for advancement in the Aryan Brotherhood first took root. He was indoctrinated with the idea of white supremacy from an early age and the natural tendency of a child to grow up without prejudices was lost with him.

That wasn't to say that his environment didn't provide him with an excuse for his racism. Through no choice on the part of his father he was raised in St. Louis, Missouri. His father was an executive with Anheuser-Busch, relocated his family near the company's headquarters in the old part of the city on South Grand Avenue. As a result of his father's position, Paniletti's parents owned a mansion in the Compton Height's section of St. Louis. The homes were large and beautiful and built in the 1904 World's Fair era. Their home was within a mile of his father's place of employment.

Paniletti's educational experience was that of a minority. He was one of very few white students in a predominantly black school district throughout his elementary and secondary education years, and his lisp did him no favors. The mocking he endured from his fellow students was a curse that followed him until shortly before his high school graduation.

It was a few days after his trip to Sing Sing before he was able to leave New York and fly out to see August. On this day, just as he always did, August was sitting on his front porch with rifle in hand when Paniletti arrived. Paniletti made a habit to greet him from a distance, as August's eyesight was worsening with age and he didn't want to run the risk of being mistaken for an enemy. Although he strode up the path in his usual manner the reception with which he was greeted was unusual. There was a solemnity about August to which Paniletti was not accustomed, and a twinge of coldness about his demeanor as Paniletti approached.

"Grüß dich," he said to August, greeting him in his native German tongue.

"You're back," August responded in an unpleasant tone. "You're late."

"What do you mean, I'm late?"

"I sent the boy, Justin Vincent. He got me the information I needed first. You're late."

"Justin Vincent? An ex-con? You're dealing with a worthless ex-con?"

"He's closer to the source and quicker than you at this point."

"He just got out of prison. How's he going to afford to do what needs to be done?"

"I gave him money," August responded. "I help those I trust. He was here first and he's hungry. He'll do anything to patch into the Brotherhood and rise up the ranks. He's hungrier than you."

"I had a failure in my spy chain. There was nothing I could do."

"This was your responsibility. You can't blame someone else."

"I'm following the trail," Paniletti announced. "I will beat the Assistant DA and I will find what you need."

"Because it's you I will give you one more shot, Troy. Find it before Justin, otherwise you're out."

"Out?" Paniletti questioned him in disbelief.

"No organization can tolerate weak allies. We have to dispose of the rubbish. Your standing in the Brotherhood will be removed if you fail."

Paniletti stared in shock. *He'll strip me of my ranking if I fail. That can't happen.*

August interjected his train of thought by reminding him of what was at stake. "If my treasure is found it will be the end of us. Not just of me, but the entire organization. I will be incarcerated, my last days will be spent rotting away in a putrid prison cell and the money I have will be locked away. Neither you nor this organization can afford to lose the financial backing I provide. My greatest secret cannot be leaked to the outside. It must be recovered and brought back to me, and anyone who sees it must be killed. That is the directive I gave to Justin and if you want to man up and prove yourself greater than a young Aryan buck, it is the directive I will give to you. Your reward for success will be sweet, but the consequences of failure will be severe. Do not disappoint me."

By this time, the man Paniletti referred to only as the worthless ex-con, was halfway across the world. Justin's flight was right on time when it touched down at the Sde Hov Airport, also known as the Dov Haz Airport in Tel Aviv, Israel. He took pride in his ability to quickly find his intended destination and immediately acquired a hotel room in a convenient location also located near a fire escape. He had easily beaten Charlotte there by several days and used the time to his advantage by surveilling the area.

Watching from his hotel window, learned that the staff of the medical clinic across the street, which he read about through the code in Isaac's *Torah*, and which he was keeping an eye on, went from four employees to one nurse at 10:00 p.m. When Charlotte arrived, as he knew she most certainly would, he would simply wait until then when there would be fewer potential witnesses and would make his move.

Justin smiled at the $100,000 check the Grand Imperial Wizard had handed him. He promised him another $100,000 after the job was done.

The money Justin had been given was for travel and supplies and then some. "Weapons won't be a problem," August assured him. He had an excellent resource for weapons in Israel. Although August hadn't returned to Europe since he left in 1945, he was still a legacy overseas in the international white supremacy community and was able to make things, like the procurement of firearms and ammunition, happen with ease.

Armed with the support and resources of the Grand Imperial Wizard the day after their meeting, Justin was on an international flight. This was the chance he longed for and there was nothing he couldn't do now.

Spending his first few days in Jerusalem, waiting for Charlotte, he was in deep planning mode. He took great pride also knowing through the coded message in the *Torah* what her next move would be even before she did. Every detail was laid out in the book including a back-up plan for his back-up plan. Just as promised, with his connection to August Bäcker, he was able to obtain guns and ammunition in this foreign land as well as a couple of extras when it came to weaponry.

Currently, he felt confident all of his bases were covered. He well established the perfect vantage point from which to scout the DA when she arrived. At the right time when he spotted her, he would make the hit undetected with the aid of a silencer on his high-powered weapon. It was not a risk he was willing to take to act from any other location than what was dictated by his established plan. He even mapped out the perfect escape route for himself after getting the job done and would then move on to the next and equally important phase of his mission. He would make the pick-up that August urged him was of the utmost importance and thereafter take the next available flight back to the U.S. With his money tucked away and the backing of the Grand Imperial Wizard, he was invincible.

On the morning Charlotte arrived he would know his target immediately. August had given him a recent photograph of her which had been covertly taken by one of the Brotherhood members. As her assassin, Justin now had a clear image in his head as to what she looked like and when the moment arrived he would be ready.

# *Chapter 48*

The next several days passed like a sluggish snail for Charlotte and Alex. The two stowaways were getting progressively weaker and their circumstances were much more blatantly affecting Charlotte. The last 48 hours were riddled with stomach pains and her digestive system was undoubtedly on the fritz. Even if she had eaten food, it wouldn't have stuck with her long. Her colon was rebelling against her. The tension in the air in the cofferdam had dissipated, but was unabashedly replaced with a horrific stench. Although their tiny space didn't particularly smell of roses prior, Charlotte felt terrible about being the main source of the odor. As her heart sank, Alex was more concerned for her health than anything. She was not looking good.

*I wish I could go outside to get food, but I can't. I'll get arrested and we don't have time for that.*

Shortly after sunset on the sixth day, however, there was a knock on the cofferdam's paneled door and both Alex and Charlotte froze at the sound. Slowly, despite their decision to ignore the problem, the panel door began to crack slightly. The bright fluorescent light in the space overhead shined in through the uncomfortably expanding opening they were sure would spell their demise.

"Are you guys down there?" a male voice asked. "I talked to Mikey on the phone and he told me you might need some food. He said you have money."

Much to their dismay, they were definitely found out. Alex cursed Mikey for ratting them out before responding assertively, "Who are you?"

"Tom Jenkins, sir. I'm a member of the crew. I've got a need for some extra money and I hear you're some type of politician with cash. Mikey said he meant to get the message to me sooner but he used the money you gave him and went to gamble in Atlantic City. I guess he got distracted. Have you been here all week?"

"That's perfect," Alex muttered sarcastically under his breath. Then not wanting to miss out on this opportunity, he asked Jenkins, "You want money?"

"I'm certainly not coming down here for my health and apparently neither are you. What is that smell?"

Wanting to deflect from the obvious, Alex answered his question with a question of his own. "Why do you need money when you're probably getting paid around the clock to be working on this ship?" Alex felt the need to feel him out to determine his credibility even though he knew he would be giving Jenkins nearly any amount he asked for in order to ensure their survival.

Jenkins answered with an almost brutal amount of honesty. "You think we're rolling in it with this job? Absolutely not. This is nothing but hard work and a semi-decent wage. I got a wife back home who's about to divorce me and take me for all she can. She's the one stepping out while I'm away. I gotta get some cash she doesn't know about. After that I'm cutting off her ass."

"How much?"

"A thousand oughta do it for today. I brought you guys some MRE's and bottled water. I'd be happy to bring more tomorrow if you keep the cash coming. Oh, and as long as you pay, you won't need to worry; I'm the only one on the boat who knows you're here. You keep the money coming and it'll stay that way."

"Well played, sir. This is capitalism at its finest," Alex remarked as the day's allotment changed hands and the $1,000 was paid in cash.

Tom provided two military style ready to eat meals.

"I'll be back here tomorrow night. I'm on watch at this time and my commander won't see me. We got a deal?"

"We've got ourselves a deal," Alex assured him. He didn't think twice about the fact that this would be the singular most expensive meal he had ever eaten. He was able to stop rationalizing about leaving the cofferdam and risking their arrest.

"Oh, wait. Just a sec," the sailor went on. His "sec" turned into 10 minutes, at which point he reappeared and threw down some toilet paper and sanitizer.

"You all got it smelling like an outhouse down there." *Of course he had to state the obvious.* "I'm not even going to ask why you're doing this. It's crazy."

At the sight of food and fresh water, the depths of despair Charlotte had managed to convince herself she was living in suddenly seemed a little brighter. *Maybe I'm not doomed after all to a slow, uncomfortable death here.*

It may have been the delirium from their confined environment or the exhaustion she felt as a result of the experience but the prisoner's cipher was starting to be a thing she was grateful for. She was learning things about herself she never before knew and realized she would ultimately be stronger for the experience.

Tom kept to his word and dutifully brought them each day after another day's allotment of food. Alex in return dutifully paid him for his service. Even in her feeble state, Charlotte was gaining even more respect for him. He was thinking of more than himself.

"I am in love with these M & M's," she said, referring to the candy that came in their MRE's and were the only things she could keep down. She and Alex were in a different world now. It was a world of isolation and tight quarters and the chocolate was a precious gift.

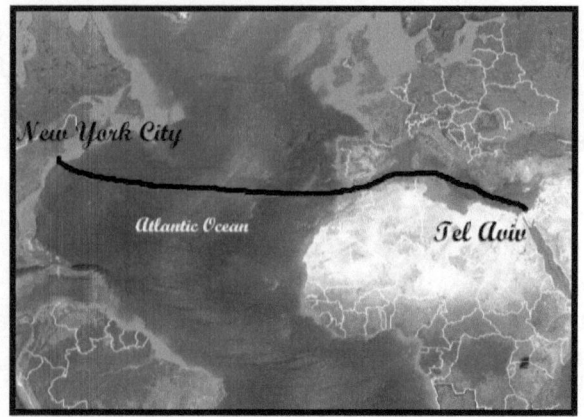

# Chapter 49

*September 24, 1988 – Tel Aviv, Israel*

By remaining captive in the cofferdam for a period of time she would never wish on anyone, Charlotte was starting to understand with greater clarity the concept of solitary confinement. The intensity of the situation just about overcame her will and her health and she gained a new appreciation for modern medicine. Alex's physical well-being was sustained by the help of their accomplice on the outside, Tom, who was being very handsomely compensated for the service he was providing.

Though her health continued to decline during their eight days of confinement, as the ship eventually docked, this meant the possibility for medical attention.

It was, as planned, after eight days and nights when they finally docked. Charlotte knew the second it happened because she was shaken by the abrupt stop, as it jolted them forward.

"I know it'll be rough, but we still have to wait three hours," Alex informed her. "The attendant warned me there would still be crew on the ship until then. We're so close now. We can't risk getting caught."

It was three hours exactly to the second by the count of Alex's watch, when they made their escape.

When Alex cracked open the cofferdam panel, they both experienced a swirl of emotions ranging from fatigue and fear to anxiousness and excitement. Fortunately, and just as they had been told, the ship was empty and as they stepped off they didn't see a soul. The coast being clear, they emerged; or that is to say Alex emerged and dragged Charlotte out with him. She was only able to assist in the slightest way in her own rescue. Her legs flailed and her arms were like Jell-O from fatigue.

"Lift your arms," he requested as he sat on the outside of the cofferdam looking in. Charlotte was able to accomplish this one small feat, which allowed Alex to reach down to grab her around the waist and hoist her out. It was painfully evident she could not walk, a detail neither of them was aware of given they had spent the last eight days in the cofferdam unable to stand. Due to the degradation of their circumstances, her time in the cofferdam had turned to a period of almost non-stop lying down. Charlotte found she preferred the fetal position.

As they made their attempt to secure their freedom from the confines of the cofferdam it wasn't just hoisting Charlotte out which proved to be problematic. Her inability to walk without great assistance required tremendous effort on Alex's part. They tried for a moment with Alex wrapping his arm underneath hers and supporting her body weight as they walked, but through no one's fault, this method proved ineffective, and recognizing the need to remove them from the area as quickly as possible, it was then that Alex carried her.

Although feeling as though his health was definitely compromised, Alex was larger and stronger in general and was in much better physical health compared to Charlotte at the moment. Although her figure was slender, Charlotte's work schedule, eating habits, and the fact she spent a large portion of her time behind an office desk, did nothing to promote a healthy lifestyle.

Charlotte had most certainly fallen victim to dehydration. Tom had informed them he would be able to provide them no more than what he was giving them, as he didn't want to raise any suspicion. Charlotte and Alex both agreed with this sentiment but with that being the case, even with Alex's drip system, the lack of adequate amounts of water over the entirety of their confinement proved to be an absence which Charlotte would need medical care to recover from. Tears may have been possible in the future but she couldn't even cry now if she wanted to. Her mouth was still in a state of dryness and her tongue again still felt swollen.

The sailor had warned that although the three hours they spent at the dock would clear out the ship, there would still be security at the gangway. To make matters worse they would need to jump and swim to shore. Alex guided Charlotte stealthily to the opposite end of the boat's key side. This was further from shore but would help them remain incognito. Alex found lifejackets and placed one on Charlotte as well as himself. He knew she would certainly need one, being in no condition to swim, and he was sure to need one since he would be essentially dragging her to shore.

"We're going in together," Alex told her. "You have to trust me."

"What do I do?  I can hardly move," she whispered faintly.

"Just hold your breath while you're underwater. I'll take care of everything."

Alex lifted Charlotte over the side of the boat and jumped off with her in tow. He clung to her during the treacherous seconds in which he kicked both their body weights to the surface after being submerged in water, and he placed Charlotte on her back when they emerged above water and he swam to shore.

Alex pulled her out of the water and began to carry her once they reached land. Successfully avoiding the security guards at the gangway and without even recognizing that he didn't know where he was going, Alex walked away from the ship. He plowed through the main road leading away from the harbor as quickly as he could, saying aloud, "A main road is our most likely path to a hospital." Fortunately traffic was light on this chilly Monday morning and he was able to carry Charlotte with very little attention.

Of those who were witnesses to this odd sight of strangers in their town, it didn't surprise him at all when no one stopped to inquire as to their welfare. He put himself in their position and contemplated what he would do if he were them. *Likely move on; I would move on out of an abundance of caution.* He concluded it wouldn't be his place to meddle or interfere.

With this analysis, combined with the knowledge he had regarding the inherent cautiousness and distance from strangers that the Israeli culture upheld, he felt no feelings of bitterness at their unhelpfulness. *I can do this. We've come so far already.*

Alex consoled himself in this situation with the knowledge that their journey was something Charlotte fully wanted to participate in and volunteered without even a moment's hesitation. Nonetheless, he couldn't help but feel he had dragged her into it. Because the livelihood of his daughter, Brielle, was the most propelling force in this matter Charlotte was compelled to be there to help him reunite with her.

Although uncertain regarding exactly where they were, as Alex plodded through the city, he observed several signs bearing the name, "Tel Aviv." They had crossed the North Atlantic Ocean and the Mediterranean Sea and travelled through the slim Strait of Gibraltar to find themselves on the coast of this country in the Middle East. A sign pointing in the direction of the airport prompted Alex to question why they couldn't have flown.

Tel Aviv was a large city on the coast of Israel which served as a major shipping town for importing and exporting in and out of the country. It was a city that due to its geography was integral in spurring the local economy and was, to Alex's surprise, very urban. As Alex walked towards town, carrying Charlotte in his arms, dawn had just broken. In the new light of day they traversed a side road of Jaffe, the port city upon whose outskirts the urban Tel Aviv was founded by the Jewish community.

Alex felt incredibly small as he held Charlotte and looked in the distance to see the giant skyscrapers towering up ahead in Tel Aviv's heart of downtown. *What in the world do we do now? We have been so focused on getting here that we didn't stop to consider our next step.*

Charlotte was too weak to offer assistance and her eyes stayed closed as she groaned weakly in his arms.

As Alex continued diligently walking along the sidewalk he noticed a flash of red ahead about 300 meters. As he came closer he saw it was a red cross. It was the symbol of a facility of the international Red Cross organization which was central in providing world-wide relief aid. In his position as a U.S. Senator he was familiar with the organization's immense contributions to society and he supported them wholeheartedly.

*Another red cross!* This was their answer and with his eyes glued on their destination, his pace quickened. Upon their arrival at the building, Alex pushed his way through the double doors of the entrance in a necessarily dramatic fashion. He approached the back entrance which was closest to the road.

The interior of the square building wherein he found them after plowing his way over the threshold was cold and metallic.

"Hello!" he yelled as he scanned the hallway he had just entered. The greeting was in English but he was confident anyone within earshot would understand it.

It took a few moments of walking down the hall and repeating a call for help before a dark-complected young nurse stepped out of a side room where she was visiting with her remaining colleagues who were there on duty that day.

"She's so pale," the nurse shrieked in Hebrew. She was petrified at the weak state of Charlotte's appearance and rushed to Alex's side to assist them.

The nurse led him into another side room and got the attention of her colleagues. Within seconds it became a group effort as they found a bed and hoisted Charlotte on top of it, gently laying her down.

None of the team rendering aid to Charlotte noticed, but as they carried her towards the room designated as hers, they passed a hallway mirror. Charlotte's eyes opened slightly and she caught a glimpse of her reflection. She instantly recognized her frail and weak appearance and noted she had lost a considerable amount of weight. Charlotte disapproved of how pronounced her cheekbones were and how gaunt her face looked when she saw herself.

The nurses were quick to lay Charlotte on the bed as comfortably as possible and quickly got to work. Perhaps the most invested in the affair was a surprisingly fair-skinned woman with golden blond hair peppered with gray strands. She was in her late fifties, but she cared for Charlotte like she was her mother. She introduced herself as Nurse LeMond and there was something very comforting about her that put Alex at ease. *Perhaps it's because of her motherly demeanor or maybe her quiet understated beauty that's not thoroughly captured by the soft strands of hair framing her face.*

Nurse LeMond immediately and gently inserted a needle into Charlotte's arm to begin an IV drip. The goal here was to provide her with a constant flow of the liquid and elements she needed to pull her body from out of the dangerous state of dehydration.

Alex remained dutifully by her side as the nurses worked their magic. They had kindly provided him with a dry set of clothes and he patiently sat in a chair in the corner of the room through much of the morning as they worked towards Charlotte's physical stabilization. They offered him a bed in another room to lie in and recuperate, but he declined in favor of staying with Charlotte. This corner chair wasn't the most comfortable, but he fell asleep regardless as he sat, waiting. *It sure beats the concrete floor we've been sleeping on for the last eight days.*

# Chapter 50

Alex woke up after several hours, and noticed Nurse LeMond still busy attending to her patient. Charlotte was now fast asleep and it was clear she was going to be out for a while. Nurse LeMond could see the stress on Alex's face.

"Ms. Weiss was grossly dehydrated and she's got dysentery," she informed him. "Don't worry yourself though. She's stable now and should recover quickly. The best thing for her is to sleep," she said to him kindly. Then in an effort to further distract him, she extended an invitation. "Come with me. I am going to the center of Jerusalem. It will take your mind off things."

Her shift was over and Alex stopped to consider her proposal. As he looked at Charlotte he realized he had never set foot in this country before, which as a United States Senator especially was something to consider. Also, he reasoned, it would be nice to get out and move around a little bit more.

"All people must see the Dome of the Rock," Nurse LeMond urged.

With that he was convinced. "Alright. Charlotte will probably still be asleep when we get back anyway."

Tel Aviv lay only 69 kilometers northwest of Jerusalem. Nurse LeMond drove and the trip took them about an hour, during which time Alex soaked in the countryside. When they arrived in the city, he saw a fully concentrated population of Israeli Jews. He recognized them immediately as they looked very similar to their counterparts in New York and Washington D.C. he was accustomed to seeing.

Jerusalem stood in stark contrast to Tel Aviv and might as well have been a world, rather than just an hour, away. One of the oldest cities in the world, it was located on a plateau in the Judean Mountains, which were nestled in between the Mediterranean Sea and the Dead Sea.

*It's much more modern than I thought. I expected a city frozen in time with nothing having changed since Biblical times.*

Nevertheless, despite the introduction of new buildings and new thought into the equation, the religious ambiance of this Holy City was not to be overshadowed.

"The city is considered holy to the three major Abrahamic religions: Christianity, Islam and Judaism and maintains that appearance," Nurse LeMond informed him. "Follow me. It's just over here behind the wall. The Well of Souls lies beneath the Dome of the Rock, which you must see."

Having been struck with a feeling of reverence at the holy place even before he got close to the Dome. Alex followed her dutifully to it. The Dome of the Rock sat atop the center of a platform referred to as the Temple Mount. The structure was octagonal and consisted of a wooden dome elevated on a drum with a circle of 16 piers and columns. Once having been covered in tiles during the reign of the Ottoman Empire's Suleiman the Magnificent, the exterior of the dome was now made of porcelain, which had the appearance of pure gold. Nurse LeMond explained this to Alex, which was the only way he could distinguish it wasn't actually gold he was seeing.

As a sign of respect, they removed their shoes upon entering the building and Alex gasped in amazement at the interior adorned with beautiful mosaics made of tiles configured into elaborate designs. They then walked through a wooden entryway leading to sixteen marble steps leading down. Along the way were several niches leading to the cave they were aiming towards, which was partially natural and partially man made. The stairway led through a cut passage, which Nurse LeMond explained was believed to date back to Crusader times.

"This is what they call the Well of Souls," she told him as they descended quietly. There were few visitors at this time and her voice echoed when she spoke.

"The floor of the dome consists of the Foundation Stone, which is unadulterated, exposed bedrock. The belief among Jews is that upon this rock lied the altar where Abraham came to sacrifice his son Isaac. It is considered the Holy of Holies in Jerusalem and Jews, Christians and Muslims come from all over the world to walk where Jesus walked and pray to God in the direction of this place.

"Non-Muslims, including Jews are not permitted to pray on the Temple Mount or even carry anything of or pertaining to a religious artifact or containing Hebrew letters. In fact, they are absolutely banned and are allowed to pray only at the nearby Wailing Wall."

Alex spent considerable time in the cavern soaking in his surroundings. He was struck by the simplicity of the Foundation Stone set against the elaborate decoration of the surrounding interior. *I see why this place is considered to be truly holy.*

Once they exited and retrieved their shoes, they arrived at the West Wall of Jerusalem; the Wailing Wall. Nurse LeMond reminded him, "This is the place where Jewish people come to pray. This is as close as they are permitted to get to the holy sanctuary."

Alex was struck by the imagery before him.

There sat rows of devout Jews praying at the wall in the direction of the Dome of the Rock. Some sat in quiet contemplation, resting in the peace of their holy place, while others fervently kneeled and prayed. Each of these individuals had taken time out of their day to come to the Wall, to take time to be holy and to take time to speak with God. Alex was impressed at their belief and dedication and reflected on his own church attendance. He was a *Christer Catholic* as he liked to refer to himself, meaning he was lucky to hit mass for Easter and Christmas in the same year. Gazing out over the worshipers in front of him, he unconsciously said aloud, "I really need to do better."

# Chapter 51

Dusk was setting and Justin had been ready with his gun pointed in the direction of the Red Cross entrance all day. He was stationed on the rooftop of his hotel lying low against the flat concrete that served as his perch, and peered over the edge like a ravenous hawk waiting to pounce on its next prey. He was relentless, but his diligence hadn't yet paid off. Night had now fallen and it was a quarter after eight. *Soon I will make my play.* Earlier, he saw the unidentified man who carried the DA inside, walk out of the building with one of the nurses. *Perfect*, he thought. *That puts him out of the way.* He had missed them earlier as they had entered through the back, but he knew of their arrival and the situation was better for Justin now with Alex gone.

Justin relished in his cleverness. His stake out point provided an optimum view with a clear shot and remained undetected. That is, undetected to most. Justin didn't know about Paniletti.

August had filled Paniletti in on the details of his whereabouts and let him loose in an effort to increase his chances of success in finding his treasure. This gave August a backup to his assassin. One of them was sure to kill Charlotte Weiss.

As Justin lay motionless on the concrete, eye to the scope of his gun, he felt a swift kick to his right side that almost knocked him off the building. Scrambling to his feet, Justin picked himself up and retrieved his bearings. His body burned with anger and as he looked up he was shocked at who he saw. There stood Paniletti, rigid and unmoving. He knew him well because he had been arrested by him several times in the past. He hated this guy.

Suddenly and very confused, Justin wondered if his parole officer sent for him. *But I'm out of the country and only one person knows where I am. How could they find me so quickly?*

As these thoughts circulated in his mind, there in front of him Paniletti stood with his gun aimed squarely at Justin's heart. Justin had incidentally lost hold of his gun with the painful kick but unwittingly ignored the barrel aimed directly for him. He dodged for his gun, which lay six feet to his right, but as Justin clumsily grabbed for his weapon, Paniletti saw a look of arrogance on his face he knew was backed only by weakness.

"You have no idea what it takes to be in the Brotherhood," Paniletti informed him with a look of smugness on his face.

Ignoring him, Justin dared to grab the gun and turn it on his opponent, but Paniletti swiftly kicked it out of his hands. The gun slid to the edge of the roof as Paniletti laughed maniacally.

Not to be so quickly undone, Justin reached for his gun a second time but was too slow on the uptake. At the instant Justin turned his back to him, dangerously close to the edge, Paniletti gave him a solid push with his foot.

*A shot in the back would be too quick and painless for this wannabe. I'd rather Justin see himself falling to his death.*

Although the building was only three stories tall Paniletti knew Justin couldn't survive the fall. Justin's body hurled over the edge of the building and fell quickly.

Paniletti scurried down the fire escape to the ground and grabbed the weapon that fell near Justin's head. It was a fine piece and was bought with money from the Brotherhood. This drain on society lying before him was not worthy of the Brand and he would be taking his gun. He took no further thought of Justin as seconds later he heard police sirens approaching in the distance. It was time for him to disappear. He had other things to take care of.

# Chapter 52

Shortly after Alex left for Jerusalem with Nurse LeMond, Charlotte awoke to a distinct nagging from the muscles in her legs that were aching to move. They were stuck in place and almost frozen from the cramped environment she had stayed in for over a week. She had been carried into the building and laid on the bed and her limbs consequently received no exercise even in entering the clinic. *It's time to walk around; at least for a few minutes.*

Charlotte drifted in and out of consciousness during the duration of her stay there at the clinic and was happy to be cognizant enough to determine they had not only made it to Israel but also that they were in a Red Cross. Immediately her interest was spurned by the name of their location, but she hadn't had the strength to do any investigating until now. The mere fact they stumbled upon the city's Red Cross, if not directly placed in a position in which they would be drawn there, was something she was sure was not a coincidence. It was time to look around for their next clue.

Given her physical ability, she would be required to start locally within the confines of the clinic. Having built up sufficient strength to walk a short distance on her own with the help of her IV pole, she wandered the sterile halls looking for anything eye-catching or out of the ordinary. Just as Alex had been doing all along, she also felt it couldn't hurt to be on the lookout for small locks that may fit the mysterious key he received.

It didn't take long, as she dragged the IV pole beside her through the clinic halls, to become tired again, but she decided to round one final corner before heading back to her room. As she made the turn, her persistence paid off. Directly in front of her at the end of the hallway was a glass display cabinet hanging on the wall. Charlotte noticed immediately the cabinet had a small lock to secure the belongings inside and she made, an albeit slow, beeline for the case. *I wish I had Alex's key. It might open the lock.* Fortunately, as she drew closer, she was satisfied to see she had a visual of everything in it.

Her eyes panned the contents of the case and were eventually drawn to its far side where an old tattered document hung against the backdrop of the bottom shelf. There her eyes rested upon the familiar symbol of a red cross. It had been quickly marked by use of a red pen and plastered across the bottom of the document. It appeared just as it did on the letter she received from Isaac and the note Alex received from the kidnappers, and it stared her in the face like a blinding light as she stood in front of it, stunned.

She looked closer to read the now faded script on the page. The document was crudely crafted and the text was quickly written. The penmanship demonstrated that the scribe was marking hurriedly and didn't take long to contemplate what was being documented. The document was written in German and through the faded lettering, she was able to make out its content.

It was a medical form dated March of 1943 and included typed information pertaining to a patient by the name of Tobias Hess. A list of ailments was written on the form and in bold letters beneath it was written the word "Behinderte," which translated into English meant "disabled" and signified the mental incapacity of the individual. Written squarely beneath that was one simple word, "Auschwitz" and the very bottom of the page was signed Dr. Bernhard Stanz. Charlotte recognized this document immediately as being a death warrant.

As she stood engrossed in what lay before her, Charlotte captured the attention of Svenda, the only remaining nurse on duty who was searching for her after not finding her in bed.

"Interesting, isn't it?" she asked Charlotte.

"Yes, it is," she replied.

Then, without any further prompting, Svenda went on to explain the contents.

"During World War II," she began, "Hospitals and clinics all over Europe, buildings just like this one we're standing in, were turned into centers for mass murders as a continuing means for the genocide resulting from the Holocaust. Such places were favored by the Nazis, and in particular, one Dr. Josef Mengele who performed many sadistic medical experiments on Nazi victims. Josef Mengele was the architect for horrific acts of torture and murder, and he had several doctors beneath him who pledged allegiance to the Nazi party and did as he directed.

"As the Nazi Chief in Command with regard to medical matters, the war crimes of Dr. Mengele were horrific. He often chose women, twins, small children and babies as victims for his senseless experiments. Often times, he would inject his victims with various poisons which produced any manner of effect from handicapping or killing vital organs to stunting their growth. He was also known to amputate any range of various body parts and sew them to another part of the amputee's body and injecting cyanide into his victims' hearts."

"For what purpose?" Charlotte asked in outrage.

"For his sadistic whims sponsored by the Nazi party, which they falsely claimed were done in the name of science. It's a tragedy we display here so the memories of these acts aren't lost with the generations. These are actions which must never be forgotten and must never be repeated. Nurse LeMond set this glass case up here many years ago and I'm glad she did. We've kept its contents displayed ever since."

"Have any of Mengele's medical records been uncovered or any more from his subordinate doctors? Surely this death warrant for Tobias Hess can't be the only paper trail of these atrocities."

"None that I have access to," Svenda told her. "Just like the Nazis orchestrated death marches and the rapid burning of as many bodies as they could in order to avoid detection, under the direction of Hitler, Dr. Mengele made certain his records were destroyed as were all records of those working for him. They were likely burned along with other human remains, but their precise method of destruction is purely speculation. All we know is that they have never been found and the very few surviving records stand as the only testaments to these medical atrocities.

"This certificate is a notice ordering the direct extermination of Tobias Hess. Mr. Hess was a paranoid schizophrenic who was deemed by Dr. Bernhard Stanz, unfit for life. Doctors such as Stanz were recruited by the Nazi party to conduct paper analyses of those who were deemed to be sub-human by virtue of their mental state. Approximately 70,000 mentally ill or other 'problem' patients were deemed unworthy of life and were given the red cross designation you see at the bottom of the page. Once deemed unfit to continue living, each of the mentally ill was then killed by poisoning, injection or the gas chamber. That one red cross was their senseless ticket to the death house. This document, along with a few other of Dr. Stanz's medical papers, somehow survived destruction.

"These 70,000 individuals were never personally seen or observed by Dr. Stanz. He made a quick decision that based on no reason other than they were placed in a mental hospital, they needed to die. He deemed Tobias Hess and thousands of others like him to be second-class citizens and useless to the world and his decision was the official Nazi determination supported by Nazi ideology."

"Whether it's in this life or the one to come, one day there will be justice," Charlotte said aloud. She had no other words.

Charlotte was previously unfamiliar with the details Svenda described. Although raised in Germany, she learned the country's history but stuck to the basics. Although she had patches of knowledge about the Holocaust, the whole truth had always been too much for her to tolerate. She was well aware that although not a member of the Operation Paperclip crowd, Josef Mengele fled Germany towards the end of World War II and avoided capture then and up until his dying day.

This wasn't to say the world hadn't been hunting him the whole time. The Washington Times, the Simon

Wiesenthal Center and the governments of Israel and West Germany went so far as to offer rewards for his capture. In dramatic efforts to hide his identity in defiance of his would-be captors, Mengele had obtained a false passport deceptively using the name Helmut Gregor. Then beginning in 1971, he used the identity card of a friend, Wolfgang Gerhard, under which name he was buried at his death. He lived all over South America as the years passed and took up residence in various places such as Paraguay and Brazil. Fortune weighed in his favor as he found success in always avoiding capture, which led his victims to wonder where earthly justice was and forced them to foster a hope for it in the hereafter.

"You certainly are educated on the subject," Charlotte praised Svenda for the information.

"I haven't always lived in Israel. I emigrated here from Germany, and I was raised there, just like I can tell from your accent you were as well."

"That's right, I was," Charlotte answered.

"As you know, for many Germans, the Holocaust is a black spot on their history and many are loathe to divulge the truth if they are even distantly descended from anyone involved in the state sponsored genocide. It's best not to ask.

"As for me, I'm not shy about declaring my heritage and I think the conversation needs to be expanded. I am one of Hitler's children in a sense. My grandfather was among the shining members of the SS and the Nazi party. Despite that, I'm not defined by my ancestry. The blood running through my body is not an inherent product of my grandfather's actions. I am my own person and I have the opportunity to gain some level of redemption for my family by making sure this part of our stained history is never swept under the rug."

"Those who don't know history are bound to repeat it," Charlotte shared.

"That's right. I know it and I will share it. This Red Cross clinic, as long as I have a say, will stand as a place of refuge where all can come for healing regardless of race, gender, ethnicity, sexual orientation or any other portion of their being. I will be here to help the wounded and aid the weary as long as I am able and I hope I am a symbol of change. It is my responsibility as a citizen in the world to do my part to ensure that memories of genocide, such as the Holocaust, are never lost. I fully support this display in our clinic and I will never stand blamed for not speaking up."

Charlotte became lost in Svenda's words. As she stared again at the tattered medical document that captured her interest, the very literal red cross on the paper bled into the words "Auschwitz-Birkenau." It was blatant the direction she and Alex needed to go. According to the document, the mandate of Dr. Stanz was that Tobias Hess be shipped to Auschwitz. It was at this concentration camp he had died in a gas chamber 45 years prior and it was there she and Alex would go to continue the journey to finding his daughter.

*This historic document is what we were sent to Israel to find. The link between the Nazi atrocities of World War II and the present agenda of the Aryan Brotherhood is unmistakable.*

Although their next destination was clear, Charlotte was unsure she would make it. She still felt incredibly faint as Svenda helped her back to her room.

"Your friend went to explore Jerusalem with Nurse LeMond. He wanted me to let you know that when you woke up," Svenda assured her. "And I know Nurse LeMond wanted to show him the display we just saw. It's almost more important to her than it is to me."

As Charlotte returned to her room, her eyes felt heavy from the sedation in her IV. She would need as much rest as possible if her body was going to be allowed to heal itself properly. Quickly Charlotte scribbled a note to Alex and asked Svenda to place it on his bed. In loopy penmanship she wrote:

Our next stop is Auschwitz. The display
case at the end of the South Hall is what
we were sent here to find. Take the next
train. If I am unable to leave with you
I will follow you there when I have
strength. You need to go immediately.

# Chapter 53

No one could have easily spotted Paniletti as he slithered under the color of darkness and quietly entered the Red Cross. He chose wisely with respect to his attire by wearing all black to blend into the night. It had served him well in sneaking up on Justin and he avoided streetlights as he sprinted across the street towards the clinic. He checked before crossing that there were no witnesses outside and planned to appropriately take care of any potential witnesses he met inside.

Silently he entered the welcoming doorway of the Red Cross and stuck like a leech to the walls of the entrance hallway in an effort to avoid detection. He scoured his surroundings, which now hours after nightfall, were desolate and empty, and cautiously made his way down to the end of the hall directly across from Charlotte's room. Peering in, he could see she was still asleep just as he hoped.

Having toured the building earlier in the afternoon he was aware of the layout. He entered earlier as if he was a lost traveler. He wore a wig and glasses as he was determined not to be found out. He knew Charlotte would recognize him without a disguise, but fortunately she had been asleep. In addition to staking out the location of Charlotte's room he knew the main office was further down the hall. If the night staff was lucky, he determined, he would have sufficient time to collect his prize unseen, and there would be no casualties. That ideal turned out not to be the case, however.

Paniletti heard Svenda humming quietly to herself as she entered Charlotte's room. He was careful to duck behind a doorway. He watched her in a mirror hanging on the ceiling across from him as she made her way to Charlotte's bed. Her care of Charlotte bothered him and the longer she stayed there writing in her chart and checking on her vitals the angrier he became. He was not going to let her ruin his plans.

Charlotte was again asleep after her stroll through the clinic, and while Svenda would not be able to hear him from the other end of the hall once she returned to the clinic office, Paniletti wasn't taking any more chances. As Svenda left Charlotte's room, Paniletti quietly followed her until she sat down behind a wooden desk in the office, remaining completely good-natured and unsuspecting. None of her innocence mattered when without hesitation Paniletti put a bullet through her heart quietly with the help of a silencer. It killed her instantly. *She'll no longer be an interruption.* Paniletti unceremoniously closed the office and quickly made his way to Charlotte's room.

# Chapter 54

Charlotte remembered her eyes popping wide open and waking up being unable to breathe. There was a cloth pressing against her face, completely covering her mouth and nose and was preventing her from breathing. She remembers struggling but couldn't see her attacker. Kicking and screaming, she made every possible effort to escape the tight grasp on her. Although already weak with strength in defending herself, she fought with every ounce of what she had.

Her unknown kidnapper made only one blurted statement, "Dammit, you scratched me." That was all she heard from him. His voice was familiar to her but she couldn't place it and he came at her from the top of her head so she couldn't see him. Whoever it was had doused the cloth in chloroform and it was suffocating her. She smelled it strongly and her resistance didn't last long.

She finally passed out and was limp and unaware of what was happening. She didn't feel her attacker throwing her over his shoulder and carrying her abrasively out a back door. She didn't feel the pull on her skin as he ripped the IV out of her arm or the pain caused by a rip in her vein which would later turn into a subdural pool of blood and a large bruise.

No, she was completely unaware. She was completely unaware of being thrown into the trunk of a car and dragged to an abandoned warehouse. She was completely unaware of being locked in a small closet with the soaked cloth having been replaced by a gag in her mouth and her arms bound behind her back. She was completely unaware and was completely unconscious as her attacker threw her into the closet and searched her entire body for the key she was supposed to have in her possession. Her unconsciousness during the full body search that took place next was a blessing as she would have had a hard time recovering if she knew her attacker had his hands all over her body. The rest she could have gotten over, but the idea of that would be sickening to her.

Charlotte didn't have the key! *It has to be somewhere. If it's not with her then it must be with the Senator*, Paniletti thought. He would have to go back to the Red Cross and hunt him down.

"I'll be back for you," he warned Charlotte's unconscious limp body. "I want to see the fear in your eyes the moment before you die."

# Chapter 55

Alex surprised himself that he was hesitant to leave the holy place where the Dome of the Rock lay, but the sun had already set when they emerged from the cavern and he knew they needed to get back.

"I need to check on Charlotte," he mentioned to Nurse LeMond, vocalizing the thought that had been ever present in his mind during their trip.

As Nurse LeMond drove back to the Red Cross in Tel Aviv, they chatted much more than they had on the trip there. Something about the reverence of the Dome of the Rock they experienced together established a bond between them. She was easy to talk to. Her demeanor served as an invitation to open up and beckoned him to tell her things he would otherwise not share with a stranger.

Nurse LeMond predominantly led the conversation and did so as if she were thankful to have someone to talk to and had been missing out on this type of company for years. She was extremely curious about Alex and his life and she listened to him with the same intensity with which she spoke. She spoke with a conviction Alex would not have expected and it was clear, more by the words she spoke than by the way she looked, that life had taken its toll on her.

They talked mainly about his life; at least as much as he could divulge about being a U.S. Senator. She seemed very interested in him in a motherly sort of way and was curious about his life. When she did talk about herself she spoke little about where she came from and more about the knowledge she had acquired. Other than relating her move to Tel Aviv 35 years prior, marrying, raising a family and pursuing her dream as a nurse, she didn't spend much time talking about her life. The fact that she was originally from Germany didn't come as a surprise to Alex as he thought he detected a German accent very similar to Charlotte's. Throughout the conversation she spoke with force and with each new topic it was as if she was sharing a small packet of her soul.

Because of the warm and open conversation, their return trip was extremely pleasant. The time passed quickly and Alex was pleased he made the choice to go with her. The conversation ended almost too soon and the culminating and final fact she told him with a flurry of emotion as they pulled up to the entrance of the Red Cross took him by surprise.

"The Nazis made lamp shades from human skin," she stated suddenly and matter of factly. "Their sadism was so prevalent they couldn't stop with mere killing. They had to flaunt their conquests. That is the truth," she said. "I have seen one such lamp with my own eyes."

With that bold statement she parked the car, and as if knowing his curiosity was peaked, she led him back inside the Red Cross building.

"I'll walk in with you," she said as they arrived back at the Red Cross. "I want to check on Ms. Weiss as well before I go home, but I also have one more thing to show you."

Alex held the door for her as they walked into the building. His sense of chivalry was kicking in for this fragile, hard working woman. They were unable to reach their intended destination however, as the peace from their visit to Jerusalem was instantly shattered with the horror they saw when entering the building and seeing Charlotte's room.

Alex was in shock and couldn't properly process the scene lying before him. Initially he wanted to believe Charlotte was somewhere in the building, possibly sauntering around, but the sight of the IV swaying in the breeze told him blatantly otherwise.

Nurse LeMond rushed through the clinic equally in a panic and having been gone for just a moment to the back office, came out panicking.

"You have to go to Auschwitz, Poland now!" she cried. "You have to find your daughter."

"Wait a minute. What? What are you talking about?" he asked her thoroughly confused.

*How did she know about Brielle? Who tipped her off? What had she just seen?*

Alex traced her steps back to the location where this sudden command was coming from. It was the back office and after running to it he knocked loudly on the door. There was no answer. It was only a matter of seconds before he banged the door so hard that it was forced to swing open and there he saw Svenda slumped over the desk. The pools of blood on the floor were beginning to dry.

Alex rushed back to Nurse LeMond. "Call the police!" he shouted.

She looked him in the eye and reasoned with him. "I already have. Now you have got to get out of here. I will tell Charlotte if she returns that you have gone to Auschwitz. That is your next destination and you must take a train. There is no time to explain. Your life is in danger!"

Alex heard the words she was saying, but he was having trouble processing everything.

*Charlotte is missing and Nurse LeMond is demanding I leave the country and travel to Poland?*

Any hope his daughter was there in Israel was dashed and he was suddenly presented with a distinct moral dilemma.

His thoughts raced. *Should I leave now to save Brielle's life or should I stay and search for Charlotte? She may be in grave danger. The police would likely have leads and I may be able to help in some way. On the other hand, Brielle's life is also in danger and now possibly mine as well.*

Nurse LeMond, who just a few minutes ago had been completely serene, continued to scream at him to leave. It was mystifying. In the heat of the moment his thoughts honed in on his family and on his daughter and rationality kicked in.

*I have no leads on where to find Charlotte and by tracking down Brielle I'll track down the monsters that abducted her and in turn track down Charlotte. I must*

*continue to follow the clues. I'll come back for Charlotte;
Brielle and I. I won't leave her stranded in Israel.*

Upon making his decision, Alex wasted no time and
rushed to his room to gather his jacket, the one possession
he had with him. Next to it on the bed laid the note from
Charlotte. He read it, but the message was already received.
There was no time to look for the display case.

To add to Nurse LeMond's mysterious behavior she
rushed into the room and forced a flashlight upon him.

"It's waterproof. Don't lose it," she demanded.

Alex looked at it quizzically before shoving it into his
jacket pocket. It was an unusual looking flashlight. *Maybe
because it's LED*, he thought. *Or maybe because it's a
waterproof model.*

There was no doubt Nurse LeMond's behavior was
extremely odd, but he had no choice but to trust her. She
gave him very specific instructions regarding what he
needed to know and they were exactly what Charlotte was
directing in her note. He couldn't help but think however
about how Charlotte's note must have been written before
she was abducted and shed a tear at the thought.

Without another moment's hesitation he stuffed
Charlotte's note into his pocket and exited the building to
run as quickly as possible to the train station. No sooner
had he run through the threshold to the outside, however,
than a bullet flew by atop his head.

Paniletti had made it back and was coming after him!
He retreated inside, locking the front door securely behind
him, and took cover. Thinking quickly, he ran to the nurse's
office and pulled Svenda's keys out of the pocket he noticed
she stored them in. He considered the safety of Nurse
LeMond but heard police sirens quickly approaching. They
would be there in seconds and she would be safe. He was
grateful there was no one else in the building. There was a
dearth of patients in the facility.

Ducking and running this time out the back to the
clinic's parking lot where Nurse LeMond parked, he tried
the keys on the only other car in the lot. It was, in fact,

Svenda's, and he jumped in and drove furiously away, tires screeching.

# Chapter 56

Charlotte's eyes fluttered open. Pain was her sole companion. *I feel like I've been run over by a semi-truck.* Her body was cramped and she was tormented with a splitting headache and no memory of what happened to her. The pounding in her head was doing little to distract from the pain and heaviness in the rest of her body. She moaned in agony and discovered the gag in her mouth. Her shoulders particularly ached as it dawned on her that her arms had been tied behind her back.

One memory did quickly come back to her amidst the pain and heaviness coursing through her body—she had something urgent to take care of. *Whoever did this went to great lengths to stop me, but I'm not letting that happen.*

Her tough-as-nails determination was strengthened by thoughts of Alex and the search they were on. Willing herself to get out of this bind, she kicked her feet and breathed a sigh of relief upon finding her legs were not bound. There was very little room to maneuver in and she found the space she currently consumed was much smaller than even the cofferdam. A tiny shred of light seeping in under the door made her intensely aware she had been stuffed in a closet. Her fear of small spaces kicked in again but she willed herself to ignore it. She didn't think it possible her body could fit into a space any smaller than where she had recently spent eight days but was being proven wrong. On the bright side, at least here she could stand, and it was her goal to do just that.

She found out exactly what she was made of when she struggled to an upright position. Forcing herself to stand, she rubbed her back and shoulders around the walls of the closet to find out what she was dealing with in this small space. Soon she felt the metal of a pipe clasp rub against her skin. She painfully backed up to it and positioned her wrists against it. She was bound with rope but fortunately, although it was looped around her wrists several times, the individual width of its strands weren't terribly strong. Because it would set her free she didn't mind the pressure digging the rope further into her skin as she rubbed against the pipe. *This may be my salvation.*

Using the friction between the pipe clasp and the rope to tear each strand away until she freed herself, she quickly removed the gag from her mouth and attempted to open the door.

*Of course it's locked.* She listened to see if anyone was around. Her initial instinct was to scream and bang on it, hoping to attract any human attention, but it wasn't until she heard only the echoes of her scream that she gave up and opted for an alternate plan. Looking upward, she noticed the ceiling of this small space was made of panels and instantly formulated the thought that if she could jump high enough and knock one of the panels out of the way she could escape.

Charlotte jumped straight up in the almost darkness with her arms outstretched. Her fingertips brushed the overhead panel. She was unsuccessful in her first attempt and imagined that if she weren't in so much pain she might have been able to make the distance. Her situation being as it was, she couldn't get the vertical height she needed.

*This is going to take some ingenuity.* She checked the height of a pipe running horizontally along the back wall of the closet. It was about a foot from the floor and would give her the extra height she needed. As she stepped lightly on it at first, she realized it could hold her weight at least temporarily. She balanced herself on the pipe with assistance from the adjacent wall and then used the extra foot of height to lift her other foot atop the door handle. She then balanced herself between the door and the opposite wall. *This would be an extremely inconvenient time for the door to actually swing open*, she thought, but knowing that wasn't going to happen she proceeded with the gymnastics.

By straddling the closet, she was able to reach the ceiling panel, lift it up and barely, using the intense adrenaline pulsing through her body, pull herself over the edge up into the ceiling. This was indeed a beautiful feeling.

Fortunately, the ceiling frame fully supported her weight and allowed her to crawl in the direction of an overhead vent, through which seeped in four dim blades of light from the night sky's moon outside. The vent was easy enough to push out and she made it into the open air. A quick survey from the roof of the large building revealed it to be a warehouse. A fire escape on the opposite corner of the building led to the ground and immediately drew her attention. She achingly made her way down the side of the building and with the help of the not far off city lights, hobbled painfully in the direction of civilization.

*I have to get to the train station immediately. I hope Alex got my note. The Red Cross isn't safe anymore.*

Embarrassingly exposed to the world aside from her underwear and now tattered hospital gown, she cleverly latched on to a small group of people who seemed to be heading in the direction of downtown. Although she was following the group, she hung back a ways.

The group's extravagant attire screamed a night of clubbing for them and the extremely high heels of the four women in the group slowed their pace sufficiently to make it possible for Charlotte to keep up until they arrived indeed in the center of town. The train station wasn't far from where she ended up when her guides ducked into a local downtown club. Within minutes from that point, despite her lack of speed, she arrived at the train station.

Penniless and without proper clothing, Charlotte climbed onto the first departing train she saw and caught it mere minutes before it inched away from the station. It was of no consequence to her where she was headed as long as she was headed somewhere else. Delirium was starting to set in due to her physical fragility and finding the first available cabin in the first available car, she let go of her body as it fell atop the bench seat. Sleep was now beyond her control.

# Chapter 57

*September 25, 1988*

"Fahrkarte, bitte!" the train attendant demanded. "Fahrkarte!" he repeated.

He poked his head into Charlotte's train cabin like a turtle trying to escape its shell as he loudly requested her train ticket.

"Fahrkarte, bitte! Fahrkarte!" he repeated himself. With each request, his frustration grew and Charlotte remained unresponsive. It was causing quite a scene as passengers began to peek out into the corridor to see what all the ruckus was about.

"Is she dead?" a colleague approached and asked with serious concern.

"She may just be pretending to avoid having to pay," the attendant responded. "That happened to me once before. That guy was a scoundrel."

"She doesn't look so good. Miss?" the colleague addressed her. "Can you hear me?" His voice carried throughout the car and attracted more than just the clueless bystanders.

This was the last train of the night and it was the train Alex had boarded as well. Alex couldn't help, just as all the other passengers couldn't help but hear the commotion, and he became one of the throng of rubberneckers. He made his way closer through the narrow train car and his jaw dropped when he saw Charlotte. He barged past the attendants to kneel by her side.

"Charlotte? Can you hear me? Charlotte?" he called, panicked. Charlotte's eyes fluttered open momentarily at the sound of his voice and he breathed a sigh of relief. He quickly addressed the train attendant and took care of her fare by purchasing a ticket. The attendant let out a breath of disgust and closed the cabin door before moving on. Slowly, the crowd began to dissipate.

"What happened to you?" Alex asked of an incoherent Charlotte. "I was so worried."

He pulled a pillow and blanket from an overhead bin and made her as comfortable as possible for the duration of the ride as she laid still on one of the two rows of seats in the cabin.

"I'm not letting you out of my sight again," he whispered to her.

Alex remained astonished for quite some time at the miracle that had taken place in bringing the two of them together again. Before the train departed he had waited at the station for close to three hours hoping she would show up, but was forced to board when the last train of the night was leaving. He knew that indirectly this train would get him to Poland and eventually to a train which included *Oświęcim* on its route. Having initially struggled to make sense of the word *Oświęcim* engraven on the key bound tightly on a chain around his neck, he had learned it was the Polish name for Auschwitz. The pieces of the puzzle were starting to come together.

Their trip would take them through Bulgaria, northeast through Serbia, Hungary and Slovakia and finally into Poland.

*A plane ride would again have been much faster*, Alex reasoned, but Nurse LeMond was unequivocal in her instructions to him about taking a train.

# Chapter 58

It was almost a full two days after leaving Tel Aviv when they arrived at their destination at which time they observed the train station at Oświęcim was small but functional. Alex had carried Charlotte each time they boarded a new connecting train. She had been awake and alert for the last hour before their arrival.

"I'm so happy to see you," were the first words out of her mouth,

"Are you feeling any better?" Alex asked her.

"A little bit. I slept long enough."

As they disembarked from the train at Auschwitz station, Charlotte immediately began looking for any type of concessions stand.

"Don't they have any food here? I'm famished."

When she became critical of the lack of restaurant or snack bar in the station Alex knew she was well on her way to a sense of normalcy.

Despite her moderately improved health at this time Charlotte could hardly keep up as Alex immediately sprinted off the train to find the keyhole he was searching for. Alex was consequently a good 10 steps ahead of her, but quickly turned around after recognizing he was leaving her behind.

"I'm coming," she chided him. "I know you just can't wait."

As they made their way through the main thoroughfare of the train station, Alex's eyes were wide open, scanning the small area and looking in all directions for a potential place to use his key. *It has to be here. Nurse LeMond was adamant we arrive at this train station.* On each train they boarded on their way, he had surveilled all areas the common passenger was privy to, as well as some he wasn't privy to. Hopping off at each connection and looking around, he also paused to search in the train stations just to be sure. Some of the stations had lockers that required small keys like the one hanging from his neck and some did not. En route he was unsuccessful in finding a compatible hole for his key.

The train station at Auschwitz was their final hope. Hope had sprung when he discovered that "*Oświęcim*" was the Polish name for Auschwitz and he was even more thrilled to learn when they arrived that "*stacja*" and "*kolejowa,*" the other words engraven on the key translated to "train station."

"This key belongs here," he told Charlotte excitedly and didn't hesitate any longer to run when he saw the bank of lockers against a back wall of the train station. This time he gave no regard to Charlotte and made a beeline for it. Charlotte happily, but slowly followed behind.

*This has to be it,* he reasoned. Now it was just a matter of trial and error to find the locker the key was made for.

"It's just as well I start at the top," he told Charlotte as she approached behind him scanning the bank of lockers, each with a separate lock. He was already busy at work, having wasted no time in inserting the key into the various locks. A few of the lockers were unoccupied so he could eliminate those from the trial and error process, and he was able to work quickly. As he approached the end his hope slowly diminishing, it was the bottom row, second locker from the end where he finally found his success. The key slid into the lock of this precious locker with ease and clicked loudly when he turned it. *What a sound!*

Expectantly, he flung the door open.

# Chapter 59

The throes of Alex's excitement were met with somewhat of an anticlimactic result. As he bent down and peered into the 80 square inch locker, he was met with a folded piece of paper and a ratty old box.

He pulled out the paper first to view it under the fluorescent lighting of the train station. It appeared to have been folded with perfect precision to fit within the confines of the small locker. As he unfolded it, they saw its folded size was deceiving as it was actually much larger than he anticipated.

"It's a map," he uttered upon completion of maneuvering the item into full view.

"See the precise longitudinal and latitudinal lines. Their increments are labelled. This is a very detailed map," he informed Charlotte.

His mind raced as he tried to make sense of it. Charlotte was able to generally make out the caption. "It's Lesser Poland, here in Southern Poland. It's a military map of Oświęcim County, right here where Auschwitz is located. Our location is on this map."

"What are we supposed to do with it? We're already here and we know where we're supposed to go next— Auschwitz Birkenau concentration camp. Why do we need a map with geographic coordinates?

"That I don't know. Did you really think we'd get a straight answer out of this?" Charlotte responded.

"Maybe the box will tell us."

Moving on, Alex opened the white rectangular box which lay remaining in the locker while Charlotte looked on in anticipation.

Instinctively, Alex jumped back in horror as the contents of the box were revealed. His shaky hands didn't drop it, although it was tempting, but his eyes welled with tears.

"What is it?" Charlotte inquired of him, very concerned.

Alex handed the box to her with tears wetting his face and Charlotte was met with equal shock and sadness. Inside the rectangular box was the small, amputated right leg of a baby. It had not recently been removed from its rightful owner's body, but was instead gray, shriveled and clearly well on its way to total decay.

"I can't believe it," Charlotte exclaimed. "I cannot believe that anyone could be capable of such a thing."

"This just got beyond personal," Alex responded with pure anger in his voice. "We are going to find whoever did this and I am going to kill them."

Quickly Charlotte's mind began to churn and she tried to piece together the series of clues they had received along the way in deciphering the prisoner's code.

"This can't be," Charlotte stated authoritatively. "Isaac promised that if we followed the clues we would find your daughter."

"Did he mention whether or not she would be in one piece? Did he mention whether or not she would be alive?"

He expressed himself with a fury that despite everything they had experienced up to this point Charlotte had not yet seen coming from him.

"That was the impression I got. That's what he led me to believe."

"It's not looking like the soon-to-be-convicted multiple murderer has been completely up front about things. I'm going—"

"Ok, just a minute," Charlotte interrupted him. "Let's calm down and think about this rationally. There's really no good reason for anyone to amputate your daughter's leg."

"Calm down?" Alex stammered breathlessly. "I think I'm about to throw up. I can't believe this is happening."

Alex doubled over and leaned against the bank of lockers, his stomach now churning with nausea.

"Do you think you can take just one more look? We need to be sure that this is Brielle's leg."

Charlotte's voice was calm and seemed to have a momentary soothing effect. Alex collected himself and stumbled the two feet to where she was standing, holding the box. First closing his eyes, he opened them for just long enough to take in the horrific sight once more. Suddenly his strained face softened.

"You might just be right, Weiss," he uttered, his voice filled with surprise.

He took the box back and examined the contents more closely.

"Brielle has a large birthmark on her right leg. It's a little hard to tell from the decay, but this child's leg doesn't appear to have a birthmark. As I'm looking closer, the skin tone also seems to be much lighter than my daughter's. She is more dark-complected than this child."

"So, you don't think this is hers after all?"

"No, it's definitely not hers."

"Wow."

They paused a moment to mentally recuperate and reassess. Charlotte was the first to speak again.

"I will never get this image out of my mind, but I am so relieved to hear that. What a tender mercy. Now all we have to do is figure out which poor child this leg belongs to. Let's get out of here then and find a hotel. We'll head over to Auschwitz first thing in the morning."

Peace of mind for the time being restored, Charlotte took both the map and the box and they headed for the exit.

Meanwhile, Paniletti watched like a hawk and saw this range of emotion that hit Charlotte and Alex. As he had done with every other incoming group from the arriving trains at the Auschwitz station that day he scoured their faces as they arrived and exited their train. Once he spotted them, his eyes never lost contact with them. He felt enraged by his lack of success at stopping Alex before he left Tel Aviv, but Paniletti was even more furious upon returning to the warehouse to find Charlotte gone.

Neither Alex nor Charlotte noticed him as he now sat lying in wait. They were singularly minded as they exited the train and headed straight for the lockers, and Paniletti was fairly well concealed behind a wide beam stretching from floor to ceiling.

Paniletti didn't know exactly what they were looking for, but he knew they would lead him to the exact location he needed to be. He watched studiously as Charlotte followed to the bank of lockers and Alex attempted to unlock each one using a key. This was the key he had been looking for and the key he kidnapped Charlotte for. *Now I won't need it. They're doing all the work for me.*

He observed Alex collect the contents from the prized locker and watched them get distraught over something in a box they pulled out. Whatever the item was, it was insignificant to him. He decided his best plan of action would be to follow his targets. He was concerned only with where they were going and with retrieving August's treasure when they found it. Alex and Charlotte were his personal compass to everything he needed, and what he believed to be his fool-proof plan, was to rob them of it afterwards. That's not to say he wasn't willing to take drastic measures if needed and kill them early, but he would strategically wait just a little while longer.

Besides, they were too easy of a target at this hour. It was getting very late and Paniletti knew they would be tired. *There's no challenge in that.* As they left the train station for a hotel, Paniletti maintained a strong confidence as he followed at a safe distance, watching their every move.

# Chapter 60

The town of Oświęcim was pleasant enough and the air of solidarity lingering at the concentration camp outside the city was hardly felt within the borders of the city itself. The residents there could live separately in the present while still being close to such an important memorial of history. Life moved on outside of the concentration camp.

Alex was able to find a hotel quickly when they arrived in the center of town and he paid for two rooms.

"I will pay you back for all of this," Charlotte assured him gratefully.

Alex handed her a room key and a handful of Polish złotys he had exchanged at the hotel and kindly responded, "Don't worry about it." After a tender pause he continued, "I'm going to turn in early now. It's not by any means a manly thing to admit, but this trip is starting to take its toll on me. The constant pumping of the adrenaline though my body has taken a nosedive so I'm just going to order room service and take a shower. I've been able to smell myself for about a week now."

Charlotte laughed knowing his last statement was true and the same applied to her.

"Having the ability to smell one's own body odor is never a good sign," she joked as they said goodnight and retired to their separate bedrooms.

Charlotte was now properly clothed as Alex had purchased an outfit for her at a clothing store in Hungary when they switched trains. She felt better about being in public, being properly dressed, but she nonetheless opted for room service as well. The plush king size bed in her room was calling her name and she couldn't have enjoyed the feeling of lying in it more. She slept well through the night despite having slept almost constantly for the last couple of days. Her body was fighting hard to heal itself and sleep was allowing it time to do that.

# *Chapter 61*

Charlotte awoke the next morning literally at the crack of dawn. After a good night's rest she was free from any feelings of grogginess as the early morning light filled her hotel room and sparked her eyes open.

*It's great to have my own room. Finally, I don't feel like I'm being watched by a stranger.*

She laid in bed motionless for a few minutes longer as she relished the momentary feeling of the soft plush bed cushioning her body in the safety of her locked hotel room.

Alex, on the other hand, was experiencing quite the opposite as he had drifted in and out of sleep all night and was angry at himself about the slightest things keeping him awake.

*Why aren't I sleeping!*

As dawn broke, he was rudely awakened by the sound of a barking dog. Although this was annoying in and of itself, he discovered he had failed to fully close the drapes in his room. A beam of light began to shine through the crack in the drapes, of course straight into his eyes. He was awake now and he was mad at the world. The chemicals in his brain were killing any last drop of dopamine that may have been present and a sense of utter despair hit him like a sledgehammer.

Laying in his hotel bed he finally had a moment to just be still and think. That was not necessarily a good thing. It was the first time silence had fully surrounded him since starting this journey. With no noise to interrupt his thoughts he was alone with them and he discovered they were steeped in negativity to a greater degree than he realized.

His time to wallow was interrupted seconds later, however, when the soft stillness with its annoying beam of light, was broken. He heard the distinct sound of paper sliding under the crack of his hotel room door across the plush carpet inside. At first he questioned if he heard anything at all. Then suspecting it was Charlotte, he remembered she called him before bed last night from her room. *If she needed something she would just call.*

His curiosity getting the best of him, he lifted his head from its position of motionlessness and craned to see what had been pushed into his room. Bleary eyed, he saw it was an envelope and like an idiot stared at it for a second before it pounded him over the head. *It may be from the kidnapper!*

Quickly and without stopping to see what it was, Alex rushed to the door and threw it open. He was met with nothing more than an empty hallway. Seeing no one, he instinctively reached down to retrieve the envelope. He first noticed the insignia on the front. It was well familiar to him as the symbol of the United Nations and the front of the envelope was addressed to him in neat penmanship.

> *To: Senator Card*
> *From: Head of Security for the United Nations*

Alex ripped open the envelope and pulled from it a piece of hotel stationary. It was otherwise nondescript aside from a pairing of words it contained written in scarlet red lettering. It was largely similar and equally mysterious as the prior two word pairings he and Charlotte received in the shape of a red cross:

K
LIMB
T
C
H
E
N

*This is the final straw.* Upon seeing the enigmatic message Alex immediately dodged out of his room, determined to find its deliverer.

Being very much a mom and pop establishment, the hotel was not large. It contained only 10 rooms and neither he nor Charlotte saw any other guests or engaged in interaction with anyone other than the hotel clerk. As Alex raced through the hall of the second floor where his room was and down the steps to the main lobby he saw no one and was out of breath by the time he raced out the front door to the street. Other than a flock of birds who took immediate flight from the tree they were perched on as he flew out the door, there was no movement to be seen.

Alex turned back to the hotel and decided to next interrogate the clerk. He was in his seventies and stood with a hunched back.

"I need to speak with your head of security," he demanded.

"We don't have a head of security. I watch the hotel and call the police if there is trouble. Is there a problem, sir?" he asked in English with a thick Polish accent.

"Are you the only employee here?"

"Yes. Me and my wife. We switch shifts."

"Where is your wife now?"

"She's asleep. She did the night duty."

These responses were aggravating Alex as he continued to hit one dead end after another.

"I just received something under my door, did you see anyone just exit the hotel?" he asked him quickly.

"No, sir. No one's been in or out all morning."

"How many guests are staying here?"

"At the moment it is just you and your lady friend and Frau Müller who is visiting from Berlin."

"Frau Müller?"

"Yes, of course. She's been staying here for the last three months. She came right after her husband's funeral."

"Thank you for the information," Alex responded.

He noticed on the back wall's key storage board that other than the keys for rooms 8 and 9, which he and

Charlotte were occupying, the only other missing key belonged to room number 3. *That must be Frau Müller's room. I'll go ask her for information. Maybe she saw something...Or maybe she's in on it.*

It took no less than 30 seconds of solid pounding on the door of room number 3 before Frau Müller answered the door. Simply knocking wasn't at all effective, hence the pounding. Inside, a small dog was barking incessantly.

Behind the door was the source of the yappy disturbance that had woken him up. *That's one mystery solved.*

Alex could hear shuffling inside and was taken aback when a frail old woman, no larger than the size of a large child, opened the door in a pink bathrobe. She was in her early eighties. Deeply apologetic, Alex begged her forgiveness for the intrusion and asked her if she had seen anyone roaming the halls.

His attempt to communicate was completely unsuccessful given she spoke only German. Alex begged her a moment, in the simplest of terms he could muster, so he could retrieve Charlotte.

Charlotte complied with his request when he came to her door and urged her to put on her robe and come translate for him. They returned to the threshold of Frau Müller's room and through Charlotte's assistance the old woman politely told them that, no, she hadn't seen anyone.

"But then again, I don't see much these days with my poor eyesight. You should have met my husband, Albrecht. His vision was so much worse. He was constantly running into things."

Alex, feeling terrible about interrupting Frau Müller in the brash manner he had, felt obligated to stay and listen as she rambled on about her husband while Charlotte translated. Despite his compulsion to stay, he was fidgeting and anxious beyond measure to get going the entire time. When she finally finished minutes later she invited them in and Charlotte snatched the opportunity to politely decline, citing business to attend to. They then thanked her as Alex slid away and again apologized for the intrusion.

"Tschüß, Liebchen," she said to them as they left, almost as if she were sad to see them go.

"She said goodbye, dears," Charlotte informed him. Not wanting him to miss a word of what she said. It was her light hearted stab at teasing him.

Alex rushed up the stairs again to the second floor to show Charlotte the letter. Immediately after conquering the flight of stairs, he noticed a breeze blowing the curtain covering a window at the opposite end of the hall. He surmised that the window must be open and confirmed this theory when he arrived at its ledge and looked out to find a fire escape.

"Dammit!" he exclaimed, realizing this must have been the means of entry and exit for the letter's courier.

His frustration seemingly oozed from his pores.

He returned to his room and handed the letter to Charlotte. "It's another incomprehensible clue," he reported angrily.

"It's from the U.N. Head of Security," Charlotte noted aloud.

"That's right."

"The UN Head of Security. He was the one who provided me with video footage of a police shooting investigation. He gave me the final link in a suspicious set of illegality on the part of a sergeant with the New York City Police Department."

"Did he tell you his name when he gave you the tape," Alex dug.

"No, now that you mention it. He simply told me he was the Head of Security and flashed a badge. I was so interested in seeing what was on the tape that I didn't take the time to ask."

"Whoever he is, he's behind all of this. I'm calling over there."

Alex furtively dialed all international codes required to reach the United Nations from his hotel phone in Poland.

"Hello, this is U.S. Senator Alexander Card," Charlotte heard him say. "Please transfer me to the Head of Security."

The response on the other end of the line was discouraging. "I'm sorry Senator, the Head of Security is currently on vacation. Can I transfer you to his assistant who may be able to help you?"

"No thank you," Alex responded, "I'll settle for his name and information about when he'll be back. "

"The Head of Security is Peter Bremer, sir, but I don't have the information about his return date."

"Peter Bremer?" he questioned.

"Yes, sir. Correct."

"Thank you very much," he responded, hanging up the phone.

"Peter Bremer," Alex repeated to Charlotte as he placed the phone back on its receiver. "Does that name ring any bells?"

"No, not at all." Charlotte replied. "Should it?"

"Peter Bremer is the Head of Security at the UN. If we knew who he was it might lead us closer to my daughter. He has her. Whoever he is, he has her."

# Chapter 62

With the name Peter Bremer in mind, but no idea who or where he was, the two hurried to get ready for the day. Knowing full well that neither the museum nor the Auschwitz-Birkenau concentration camp would be open for another two hours, Alex was motivated now more than ever to get over there.

*Peter Bremer may very well be there,* he thought, while waiting somewhat impatiently for Charlotte to finish getting ready. Fortunately, she didn't take long, almost just as anxious as he was to get going and try and make sense of everything. *Getting to the site of Auschwitz-Birkenau early won't hurt anything. We can canvass the outside of the premises first.*

They were hasty to leave the hotel and walked quickly along the road which marked the direction of the path leading to Auschwitz. This path would lead them to the abandoned railway which once provided the track to usher in the prisoners to the death camp. The iconic tracks, which crossed each other just before breaching the main gate, stood in the same condition as the Nazis left them when they fled.

As they drew closer, there was an impending air of solemnity that grew stronger and begged reverence even before they reached the entrance of the historical remains of the largest and most destructive concentration camp the world had ever seen. The atrocities of the past lingered in the air as an almost intangible presence and the passage of time did little to diminish that feeling. Charlotte got chills from being on the grounds and now properly hydrated, a tear fell down her right cheek. She was touched beyond measure.

Other than the bleak somberness of the area, Alex and Charlotte saw nothing of note by the time the museum was to open, and they approached the entrance just as the elderly museum matron unlocked the door. They were the first visitors of the day and the matron smiled and greeted them warmly. Her silver hair was cut short and curled.

"Dzień dobry," she greeted them, warmly wishing them good morning.

Although her greeting was addressed to them in Polish, the meaning was clearly understood. She was happy they were there and eager to share what stood within the historic place.

Alex purchased their admission tickets and the matron pointed them in the direction of the museum halls. Unassuming at first, the museum entrance proved to be the mouth of a place which testified boldly through word and pictures of the atrocities of the Holocaust and Alex and Charlotte initially stopped to admire a sculpture at the entrance. There were sculptures throughout the museum, some more abstract than others, but this one struck Alex profoundly. It was titled *"Starvation"* and depicted a huddled mass of bodies. As they continued to tour the museum, the other sculptures were equally heart wrenching and in their own way depicted the personal tortures inflicted upon those at the camps, but *"Starvation"* hit him hardest.

Throughout the museum was a wealth of pictures and mementos, each one standing as its own testament of the past.

"It says here this is Josef Mengele," Charlotte said to him, pointing to an old black and white photograph hanging unpleasingly on the wall. "Svenda told me about him. He's a true villain."

They walked each of the museum's halls in silent reverence, almost breathless at what they were seeing, until they made their way through the exit leading out to the camp. Outside, the rows of barracks were like haunting tombs in and of themselves. Each building in the camp was numbered and each one served a purpose. The barracks highlighted memories of their victims and provided sanctuary for all that remained of them on earth.

Among the displays that served the most poignant message was that of a giant mass of shoes in the first building they entered. As Alex stood before the display of the mountains of footwear, removed viciously from the feet of the concentration camp victims, a tear fell down his cheek. For just a moment he forgot about his own burdens and reflected on this part of history and the testimony born in the camp of the reality of the Holocaust. Alex remarked on the various types and sheer number of shoes. There were shoes of all shapes, colors and sizes. There were male shoes and female shoes and perhaps the most saddening, baby shoes. These shoes were valueless to those who stole them, but were of infinite value to those from whom they were taken.

As Alex and Charlotte moved on to another nearby building they saw a display of large quantities of desecrating hair. The caption below the display case explained that the hair had been tested. It had been removed from the victims' bodies post mortem, which fact was evident because of the presence of Zyklon-B cyanide woven within and throughout the strands. This meant the victims were subjected to the Zyklon-B before they died and these facts made it impossible to argue that the Holocaust had not occurred. The victims from whom this hair was taken were doused with heavy amounts of the poisonous gas which killed them.

The imagery of the desecrating hair was ghastly. Under normal conditions the human hair would not have deteriorated and would have retained its original composition throughout the decades. This hair, on the contrary, having been ravaged with poison, was slowly beginning to break down. The disturbing masses of ill-gotten strands were swirling together into a massive heap, which would, in time, fail to resemble the human hair of all different colors, lengths and textures that it once was. Alex pondered this deeply. *It wasn't supposed to be sitting in a case. It was supposed to have stayed with the bodies of those it belonged to and it was supposed to be spared from the toxins of lethal gas.*

When Alex and Charlotte pulled themselves away and moved on, they reached the building containing the display of prostheses, which included a collection of man-made arms, legs, hands and feet. This area was most unsettling to Charlotte. She gasped, seeing the stacks of prosthetic limbs, all varying in size and design, realizing they were ripped from the bodies of those who relied on them and that their rightful owners were forced to do without them at the time of their deaths.

Leaving the building containing the artificial limbs was a relief for Charlotte as it was painful to see, but as they next moved to the standing cells, the environment failed to lighten in spirit. The standing cells were used during the Holocaust as a method of torture, wherein the prisoners of the camp were placed for long periods of time, unable to sit.

"This reminds me of the cofferdam. It's so cramped," Alex commented. "Luckily, we weren't literally driven mad like some of the Holocaust victims who were banished here."

It seemed unimaginable, but as Alex and Charlotte continued to explore they discovered the crematorium, housed in a separate building, was even worse. The crematorium could easily be analogized to a human oven because that's exactly what it was. It was a furnace formerly heated to unmentionable levels to incinerate the camp's dead bodies which had been gassed, poisoned, or otherwise murdered. The walls were blackened and damaged. The fire which had burned in them had taken its toll. Charlotte and Alex moved quickly away from this area. It was too hard to stay.

They next made their way to the barracks which served as poor excuses for the living space cruelly provided to the camp's prisoners. The barracks contained cramped slats of wood nailed together. Once considered by the Nazis to be prison beds, they were nothing more than a human shelving system. They were meant to cram in as many bodies as possible with the actual number squeezed in far exceeding the maximum occupancy.

These were the only resting spots, despite all their discomfort, for the weary and mistreated laborers in the camps. The sight took Alex's breath away. The wood was stained with blood and embedded with the illnesses of its many former occupants. These physical reminders were striking just as were the fingernail markings on the walls.

Perhaps most damning of all for Alex and Charlotte as they moved on, was the sight of another of the iconic symbols of the Holocaust—the gas chamber. Inside, the walls of the chamber were covered with thick soot bleeding down as if still trying to escape the past and weeping for the atrocities that took place therein. Here too were horrific fingernail markings embedded into the walls. They were reminders of the desperate cries of the murdered and the clamors for help that never came.

The voices of those who had their mortal lives taken from them in this place spoke plainly to Alex that the Holocaust had occurred. It was in this chamber, where it was as blatant as the shining sun that he was standing in a place of historic and real genocide. It was also in this chamber where it dawned on Alex the essence of what he was meant to learn and what the purpose of their arduous journey to find his daughter was.

Alex, the stoic United States Senator, was struck at the power of the images and information he was receiving through his tour of Auschwitz-Birkenau. His mind reflected upon the last time he considered the Holocaust. It was right before Brielle was kidnapped. He had voted against the Genocide Prevention Act.

The Genocide Prevention Act was a bill that sought to punish the country of Iraq. During the Iran-Iraq War that had occurred in March, six months prior, Iraq had been initiating chemical weapons attacks on the Kurds at the town of Halabja. Between 3,200 and 5,000 individuals, mainly civilians, were killed needlessly by these forces. This terror called for sanctions on Iraq and an end of support from the United States.

It was then Alex's position that the Genocide Prevention Act was inappropriate because of the financial cost it would incur and its inability to have any real positive effect on ending genocide. Now, as he stood on the memorial grounds of one such act of genocide, he realized he had been dead wrong in his thinking. He realized the costs to the United States would be far greater both financially and morally if they failed to act. *I lost sight of the lessons taught to me in the past when I cast that vote.*

On Senate voting day, just a few weeks prior, he failed to foresee the decay and damage which could come by not taking a stand. He hadn't understood that failing to speak up, and even the mere presence of apathy, kept the door propped open for hatred to enter and thrive.

The Genocide Prevention Act failed to pass largely because of Alex's loud and vocal opposition which he had openly shared. Thereby, he made a step forward in the downward direction of the slippery slope that one day, if unguarded, could result in the memories of past genocide being lost. Ignoring the issue of genocide and human mistreatment would leave the world with an opening for the past to repeat itself and a paved way for those who discriminate against and destroy those they view to be less. He now realized this.

Time passed quickly now as Charlotte and Alex walked through the concentration camp, but in many respects it felt as if it had stopped. Where they initially came to hurry through and search for the missing link to the set of clues they were given, they now wandered slowly, momentarily forgetting themselves, becoming lost in the realities of the past and undoubtedly coming out changed.

As they exited the gas chamber and found themselves at the end of the tour, literally half the day had passed.

"I understand the message now," Alex said. "I never before bothered to come here and now I'm so grateful I did. I get it. But I still don't know where to turn next."

"I feel the same way," Charlotte concurred. I'm getting the impression this was a big part of the plan and I think we should review the remaining clues in light of everything we've just seen. We have the three remaining word pairings and a map, which is clearly supposed to lead us to your daughter. Maybe a fresh perspective will give us a different viewpoint on what to make of the mysterious messages we've gotten."

"It's a pretty big map, Charlotte."

"And that's why we need to figure out how the clues we have relate to each other."

Pulling the map out of a satchel he had acquired, Alex voiced his thoughts, "A map is only good if you know your destination. This map isn't of much use given we have no coordinates and still no idea of where my daughter is."

"You're right about that," Charlotte conceded. "We do need numbers to figure this out. The only numbers we've been given so far have been '12,' '22' and '23,' from the symbols on the key for the enigma machine. Even if we put those together we don't have an articulated point either vertically or horizontally on this map. We need a precise latitude and longitude—"

"Latitude and Longitude, that's right!" Alex exclaimed cutting her off. "The horizontal and vertical coordinates of locations on earth! Longitude is the geographic coordinates which specify the east-west position of a point on the Earth's surface and Latitude is the geographic coordinates which specify the north-south position of a point on the Earth's surface. It's been right in front of us."

"What's been right in front of us?" Charlotte asked.

"Latitude and Longitude. The vertical and horizontal combinations of words." Alex said as he excitedly pulled the three scarlet-lettered word pairings out of his wallet and began to study them.

Charlotte did a replay. "When they left your daughters shoes they intersected the word 'shoes' with 'chamber.'

When they cut off a lock of her hair they intersected the word 'hair' with 'theater.' The last clue we got was the word 'limb' intersected with the word 'kitchen.' We just saw the gas chamber at Auschwitz and there was also a theater and kitchen."

It struck her instantly. "The numbers on the respective buildings must coordinate with the longitudinal coordinates we need and the building numbers with the displayed shoes, hair and prosthetic limbs then likely coordinate with latitudinal coordinates."

"That would make all the clues match up to lead us to a specific point," exclaimed Alex.

Charging back through the concentration camp, they revisited each of the respective buildings to obtain the necessary building numbers.

The barracks building housing the thousands of shoes was labeled building '50', the chamber was marked with a '19' above it, and the display of hair was in building '18.' Rushing forward they headed to the theater, which had been converted to a warehouse during the Holocaust. This was building '17.'  The barracks holding the prosthetic limbs was marked with '22' and finally the kitchen, which was at the time not a building open for viewing and one that was bypassed on their original tour, was marked as building '12.'

Charlotte recorded each of these numbers, and once she had all six, they both stared at the numeric series in front of them.

"Horizontally we have 50, 18 and 22. The vertical numbers are 19, 17 and 12. If we put them together that gives us 50.1822 degrees latitude and 19.1712 longitude," Charlotte announced.

"There must be something hidden there and it better not be my daughter because we're likely going to have to do some digging. Quick, let's take a look," Alex responded.

Charlotte focused her attention on the large map and they zeroed in on their location. Alex traced his finger along the approximate vertical axis at 19.1712 degrees and

Charlotte did the same following as close to the correct horizontal axis as she could until their fingers met.

Both their jaws dropped.

"But that puts us under water," Alex remarked as they both looked up and saw the obvious Sola River right in front of them.

At first legitimately confused, Charlotte tried to find their error. As she did so, her mind reflected back on the words Isaac said to her in the prison. *The middle is where answers are found.*

*So this is what Isaac meant,* she realized. It was in the middle of the Sola River where they would find what they were looking for.

Isaac's statement was certainly playing a substantive role now as she contemplated venturing out into the middle of the large river. She wasn't afforded much time to worry about it though as her thoughts were interrupted with the sound of Alex's voice.

"We better get a boat," he said.

# Chapter 63

Naturally, the process of obtaining a boat was not as easy as it sounded. There wasn't exactly a boat harbor in the area, but fortunately they did see a house about 400 meters up the river with a small dinghy tied to a small dock on the shore.

"It looks like we're going to have to call in a favor," Alex said.

As they walked to the house they heard the soft sound of water flowing. The Sola River was 55.2 miles long and flowed northeast, passing Auschwitz and coming at one point within meters of the historic camp. The geographic coordinates they were focused on crossed at a part of the river which was close to the northeastern corner of Auschwitz and it would be important they stay at those coordinates.

"I hope the river's not too deep," Alex said.

As they arrived at the house of their desired dinghy's owner, they knocked on the door. They waited for several minutes but no one answered. As they looked at each other with a knowing glance, Alex said to Charlotte, "It looks like it might be best to ask for forgiveness than for permission. We need to get out there as quickly as possible."

"If it makes you feel any better we're not stealing, we're simply borrowing. We can't really be prosecuted," she responded.

Charlotte knew this wasn't a correct legal analysis, but it made him smile. They both convinced themselves their actions were for a greater good and they had sufficient rationale to take something that didn't belong to them.

"I hope the owners don't come out looking for the boat before we're done with it," Alex lightheartedly said as they traversed the yard behind the house and made their way to the back where the boat was docked.

The dinghy they were borrowing was simple with no motor and two paddles. It was clearly used only for casual recreational outings on the river.

"I swore to myself I was never going to set foot on any form of water vessel again. Not after eight days confined in a cofferdam," Charlotte remarked.

"You're gonna have to break that promise to yourself, Weiss. We're both going. I'll swim when we get to the coordinates but you have to keep the boat in my location while I'm underwater looking for who knows what is down there."

They wasted no more time in preparing to launch and after untying the dinghy from the dock they were finally on their way. Alex pushed the boat from the shore and jumped in. The dinghy glided across the surface of the water from the momentum. Alex began paddling while Charlotte served as the navigator. She used the coordinates she recorded to know where to steer the boat. Within minutes they reached the point as close to 50.1822 degrees latitude and 19.1712 longitude as they could find on the map.

"It's around here somewhere," Charlotte announced as Alex, following her direction, stopped the boat. Holding the oar into the water to try and determine its depth, he couldn't find bottom.

"Looks like I'm going for a swim here," he announced. He removed his shoes, socks, shirt and pants and prepared to dive in. As he was removing his jacket, he felt the flashlight that Nurse LeMond gave him. It had been stuffed in an inside pocket and he had been carrying it with him ever since. He was quick to recognize the wisdom in this gift which he had initially found extremely odd. She obviously knew much more than he had given her credit for.

Alex removed his watch and held the flashlight under water to ensure it was in fact waterproof.

"Even though it's daylight I'm sure my visibility under water will be zero without this flashlight."

"Good luck down there," Charlotte responded. "I've got two fixed markers on the shore to keep my bearings with."

"Great thinking," Alex assured her. "I want this to go as smoothly as possible. Heaven only knows what's down there."

Alex was now in just his boxer shorts and although Charlotte didn't mind the handsome sight at all, she looked away after taking a solid look. *A lot is riding on this moment. This is no time for distractions*, Charlotte thought.

"I hope it's not too deep," he said, not noticing her initial stare. Taking a deep breath, he then dove head first into the water.

The water rippled and bubbled as Alex dove in. The water was cold against his skin, but he hardly felt it. His eyes burned as he opened them to see that the flashlight was, in fact, emitting a glowing beam that remarkably shone through the dirty water. His discomfort was negligible, however as his thoughts raced consciously avoiding the thought that he would encounter the body of his baby girl. *I hope whatever I'm looking for isn't too heavy. We don't have any tools to pull it up with.*

These diverted thoughts were interrupted when he quickly reached bottom. As he peered through the water he saw a layer of mud and rocks. Traversing the bottom with his eyes, he was running out of breath. Just as he thought he would have to return to the surface for air, his eyes spied a metal box partially embedded in the mud. It was no larger than one cubic foot. He forced his breath to hold as his adrenaline pumped and he dug until he was finally successful. Pulling the box from the bottom, he tucked it under his arm and used the river bottom to propel his body upwards.

As he broke the surface with an astonishing speed, he took a tremendous gulp of air. Charlotte herself breathed a heavy sigh of relief.

"It's really not that heavy which probably means it's not buried treasure," he joked.

Cheerfully, an emotion Charlotte had yet to see from him, he hoisted first the box and then himself onto the dinghy.

"It only took one dive," he said with a smile. "Not bad if I do say so myself."

Charlotte smiled and began to paddle back to shore as he attempted to pat himself dry with his clothing and then redressed himself. She couldn't shake the still nagging feeling as they glided along the water that they were being watched.

Other than that uneasiness, it was literally smooth sailing along the water until the moment when their progress was severely hampered and the excitement of the moment was cut short. No sooner had they gotten halfway back to the water's edge than they heard the sound of a gunshot. Looking up and surveilling the area, they couldn't see the shooter, but were unable to miss a bullet careening into the water near the edge of the boat.

# Chapter 64

Justin winced. The sharpness of the pain made it almost impossible for him to hold his rifle straight. He was missing his targets. As he peered through the rifle's scope, he was continuously caught off balance, having to support himself on just one leg. Although he was now relegated to walking with a considerable limp, Justin was still dedicated to killing both Charlotte and her companion, the Senator. He had reemerged for this purpose alone. Having been left for dead in Jerusalem, Paniletti had been confident Justin would no longer be a problem after shoving him off the ledge of the hotel. Paniletti was wrong. The sound of the oncoming police sirens had prompted him to leave the scene of Justin's fateful fall and there was no time to confirm his victim's death. His assumption, based on arrogance and speculation, was that the fall killed Justin Vincent.

Since he wasn't around to confirm the death, Paniletti additionally wasn't around to see Justin found by medical staff and carried off by ambulance. He also wasn't present when the medics failed to realize the bushes he landed on were paramount in ensuring the trauma he experienced was not life threatening. Thinking him to be on the verge of death and unable to move, the medics failed to secure him into the ambulance, which allowed Justin to spring off the stretcher and run out the ambulance doors as soon as they were opened.

Despite a severe injury to his leg, the adrenaline coursing through Justin's body ensured he didn't feel a thing as he sprinted away. Those integral in assisting him in the ambulance were astonished as he bound out and weren't able to apprehend him once he made his escape. He had been so successful in that escape that he was able to follow the directions given to him by August and again meet up with Charlotte. As he now stood, focused again on his target, the same adrenaline he experienced from his fall rushed back. His standing with the Brotherhood depended on it. He would be successful this time.

# Chapter 65

"This has not been our day," Charlotte announced as Alex grabbed her head and pushed it to the floor of the boat. He catapulted his own head downward as well.

"Stay low," he warned her. "We'll flip the boat and use it as a shield."

"How will we make it back to shore?" she asked him, panicked.

"The bullets came from the opposite bank so our best bet is to head back in the direction we came."

"What about the box?"

Alex was a step ahead of her and was securing a knot in the rope that he tied around the box.

"I'll take care of it. And you, on my count of three, tip the boat to the east bank and prepare to jump ship. Hold onto the sides and we'll use the air pocket under the boat to breathe. You got that?"

Charlotte nodded yes, scared out of her mind, but grateful he had the wherewithal to execute a plan.

Another bullet flew overhead, nicking the side of the boat.

"Remember, towards the east," he reminded her as they prepared to be submerged into the water. "One...two...three."

In a synchronized fashion the two flipped the boat and jumped into the water. By now the contents of the satchel he had, including the map were drifting in the river but Alex made sure to keep hold of the box. He wrapped the second end of the rope around his wrist to secure the box to his body and even with this extra burden he was able to quickly swim his way up to the surface under the boat.

Charlotte, on the other hand, experienced a slight delay in taking proper cover. As she submerged herself in the water she rose to the top on the outer edge of the boat rather than underneath it. Taking a quick breath and getting her bearings, she heard the sound of another gunshot and dunked herself underwater, taking cover in the air pocket underneath the dinghy.

"You're ready for the Navy Seals," he said, out of breath but trying to stir up motivation when they were both inside. "Grip the sides and paddle with your feet toward the bank. I'll take the front."

Quickly they commenced kicking and began to gain momentum and propel themselves forward. Charlotte found it extremely disconcerting that there seemed to be a constant stream of bullets hitting the water and plunging dangerously close to them. The small bits of metal, which shot out of the gun towards them made a surprising impact in the water after penetrating the surface. The bullet cut through it like butter and left pockets of air in their wake.

Largely due to Alex being in excellent physical shape prior to leaving New York, his stamina helped them in this situation just as it had when Charlotte's energy was completely sucked from her in the cofferdam.

Together, they were able to make their way to the bank much more quickly than either of them, and most certainly she, would have been able to alone. The gunshots continued with only momentary pauses and stopped as the pair drew closer to shore. Just as Charlotte would breathe a small sigh of relief however, the bullets started up again coming from another direction. Clearly the shooter was moving around and trying to get closer to them on the other side of the river.

"Make sure you keep yourself covered with the boat," Alex said with a look of consternation on his face she could sense but couldn't see. "We're almost there."

As they made their final ascent to land, the danger grew worse with the shooter hitting the boat more often than not. The strength of the wooden boat prevented the bullets from ripping through to their bodies but the situation filled Charlotte with intense fear nonetheless.

They continued to use the dinghy as a shield when they returned to their home base on the side of the river. It covered them as they ran to take shelter on the side of the house. Throwing the boat to the ground in a manner that would surely leave its owners questioning what had happened if the bullet holes did not, they spotted a shed about 100 meters away.

And not a moment too soon. The bullets were now coming at them from two separate places!

"We've got enough time to make it over there if we run fast," Alex ordered. "There's another shooter on the other side of the house."

*Two shooters,* Charlotte thought to herself quickly. *That would explain the barrage of bullets coming from multiple directions.*

Running for their lives they made it to the shed and threw the door open. Quickly locking and securing the door behind them, they waited with their heavy breathing being the only sound they could hear. Everything was otherwise perfectly quiet, which in and of itself was frightening. The small shed contained slats in the door, which while leaving them with less security, allowed them to see what was happening outside.

A bird suddenly chirped in a tree above them. Given the current silence, it was presently unaware of the lurking danger. Charlotte prayed their hiding place wouldn't be found but started to doubt the power of her prayer when she saw a man with a shaven bald head, wearing red suspenders and Doc Martens, pacing the yard in front of them. He was carrying a large rifle with a look of intensity on his face. Charlotte knew she and Alex would either have to devise a brilliant plan on the spot or risk being executed.

It took her just a moment realize it but the man she was seeing was Justin Vincent. She was the one who had put him in prison. As he walked next to the side of the house searching like a bloodhound, he spit a wad of chew out of his mouth and onto the ground. Charlotte easily spotted the red swastika and an iron cross tattooed on either side of his neck. She remembered him from his sentencing hearing in court and recognized this as a new acquisition. *He must have gotten inked in prison. I definitely would have remembered that. It's disgusting.*

Now, as he stood in front of her, much too close for comfort, Charlotte noticed his limp. It was severe, but she was oblivious to how he sustained the injury and was frankly quite unconcerned. She was disturbed to see that although he was limping, the injury did nothing to stop the fervor with which he was tracking them. While their heavy breathing had largely dissipated, Charlotte was still uncomfortable about the decibel level of her breath. As they hunkered down in the shed, she felt her breath quicken and her heart race at the sight of the man in front of her trying to murder them.

"If he gets close and we have no other option, we can knock him on the head from the roof," Alex whispered softly, interjecting her thoughts.

Alex was removing the pane of glass from a small window at the back wall of the shed and stepped on a ladder to work his way out.

"Hand me that sledgehammer," he told her, pointing to a heavy tool being stored in the shed.

Charlotte readily complied with this instruction.

"You stay in here with the box no matter what," he said to her. "I'm going to crawl up to the roof through the back so he won't see me. I'll stay low and as soon as I have him in a position to drop the hammer I'm going to do it. From up above, it'll catch his head first and he'll be out."

Swallowing loudly, despite a dry mouth, Charlotte could do nothing more than nod fearfully.

After he climbed out, Charlotte could hear Alex above her sliding over the rooftop towards the edge as she simultaneously watched Justin draw closer. She winced as Justin's eyes caught sight of the shed and he started towards it.

Alex was laying too low for their attacker to see him atop the shed and as Justin moved in, Charlotte could hear Alex getting into position. Justin's eyes were focused on the door and she was grateful to know that Alex remained undetected. As the enemy drew dangerously close.

Charlotte remembered what Alex told her. *Stay in the shed, no matter what.*

Despite his admonition, her instincts took over and her hand beat his to the door handle in a last ditch effort to defend herself. She was however too late to reveal herself and jumped back at the sound of a gunshot in front of her. Greatly surprised as she looked up after gaining her bearings, she was half expecting to have been shot there were no bullet holes in the door. Noting that she wasn't shot, she instantly panicked with worry about Alex and rushed back to the door slats to see what was going on.

There in front of her lay Justin Vincent. His body was now too far away to have been pummeled by the sledgehammer and it was clear he himself had been shot. He had not noticed a second set of bullets being shot at his targets in the water and had not been on the defensive against a second shooter. Blood spewed from his neck as he lay on the ground. Charlotte was tempted to run out until she saw the source of the bullet. *It's Paniletti!* The cocky devil he was had his gun pointed directly at Alex and she knew he would be coming for her next.

There was a burning inside Charlotte. It was a fury of anger ignited in that instant and rekindled from a place deep inside her she had kept buried until now. Paniletti was a murderer and he was not going to get away with it again!

Without another thought, with no regard for the consequences and in an effort to distract him from Alex, she threw the shed door open and confronted him.

"I will kill you just as surely as I killed Saul Adler," he said to her with pure evil in his eyes. Pointing the rifle at her head, he continued, "The dream team is done."

The words spewing out of his mouth, Charlotte realized he had just admitted to Saul's murder. She was beside herself with shock at the news, but not so much so that she couldn't see, with his rifle in her face that Paniletti was going to have the last laugh after all...

And then he fell to the ground.

Charlotte saw it before she heard it. She now felt numb to the sound of gunfire and hesitated before she realized

Paniletti too was shot. Perhaps it was the shock of the realization he murdered Saul that dulled her senses, or the trauma of everything she experienced that day, which caused her to feel immune to another dead body in front of her.

Moving her head slowly to the left when it occurred to her that direction was the origin of this latest death blow, Charlotte saw a man in military fatigues. It took her just a moment but she realized it was Peter Bremer. It was almost as if he were a ghost appearing out of nowhere and saving her life. Charlotte stared at him mystified as their eyes locked.

She looked up quickly behind her to see Alex, who remained unscathed, was also staring at Peter in disbelief. Charlotte's jaw dropped. Peter Bremer, Head of UN Security and author of the cryptic cross codes, had just saved their lives.

She looked back at Alex in equal disbelief and wondered whether he was piecing this all together. She then turned her eyes back to Peter, but just like that, just as quickly as he came, he was gone. Their efforts to track him down were unsuccessful even as Alex jumped off the roof and they ran toward the road where Peter had stood. The man who saved their lives was nowhere to be seen.

Resigning herself to the fact that their journey was not yet over, Charlotte remembered the box they had found and returned to Paniletti's corpse which lay before them. *What was he doing? Why was he here? Why did he murder Benjamin Stansfeld and why did he murder Saul?*

Charlotte was immediately struck by the soles of Paniletti's boots, which had a red swastika embedded into the rubber. She recognized these as being typical of modern day Nazis and noticed Johnny wearing a similar pair as he sat cross-legged on the couch during the gathering at his home. Ordinarily, the sight of a law enforcement officer wearing a Nazi symbol would prove to be quite the dichotomy. Unfortunately, given who she was dealing with, Charlotte was not the least bit surprised. Charlotte carefully lifted his shirtsleeves, afraid of what she might find tattooed on his upper bicep. There it was, the Nordic rune symbol for life. *It's the same type of symbol that was carved into Saul's skin!*

The gravity of his offenses sunk in for Charlotte immediately when Alex flipped over the body to get a closer look and a small pouch fell from his pocket. Charlotte lifted it up and opened it observing the contents that were shiny against the cloth. She pulled it out and was overcome at what she saw. It was a sharp metal throwing star with four separate blades with jagged edges and bent in the shape of a swastika. The Nazi Eagle was emblazoned across a middle circle connecting the four small blades. *This was the weapon. It was the weapon Paniletti used to kill Saul.* Charlotte knew it and she was taking it with her.

"Let's get this box to the hotel," she said to Alex unapologetically referring to their acquisition from the Sola River. "The police will find these bodies eventually."

# *Chapter 66*

Peter returned to his hotel room knowing the two men he had just killed needed to die. The thought wasn't pleasant but he did find solace in seeing his wife lying peacefully on the bed. Having left so quickly, he arranged a flight for her to Israel the day he arrived. The photos he brought with him across the ocean had been developed and Peter reflected on the day of Benjamin Stansfeld's death several weeks prior. Peter had remained unseen by police in Benjamin's car right before the shooting as Benjamin took a strategic turn down an alleyway one block from the UN and dropped him off. When police gave chase that day, the two of them were on their way to the newspaper where Benjamin worked. Their purpose was to publish the incriminating photos that Peter had been holding close ever since. Peter had been in the back seat behind his journalist friend he liked to call Benny and remained covered by the heavily tinted windows of the sedan as Benjamin rushed through the city streets. Paniletti stayed hot on their tail, but as far as he could see, Benjamin was working alone. The Police Department had received a tip about Benjamin being in possession of photos of an incriminating nature and Paniletti was determined to rid him of them.

As the police chase continued, Paniletti stuck with the sedan but Benjamin, as stubborn as a mule, refused to back down. Because of his determination Benjamin was able to avoid capture for quite some time. In addition to being quick thinking, he was surprisingly agile for his age. He was both creatively and physically adept and his profession as a journalist did nothing to diminish his physical abilities, which included skill behind the wheel of a car. He led the police chase unapprehended for a period of time that many would be in awe of. So persistent was he to make it back to the newspaper that he was not giving in under any circumstances voluntarily.

When the pursuit turned almost too hot to continue and it seemed as if they would be run down and captured, Benjamin took a quick right turn before First Street to cut through an alley. In order to spare his friend from being captured with him, Benjamin determined he needed to let Peter out of the car. The turn was too quick and too sharp for Paniletti to negotiate before passing it by with lights and sirens blaring. Peter gave his friend one last piece of advice. He told him about the video cameras on First Street in front of the UN Building, and since it looked as if he would be forced to surrender, the whole thing would be caught on film. It was under the darkness of the alley where the buildings cut off the sunlight, where Benjamin realized the inevitable.

"Goodbye," he said somberly to his friend as he, handed him the camera film they were on their way to deliver and stopped momentarily to let him out.

"I have to trust you now to finish what we started."

He then barreled through the alleyway alone before emerging on the other side as if he hadn't skipped a beat.

Throughout the chase, no one in the pursuing Police Department was the wiser as to Paniletti's true motivation and thought nothing of the fact that Paniletti was first on the sidelines when Benjamin emerged at the alley's exit. Paniletti sped around the block to the opposite side of the alley in sufficient time to divert his path and force Benjamin's sedan into another patrol car which cut him off in the front.

It was then when the last crucial moments of Benjamin's life unfolded, all captured on video.

The photos Peter held in his hand were the reason Benjamin was killed. Paniletti knew Benjamin had taken them and he thought he had them with him when he died. He was wrong. Peter had them now. These were photos which would certainly damage Paniletti's reputation and put a black streak on his credibility if they were ever revealed. As Peter stood in his hotel room in Auschwitz, having just exacted revenge, he was going to make certain the photos were revealed.

# *Chapter 67*

As Alex and Charlotte arrived back at their own hotel across town, they felt the day had been like a dream; it was all so surreal. The string of intensity that occurred was difficult to process all at once. Everything they saw at Auschwitz, fearing death, being forcibly submerged under a boat in the Sola River and witnessing two deaths by gunshot, one right after the other, struck them to the core. Charlotte, slow in her movements now, was wholly affected. She was still reeling especially having learned about Paniletti being responsible for Saul's murder, but there was one piece of wisdom she was able to pluck from her brain— she wouldn't understand it all right now. She needed time to process the information and that was okay.

Alex, at least outwardly, didn't show any similar signs of pensiveness. It was obvious to Charlotte that he was processing the day's events in his own way and was deeply affected. The tear she saw run down his face in the gas chamber was a major signifier of that.

Deep down, on their walk back to their hotel, Charlotte hoped she would catch a glimpse of Peter Bremer again but she knew better than to think it would be that easy. Whatever his reasons, he had an agenda and he intended to follow it through to the end. Alex didn't waste a minute prying open the discovered box when they returned safely and gathered in his room.

The box was sealed extremely well but Alex was able to open it without much effort after he broke the lock. Initially thinking the contents must be waterproof, he changed his mind when he saw a smaller box sealed in airtight plastic within the box and unlatched the second box's tight seal to reveal another fully sealed plastic bag further protecting its contents from possible water contact.

Among the items in the bag were a few pieces of gold and some antique German currency. Aside from that, and by far most importantly, was an item which most needed the multiple layers of sealing. It was a leather-bound book. Its pages had turned yellow not so much from the lignin of the paper being exposed to sunlight, but from the air it was sealed in for the last several decades.

In beautiful gold leafing on the front cover was embossed the word "**TREBLINKA**" and underneath it on the bottom right hand corner of the cover was the author's name also written in gold, "Dietrich Rüpel." Alex and Charlotte carefully opened the leather-bound book. They didn't know going into its discovery, but what lied within it was of a magnitude they couldn't have possibly contemplated. It appeared to be a journal; its pages were handwritten and dated. On the front pages was a list of names. There was also a list of names at the beginning of each of the numerous dated entries. Charlotte and Alex were intrigued and it sucked them in immediately.

# Chapter 68

*January 16, 1945 – Auschwitz, Poland*

Otto was cold. His thin pants, held up loosely by worn suspenders, encased his body like a balloon. They used to fit, but with the extreme lack of food over time that was no longer the case. The wind and chill therefore had an open invitation to blow against his bones, which almost protruded through his skin. His nose was frozen and although he enjoyed seeing the constant cloud puffs wafting from his breath, each time he inhaled the chill was no longer fun.

During Violet's brave escape that would get them out of the camp, Otto was not privy to the plan and was unclear as to what his sister was doing over there at the window. As much as he disliked the tight living arrangements in the barracks, at least the mass of bodies kept him warm. Part of him wished he were back there instead of out in the cold with his sister. As shoddy of an alternative as the barracks were, they were better than battling the freezing temperature alone. *Besides, mom should be coming back anytime.* He was keeping a wide eye out for his mother and feared they would miss her return if they left the camp.

Clasping his hands under his armpits to warm them, he had no gloves and the sting of the air was bothersome. Violet continued pushing on the window of the warehouse. *It's not moving. Why is she even trying? Maybe if I walk around a little bit it will help me warm up. Standing here will only turn me into a human popsicle.*

Out in the distance he saw a figure. There was a man on a boat in the middle of the river, which was not yet frozen. Otto had monitored the water over the course of the last several weeks, ever since the cold started to get really bad. He was anxious to see it freeze. When his mother came back they would go ice-skating. He was sure of it because she had taken him the last two winters.

*What is this man doing? I need to know.* He glanced back at Violet who was still focused on her task at hand. *She'll be a while.*

His small feet made equally small prints in the fresh layer of falling snow as he proceeded toward the edge of the fence, which would be his best vantage point to see what the man was doing. It wasn't until he made it to the fence at the northeast boundary of the camp that he could make out what was happening. The man on the water arrived at a point very close to the exact middle of the river and looked around. The snowflakes falling obscured the man's view, and he remained completely oblivious to Otto in the distance. He didn't so much as even look in his direction as he stayed on the cold but not yet frozen water.

Otto watched, wide-eyed and wondering, as the man proceeded to lift a shiny metal box over the side of the boat. The light of the moon reflected off the object and Otto was enthralled. *Oh, how I wish I was out there, not just to wait for the ice to freeze but to be outside of the fence.* His longing was strong but he knew he shouldn't go. His thoughts turned again to Mother. She would be coming back for them.

Otto continued to watch as the captain of the ship threw the treasure overboard. *What was inside?* Imagining the contents was a fun mental game for him to play. A smile crossed his face as he imagined the springtime and diving into the lake to recover what was certainly a treasure chest. For a moment, he imagined he was in another place, at another time, with his mother. She would hold his hand and clap and shout for joy at what a strong boy he was and how well he could swim in the water, having learned the summer before.

These pleasant thoughts distracted him for a blessed moment but were alarmingly disturbed as the figure on the boat turned to head back to shore. Otto caught a glimpse of his face and he gasped in horror. *It's the cruel man who took mother away on our first day in the camp.* Otto wanted to scream at him and yell at him to return his mother immediately but he couldn't. He was numb with fear and the words wouldn't come. Something was holding him back as in that moment Violet grabbed him by the shoulder.

"Komm' schon! Let's go!" was his sister's immediate command. "We'll get caught."

She hadn't noticed and consequently wasn't fazed by the man on the icy cold river, who just dumped a box into the water. When they returned to the warehouse, Otto was happy she dragged him back because she had finally gotten the window open. She boosted him up through it into the warehouse where it was warm and they were able to lay among a large pile of clothing. Although he was freezing, here he would get warm. It was the best he had felt in a long time. He fell asleep soundly and at Violet's insistence stayed absolutely quiet when morning broke.

Otto never got the chance to tell her what he saw in the middle of the river. When they arrived in the city, he was covered again with clothing as they were dumped at a new location. He closed his eyes like Violet told him to and started to count. Sadly he felt the loosening of Violet's grasp, which was keeping them together, until he couldn't feel her at all. He heard the rumble of the truck they arrived in as it drove away, and when he dutifully finished counting, he opened his eyes and she was gone. She had told him he would see magic just like their friend Mathias showed them, but he didn't like this disappearing act at all.

Her words to him to wait for the magic were the last words he ever heard from her. He never saw her again.

# Chapter 69

As Alex and Charlotte stared at it more, they realized the leather-bound book they had found was ostensibly a journal and although it was written in German in neat, cursive penmanship, the messages of the writing emanated from the pages and provided a sense that the contents were not all pleasant. Scattered throughout the pages were black and white photographs of images captured before the end of WWII. Some of the photographs contained the date but for those that weren't dated, the time period was undeniable. As for the journal entries, those stopped on January 16, 1943.

Because it was written in German, Charlotte translated aloud for Alex. She focused first on the lists of names at the beginning of the journal. It was a very long list; both surnames and first names. They were split into categories and labeled accordingly.

*Juden*, which Charlotte knew to be Jews, as well as *Gypsies, Poles, Slavs, homosexuals* and *Behinderte*. The section of lists was titled: "*Meine Eroberungen*," very boldly calling the lists, "My Conquests." When Charlotte read this heading, she could scarcely bring herself to say the words in such a context.

Instantly her mind snapped to judgment and it was a judgment that, as she dug deeper into the book, would prove to be entirely fair. Charlotte could never have imagined a person to be so cruel and sadistic as to go to the lengths of criminality which were documented in the contents of this journal. Charlotte knew hate crimes. She was exposed to the criminals who committed them on an almost daily basis and worked diligently to punish those offenders. In a way she had become desensitized to reading about or prosecuting race based acts of violence and underestimated the evil surrounding them, but she had never been privy to the inner workings of a mind as evil as what she saw being manifested in the depravity of these journal pages.

It was evident from the writings that the book's author was a high-ranking official in the Nazi party. He was a person endowed with a level of power which put him in a position over the lives of others and which he used to blasphemously play God when it came to deciding who lived and who died.

The list of names continued for quite some time as Charlotte and Alex scoured the long section of pages it covered until it eventually stopped. At that point the names were no longer transcribed, apparently having become too numerous and burdensome. Names were relegated to numbers and lives of concentration camp victims became nothing more than statistics.

The sadistic nature of the author, Dietrich Rüpel, was incomprehensible as he tallied in writing each and every victim whose death he was responsible for at the Treblinka Concentration Camp and then became so arrogant and heinous that it became an inconvenience for him to identify them as anything other than a collective number on each individual day.

As Charlotte read, she resolved this book would become available to the world. Instead of using it for its intended purpose as a record of achievement, it would be made public as a testament of the truth and horror of what occurred during the Holocaust. The critics could deny all they wanted, but science was advanced to the point that the age of the paper pages in the book could be confirmed.

Charlotte was struck as she translated and read aloud the journal's dated entries and came upon one extremely poignant section. It was almost poetic in the way it was written, which was a slap in the face to the horrible truth it was describing.

*May 9, 1942*
*The naked and exposed prisoners
have walked into the cottages to take
the poisonous shower that lead them to
their deaths day after day for many
months now. The peaceful cottages built
just for them beckon them come as they
gladly walk under the blossoms of the
blooming trees. They, like lambs to a
lion's den covered in fresh sprigs of
grass, walk towards it unknowing that
the blossoms would be the last signs of
life they would see as they are ushered
into the disguised gas chambers..*
*Some of the children laugh and
play with their toys as they walk along.
When it comes to the children, they are
not the enemy, but it is the blood that
ravages inside of them which is the
enemy. Their blood is what must be
destroyed before it ravages and destroys
us.*
*I have received my orders from
Hitler and I will execute them. These
mass exterminations have been deemed
justifiable and lawful. My orders come
directly from Der Führer, and I am
happy to comply. I have no empathy in
my heart for these scoundrels.*
*Those in the line today and
everyday are enemies to our people.
They are ushered to their extermination
peacefully and it is with grace we lead
them before the hour of their knowing
arrives.*"

Skimming the entries and wanting to select the most
poignant for Alex, Charlotte felt compelled to read several

last entries from January of 1943. The tone of the writing changed dramatically from proud to anxious towards the end:

> *January 1, 1943*
>
> *I have been informed by Der Führer on this first day of the new year that I will now be leaving Auschwitz. I have done something to upset him but I don't know what. He has placed Rudolf Höss as Commander of Auschwitz and I am to go to Treblinka. I cannot understand this. I am a chemist and I can make the formula for Zyklon-B even more powerful and stronger. But I will do what I'm told and I will make Treblinka my kingdom. I will be the ruler. I have been given my first assignment and I will carry it out with exactness. Hitler will see what I am capable of.*
>
> *January 16, 1943*
>
> *I have had some days to consider my next assignment. I will focus on the good of my new position. I will use it to my full advantage. I will bring my dear wife, Ingrid and my daughters, Brigitte and the blond-haired beauty from Auschwitz. I am so happy to have her. She looks just as my little Eva would have looked. My pride and joy, my precious daughter, Eva, will ever live in my heart even though she is now gone.*
>
> *There, at Treblinka, I am the Captain. No longer will I walk in the shadow of Rudolph Höss. I am a Master in my own right.*

> *My accomplishments will carry on as a legacy to the power of the pure race.*

"And there's a photo attached on this page," Charlotte stopped reading to tell Alex. "It's two little girls."

Charlotte stared at the photograph of a beautiful blond headed girl standing, shoulders slumped with sadness, next to a plain looking brown haired, dark eyed girl of a similar age.

"They both look so sad," Charlotte continued.

Charlotte turned the book towards him so he could see the photograph. She didn't want him to miss any of it.

As Alex gazed at the photograph, he stared hard. Drawing the book closer to his eyes he looked intently as if looking for something within the photo that couldn't be seen by natural eyes. He carefully removed the glued photograph from the yellowed page and turned it over expecting to see something else. He was disappointed, however. There was no date or identifiers on the back.

"Please repeat the last section where he talks about loving his biological daughter. What did he say was his daughter's name? I need you to be sure."

"I will bring my dear wife, Ingrid and my daughters, Brigitte and the blond-haired beauty from Auschwitz," Charlotte repeated.

"I know these girls," he said.

"How could you possibly?" Charlotte asked. "Other than you probably saw a similar photograph of them in the museum. There were many photos of the Nazis. Likely some of their children were caught on camera."

"No, that's not it. I know them."

He stared at the photo intently with his eyes fixated on the image, then looked up at Charlotte with tears in his eyes.

"This is her," he said to her, pointing to the curly, blond haired girl in the photo. "It's the little girl who came to me in my dream the night I called you." He paused as if in deep thought before continuing, "And this is my mother." He pointed to the second girl in the photograph with a tear in his eye.

"My mother's name is Brigitte, but she always went by Bridget. I've seen this young face before."

"Your mother? Are you sure?"

"Yes, I'm sure. It's my mother. I know her face. This is the same face I have seen in many pictures of her taken as she was growing up. She was always alone in the pictures I saw though and was never with this girl.

"He writes that his daughter, Eva, had died. Maybe Eva was preferred by her parents over your mother."

"That may explain why my mom never smiled even as an adult. The sadness she carried from childhood must have stayed with her the rest of her life. Now I understand why she refused to talk about her past and why she always wanted more for me. She was trying to fill the void of her own unhappiness. She died three years ago, but she was always so proud of what I had become. She told me I gave her hope."

After a moment of pondering, Charlotte continued reading from the journal, hoping to learn more. She was astonished at the discovery of Alex's descendants, and with the story told through the journal she was able to put together the jumbled pieces of the last two weeks. The answers came quickly.

As his writing moved forward, the author, who they now knew to be the grandfather Alex never knew, continued writing more self-accolades prior to his last entry. He wrote admiringly about Josef Mengele and how he revered his scientific mind. He expressed pleasure that Mengele trusted him with the extermination of those people found to be unfit for life. They would be gassed at Auschwitz and Treblinka and Dietrich recorded his honor from the gesture.

He then went on to relish further, in what he considered his great achievements, as Charlotte read the transcription of yet another lengthy list of 287 names. These were Mengele's victims who were brought on one day alone to be gassed. It appeared as if Dietrich took as much pride in recording the deaths as he did executing them.

Charlotte passed the journal back to Alex when she turned to the last page and saw a familiar symbol at the bottom. They both gasped when they saw the form of a red cross. Just as had now seen many times before, it was the same symbol which brought them to where they were in the first place, only this time, Dietrich took a creative liberty with the symbol and perverted it even further.

After the image of the cross he wrote the letters "R-E-B-L-I-N-K-A," thereby creating his own sadistic logo for his new assignment. Beneath this logo he had written, *"Here will lay the Pride and Joy of the Pure Race."*

The pieces of their mysterious journey were falling together even more. There was a specific reason they were led to this journal in the way they had. The words of Isaac Kanzler were right all along and he had led them on the path of greatest understanding. The clues they had been given were leading them to hidden answers and to the discovery of Alex's ancestry which included a man who forever changed the course of history in the most vile of ways. It wasn't until Charlotte and Alex made this journey that they could fully understand.

Isaac led both she and Alex to be introduced to an inner circle of the Aryan Brotherhood that led to their captivity in the cofferdam and the subsequent trip to Auschwitz. The trip to Auschwitz was made poignantly meaningful because they were forced to look thoroughly at a past many will turn a blind eye to. This was why Isaac had gotten Alex involved. *This was for Alex too and perhaps, most of all.*

As Charlotte continued translating the words of the book in front of her, Alex suddenly cut her off, almost begging her to stop as if he couldn't stand to hear any further detail. "It's clear to me from this journal which direction we are being pointed towards. 'Here will lay the Pride and Joy of the Pure Race.' He also referred to his daughter, Eva, as his pride and joy. Our answer is in Treblinka. That has to be where my daughter is."

"I completely agree," Charlotte concurred, realizing they found their answer.

"Then let's get out of here," Alex responded affirmatively as if it was almost foolish they were still sitting there in a hotel in Auschwitz.

Hurriedly, they gathered what little belongings they had. Alex was exceedingly careful to repackage the journal with the remaining contents of the box and latch it shut. Checking out of the hotel and heading straight for the train station, they were fortunate when they arrived to have to wait less than an hour on the cold, plastic chairs available for them to sit on. As the next train out of town pulled up, they were on it, and were consequently on their way to the Village of Treblinka. Their destination: Treblinka Extermination Camp.

# *Chapter 70*

Their train ride was much smoother this time around. As it glided along the tracks, there was much time for contemplation. Alex focused out the window, staring at the world as it rushed by. This was soothing in a way. The trees came in and out of view in rhythm with the consistent hum of the train.

For a portion of the trip, Charlotte and Alex shared a cabin with a small family consisting of a husband and wife and their two toddler daughters. The tow-headed of the two young children strongly resembled her mother and the other's black skin clearly meant that she was adopted by her fair-skinned parents. The girls entertained themselves in the cabin with laughter and cheerful playing with each other. At one point, the little blond girl smiled at Charlotte and her sister followed her lead and did the same. They then resumed playing together. As the family deboarded the train, Charlotte wasn't remiss in commenting, "No one's born a racist."

Alex smiled.

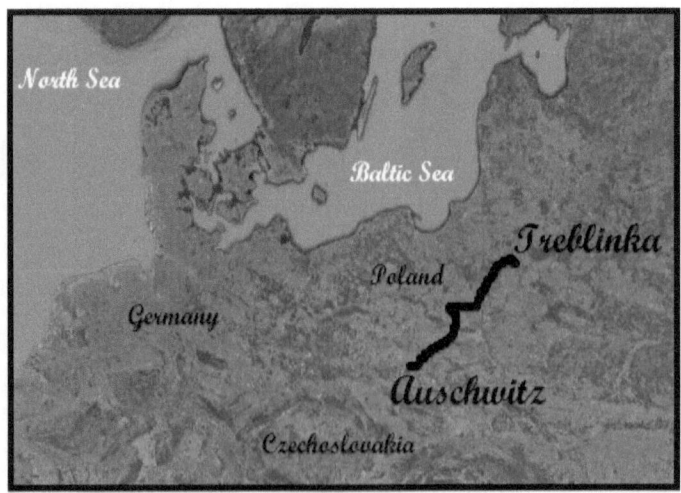

When their time came to exit the train and the Treblinka Village railroad stop was reached, Charlotte didn't think twice about making the necessary trek by foot to the Treblinka extermination camp. They found it, however, to be a long walk. This smaller variety concentration camp was much further off the beaten path than Auschwitz was.

The area smelled of a fresh pine scent, which was magnified by the crispness of the day. Under much different circumstances this would have been a cheerful and festive area. The wind rustled through the trees and there was an eerie silence in the area they travelled. It took some jockeying through the foliage to keep going. The dirt road leading to Treblinka had long since worn away since the camp's desertion. What remained of Treblinka and the surrounding area was a ghost town both in the figurative and literal senses. No one else was around. Although the area was desolate, the almost tangible presence of the lives taken there was incredibly palpable just as it was at Auschwitz.

They first came upon Treblinka I, which was the first of two camps containing the name Treblinka. A short distance away laid the former killing center of the camp, Treblinka II. They began their continued search first with Treblinka I as they made their way to a knoll after climbing a gentle slope. The air whispered to them. Its message was one of remembrance and it spoke with a warning—*If the world fails to remember the tragedies of this place, the camp will disintegrate and take the memories of the past with it.*

All remains of the camp had been destroyed after WWII and in front of them lay a symbolic cemetery crafted from 170,000 various stones. Of the differently shaped and colored stones, 130 represented cities that the almost 900,000 victims of the camp originated from. Like small soldiers parading in a circle, the upright stones stood in solemnity.

Almost breathless at the sight as they passed, they made their way through this open space further into the deep woods to Treblinka II. The lingering history of Treblinka I held a deep lesson, but no Brielle.

They traversed a row of cement pillars lined up parallel to the ground. The pillars stood as a memorial, marking the rail spur, which once led prisoners from the Treblinka I labor camp to Treblinka II, the killing camp, and lay as cold and rigid as the rest of their surroundings.

Eventually, they made their way to Treblinka, which was the first of two camps containing the name Treblinka. Treblinka II was distinguished with the Roman numeral behind it and their instincts told them to start with the first camp. Although the path was longer and far less traversed than the prior walking path they took to Auschwitz, they felt much more confident than at any other point in their journey. They were close to the end and they knew it.

"This next section has to be it, Charlotte," Alex said. "If my daughter's not here I don't know if I can take much more."

His confidence in success was raised minimally knowing that Peter, the elusive Head of Security, was very likely in the area. *Some vacation*, he scoffed to himself, recalling his phone call to the United Nations. Given the long arduous code-laden trail they had followed and all the enciphered messages delivered, which now were coming to a head, Alex still felt empty knowing his child was not in his arms.

The air was cold as they continued. Alex took to walking so briskly in anticipation at times that he was essentially jogging. Given he was not in this alone he would regularly force himself to slow down to accommodate Charlotte who was not moving as quickly. Her road to recovery was definitely on the right track, but she was still unable to keep up with his swiftness.

As Charlotte and Alex entered the camp, the fallen leaves from nearby trees cracked under their feet. They entered through the single gate leading into the camp. It was positioned wide open, as if to beckon them in, and unnervingly signified someone was expecting them. As they arrived and crossed the threshold into the death camp, a chill ran down their spines. Looking fervently for any signs of life, namely his daughter's, Alex took a passing glance over the entirety of the camp hoping to get some sense of where he should go to look. The silence returned no clues.

The two proceeded forward. Treading cautiously and not knowing what they might find in the deserted camp. The eerie ambiance of this place reminded Alex that he had purchased a weapon after Charlotte's abduction in Israel. He hadn't wanted Charlotte to worry unnecessarily and hadn't told her about it. He had been extremely discreet about it, keeping it tucked in his pants and concealing it even when he had undressed to find the journal. Charlotte had no idea he was previously in possession of the weapon, but it didn't matter now. Between clinging to the box and fleeing for safety, the gun was one item lost in the Sola River when they were forced to overturn the boat.

On one hand, he regretted the loss because things could have gone much differently at the riverbank had he been armed, but on the other hand, he was happy in hindsight to have not been the one to kill Justin or Paniletti. Taking a life was a depressing prospect for him under any circumstance.

The care with which Alex and Charlotte proceeded quickly evaporated when the silence was broken by the cry of a baby. Alex's pace immediately quickened and in no time he was in full sprint mode. *It was Brielle!* He knew it just by the sound of her cry and tears rolled down his face at the thought of finally finding her.

Turning left toward the direction of the call, he saw, nestled between the dense trees in the distance, a small building detached from the camp. *Someone must have lived on the outskirts of the camp*, Alex thought. Smoke was rising up and billowing out through the stone chimney on the roof. Wasting no time after laying eyes upon it, Alex entered the metal, gated yard of the residence and ran to the door.

Frustratingly, it was locked and wouldn't budge. Charlotte wasn't far behind and when she arrived they united their strength to get the door to budge.

"It's solid wood. It's not going anywhere," Alex reported.

The home appeared dim inside and the windows were covered by bars. Curtains also hung in front of the windows making it impossible for them to see anything within. They circled the house and eventually made their way back to the front door, staring intently at it and trying to figure out another way in.

As Alex considered scouring the area for a hatchet, ax or any other tool to make entry, he was kicking himself for losing the gun. His thoughts of anger toward himself were interrupted, however, by the slow sound of the clanking metal gate behind them. Without any hesitation, they both turned and were thrown into momentary shock to see their personal enigma. It was the man in the military fatigues, the Head of Security for the United Nations. *Peter Bremer!*

Securing the gate with a lock, Peter was holding a rifle upright with the butt of the gun cocked against his arm and his finger on the trigger.

"There's no escape now, Senator," Peter warned.

# Chapter 71

"I want my daughter!" Alex replied sternly, taking courage in the thought that this man once had the opportunity to kill him but didn't take it.

Peter stood motionless, simply staring with the weapon firmly in place.

"I want my daughter now!" Alex repeated angrily.

Peter remained unresponsive as Alex finally broke and went after him. Lunging forward, he bulldozed his way toward Peter, risking his life in the face of a gun, and not ceasing until Peter shot three loud bullets into the air.

A nearby flock of sparrows took flight and in a cloud of black flew away with haste. They had zero interest in wanting to stick around for more. The sound of the gunfire, being in such close proximity to Alex and Charlotte, was deafening and Alex was forced to retreat at the intense sound and the seeming shaking of the Earth.

Simultaneously, Brielle's shrill cry was heard again. Alex looked back at the old brick house in the direction of the cries and then returned his gaze to Peter to gauge his response. Alex sensed the distinction in this cry as opposed to the cry that welcomed them into the camp. This cry was loud and shrill and though Brielle sounded as if she was in torturous misery, his heart swelled with the simple knowledge of her being alive.

Charlotte stood silently, hoping to remain invisible and out of any line of fire. Peter remained staring at Alex. He seemingly had an unhealthy fascination with the Senator as he went so far as to abduct his child and this obsession was evident in his stare. In complying with her strategy, Charlotte thought, *It's best to remain frozen. I'll wait until the man with the gun addresses me.*

The wheels were turning in Alex's head as flashes of ideas filled his mind as to what to do next. As if knowing what he was thinking, Peter responded by grabbing from Alex the precious box containing Dietrich's journal and then reaching into his own pocket and retrieving two pairs of handcuffs. Charlotte winced at their sight.

Approaching Alex and bidding Charlotte to stand beside him with the gun aimed at chest level towards them, Peter threw the handcuffs at their feet and directed them to put them on each other with their arms in front of them. He then bound their handcuffs together with a third set so as to make it impossible to escape.

"If you want your daughter to live you will do as I say. Exactly what I say," he ordered.

"What do you want?" Alex responded, acknowledging to himself he had no choice but to listen.

Charlotte continued to remain silent.

"We've done everything you've asked of us, haven't we? We've played your game. Followed the clues."

Charlotte cringed with worry that his verbal backlash would set Peter off again. She didn't want to see the rifle fired any more.

"You will exit through this gate," Peter commanded, pointing to where they entered the house's front yard. To Charlotte's pleasant surprise he was simply ignoring Alex's snide remarks. "I will be right behind you with this gun pointed at your backs."

Alex and Charlotte did exactly as he commanded and continued to obey his will when he ordered them to turn immediately right and walk straight ahead. Awkwardly, with their wrists bound together they negotiated the turn and began marching straight ahead as Peter followed closely behind as promised. The barrel of the gun rubbed against their backs in moments when he got too close. They marched in silence, not knowing what was in store for them.

At the halfway point Peter advised them, "It's 300 meters more just down that decline."

Sure enough the dirt directly in front of them started to decline and slope downwards at a 15 degree angle. Charlotte and Alex continued down obediently, being careful to do exactly as instructed and not providing any more reason for discontent. They were being led back to the site of Treblinka II.

As they drew closer their eyes settled on a slight mound memorial stones of melted basalt set atop a concrete fundamental plate stretching about 200 feet long and 15 feet wide. They both wondered nervously what it could be. *Where was he taking them?*

As they got closer, they realized the pile of dirt was, in fact, their destination and they continued to walk until confronted with a small hole directly before it. The freshness of this hole's existence was apparent by the shovel lying beside it.

"Stop here," Peter ordered.

Glad for that one command, they both stopped just short of falling with one leg each into the hole. It was rectangular with unique dimensions. Approximately six feet deep it was only three feet long by three feet wide.

"I want to tell you the story about a man," Peter began. "Senator, you now know him to be your grandfather. His name is Dietrich Rüpel and he is one of the cruelest human beings to ever walk the face of this Earth"

*If Peter didn't have Alex's attention before, he certainly did now. This was about Alex. It was all about him.*

Peter continued, "Dietrich Rüpel was the Commander of this camp during its operating years. He was appointed to the position directly by Adolf Hitler. I'm sure you're familiar with him," he said with sarcasm. "Dietrich kept something that was so sacred to him that he made sure it would not be lost, and buried it securely in the water of the Sola River. He made sure to drop it in the deepest part of the river and in a place he was certain would never be discovered by anyone until he could return for it. That opportunity never came as his presence back in the country of his crimes would surely mean his imprisonment and death.

"He received word that the Americans were infiltrating the Nazi camps and he fled to the United States. He was recruited by the U.S. government to work as a chemist in what was a sad compromise on the part of the United States rationalized by their need for scientists.

"Dietrich Rüpel is a heartless and soulless man who did only one kind thing in his life. He spared the life of Violet Bremer, who he gave the name of Eva, and who is now known in the world as Violet LeMond."

Charlotte gasped. *He was talking about Nurse LeMond!*

Peter continued, "And your grandfather only did so because of his fondness for Violet. He was obsessed with her physical beauty. As a young girl she looked the part of the perfect Aryan. If she hadn't been so fortunate she would be dead.

"Before Violet was forced into his family, she was ripped from her home by Nazi soldiers, stripped of her mother and taken from the grasp of the only person she had left in the world, her younger brother, Otto Klaus Bremer. He is my father. I am proudly his son, as is my brother, Isaac Kanzler Bremer."

At this time, Charlotte could not contain her surprise. Her eyes opened wide like saucers and she stared back at him in almost utter disbelief. *Everything is coming together. Peter was Isaac's brother. They in turn are related to Nurse Violet LeMond who had said nothing to them about it, but in her early life suffered gravely at the hands of the Nazis.*

"Dietrich Rüpel took everything from my family," Peter continued. "My father, Otto, knew there was a secret being buried in the Sola River. He saw it the night your grandfather dumped it over the side of his boat. Even as a small child my father recognized the distinct evil within him and understood he had many things to hide. He knew there would be secrets contained in the book and he longed for them, however he too would never return. He couldn't bear to come back to the place where he was tortured, even if it meant getting proof of the atrocities born by the victims of the Holocaust.

"My Aunt Violet is a strong kind girl who in her youth with boldness led my father in escaping the horrors of the Nazi concentration camps. She saved his life and her own and for all the years after she has loved strongly and sweetly and made the world a better place."

Peter squared his body and looked Alex firmly in the eyes. "She, as my father's sister, left the grips of her Nazi upbringing as soon as she was able. Later in life she acquired a successful career which she loves and married and bore two beautiful children of her own. She has fought hard to suppress the grief that has come to consume her by virtue of the things inflicted upon her in her early years. She has been luckier than my father, who after escaping from Auschwitz was taken in by a loving man and wife who were unable to bear children of their own. Sadly, his strength to cope with the pain of his past gave out and he took his own life at the age of 44. Nevertheless, his memory and posterity live on as a grand legacy through myself and my brother Isaac Kanzler. We will make sure he is not forgotten."

Charlotte audibly gasped. She was struck by the sadness of Peter's family's life and the demise of his father, Otto, struck Charlotte to the core. She realized there was a reason Peter looked familiar. He was the brother of Isaac Kanzler, and thereby also a Jew. They resembled each other in many respects.

"My father shared with his sons the witness of his experience in Auschwitz," Peter went on. Referring to the box he was holding he said, "He always wanted to recover this secret box. He always wanted it to be exposed, whatever it contained, and was certain it would serve as living proof of the atrocities of the Holocaust. He passed on the information as to its whereabouts to my brother Isaac and I in an effort to ensure the struggles of the Jews weren't for naught. Though he told us years ago where we could find it, my brother and I knew no one would believe us if we dug it up ourselves. Though my father could never bring himself to come back to the place of his struggle, I am his mouthpiece and I am the mouthpiece for those victims of genocide who can't speak for themselves.

"Sadly, he never saw his sister again. She had a new name and neither one of them had the resources to track each other down. My brother and I have been able to find her just in the last year. We told her about our father and our plan for you."

"What do the sins of my grandfather have to do with my daughter?" Alex questioned after hearing what Peter revealed to them. "Why have you kidnapped her? You can't redeem evils of the past through vengeance now."

"I'm glad you asked, Senator, because I've been anxious to tell you. The answer to your question lies in the entire reason your journey to this place was so elaborately arranged. You would not have understood any other way. You have been exposed on your journey to the treachery of confinement, hunger, thirst and illness. You have had the opportunity to see from the inside, the mechanics of the Aryan Brotherhood that continue to perpetuate the Nazi ideologies of the past and carry on the fight for ethnic cleansing. You read the letter I wrote, which I left in your daughter's bed; the letter putting you on the path to this moment. You have a choice to make."

"I still don't understand," Alex responded sincerely, even though he would never forget the encrypted letter.

"Dietrich Rüpel, as one person, took hundreds of thousands of lives. He robbed them of the opportunity to live life and eliminated all prospects of a future for them. It was that same man who took everything a nine-year-old Otto and a thirteen-year-old Violet held dear, and made things such that I never got to know my grandmother, Katherine.

"Nonetheless, I have become the man I am today because of who my father was and because of who the senseless victims of the Holocaust were. My father intended to make sure their legacy is never forgotten and I will see this through until my dying day. I have served in the United States Army for the last 15 years. With the help of our father's instructions and my ability to acquire a military grade map of Poland, Isaac and I were able to set you on the right course. We have been working towards this for many years.

"Prior to my current position with the United Nations, I was stationed for the last four years of my military career in South Korea where with my fellow American soldiers we offered protection and strength along the North Korea border.

"I have felt the consequences of what occurred because of Hitler, an evil dictator, in World War II Germany with his hate-filled ideas and genocide. I have also seen the atrocities which occur at the hands of Kim Jong-il, an evil dictator in North Korea with his own hate-filled ideas and horrific genocide. Because of this, the terrors of the Holocaust are not in the past and its modern day equivalent is occurring as we speak. It is happening today, right at this moment, and I have seen what can happen when no one speaks up. I am speaking up now, Senator, and I am urging you to do the same."

Directing their attention to the mound of stones in front of them, Peter continued, "I want you to take a look at what stands in front of you and what stands right below you. The stones of basalt you see laying in a line, as if covering a long dark secret, are exactly what they appear to be. This is the sight of one of the horrific mass graves of the Holocaust. Here marks the cremation pit where bodies of innocent Jews were burned. Below that dirt lays thousands of bodies of Jews who didn't deserve to die, but were nonetheless killed and buried here over four decades ago before they were burned.

"What is shrouded in stone was once a large open pit descending 20 feet into the ground. In small groups Nazi soldiers ordered the victims who now lay in this grave to stand in front of it where each one was shot at point blank range. When the Nazis had no more place for those gassed with cyanide in the chambers, they dumped their bodies here also, on top of those who already lay in death."

"I am truly sorry for the torture your family went through," Alex said in sympathy. "It was just in Auschwitz where I learned that Dietrich Rüpel is my grandfather. My parents told me nothing about him. Ever. And I assure you my family has nothing to do with him, nor do we intend to."

"That is precisely the problem," Peter responded. "You have nothing to do with him. You have stayed neutral and have not spoken up against him or his cause. He has continued to ravage the United States much like he did in Germany and Poland, only this time he has been shrouded in secrecy and hidden like the journal that evidences his crimes.

"After coming to America Dietrich Rüpel went on to become a person of large influence in the world and secretly helped shape the course of history there too. Just as the atrocities he committed here in Treblinka, in Auschwitz and as a leader of the white supremacy ideology, he has continued to make changes in people's lives for the very worst.

"He has pushed forward a culture of hatred and cruelty. He brought his prejudices and capacity for evil with him to the United States. He has participated largely in the Ku Klux Klan and became a founding member of the Aryan Brotherhood."

"What do you want from me?" Alex questioned him, still looking for answers.

"Do you remember the recent Senate vote surrounding the Genocide Prevention Act? The vote that was placed before you and each of the members of the United States' Senate?"

Of course Alex remembered this bill. It was put to vote only weeks prior—the day before Brielle's abduction. He recalled it was Senator Timothy Carlisle who eloquently summarized the bill when he said, "This legislation will help demonstrate to the Iraqi regime just how seriously our country views its campaign against the Kurds. In addition, it will help assure that US tax dollars do not subsidize the Iraqis."

Nevertheless, there were the critics and naysayers, and Alex was at their lead. Clearly his public opposition to the bill caught the attention of Peter.

"Yes, it was just a couple of weeks ago," he admitted. "Right before Brielle—" he couldn't finish that statement; not with the man who abducted his daughter.

"And do you remember that you led the Senate away from passage of the bill?  There were many who were in favor of stopping the spread of hate at its roots and speaking up to say 'it's not okay to stand idly by while hate moves forward.'"

Peter continued without letting him respond, "And you, as a voice of the Nation, said 'No.' No, because you do not value even the slightest of efforts to stop racial hatred. You have done nothing to hinder the spreading of the legacy of hate your grandfather has devoted his life to even though you are in a position to do so.

"For your information, after immigrating to the United States, your grandfather has risen to become the most high-ranking member of the Aryan Brotherhood still alive. He continues his work and serves as the lifeline on the outside for financing the Brotherhood's desecrations under the name August Bäcker."

"You mean to tell me he's still alive?" Alex asked in shock, hardly able to believe what was being said to him. Charlotte, for her part, was floored she now had this monumental piece of information she sought after for so long.

Peter turned to Charlotte. "Ms. Weiss, you're welcome. He now is known as August Bäcker of North Dakota. That along with the identity of your friend's killer is the information promised to you by my brother if you were successful in this journey."

Turning his attention back to Alex he said, "And yes, he's still alive and he's still continuing in the work. The only reason I haven't killed him myself is because one member of my family has got to stay out of prison and I would surely be arrested for murder in the United States. We can't share the truth otherwise. Also, equally important to me now is that I have a family of my own. I have a wife, Myung-Hee, who is from North Korea and is a witness to the modern day Holocaust happening as we speak. Senator Card, you have got to act. You are one of the few who can pave the way for change."

As she and Alex stood in front of a mass grave, still bound together at the wrists, a burst of excitement sparked inside Charlotte despite the gravity of the information being revealed to them. Isaac Kanzler knew it all along, but he wanted her to find out for herself and gain a better understanding of the impacts of her work. She knew what her role was to be at the conclusion of this turmoil, but Peter's ambition for Alex was still unclear to her.

Peter clarified that question with his next instruction to Alex. "You must change your mindset, Senator Card. You are in a rare position of supreme power to change the course of history and bring redemption to what your grandfather and the Nazis took from millions."

His message was becoming clearer as his words stopped suddenly. The mood grew even heavier as they heard footsteps coming up slowly behind them. Peter remained unflinching as he knew what was coming, but Charlotte feared the worst and waited with bated breath.

# Chapter 72

Whoever it was that was approaching was coming eerily close, but instead of making contact, passed by Charlotte and Alex to arrive at Peter's side. Peter then led the thin and beautiful North Korean woman to the other side of the small hole.

"I would like to introduce you to my wife, Myung-Hee. She is very aware of you Senator Card, and though she doesn't speak English she has a message for you."

Alex stared in horror as he studied her and noticed she was clinging to a small wooden casket just large enough to contain a small infant.

Alex gasped and shouted. "I've done everything you've asked of me. I've listened to what you've said, but if you've killed my daughter, so help me God, you can destroy me and I don't care whether I live or die. I will <u>never</u> do anything for you!"

Myung-Hee began to tremble at his screams. Peter placed his arm around her shoulders for comfort and in a calm voice responded, "When I was stationed in South Korea I felt the tangible sense of impending doom that plagues the people of Korea every second of every day. From the South, there was the unceasing, constant threat of an attack by North Korea and an obliteration of their society."

Peter was making it a point to stress these details to ensure Alex was aware of the harsh realities he had witnessed in Korea.

"That is daily life in the South. But in the North it is much worse," Peter continued. "Despite the gravity of the concerns of each and every South Korean, tyranny is much more real and tangible on the North side of the Korean Demilitarized Zone. It is a plague that serves as a modern day Holocaust under our noses and Myung-Hee is a living witness of it."

Next turning to his wife he elaborated, "Myung-Hee is one of the very few and very lucky ones who were able to escape North Korea. She was confined to a prison camp for five months and when her beauty caught the attention of a high-ranking guard, she found herself in a position that gave her a sliver of a chance at survival and the hope of gaining freedom.

"Because of the abuse she has suffered and the agony it has instilled in her mind and body, she can never again bear children. For this she is very sad but is also grateful. The North Korean guard who later took her by his side and repeatedly raped her each and every day could not impregnate her as a result of an earlier abortion. The child she once bore within her was murdered. It was involuntarily aborted in a very violent way at 35 weeks along. The baby was fully formed at the time but the gruesome method of its delivery was carried out by Myung-Hee's imprisoners. They murdered the baby inside her before it had any chance of life outside the womb.

"You can't see the scars inside her which will prevent her from procreating again, but you will see the marks on her wrists and ankles from the pressure of the shackles that bound her while she was stuffed in a prison camp cage. Myung-Hee was literally surrounded by thousands who were equally mal-treated; confined like gophers in a flooded hole.

"They were, and still are, often forced into positions standing for long periods of time with their arms locked behind their backs in an elevated position that make it difficult to gasp for air. They are confined in cages like animals, unable to stand when locked in horizontal cages and unable to sit when confined in vertical cages. Often desperate for the slightest bit of food or water, the prisoners are emaciated beyond recognition and the otherwise disturbing inhabitation of rats in their filthy conditions is a welcome addition. The captives spend their small bits of energy trying to capture that one thing that could provide them sustenance."

As Peter spoke, Myung-Hee stood shaking in the cold Treblinka air, still traumatized and unsure of what would ultimately become of her.

Peter continued, "Myung-Hee has told me her story and wants me to share it with you. She feels a longing to help those who are still left behind and speak for them where they cannot speak for themselves. She was one of the exceptionally lucky and feels an obligation to inform the world of the dark underbelly of the North Korean prison camps."

Myung-Hee stood, still trembling, as he finished his words. Despite her trepidation in the moment, she refused to let the language barrier hinder her from communicating with Alex and she used drawings to raise awareness of the perversions occurring in her country of birth. Tenderly setting the small coffin onto the ground in front of the now obviously perfectly sized hole, she reached into the pocket of her plain oversized dress, pulled out a small sketchbook and presented it to Alex. This was a gift for him. She carefully flipped through the book and approached him as she meticulously turned to each page. Being that he was at present in handcuffs and rendered unable to move, she had his full attention. Alex observed that it was with great ability she could translate images from her mind onto paper and graphically illustrated what others could not see for themselves. There was a look of consternation on her face and moisture in her eyes as tears welled as she showed them to him.

Isaac and Peter had laid out the plan for this moment and she had anxiously anticipated Alex's arrival with excited nervousness. She was told who she was talking to and this was her time to make her plea. She was so invested in this meeting she was willing to sacrifice a part of her own child's body to communicate. It was her baby whose limb Alex had retrieved from the locker in Auschwitz.

After showing him each horrible drawing of real life North Korean prison camps, she placed the book in Alex's pocket and returned to the small casket.

Alex winced as she slowly opened the casket to reveal a small, dark-skinned baby girl lying on a cushion of pure white material. As horrific as the sight in front of him was, he breathed a sigh of relief to see it was not Brielle. Myung-Hee had done her best to dress the wounded baby and cover the scars and amputations it sustained from its murder in the womb. Underneath the clothing, both her legs and one arm were cut off and her tiny right eye was gorged out.

Myung-Hee had been pregnant when she arrived at the camp and it was immediately upon her arrival that the abuse and violations against her body began. The baby inside her was her first and only child and it was quickly executed inside her, ripped out and dismembered. The remains of her baby that were returned to her were meant to serve as a further act of cruelty, and she had clung to them, carrying them in a small burlap sack whenever she could. She remained with her child until this day, in which she would provide a proper burial.

None of the four present could hold back tears at the body in front of them. The intensity of the moment and the gravity of the small life and desecrated remains lying before them stirred their emotions to the point of weeping.

Peter was slightly less emotional than the others. He had prepared for this moment for what seemed like a lifetime.

Scanning the length of the mass grave he spoke up again, particularly addressing Alex, "This camp, and the numerous concentration camps which remain standing today serve as a reminder of our obligation to speak up. This massive grave serves as a reminder that one person has the ability to make and take lives and to penetrate the world with good or evil." Motioning to Myung-Hee he said, "This woman and this child are a symbol of the hate and discrimination continuing to plague the world today."

Myung-Hee then kissed the remains of her child. With the exception of her eye and right leg that Alex couldn't bear to have kept with him, the baby girl's limbs were all now in the casket. She closed it slowly and carefully tied a rope around the casket. She then ceremoniously lowered it into the hole, bowing her head further as the fragile body descended into the earth. Its last moments above the ground having passed, Peter cut the rope with a knife and pulled it from the grave. Myung-Hee joined him in the process of placing the fresh dirt atop the coffin. The dirt was waiting in a pile near the hole after being dug from the earth for this very moment. Peter then plucked a nearby pink wildflower from the ground and placed it on the tiny grave.

Charlotte and Alex were both moved to the point they were brought to their knees and bent to the ground. The tone immediately softened and turned from one of confrontation to one of grieving. In what had to be a mutual effort, the two gathered handfuls of dirt and assisted Myung-Hee in the burial. They wept with her until she had no further tears.

When the grave was filled, Peter tenderly patted the earth as Myung-Hee took one last dip to the ground to hover over her daughter's body. He then guided her up sweetly, lifting her back to a standing position. Slowly as Alex and Charlotte also rose, Peter reached inside his pocket and retrieved the handcuff key, holding it in front of them.

As he did so he made sure to say, "The end goal, Senator Card, your hope of being reunited with your daughter, has been hard fought.

"Your journey here has all been arranged because of my obligation, my wife's obligation and my brother's obligation, as members of humanity, to speak up against genocide in all its forms. You have been a target, Senator, in a very real sense because you hold an incredible gift. You hold a position of power which comes with an incredible responsibility. You are a mouthpiece for the United States. The goal we have sought in placing your daughter, in jeopardy has been to force you to see the magnitude of the consequences that come from failing to speak up and failing to act. Those consequences are grave."

"I'm very sorry," Alex tried to reason with him, eyeing the key. "What you're forgetting, however, is that it's not so simple. What you're asking requires global cooperation. China, for example, has major ties with Korea, and as one of the three top powers in the United Nations it's impossible to convince them that action must be taken."

"Senator, you now have an obligation, given what you know, to speak up and make a difference. If you fail to do so, there will be serious consequences. You must tell other world leaders what you now know and what you have personally been a witness to. With this knowledge, you can no longer fail to act."

"If you give me my baby, I will do everything in my power. You have my word," he promised Peter.

With that, Peter bowed his head and turned to Myung-Hee. Touching her shoulder, he gave her one last opportunity to rest her eyes upon her daughter's grave. He then lifted his rifle, pointed it straight into the air and shot 21 deafening bullets in reverence for the child whose life was taken far too soon. There was a look in his eyes signifying his heartfelt intent to honor the little bit of life she lived inside her mother's body.

As the final bullet rang, the shrill sound of a baby was heard again in the distance at Treblinka. Peter unlocked their handcuffs and in a final gesture handed Alex the box they risked their lives in the Sola River to get. Atop the box he placed a second key. This one had no engraven images and no clues to decipher. *Finally.* It was a simple key that unlocked a very important door.

A look of trust filled Peter's eyes.

"We have done all we can do now. The rest is up to you."

As the wind waved through Myung-Hee's long black hair she led Peter away towards the exit. Hand in hand they walked, leaving behind a past they had given their all to make sure was never repeated.

Charlotte waited with Alex and watched them walk away, confirming this was really their opportunity to retrieve what they came for. Just seconds passed as Brielle continued to cry in the distance and being able to wait no longer, Alex ran once again toward the sound of her voice. He didn't pause further to see whether Peter would react, and Peter and Myung-Hee didn't so much as flinch or look over as he passed them by and ran towards his child.

Approaching the building, Alex raced to the doorway and just about jumped for joy to find the key worked to unlock it. Running inside, he saw there in the middle of a small room, a wicker bassinette with the beautiful sight of Brielle carefully swaddled and crying for him. She was well dressed and well fed. The set of pajamas she was taken in had since been washed and were lying neatly folded beside her. Her hair was combed and she had new shoes. Alex picked her up and held her close. Soothing and calming her, her cries soon began to fade into a steady breathing that was the hum of perfect peace.

Charlotte approached behind him.

"That's the most beautiful sight I've seen in a long time," she remarked.

Inside the bassinette she noticed a full bottle of formula and a small baby bag filled with diapers and supplies for their trip back to New York. Much less conspicuously, tucked in the corner of the bassinette, was a single color photograph. Left meticulously by Peter, it was the photograph that Benjamin Stansfeld was killed for and was the crucial piece of evidence Charlotte would need to bring the Aryan Brotherhood to its knees. It was clear the picture was taken without its subjects' knowledge, but was even clearer as to the subjects' identities. Plain as day it was a photograph of Paniletti standing closely next to Dietrich Rüpel. Both donned in white robes with tall white hoods of the Ku Klux Klan in their hands, they smiled at a blazing fire in front of them.

# *Chapter 73*

This time they took an airline home. Alex bought first class tickets so Charlotte could sleep and he could comfortably enjoy just holding his daughter. Charlotte slept the entire way back to New York City, as did Brielle, and Alex was content to see that. A look of sheer peace covered his face. He held the pad of Myung-Hee's drawings close to him along with Dietrich's journal. Each was a record of infinite value

His time in the air was sufficiently long enough to come to terms with the fact that his marriage was over. He accepted what he had known all along but wanted to ignore; his wife would be reunited with their daughter but she was never coming back to him. He dismissed this reality for the time being by taking solace in the fact that his daughter was alive. That was the only thing that mattered.

The ten hour and 39 minute flight back to New York from Poland flew by in the most literal and figurative of senses. Using almost all the time for pondering, Alex stepped off the plane a different man than when he left New York. He walked off triumphantly with a plan in place.

The timing of their plane's arrival put them back on home turf at John F. Kennedy International airport mid-morning on a Sunday. This was opportune given concerns over jet lag. Without luggage of any type and rolling into town like vagrants, Charlotte hailed a cab to take her home. Before getting in was strongly tempted to kiss the ground beneath her feet.

Alex was much more concerned with his next course of action. Turning to her, he made a request, "I'd like you to meet me at the United Nations Compound on Wednesday morning if you can. There's something I'd like to go over with you."

"The UN? Fancy. I'll be there," Charlotte assured him. "Today though I'm going straight home to sleep in my own bed and enjoy a state of comatose that will hopefully last until then."

Alex leaned over, with Brielle still in his arms, and hugged her. He kissed her on the top of her head before she entered the cab and was driven away. Then when she arrived home, just as she said she would, she slept on and off until Wednesday morning.

Charlotte had not been remiss before her journey home, however, in placing a very important call while at the airport in Poland. She alerted the authorities to the true identity of August Bäcker and knew his arrest was underway. Alex was keeping the journal and photograph with him and knowing the evidence to seal Dietrich's fate was secure with him, Charlotte was able to sleep peacefully.

# Chapter 74

Charlotte would see it later as it was repeated continuously in the news over the next couple of days. Alex held a press conference the day after their arrival in New York. He took the opportunity almost immediately upon arriving back in the States to inform the news media about the gruesome history he learned on his overseas voyage and the heritage from which he came. It was also at this time that Dietrich Rüpel's journal was revealed to the world. It was written in Dietrich's hand and contained photographs of his descendants. The life he lived for so long in the United States under the color of another identity was now stripped from him. No longer could he remain without his secret being known.

Dietrich himself was made aware of the discovery of his journal with the live media broadcast of the press conference. The light from his television seemed brighter and burned his eyes as his precious journal was broadcast to the masses. *Why did the camera have to zoom in on his book? This is the day I have dreaded.*

Previous to his journal's unfortunate reveal, he wondered what had happened to Justin and Paniletti when they didn't return with his book. This was not because he cared for them, however. It was insignificant to him whether they were still alive or died a horrible death, but rather his anger was spurned that they had failed to complete their assigned task and obey his orders. This was perhaps his most important ordered task to date as Grand Imperial Wizard, and it was essential one of them return with his journal. *They both failed.*

Dietrich looked out the clouded window of the home in Hannah he had carefully created. He looked out at its obscure entrance points, knowing well that the solitude in which he had lived couldn't save him now. The drone of the television sounded in his ears as his eyes stared desperately and the broadcast hadn't even ended when he heard the police sirens blaring in the distance. They were quickly approaching. He watched as the dust from their speeding patrol cars kicked up on the nearby dirt before penetrating the barrier of his property.

His life of anonymity was now over. At all moments after he fled Europe in 1945, he had lived a life with one eye always open.

Forty three years of looking over his shoulder was now at an end. Being too old and too weak to evade the police any further he made the conscious decision he would not be taken alive. He had lived his life completely on his terms and wasn't about to stop now. To his last dying breath he would reign supreme. He had controlled how he lived and he would control how he died.

On this day, he was 89-years-old, and Dietrich's muscle, which once held the aiming pistol on the naked Jews in front of the mass grave at Auschwitz, was long since gone and his skin was thin and frail like those he had victimized in the concentration camps in decades past. He closed his eyes as he leaned back in his aged recliner, still clutching the rifle he always carried. He took a deep breath and his mind raced. It was like a steel trap, cold and unforgiving like the memories rushing through it which could not escape.

*I wonder if this is how the Jews felt,* he thought for a mere second as he closed his eyes. The room was dim as the dusk outside leaked its way in through the window. The rhythmic ticking of the grandfather clock down the hall echoed in his ears, interjecting the noise of the sirens surrounding him. He felt alone. The pockets of his heart were empty and he was haunted by the thoughts of what might have been if he had chosen to live his life differently.

As the dimness continued to enshroud him, his eyes opened and he looked to the nightstand and saw his token bottle. Filled with cyanide, it beckoned to him and he knew it marked the end. It had to be done. He clutched the small bottle in his feeble, wrinkled hand and felt the coldness against his thin skin. Although his mind raced, he was eerily calm. This bottle was like an old friend coming to take him home. Soon he would be breathless; lifeless. That was the way it had to be.

One more breath, and then it went down, stinging as it passed his tongue and throat. Setting the bottle back on the nightstand, it was now time to wait. It would only be a minute. His chest began to heave while he took in his last view of the world as the sun finally sank. His pulse raced and his throat tightened. Slowly the breaths began to elude him as the clock continued to tick. One more gasp and his eyes closed, shutting out the world around him. His body went limp and then it was over. For a second time he was dead.

# Chapter 75

*October 3, 1988*

Charlotte arrived in the lobby of the United Nations Headquarters on Wednesday morning looking clean and beautiful. From there, she was personally escorted down a long hallway by Alex. His arrival back in New York was a welcome event for his staff and his top advisor was happy to set him up to present to the UN. He was slated to address the quorum of ambassadors this morning.

By now the die was cast. Alex had made up his mind and he knew exactly what he needed to do. He was turning to this group of world leaders for help. Given his historic approach to problem solving within the realm of foreign relations, his next move would come as a proposition that had never been contemplated he would be the initiator of. With all he and Charlotte had gone through, he wanted her to be there to see it.

It came first as a plea and well-documented plan to the United Nations Assembly. In as powerful and poignant a speech as he had ever given, Alex unfolded to the Assembly, and thereby the world, the truth of what he learned in his journey across the ocean. He introduced them to a concept that would be novel in the making and which required cooperation of the international community to support.

He was prompting a movement which would take the cooperation of not just the United States, but also the member states of the United Nations and the international community in order to recognize the importance of stopping genocide.

"This is our world," he vocalized loudly as he stood at the podium before the elite group. "We have an obligation to stand up for what is right if we want to keep that world from crumbling. We must stand together and speak up against evil acts of torture, desecration, murder and infringement of human rights and stomp them out!

"Remember the Ottoman Turks in the Armenian Genocide from 1915 to 1923? Mao Zedong in China, 1949 to 1976? Stalin's death camps in the USSR with their atrocities that plagued the Earth from 1929-1953? The Khmer Rouge in Cambodia was just in the last decade. All over the world and throughout history. People have been killing people, and for what?"

"We have failed to learn from past mistakes, but must no longer. These atrocities can never happen again. We must fight together."

"I now turn my remarks to the topic of North Korea, the terrors under which its citizens live and the modern day genocide occurring in death camps as we speak. There may be some who reject the fight for this cause, but I trust those will be few. I propose we treat them with every bit of kindness that we do our other fellow men, but that we unequivocally say we will no longer support them. There will be sanctions against them and those sanctions will be enforced and will be harsh. I propose that if China continues to partner with Korea that we sanction them both, that we make it financially impossible for them to function without the support of any other world power and that we refuse to cooperate with them on anything else.

"I propose that we as world leaders gather together, combine our efforts and not back down. To my Chinese friends, I respectfully implore you to do the right thing. Your alliance with North Korea can only bring you down. A system which rots from within ultimately cannot survive. And to my other friends of the world, of which I include everyone, let us unite as one and work together to demand tolerance. In so doing, we will each preserve our own rights.

"I understand the full complexity of what I am proposing. We, along with victims of North Korean death camps, have allowed ourselves to be intimidated by that country's threats of nuclear war. I say to you: if we are one they cannot beat us. A bully cannot defeat a combined world power. A combined world power is far too great and far too strong to be taken for anything!"

As Alex concluded his words and had fully outlined his plan of unifying the ambassadors of the world's nations to force a stop to the modern day Holocaust in North Korea, it was his one voice, in front of a room full of world leaders, that held their absolute attention. The world leaders were listening.

Only time would tell which actions would result from his speech, and as time passed, although Alex considered his reunion with Brielle to be the happiest of endings to their journey, the aftermath with the UN would initially be no fairy tale. His oration to the Assembly was powerful and strong. It rallied the proverbial troops, but at that time it was not the entirety of what was needed. The world wasn't fully ready for his proposal and the numerous politics plaguing the United Nations could not be fully overcome. There were still the skeptics and those doubtful of the validity of Dietrich's journal, and there were strong economic and otherwise political ties which would not be broken solely by his strength.

Despite this, his words planted a seed and he would keep working. During the next legislative session, he would go on to be a co-drafter of a new and improved Genocide Prevention Act and he would be its strongest supporter. Despite changes happening as a process over time, one great and immediate victory was that he, as one person, demonstrated to the world the sheer power of speaking up in defense of others. This was a requisite for humanity.

# Chapter 76

*October 4, 1988*

The day after his speech, Alex returned to his New York Senate office with a sense of true satisfaction. As he sat at his desk for a moment of serenity after letting the events of his speech all sink in, his desk phone rang, startling him. Flinching at first, he reached for the receiver.

"Hello," he said simply, still coming out of his daze.

"Hello, Senator Card?" questioned the man on the other line.

"Yes, this is he."

"My name is Carson Stebbens, I am an attorney and I represent the estate of Dietrich Rüpel. With his passing, I must inform you that you are listed in his will."

What Alex didn't know but would soon find out was that Dietrich's lifeless body was found shortly after his suicide. The police entered his home moments after the suicide and in a ceremonial act, handcuffed his corpse. Though strongly inclined to kick his lifeless body out of anger towards him, the officers restrained themselves. Paramedics wheeled his dead body out of his house and in the subsequent days it came to light that he had a will. Dietrich Rüpel had retained an attorney, and though he didn't know it, his attorney was a Jew. This was something Carson Stebbens never revealed to Dietrich just as he never revealed Dietrich's secrets to the world. Stebbens' ethical obligation to uphold the attorney client privilege Dietrich was entitled to trumped his feelings of hatred for what his client stood for. In reality, his heart was glad when he discovered Dietrich Rüpel was dead. His death lifted a tremendous burden swiftly from Stebbens' shoulders.

As he continued on his call to Alex, he reported, "I understand you are just now being made aware of the will and I know you didn't know him before, but please understand that he knew you. I understand your mother disowned him. You should know he was heartbroken at her passing. With these things in mind, like it or not, you are blood and he has made generous accommodations for you at his passing."

This news pummeled Alex in the face. The news of who his grandfather was, the impact he had on history and the existence of his will all came as a shock. With this most recent news, Alex was unclear whether he even wanted to accept his role as beneficiary of the will. He had obtained information about his grandfather which went beyond even his wildest imaginings and he didn't like it.

"Where did he get his money?" Alex asked, begging for verification of the reality of his grandfather's criminal past.

"Due to my ethical obligations and the privilege between attorney and client, I cannot answer any questions or provide you with any information about the source of his money. What I can tell you is he has a considerable estate and you are one of two sole remaining heirs."

*Two remaining heirs? The other must be Violet LeMond,* Alex reasoned. *Although she wasn't blood Dietrich loved her like his own, if not eerily more so.*

"Your grandfather was careful to ensure that the people he wanted to have his money got it and that it didn't fall into the wrong hands. He has a list of beneficiaries in the order of who the money is to go to. If the first on the list is no longer surviving or cannot receive the money, it is to be granted to the next beneficiary on the list and so on until the final name is reached.

"I have gone through the line and verified that each and every other person is no longer eligible. I have to be honest with you, and you may be very surprised to hear this, but his first names on the list for half of the estate to be split between them were a Sampson Barrett and Joseph Simms. They are both now dead. Your grandfather apparently also maintained close ties with the New York community. He had named next, former Detective Sergeant Troy Paniletti who also no longer survives. After him is a man by the name of Brent Somers, the current New York District Attorney. I have researched Mr. Somers and verified his status. He is the first and only other person on the list who is alive, however his assets have been frozen. He cannot withdraw any funds and I cannot deposit them to him. He must forfeit his claim.

"A separate portion of the estate was bequeathed to your mother, of course, and to a woman by the name of Violet LeMond. If they don't survive then the money goes to their offspring, which leaves you in your mother's line as she has passed on.

"This means you will be splitting your grandfather's estate with Ms. LeMond. It is in the tens of millions which doesn't include the value of his land that will be split in half as well. I will follow up with you on those details."

"You know Violet wasn't his biological child, didn't you? He ripped her from her own family," Alex blurted without thinking.

The knowing look in Stebbens' eyes that Alex couldn't see was a solid tell as Stebbens replied, "I am not at liberty to expand any further than I have."

Alex thought seriously for a moment, reflecting on the words he was hearing. "Thank you for your time, Mr. Stebbens," he responded matter of factly.

"I will be in touch," Stebbens told him before gently hanging up the phone.

Alex knew every cent received from Dietrich Rüpel would be blood money, but he would cleanse it— the money would be donated. A portion of it would go to Peter and Myung-Hee, an act of solidarity on Alex's part meant to serve as reparations. Every remaining dime after that would be donated to the cause of fighting genocide. With this money Alex had more than the ability to advertise and raise awareness for those victims who are often forgotten and who were being tortured on his time and right under his nose. The world would no longer be devoid of his advocacy for the end of hate and genocide.

As for DA Somers, his role in the white supremacy movement did not remain a secret in any sense of the word when Stebbens read the list of beneficiaries to Dietrich's will. Upon hearing it, Alex immediately made a call to the police about Somers and his ties to the Aryan Brotherhood, but he soon learned an anonymous tipster had already informed them. The tipster refused to identify themselves but Alex knew Carson Stebbens was the only person in the world, besides himself, who knew the truth. *Even Stebbens could no longer keep Dietrich's dirty secret.*

When it was discovered that Somers was the first name on the list of beneficiaries it became clear that Dietrich had been a major source of his District Attorney campaign funding and would have continued with the financial support. This news was the answer to many questions raised about Somers' campaign's financial bounty. Not only had Dietrich lived a life filled with hate propaganda and promoting the agenda of the white power movement with his money, but he was using the new District Attorney to move it forward.

Charlotte was overjoyed to learn about Somers' prompt arrest after the will was read and it became known he had accepted bribe money. Somers was dirty, he and Paniletti both had close personal ties with each other and with Dietrich, and she no longer needed to struggle to prove he knew about, and was behind, Saul's murder.

Desperately wanting to be present at Somers' arrest, Charlotte got special permission to tag along. The opportunity proved to be invaluable as the look of angst on Somers' face was priceless when he was taken from his home that very evening. Fear penetrated his face when he was booked into jail and the thick band he had wrapped around his right ring finger was removed. On the bottom was the unmistakable mark of a swastika. His life as he knew it was over.

# Chapter 77

The sun was just beginning to peak through the cloud cover when Charlotte returned to work the day after her trip to the UN. She stepped into the District Attorney's Office to see a once familiar environment which now seemed so foreign after her weeks of time off. The job that had consumed Charlotte's heart with passion, felt now just a burden. She was at a precipice in her career. It was a summit she had struggled to attain and it was time for a respite.

As she set foot in her office and made her way to her government issued faux leather desk chair, there was an almost undeniable force wielding her back out the door. She had always wondered when this day would come—the day when it would be time to leave. She always knew it could be at any moment and on the silent grounds of Treblinka she decided now was the time.

Her recent journey made her tired and it was more than just a physical fatigue. She was tired in spirit. Little by little, day by day, the job of prosecution had been chipping away at her stamina until it came to a head and drained the last bit of determination she had left. It was time for a break.

Everything had changed. Including her. Saul lost his life over the job and she refused to let the same thing happen to her. There was a world out there she rarely saw from the confines of the court, and a majesty in her surroundings she never took the time to appreciate due to the professional demands on her schedule.

The politics plaguing the office since the inception of Somers' administration had rotted the office so intensely that Charlotte could no longer avoid the stench. Despite the inherent goodness of many of her colleagues, Charlotte was saddened to see that hate had entered the office walls and that sheer intolerance in the form of racial discrimination, which had demonstrated itself throughout history, had not been swept away with the past in the District Attorney's Office. Prejudice and discrimination had, up until Somers' arrest, been alive and well and it was nothing less than shameful. It left a bitter taste in her mouth that replaced the former taste of justice.

She realized that Somers' downfall was a prime example of evil in the world running its course, but being unable to sustain itself forever. If Isaac had taught her anything, it was that—the day would always come when evil would fall. In the end, hatred will turn on itself and any organization wherein it serves as a foundation will eventually rot and crumble. Just as with the downfall of Dietrich Rüpel, Brent Somers, Troy Paniletti, Justin Vincent and the Aryan Brotherhood of the New York state prison system, the dark seeds of evil would eventually be quashed.

*Maybe in time,* Charlotte thought, *I'll come back. Maybe I won't.* For now she was sucked dry and even her bones felt wanting for strength. She felt as though they had turned to volcanic rock, filled with holes and crevices by the energy drawn from them. Nonetheless, she felt an onslaught of overwhelming satisfaction. At this moment, she had accomplished what she set out to do when Saul died. She learned the Aryan Brotherhood had a master leader and with him as the organization's head having been chopped off, her goal was reached. As she turned around and started walking towards the exit, she had never felt more free.

The burdens of her profession drifted away as she let herself go and set foot out the door into what became a sky full of sun. She wandered down the concrete sidewalk to the park adjacent the nearby courthouse. Historically, she always walked past the park as she made her journey from the office to the courthouse. This time, however, the courthouse was not her destination.

This time she noticed the park's birds and trees and its visitors stopping in for a visit. Though she had passed the park countless times before, she had never stopped to take it all in. She walked deeper into the park and found a grassy spot surrounded by lush green oaks nestled among the hundreds of trees in the park. Light shone through the branches casting glimmers of hope on the ground below.

Without a second thought she laid on the ground, back against the grass, with her eyes looking heavenward. *This was ecstasy.* The feeling of bondage her job had turned to giving her was removed. She had little idea what she was going to do, having just left what was once her dream job and having walked away from her reason for living. Completely uncertain of which direction her life would take, she didn't give it a moment's thought more. That could be considered tomorrow. Or maybe the day after. That was all of no consequence. For now there were trees.

# *Epilogue*

It was 22 years later and Isaac Kanzler had failed to file an appeal. He had ultimately been convicted of the murders of the 11 prison inmates in Sing Sing, although due to legal complications, the conviction took over two decades. A jury eventually found him guilty of all 11 murders of the Aryan Brotherhood members he poisoned to death.

"It was the sheer number of dead bodies," a juror reported after the trial, "that provided any level of jury appeal. It wasn't so much the character or affiliation of the murdered white supremacists that urged us to convict, but rather the number of them who were once living and were now dead."

In addition, the jury found death to be an appropriate sanction for Isaac's crimes.

Upon the passing of sentence, Isaac's permanent residence was death row, a fact he simply accepted. He advised his attorneys to take no further action. There would be no writs on his behalf, no plea for a new trial or reconsideration for an overturning of his conviction. There was no suggestion of habeas corpus.

The trial received strong media coverage and stood as an example of evil fighting against evil, with neither being victorious. Isaac did nothing to reignite the interest in his situation after the trial concluded and the world eventually turned its attention to other more current events. He was quiet, day after day, month after month and year after year as he waited until the final day came—execution day.

For that day, he had requested the gas chamber. Though it was now abolished in New York, his request was placed prior to its abolition. On his final day of life, it would have been too late to make the request. It was currently deemed too cruel to be exercised as a form of punishment.

As for Isaac, it was important to him that he die in this way; that he lose his life as his Jewish grandmother did in the concentration camp. Though she was guiltless and undeserving of her death sentence, he would be truly paying for his crimes and was content to do so. He had lived a life he felt had purpose and he had accomplished the last goal he sought after. With his brother, he arranged a series of events that propelled a United States Senator to use the power he had to incite a change in human history. He had spoken up.

Charlotte attended Isaac's execution. He requested she be there. She watched him through the thick glass from her vantage point in the adjoining small viewing room. Alex came as well and sat by her side. It was his choice and support Charlotte. From a rocky introduction between them after the abduction of his daughter through a difficult journey, she had been by his side ever since his speech to the UN. After the loss of Alex's wife, a romantic love for each other had grown in he and Charlotte's hearts through the years and their journeys together hadn't ceased since finding Brielle.

In his travels throughout the world as he spread his anti-genocide message, she was his companion. It had, in fact, been just less than a week since they returned from their most recent trip to Istanbul.

In this important moment, Alex sat with her, his arm enveloping her shoulders. As they both sat in the otherwise empty viewing room moments before the execution, they were alone. The Governor did not call to issue a last minute pardon, and Isaac was sitting in the chamber's chair, strapped in and ready to die.

*There is no one present to speak for him,* she thought as they sat in the dark stillness, but no sooner did these words cross her mind than she heard the viewing room door creak open. Turning her head back to see who the last minute observers were, she saw Peter Bremer and Myung-Hee. Charlotte easily recognized them despite their now wrinkled skin and graying hair. Without a word, they made their way to the third and last row of seats in the viewing room as Alex and Charlotte remained sitting in front. They sat quietly, hand in hand, and stared in silence at the chamber.

Isaac was given the warning. The gas was to be turned on. He had eaten a thick steak with mashed potatoes as his final meal and a Rabbi had given him his last rites. It was now his opportunity to make a final statement.

His words were simple, but poignant, as he stared through the window at the four people who were present to watch him leave this life.

"I am the son of Otto Klaus Bremer, the brother to Peter Jan Bremer, nephew of Violet LeMond and I am a Jew. I know what I have done to get this sentence of death and for those acts I will now pay. At this time I go to meet my maker and will finally feel peace."

That was all. Those were the words he chose to say at the end of his life, leaving a legacy of equality, that there is no superior race, ethnicity, culture or group. There is only one God wherefrom we all come and it is impossible for Him to love any of His children more than the other.

After Isaac took his last breath, Charlotte left the room with mixed emotions. She had kept in correspondence with him on occasion over the years as he sat on death row. She filled him in on the news of the outside world and he shared with her more of his history and wisdom. She grew to consider him a friend despite his crimes, and although she knew the ends of justice were being served with his execution, she couldn't help but grieve at the loss of him. Despite this, a small part of her felt just as happy as the day she left the District Attorney's Office. She was devoting her time now to several charitable causes and became a Guardian ad Litem. She was a lawyer for child victims, speaking for those who couldn't speak for themselves. She felt peace.

Alex had eventually been able to successfully rally Russia and many other major UN member states. Throughout the last 22 years, the world had been slowly coming together for the cause of ending genocide. They placed sanctions on China for continual support of North Korea and eventually convinced them that their allegiance to a country wrought with genocide would ultimately cause them much more harm than benefit.

Of course North Korea had threatened war and threatened to deploy their nuclear bombs but when that happened the rest of the world was in uniformity in taking a stand against Genocide and openly declared, "Not on my watch." North Korea had no choice but to accept they could not win. The bully was becoming the bullied and a united army of international soldiers swept in to liberate the North Korean prison camps, just as the United States did in the Auschwitz Concentration Camp on January 27, 1945.

At the time of Dietrich's passing, Violet, though a beneficiary of Dietrich Rüpel's estate, did not leave Israel to collect it. Her work was there in Israel. She fled from him when she was only 17-years-old and she had no desire to ever be in the area of his covert American home. She had no interest in the dismantling of his estate either. The money she was allotted was wired to her bank account and that was the last she was to think of him again. The Red Cross did, however, receive an extremely sizeable anonymous donation right in the exact amount of her inheritance, and its Holocaust memorial display was expanded.

"It's just a coincidence," she would say, if asked.

Violet's absence from the dismantling of the estate left Alex to do it alone. He also had no interest, but if he didn't do it, no one else would. Dietrich's house was sold immediately at a rock bottom price and Alex kept none of its contents, with two exceptions— a *Torah* with the cover of a *Bible* and a lampshade. The fruits of Dietrich's life and all his worldly possessions had been purchased with blood money and he wanted nothing to do with any of them.

As he sifted through the belongings of Dietrich's estate, and placing his possessions into a large trailer to be hauled off for charity, Alex's eyes had lain specifically upon the lampshade and the words of Violet rang in his mind.

*The Nazis made lamp shades from human flesh*, he recalled her saying.

He would never forget that and instinctively knew what he had. He couldn't prove it yet, but he hoped one day the time would come when proof would be possible, and he took it with the hope it would further help the world to see the truth.

Twenty two years later, as Alex sat in the gas chamber viewing room, Brielle, had grown into a strong young woman and had strong ambitions of her own. She in no way wanted to follow in her father's professional footsteps and subject herself to disingenuous politicians. The truth, however, was vastly important to her and she worked hard to find it and disclose it. She was gifted in this regard and she excelled in her college history courses.

Advancements in DNA research had been skyrocketing since four years prior in 2006, and she was able to use that technology to her benefit. She was fascinated by the stories her father repeated to her time and time again about her abduction as a baby, where he had gotten the strange lampshade he kept in a box in a corner of the attic and how he believed it to be made of human skin. She took it upon herself to set the wheels of discovery in motion when it came to that disturbing piece of history.

The test results were being processed. Brielle knew her father was waiting for this opportunity and she too was wildly curious. She had taken the lampshade for samples from it to be studied at a molecular level including the thread binding of the lampshade and its metal frame. She acquired the services of the best of the best in DNA analysis and was to be notified of the results any day. Her father had hoped they would be available by Isaac's execution day. He wanted to confirm what he already knew to be true and he wanted to tell Isaac and Peter.

Finally, Brielle got the results, but unfortunately not until ten days after Isaac's death. It was confirmed by consensus of several different scientists that the lamp, in fact, had come from human elements. Specifically, the shade was made from human flesh. There was no way to confirm the identity of the victim, she was told, but the time period from which the materials came was that of World War II and the origins of the shade was human flesh of Jewish lineage. Science could not be argued with and no one could ever dispute this reality. Upon making this discovery, Alex donated the lampshade, which was immediately scheduled for display at the Smithsonian. With that, a piece of undeniable historical truth would be forever enclosed in a sealed glass case for all the world to see.

## Auschwitz Concentration Camp
## Poland
## 1940-1945

## Kaechon Extermination Camp
## North Korea
## TODAY

© S.E. Francis

**S.E. FRANCIS** has been practicing law for over a decade. She specializes in felony prosecution and currently practices in the Mountain West where she lives with her dog, Schwarz.

**www.sefrancis.com**

www.ingramcontent.com/pod-product-compliance
Lightning Source LLC
Chambersburg PA
CBHW020245200626
46816CB00001BA/143

* 9 7 8 0 9 9 6 1 3 1 9 3 3 *